LOVE
ON
display

DANA LeCHEMINANT

First Printing: October 2022

ISBN: 978-1-951753-15-3

ONE

THERE WERE TWO TYPES OF runners in the world: those who did it for their health, and those who did it so they could brag about it to anyone who would listen. Okay, so there were probably some others thrown into the mix, like the family who thought it would be a good bonding experience until they realized they were paying money to get up at four in the morning and run. But generally, Kailani only encountered the first two.

Well, while she was at it, she figured she should add another category, the one where she fit in: the people who hated running with a burning passion but did it for the people they loved.

The grumbling family probably fit into that group too.

So there were three types of runners in the world: those who did it for their health, those who hated it but did it for their loved ones, and the worst group of all.

Those who did it to inflate their own egos.

Kailani first saw the meathead when she was crossing the parking lot to the start of the course. He'd been pretty hard to miss, massive as he was, and that smirk of his was seared into her brain. She'd seen it once before, when he hit on her at her favorite climbing gym, and she had hoped to never see him again.

Fate was not on her side, and he'd nearly walked right into her a few minutes later when she was stretching.

"Hey," he'd said in his deep voice.

She'd ignored him, pretending she couldn't hear him over her music despite her ear buds playing absolutely nothing at the time, and she had walked away without giving him a passing glance.

Now, however, he was talking to one of the sponsors, which was exactly why Kailani had come over this way in the first place. The race was about to start, and she had a short window in which to talk to this particular sponsor, The Healing Well. It was the whole reason she was here. Well, that, and she'd promised Isla she would do the race.

Her sister had no real reason to want Kailani here, but she'd begged Kailani to promise she would race. Something about it projecting a good image. And Kailani, being the sucker that she was, hadn't been able to say no. Only after she'd realized The Healing Well was one of the sponsors did she have any real desire to show up. Maybe Isla had known they would be one of the sponsors…

Kailani shuffled a little closer to the booth, bouncing on the balls of her feet to keep her legs limber. Isla could pretend all she wanted that she had no idea how business worked, but she kept doing things that completely contradicted that idea. That girl was going places.

Kailani, on the other hand, was stuck watching Meathead do his thing because he was standing exactly where she wanted to be.

He seemed to be charming the pants off the girl at the Healing Well booth, leaning on the table and giving her a seductive look that had probably worked for him so many times. The girl, to Kailani's disgust, was clearly into it, as if a well-formed pectoral was all a guy needed to recommend himself.

Honestly, it was remarkable anyone could see anything beyond his ego.

"I'd love to keep talking," Meathead said, "but I think the race is about to start, so I'd better skedaddle."

Skedaddle? Who even used that word anymore?

"Can I convince you to share a free banana and granola bar with me after the race? My treat."

The girl giggled.

Kailani scoffed.

For a guy with so much muscle mass, he moved quick, spinning around and turning red as if he hadn't expected anyone to be nearby.

Kailani raised an eyebrow. "Are you done?"

He glanced at the girl, who bit her lip as if she'd been caught doing something wrong. It wasn't her fault. She was young, and guys like Meathead had a habit of preying on the weak and vulnerable. For all their time spent building muscle, they never seemed to want an actual challenge.

"Hi," Meathead said, and then he clenched his jaw so hard the muscle by his ear bulged. "I know you, right?"

If she looked familiar at all to him, she knew he wouldn't remember where they'd met. He probably spoke to anything that breathed, and she was just one of hundreds. Rolling her eyes, Kailani turned to ask the Healing Well girl if they could talk after the race.

"The climbing wall."

She froze.

"My friend and I were sitting beneath the bouldering wall, and we were in your way."

She looked back, surprised to see an apologetic expression. She certainly hadn't expected recognition let alone repentance.

"I was an idiot," he added, and he threw in a smile that only climbed half his face.

Kailani had always been a sucker for a crooked smile, especially when it accompanied humility. Though the announcer had started pumping up the racers and getting them ready, Kailani shifted just a little closer to the gym rat, curious to know what he would say if she let him keep talking. This was a much better encounter than the last one, when she'd been amazed his head could hold such a big ego. Not so big, apparently…

With his smile still intact, he ducked his head and took several steps away from the booth. Probably so the Healing Well girl wouldn't be privy to their entire conversation. Kailani followed, too curious not to. "It's a curse," he said. "No matter what I do, I always get flustered around beautiful women, and I turn into a…a…"

"A tool?" she supplied, hating that his little compliment got to her.

He nodded, back to clenching his jaw.

And Kailani's heart softened a little because he looked so worried about what she thought of him. "You're trying not to say anything stupid right now, aren't you?" Another nod made her laugh, and she folded her arms as she examined him a little more closely. Maybe there was more to this meathead than muscle (of which he had a whole lot).

"I'm Kailani," she said, holding out her hand.

His smile morphed into a white-toothed grin that caught Kailani off guard. Wow, he was handsome. With his muscle definition and bronze skin, he was undeniably attractive.

"Cam," he said, but he didn't take her hand. Instead, he offered a fist bump.

Kailani raised an eyebrow.

"I'm, uh, careful about where I put my hands." His eyes went wide. "I did not mean that how it sounded. I mean, I don't take just anyone's—no." He blew out all of his breath, then ran both hands through his thick, dark hair. "Such an idiot," he mumbled under his breath.

As she stood there biting her lip to keep from laughing, Kailani was really enjoying this man's bumbling. He definitely wasn't what she'd expected, and she was curious to know more. Was Cam the jerk at the climbing gym, or this bumbling babbler who really packed a punch with that genuine smile of his?

"Tell you what," she said, and he snapped to attention. It wouldn't hurt to put him to the test. "If you can keep up with me for the next thirteen miles, I'll buy *you* free fruit and granola."

"Thirteen point one," he said, and then he slapped a palm to his face. "Sorry. I know what you meant. Yes, I'd… Yeah."

When the start gun fired into the air a second later, Kailani patted Cam's impressive tricep and took off running, refusing to look behind her to see if he was following her. If he was truly attracted to her and wanted to get to know her, he'd catch up.

She almost hoped he did.

Cam hated running. He hated it with a fiery, burning passion. The only reason he was even here was because he'd made a bet with his friend Oliver, who thought he couldn't make it past mile five before he collapsed, and Cam was determined to prove him wrong. How hard could a half-marathon be, anyway?

If the likes of Oliver Hamilton could run a race like this, anyone could. The guy put the bare minimum effort into everything he did.

The problem was it was only mile three, and Oliver had long-ago disappeared up with the race leaders despite breaking his foot eight months ago. Cam hated to admit it, but there was a slight chance the man was genuinely good at running. And Cam hated that. Especially because his lungs were burning, and he was pretty sure he sounded like a dying horse as he wheezed along. He hadn't done continuous cardio since high school, and his inability to keep up with the bulk of the runners was making that painfully obvious.

That's not to say he didn't try. He could still see the back of Kailani's head, and the fact that the woman had even given him a chance was quite the motivator to keep him moving forward. It may have been three months since he saw her at the climbing gym, but he hadn't been able to get her out of his head. Seeing her in the parking lot this morning had completely disarmed him.

"What's wrong with you?" Oliver had asked when Cam went stiff.

Cam had kept his mouth shut in case he accidentally told Oliver everything.

He liked to think the fact that he and the incredibly attractive Kailani were both running the same race on a late January morning was a gift of fate. For once, something had gone his way, and he was not about to mess this up.

He had to catch up to her first, though.

Clearly a natural runner, Kailani hadn't slowed down even once since the start of the race. Though she remained fairly middle ground in terms of placement, she was more consistent than anyone Cam had ever seen. He'd been watching her long brown ponytail swish back and forth for the last half an hour, and other runners had passed her and been passed by her. Kailani hadn't given them a moment's notice, and she'd kept her eyes fixed ahead.

Cam would catch up to her eventually. He had to. Watching her from behind—as enjoyable as it was—was nothing compared to actually talking to her. Seeing her smile. Hearing her laugh. If he wanted a chance to get to know this girl, he had to pick up his pace and close the distance between them.

His legs protested the push as he forced himself faster. Somehow, his lungs burned even more. But with every second, he was gaining ground, and he repeated the mantra of "body over mind" again and again, telling himself that his only limitations were the ones he put on himself.

Almost there.

"Hi," he gasped when he reached her side.

Next thing he knew, he was looking up at Kailani from the ground, his head spinning and his tongue feeling like cotton in his mouth.

"Welcome back," she said. Her voice was low and soothing, her dark eyes kind, and Cam became distinctly aware of the warmth of her fingers resting on his arm. Even through the smooth fabric of his athletic shirt.

"Back?" he asked. Brushing a hand through his hair to push it back from his forehead, he grimaced when his fingers came back dripping with sweat. He was simultaneously burning and frozen, the cold seeping into his back from the pavement where he lay. "What...?"

She smiled, but it was the kind of smile that meant she felt sorry for him. Cam hated that smile. "You fainted."

He groaned. "You could at least say 'passed out' so I don't sound completely pathetic," he muttered as he struggled to sit up. Dizziness threatened to knock him back down, and he paused for a second, taking some deep breaths. "How long was I out?" There weren't any other racers around, but with the sky gray with low clouds, it was impossible to know how much time had passed.

Kailani's smile twisted a little, giving way to some genuine amusement that Cam would have appreciated if he hadn't been the source of it. "Just a couple of minutes," she told him. "Did you eat enough breakfast this morning? I know some beginners tend to go too light before a race."

Not that Cam was checking her out—he totally was—but she had the muscle definition and lean frame that came from good nutrition and an active lifestyle. The fact that she'd asked that question without sounding condescending made him like her all the more, but he didn't want her to think he was totally clueless.

"I forgot to increase my carb intake," he grunted, wiping his sticky forehead with his sleeve. "And I didn't get a chance to do any endurance training."

She cocked her head. "So why are you here?"

"Because I want to drive the Benz." Cam clenched his jaw. "I mean, I want to beat Oliver. I mean—"

She snickered, sitting back on her heels and folding her arms. "You were forced into it too?"

Cam breathed a sigh of relief. "I don't like to back down from a challenge," he said. "My friend promised I could drive his car if I did the race with him. It's a nice car. What's your excuse?"

"Promised my sister." The answer came with a shrug. "Truth be told, I kind of hate running."

"Oh, thank goodness." He smacked his face with his palm. Why, oh why, did he have to say everything that came to his head? It didn't help that she was completely stunning, with her golden-brown skin and eyes so dark they were almost black, and then there was the whole fit and athletic thing. He was desperate to impress her, and that meant his tongue was determined to take the lead.

Giving her a sheepish smile, he hoped he could wipe that confused look off her face. "I turn into an idiot around pretty girls, remember? Even more of an idiot around ones that intimidate me." And if he could just lie down and die of embarrassment right now, that would be great.

For some reason, Kailani smiled. "I intimidate you?"

"No." He cringed, his stomach churning and threatening to launch his protein-heavy breakfast onto the ground next to him. "Yes." His stomach settled, but only marginally, as if it knew he might try to lie again.

She couldn't seem to decide what to make of him, and he hoped that was a good sign. True, he knew nothing about her, but she seemed entirely perfect. He refused to let her go without at least trying, knowing he would probably never find another girl like her.

"You didn't have to hang around," he said, wincing as he examined a scrape on his arm that had just begun stinging like crazy thanks to the bits of asphalt lodged in his skin. A nice hole had torn through the brand-new shirt. "But thanks."

She grinned. "Well, technically you fell right into me, so you seemed to want me around."

That was when Cam saw the hole in the knee of her leggings, and his stomach dropped. "You're bleeding!" Without thinking, he grabbed her leg and tugged, knocking her backward and twisting her into a ridiculous position because the other leg was still folded beneath her. He cursed as she landed on her elbows, and then he scrambled forward to scoop her up before he injured her further.

Only when she was safely cradled in his arms, one arm around her back and the other tucked behind her knees, did he stop moving, freezing as he knelt on two equally scraped up knees that did not appreciate holding his weight.

"Sorry," he whispered, waiting for her to fly out of his arms and take off running. She didn't move, staring at him with wide eyes and an expression that was either terror or complete panic. He wasn't sure which. "Um. How's your knee?"

Her eyes flicked down to the knee in question. "I hadn't noticed it," she said, a little breathless. She was probably terrified and waiting for him to have his way with her on the trail or something.

His arms started to shake at the idea of anyone being afraid of him, especially her.

She noticed the trembling, her eyebrows pulling low. "You can put me down. I weigh more than I—"

"You're not heavy," he blurted, and instinctively he pulled her a little closer, though that didn't stop the shaking. "I'm just worried that I really hurt you." If anyone was heavy, he was, and she'd said he fell right into her when he fainted—passed out. Had he landed on her?

Smiling a little, she shook her head. "I'm fine. I'm just glad I was able to catch you so you didn't get more hurt."

"You caught me?" Was this girl for real?

"Well, I slowed your fall. You are kind of huge."

Cam chuckled, his arms feeling steadier the longer he held her. Despite actively building muscle on a daily basis, he didn't usually like people pointing out his size. But she seemed to appreciate it. "I guess I should thank you for that. And I really am sorry."

Her eyes burned with something new, making Cam wonder what emotion fueled that fire. When she pressed a hand to his chest, the fire jumped over to where she touched, burning hot and steady. "I'm not. You can fall into me anytime."

His heart stumbled in his chest, which was probably an early warning sign of a heart attack. He didn't care, not with the way Kailani was looking at him. "Only if it means I get to hold you again," he said.

Her full lips parted with a little gasp. "I'd be okay with that," she whispered, lifting her mouth closer.

"You guys okay?"

The sound of an unfamiliar voice startled Cam so much that he nearly dumped Kailani onto the ground. Cursing under his breath—he really hated getting startled—he gently set her on the pavement and did his best to ignore the way she seemed about to laugh.

The poor race volunteer was so red in the face, he was probably in danger of his own heart attack. "Someone said there were a couple of injuries. But it looks like you're…"

Kailani grinned as she hopped to her feet. "I'm fine. Cam is the one who fainted."

"Passed out," Cam corrected, though he was quickly realizing that didn't sound much better. He wasn't nearly as lithe as he slowly made his way upright, every limb protesting.

"Need to hop in the golf cart?" The volunteer glanced between them.

The last thing Cam needed was Oliver finding out he'd been carted back to the start line. He bent his legs, testing the resilience of his still-weak knees. "I can walk," he decided out loud, though he was eager to get into the steam room at his gym to soothe the ache that was building all over his body. He must have fallen hard.

And Kailani had taken the brunt of that fall.

"I'm sorry for ruining the race," he told her, knowing that apology hardly covered it.

She flashed a brilliant smile. "Don't be. I'd rather rescue you than spend the next hour and a half stuck running."

Cam nearly fainted again. *Passed out.* "Wait, that's how long it takes to run a half marathon?"

She grimaced. "Terrible, right? And with how pale you look, I think you need someone to escort you back to the parking lot in case you fa—pass out again. I'd be happy to walk back with you."

The volunteer gestured toward the golf cart waiting behind him. "I can—"

"That's incredibly kind of you," Cam said to Kailani, smiling despite the pain. She genuinely seemed to want to walk with him, and he definitely wanted that to happen. "It might be a long five miles back, though," he warned, just in case she hadn't thought through what she had offered.

"I'm counting on it."

"Really?" Cam almost slapped himself. If he would stop questioning everything, maybe something might actually come of this unfortunate incident. And as the volunteer drove off, leaving them behind, he hoped Kailani didn't take his question as wanting her to go on without him. Otherwise, he wasn't sure he would make it back.

Chuckling, Kailani nodded and grabbed Cam's arm, slinging it over her shoulder so they could start walking. "How else am I going to get to know you?"

Beautiful, strong, *and* confident. Cam was pretty much in love.

"So," he said, hoping he didn't make a fool of himself as he tried to find a conversation starter. "Kailani. Is that Hawaiian?"

"Yep. I was born there. Dad went for the surf, stayed for my mom."

"What brought you to Diamond Springs?"

She seemed to think about that, like she wasn't sure how to answer. "When I was twelve, my parents came back to look after my grandparents when they got old. So here we are."

"Do you ever think of going back?" *Please say no.* Although, Cam wouldn't mind the excuse to take a trip to Hawaii to see her. Not that he could afford it.

Kailani thought over that question as well, her eyes distant. "Sometimes," she admitted. "I miss surfing, especially. But my family is here, and my parents need…" She shook her head. "You don't need to know all my drama."

"I would love to know your drama." He coughed. "I mean, only if you need a listening ear."

She smiled, and the expression lit up her whole face. Cam had never met anyone so expressive, and that was saying something. His friends were definite characters. It probably came with the territory of calling themselves the "Wonder Boys," a name courtesy of their shared little sister, Madi.

Well, she wasn't Oliver's adopted sister anymore. Now she was his wife, and that still threw Cam for a loop sometimes. He'd always figured they would all stay single forever, given how long it had taken Oliver to finally commit to something. Ben wasn't far behind on the whole marriage thing, from the looks of it. Cam just had to hope his best friend, Kit, didn't suddenly decide to break character and make a life change again.

If Kit decided to start dating, that would leave Cam entirely on his own.

A shudder ran through him at the thought, his heart rate picking up speed.

"You okay?" Kailani paused and put her hand on his chest.

The physical pain had dulled, but Cam's vision tunneled a bit as his chest grew tight, so he shook his head. "I just need to sit down for a second," he said. Nausea bubbled up into his stomach, and he hoped that was just from the dizziness. Not because he was lying. The loneliness and fear would pass, like it always did when he inadvertently thought about being left behind.

Kailani led him to the side of the path, where a fallen log provided a decent place to sit. Once he'd settled, she sat close enough that their arms pressed together. "I take it you don't do much running," she said.

That wasn't the problem, but he decided to run with the topic. "My focus is high intensity interval training, not marathons."

"Technically it's a half-marathon."

"I know it's—" He cut himself off when he saw her smile. She was *teasing* him. That had to be a good sign, right? He chanced a grin back at her and was pleased when she blushed a little. He'd never had Oliver's and Ben's skills with women, and he'd never understood how they could steal hearts with only a smile.

Maybe he'd just been smiling at the wrong people. All of his past girlfriends had taken some time to warm up to him, and none of them had ever lasted long. Not that he'd been surprised by that.

"You'd think I would have learned by now to do more cardio," he muttered, still grinning. "But at least my embarrassment gave me a chance to sit next to you."

"Oh, is that why you fainted?"

"Passed out."

"Still out cold on the ground."

Chuckling, Cam bumped his shoulder into hers as gently as he could, though it still knocked her over a couple of inches.

"I think that's the first time I've ever passed out from exercise," he said. Which, honestly, surprised him. Some days he pushed himself so hard that his body should have given out long before now.

Her eyebrows pulled low, and she seemed to look him over for a second. "Does that mean you've passed out for other reasons? How often do you fall on top of unsuspecting women?"

Since he definitely wasn't about to admit anything that alluded to his anxiety getting the best of him or fists knocking him out cold back when he used to get into a lot of fights, Cam opted for another joke. It would keep things light and easy, and hopefully it would give him a reason to stop thinking about unknown situations and focus on the moment. "I save that move for the extra special ones."

Blushing again, she gave him an impressive shove. "So why did you waste it on me? You could have saved yourself so much pain, and I probably would have walked with you anyway."

Cam couldn't help but grin at her as they sat there watching each other, like his full attention had been locked onto her with no chance of deviation. He knew next to nothing about this girl, and yet he was convinced he'd been made to be at her side. Like this, forever. Though, maybe without the after-effects of passing out...

"Are you ready to walk again?" she asked, a bit of laughter in her voice as her eyes traced his face. He had no idea what was in his expression, but he knew any chance of being calm and cool was out the window.

He nodded, not as confidently as he'd like. His knees already felt stiffer than they'd been a minute ago. "I'm seriously embarrassed about all of this," he muttered as he struggled to his feet. "How am I supposed to impress you when I make a fool of myself every time we meet?"

To his immense pleasure, Kailani tucked herself under his arm again as they set off down the tree-lined path. "Maybe you just need more chances. I definitely like you better today than I did the first time we met."

He cringed. They'd met at the climbing gym, and something had broken in his brain the moment he saw her rhomboids. Back muscles like that should have been outlawed. "Have I apologized yet for being a tool?" He had gone all macho and hit on her, and he felt sick just thinking about it. "I promise I'm not usually like that. Just when I'm around strong, beautiful women who scare the crap out of me."

Her laugh sent a thrill through him. "You are surprisingly refreshing, Cam," she said.

"Is that a good thing?"

"I guess we'll see."

"Think you can forgive me, at least?"

She laced her fingers through his at her shoulder, her dark eyes twinkling with what Cam hoped was affection as she gazed at him. "I can definitely do that. If you can forgive me for automatically thinking the worst of you."

"Easy."

They spent the rest of the walk back to the starting line talking about anything and everything. Kailani was open and confident, and she was easy to talk to because they had so many similar interests. And for the first time in his life, Cam didn't spend the entire conversation thinking about what he might say wrong. He didn't imagine her getting tired of him and leaving him on the side of the road so she could finish her run.

He was simply there. Fully in the present and enjoying every minute of it.

He didn't want it to end.

A quick trip to the first aid tent and several bandages later, Kailani grabbed a couple granola bars and joined Cam on the small patch of dead grass that lay next to the parking lot. Cam had said he would have to wait for his friend, and he practically begged her to stay with him to soften the embarrassment that would come from admitting what had happened.

The fact that he so openly expressed his fear had Kailani's heart twisting into knots. She'd never met anyone so honest, and if a big strong guy like Cam could talk about how much he didn't like being teased for anything physical, something had to be wrong with the rest of the world. Everyone else always had something to hide.

Cam didn't, and Kailani wasn't sure how to feel about the thudding in her chest that got stronger every time he smiled at her. Despite avoiding any personal topics, she'd been more open with him than she was used to, mostly because she figured she would never see him again. But her heart seemed to be telling her she *wanted* to see him, and that complicated things.

It was his fault. She'd spent the whole race—the five miles of it she'd actually done, anyway—forcing herself not to look back and see if he was there. Even without turning, she somehow knew he was right behind her until the moment he caught up to her and immediately passed out. The poor guy clearly wasn't built to run, but he'd put in full effort to do as she'd asked and catch up. That alone had made her want to get to know him better, and then the walk back had convinced her he was absolutely worth knowing.

"I know I said otherwise, but you know you don't have to keep hanging out with me, right?" he said as she handed him a granola bar and sat beside him. "You brought me back safe and sound. I can't ask you for more than that."

She grinned, loving the way his eyes squinted as he waited for her to up and leave. "I want to stay." Truthfully, she probably should go talk to the girl at the Healing Well before the booth got crowded by finished racers, but the last hour had been one of her better hours in a long time.

All thanks to the guy next to her. Though neither had really shared anything personal, they'd talked about so many different topics that no one could argue they didn't get along. In fact, she'd never connected so easily with anyone, and that had to mean something.

Then there was his body.

As he leaned back on his hands and stretched out his legs, Cam put his muscles on full display beneath his polyester blend. She'd gotten up close and personal with a lot of him when he'd passed out, but now she had a great chance to take him all in without worrying about him hitting his head on the pavement. Every inch of him looked sculpted from stone, from his trapezius to his calves, yet he didn't look like those guys who tried to get as big as they possibly could until they looked disproportionate and unable to wear anything with sleeves.

Cam simply looked *strong*. Like he understood the balance between working out and living life. He looked like he could take on any challenge with a smile and never back down because he had the strength to meet it.

He looked like the kind of guy who could handle a little chaos, and that was exactly the kind of guy Kailani needed.

"You're staring at me."

Heat rushed into Kailani's face, and she forced her eyes away. It wasn't easy. "Sorry!"

"I don't mind."

Peeking back at him, Kailani narrowed her eyes when she saw his easy smile. "I can't tell if that's you being egotistical or if you really don't care."

He shrugged. "I'm a personal trainer, and for a while my clientele was full of women. I've gotten used to people staring."

He lifted the hem of his shirt, giving Kailani a clear and breath-taking view of his abs. *So many abs.* "These tend to be a favorite."

She could see why. Even being around gym rats all day every day hadn't desensitized Kailani's appreciation for a good oblique. Brushing her mouth to make sure she wasn't drooling, she shrugged as if she didn't want to admire this man's body all day every day.

"How do you say things like that and not sound like a total jerk?" she asked. Anyone else, and she would have left by now.

Cam chuckled. "Probably because you actually know what a latissimus dorsi muscle is. And you've seen me pass out because I'm awful at running." He leaned his head a little closer. "And you can probably beat me in an arm wrestle, so there's no point in me showing off."

With the size of Cam's biceps, that definitely wasn't true, but Kailani appreciated the praise all the same. She liked to consider herself strong, but it wasn't always obvious from the outside.

Fighting her smile, she moved her own head closer until their foreheads touched. She couldn't help it; something about him just pulled her in. "I don't normally do this," she breathed.

He didn't seem to breathe at all. "Do what? Kiss a guy you just met? I mean, not that I was assuming anything. I wasn't thinking about kissing you. I—" Suddenly he was gone, leaning over to his other side as he vomited onto the grass.

She felt bad for the guy, of course she did, but she was more disappointed than anything. With how well he'd mastered the rest of his body, Cam was probably a *great* kisser.

"Sorry," he moaned, his whole body shaking as he sat back up. "That was—"

"What happened to you?" a new voice asked.

Both of them looked up at the runner who had just arrived and stood there watching the two of them.

"Did you even run?" the stranger asked Cam, one eyebrow rising.

Looking ready to strangle the guy, Cam struggled to his feet. "I had a mishap."

The guy snorted, probably a little too entertained by the idea of something happening to his friend. "What kind of mishap?" His eyes jumped back to Kailani, making her feel accused of something she didn't do.

She definitely didn't like this guy.

She hopped to her feet, if only to get to an even playing field. Sure, Cam's friend had been among the first to come back to the starting line, but he only had superficial muscle. He probably ran more than anything and wouldn't stand a chance in a fight. Not that fighting was a good idea. But if he was friends with Cam, surely he felt inadequate often enough to know it was a bad idea to push things too far.

And poor Cam still looked sick to his stomach, as if he knew the teasing wouldn't stop anytime soon.

"He was helping me," Kailani said loudly, pulling both men's attention back to her. "I ended up on the ground, and Cam was nice enough to walk back with me." It wasn't technically a lie.

Cam's smile might have been worth a lie, with the way he grinned at her now. "I did walk back with her," he agreed, perhaps a little unnecessarily. "Oliver, ready to—"

"How did she end up on the ground?" the guy—Oliver—asked Cam, laughter in his voice.

Before Kailani could come up with a strategic answer, Cam said, "I fell into her. I mean—"

"You tripped?" Oliver asked.

Again, Cam spoke too quickly. "Fainted." His eyes went wide. "No, I didn't—" He turned and threw up again, shaking hands pressed to his knees.

And Oliver laughed. Kailani now officially hated the man and couldn't help but wonder why Cam considered him a friend.

"Has someone been telling lies, Cam Ma—"

Cam was up in an instant, wrapping Oliver in a headlock and tucking him under his side. "If you don't stop talking right now," he warned, and then his eyes found Kailani. "I'm so sorry," he said, though she didn't know what, specifically, he was apologizing for. "I should probably go. But it was nice to meet you. Officially."

He stood there for a moment, Oliver still tucked under his arm. (Apparently Oliver was smart enough to realize there was no point in him fighting.) Was he waiting for something? Kailani hadn't dated nearly enough to know how to ask him for his number before she had to go another few months before she saw Cam again. *If* she saw Cam again.

"Can I—" she said at the same time Cam said, "Maybe I could—"

They both stopped, grinned, and then Kailani, who must have been possessed by someone far more daring than her, reached forward and grabbed his phone from the hidden pocket on his waistband, poorly ignoring how close her hands came to all of his impressive muscle. Then she shoved the phone in his face to unlock the cracked screen and typed out a text to herself. Sending it, she waited for the buzz on her arm before she put the phone back in his pocket.

"Just in case," she said, though she wasn't sure what to make of the wide-eyed expression on Cam's face.

At least, she didn't understand it until she realized her hand had strayed from his waistband to his stomach, where each of his six glorious abs had shown up for roll call beneath her fingers. She'd gone under his shirt, straight for his skin like a creep.

Even Oliver was staring at her, and her face burned as she took a step back. Maybe the distance would be a good idea.

But Cam dropped Oliver, who landed with an *oof*, and crossed the small space between them. As much as she wanted to kiss the guy, she was glad he left a lingering kiss on her cheek and not her mouth, what with all the vomit and everything. But if the heat that shot through her was her body's reaction to a kiss on the cheek, she couldn't wait to see what a real kiss would feel like.

"See you around," he said, his voice low and husky, and then he was gone, leaving Kailani reeling with a stunned Oliver on the ground next to her.

"Where in the world did that come from?" Oliver asked, as if he'd never seen his friend with so much game before.

Kailani hoped that was the case. She hoped she was the first person to ever get under that man's skin, because she didn't want to share him with anyone else. She wanted him — and that crooked smile he threw back at her as he walked away — all to herself.

TWO

"YOU'VE GOT TO BE KIDDING me." Cam stared at the flier on the light post right outside his gym, Riptide, advertising free protein shakes for a month for anyone who joined the gym around the block. For a *month*!

"What's wrong?" Sasha asked. She hadn't seen the sign yet because she was busy unlocking the front door, but when she turned around, her jaw dropped. "Oh dang, they're giving out the good stuff."

"Not helping," Cam growled.

He had been open for less than a month, and it had been a never-ending battle with Horizon Gym, the gym only a quarter mile away. The gym that had stolen his dream location and opened only two days after he did. The gym that had been stealing his clients and making him wonder if his business would be dead before it even had a chance to live.

Sasha let out a sigh as she tore the flier down. "It's probably fine," she said, though she wasn't very convincing. "We have protein shakes too."

"For purchase," Cam argued. "We can't afford to give them away for free." As he followed his head trainer inside and flipped the lights, he did his best to ignore the tightness building in his chest. He had half a dozen clients coming in today, and he couldn't afford to be off his game any more than he could afford free shakes.

He knew starting his own gym wasn't going to be easy, but he hadn't counted on having a rival. The other gym owner—some guy named K. Adams—had been a thorn in his side for weeks, and it had taken a whole lot of self-control to keep Cam from marching over there and giving the guy a piece of his mind. Whatever his name was—Kenny, Kevin, Kyle, it didn't matter—he had quickly made himself Cam's most hated person.

"Hmm."

Stashing his stuff in his tiny office behind the front desk, Cam narrowed his eyes at Sasha. "What does that mean?"

She was still looking at the flier for Horizon Gym, though she quickly held it behind her back. "Nothing."

"Nothing, huh?" Cam's voice had dropped to a growl. Sasha had never been afraid of him—she had seen him cry over a client's progress one too many times at the old gym where they used to work together—but that didn't stop him from trying.

Rolling her eyes, she crumpled the paper up and started backing away. "It's not important."

Cam leapt over the counter. "Give it to me."

Undeterred, Sasha continued her backwards retreat, narrowly avoiding weight machines as she moved in the direction of the hot tub. "I shouldn't have said anything, Cam. I promise it's not—"

Cam dove, catching hold of the flier as Sasha held it high, but he only managed to get half. The other half ended up in the tub, but it didn't matter. Cam's half had enough: *sponsored by the Healing W-*

"He got the Healing Well," he breathed, his stomach sinking. The nonprofit had been his best chance at getting enough money to really get the gym going; their focus was educating as many people as possible about the benefits of a healthy body. Cam had been talking to reps for months, hoping to convince them to donate to his gym so he could offer lower rates and get more people taking control of their health.

Becca had told him at the race a week ago that things were looking promising.

Apparently not as promising as she'd thought.

"Look on the bright side!" Sasha said as she fished the rest of the flier out of the water and led the way back to the front desk. "That probably means Horizon isn't in the black either."

It was a tiny consolation, but not enough to give Cam much hope. "How many people signed up over the weekend?" he asked, holding his breath. He wasn't sure he wanted to know the answer.

Sasha turned on the computer, and a few clicks later she made a face.

Cam's stomach twisted. "Is that a good face or a bad face? I can never tell with you."

She shrugged. Equally unhelpful. "We had thirty-six signups."

"That's good, right?"

"Unless you remember you offered everyone their first month free."

Grimacing, Cam tucked his hands under his arms to warm up his fingers. He didn't usually get cold, but anything business-related made him clammy. "It was the only way to get enough attention as a startup," he argued.

Sasha rolled her eyes again, which meant she thought he was acting stupider than normal. He knew that much about her, at least. "Horizon Gym didn't offer a month free, and they've been full from day one. I walk past it every day on my way home."

Cam groaned, running his hands down his face. "Admit it. You regret coming to work for me."

"Not yet, Martinez. But you're going to have to think of a way to get ahead of this protein shake thing. Without offering anything for free unless we can also get it free," she added, likely seeing the look on Cam's face. "You still have to bring in money, or we're both out of a job. Henry too."

That much was true. But Cam refused to fail when this was the first thing he had truly committed to in his life. This gym was entirely his, and he couldn't give up on it or the two trainers who had believed in him enough to join him.

"I'll think of something," he told Sasha as his first client stepped through the door.

He had to.

Kailani had never been one for working the numbers, but she'd been stuck in front of the computer for an hour now, staring at the spreadsheet her accountant friend had sent her. She didn't understand most of it, but it didn't look good.

Dialing Trish's number, she put her office phone on speaker and drummed her fingers on the desk while she waited for her to pick up.

"I'm guessing you've seen the numbers," Trish said by way of greeting.

Kailani groaned. "What am I looking at, Trish?"

Trish had never been much for showing emotion, and the fact that she let out a sigh now had Kailani worried. "Basically, you need better marketing. You need more clients."

"What about the protein shake thing?"

"That's already in there."

Kailani had been afraid of that, and she didn't want to know what the spreadsheet would look like without the money from the Healing Well. Thank goodness the girl at the race—Becca—had agreed to set up an appointment with the board first thing last Wednesday morning so Kailani could plead her case for some grant money. But if she didn't get enough paying, lasting clients, she was never going to be able to start an after-school program like she planned.

If she couldn't do that, she would have to return the grant, and she definitely couldn't afford to do that. All of the money had already purchased the protein shakes and the fliers.

"What kind of marketing do you suggest?" she asked Trish.

She scoffed. "I don't know anything about marketing, Kailani."

"I know. I just thought—"

"I've got a client who just came in, so I have to go, but I'm sure you'll think of something."

"Thanks," Kailani said, holding back a moan. "I owe you one, Trish."

"No problem."

As soon as she hung up, Kailani dropped her head onto the table and gave herself five seconds to wallow before she was back up again. The thought popped into her head that she could ask her parents for help, but she shut that down immediately. Why would they ever help her? Besides, they could barely take care of themselves let alone anyone else.

Rising to her feet, she wandered closer to the window to look out over her gym. Now that it was evening, the space was decently full of people working out and following Kailani's training videos. Her two trainers were out on the floor keeping an eye on things and fixing posture and position, but most of the people on the floor were doing basic exercises. Nothing that would really turn them into athletes.

If she didn't find actual clients, all of her work would be for nothing.

As she wandered back to her desk to stare at the spreadsheet a little longer and try to make the numbers fix themselves, her phone buzzed with a text and sent her heart racing as soon as she realized it was Cam from the race.

> Cam: Is it depressing that I would rather be passed out on the pavement right now than what I'm currently dealing with?

Kailani grinned, even though it sounded like Cam was having a bad day just like she was. They had been texting sporadically back and forth for a week now, and every text sent a little thrill through her. It felt like they'd known each other for years, with the way they jumped right into conversations even when they went a while in between texts.

> Kailani: As long as I'm there to catch you.
> Cam: I think I preferred the other way around, when you were in my arms.

As her cheeks burned with heat, Kailani pressed her palms against them and willed them to stay a normal color. Her office was made entirely of windows, and she wasn't keen on the whole gym seeing her blush. It usually wasn't easy to tell, with her darker skin, but Cam somehow made her blush way more than she ever thought possible.

"Who does that?" she muttered, staring at the text Cam had sent. No games, no lies. Just honesty and directness.

Before she could tell him she preferred being in his arms as well, he sent another text. Then another.

> Cam: I'm sounding like a tool again, aren't I?
> Cam: Sorry.
> Cam: I think I might be better if you weren't so beautiful.
> Cam: I didn't mean that.
> Cam: I mean, I did mean that you're beautiful. I didn't mean to come on to you so strong.
> Cam: I'm just going to lose my phone now, okay?

When she was sure he was done, Kailani typed out her response with a ridiculous grin on her face, feeling braver than she'd been all week.

> Kailani: Please don't do that. How else are we going to figure out where our date will be?
> Cam: Date???

Cam: Are you asking me out??
Kailani: Don't tell me you're all about the man having to
    be the one to make a move.
Cam: I'm just mad you beat me to it. I was working up to
    it. I had a whole plan.
Cam: Will you at least let me plan the date?

Kailani squealed a little, glad her office was relatively soundproof if not hidden behind walls. Seriously, how was this guy so adorable? He had the appearance of a gym bro but the personality of a total gentleman, and in her experience, guys like that were rare. She'd almost given up hope that they existed.

Kailani: I can concede, as long as you let me pay.

Truth be told, she probably shouldn't have offered that. She could barely afford dinner for herself as it was, and if she didn't find a way to get that spreadsheet looking a little less red, she was dead in the water. She'd known making money with her gym would take some time, but that gym on the other side of the block—Riptide—had complicated things. How had she not realized it was opening until it was too late?

Just like that, her good mood was gone, and she glared at her computer. Whoever Mr. Martinez was, he had been the biggest stress of Kailani's life. Who even offered a free month at a brand-new gym? That was the stupidest small business decision Kailani had ever heard of, and yet it was the reason most of her clients were currently members who had only signed up because they were friends of her parents or from the neighborhood and wanted to support.

None of the people out there doing half-hearted exercises were going to last.

So she'd gone to extreme measures and used all of the money that had come from the Healing Well sponsorship toward advertising and protein shakes. It was risky, and she couldn't rely on third party products to keep her place afloat for long. But hopefully the incentive would bring in some real clients.

As her phone buzzed with a text, Kailani tried to be excited about it, but the stress of her gym dampened the thrill.

Cam: Okay, but only because I believe in feminism. Date
two is on me.

Kailani *really* hoped Cam would be different from everyone else in her life. History had taught her otherwise, but maybe there was someone out there who would show her that love was possible. Maybe it would be him.

THREE

Cam was supposed to be doing a second training session right now, but the guy hadn't shown up. He wouldn't have cared — a lot of people quit after the first session — but he had a bad feeling that several of his missing clients had changed their minds on which gym they wanted to attend. Apparently free protein shakes were a big draw despite the cost of personal training being much higher at Horizon Gym.

He'd thought he would have his first date with Kailani to look forward to, but she'd just canceled on him. Again. He understood being busy — he'd had to cancel their first attempt at setting something up a few days ago — but he feared their respective jobs would continue getting in their way and he would never get a chance to prove to her he was a decent guy.

But now he was stuck in an almost empty gym, no clients to train and nowhere to put his restless energy. The bench press was calling to him, but first things first. He had to text Kailani back before she thought he was mad at her for rescheduling. He wasn't mad; just disappointed. Apparently to the point where he was starting to sound like his friend's parents.

He groaned as soon as he hit send.

Cam: And I mean that in the least creepy way possible.
Cam: I promise I have no plans to force you into anything.

How was it he managed to stick his foot in his mouth even while texting?

As if summoned by Cam's embarrassment, Kit's name lit up his phone. Cam took several breaths before he answered, knowing his best friend would catch on to any emotion he didn't keep tamped down.

He answered at the last possible second. "Hey, Kit. What's up?"

"Are you with a client?" Kit asked.

If only. "Not right now."

"Good."

When Kit went silent, Cam cleared his throat and grabbed a rag so he could start wiping down machines as he talked. He could at least be semi-productive until the last few stragglers left the gym for the night. "Did you have a reason for calling, or…?"

"Right. Sorry. I just got the feeling you might need to talk."

Cursing under his breath, Cam quickly made his way back to his closet of an office. With people still working out and him being the closing trainer, he couldn't disappear entirely, but he planted himself in the doorway and tried to pretend no one was paying him any attention. Not easy, when the three girls on the mats in the corner had been watching him all night as they pretended to do yoga.

He blamed the stupid hashtag his coworker had started a year ago. Sure, it had gotten him enough attention to get him a few actual clients from his old gym, but he wasn't sure how long he could make that unwanted publicity last. They weren't really here to work out; they were more interested in watching *him* work out. And he wanted to, if only to get out some energy, but Kit's call had made that difficult.

"Why would you think I need to talk?" Cam asked with a grimace. He couldn't have sounded more defensive if he'd tried.

"Because I haven't seen you in over a week, Martinez. Now, spill it."

Kit had been his best friend for more than fourteen years at this point, and that meant Kit sometimes knew him a little too well. Cam had done his best to pretend everything was going great with his gym, but because he was terrible at lying, that also meant he'd been avoiding his friends as much as possible.

"What do you want me to say?" he asked with a sigh.

Kit probably shrugged. "Whatever you need to. How's the gym?"

"I don't want to talk about that." Though, according to the churning in his stomach, that wasn't fully true. "I'm just having a hard time keeping things going with this other gym around the corner. Whoever this guy is who owns it, it's like he's matching my every step before I take it."

"Maybe you need a break. You should come over and we can play some basketball or something. I'll even throw a ball with you if that's what you need."

As nice as that sounded, Cam didn't have the time to spend with his friends when he could be using it for something to help his gym. Maybe if he offered up nutrition counseling to anyone who signed up for personal training… He already had the know-how, so all it would take was some time and energy.

Not that he had much of those things to spare.

"I gotta go, Kit. If I don't figure out how to get in the black, you're going to have me moving into your spare bedroom and organizing your nightmare of a closet."

Kit laughed. "That might be the strangest threat anyone has ever made against me. Don't work yourself too hard, okay?"

Cam mumbled something that barely resembled words, mostly because he didn't want to lie. Until he stopped wanting to tear his hair out every time he looked at his finances, the only thing he was going to have time for was work.

He just hoped he could fit some time in with Kailani somewhere in there. If anyone could make him feel better about his situation, hopefully she could.

Cam: I know you and I are both busy, but I'm not giving up on you yet. How about a twenty-minute coffee date next Thursday sometime between 10 and 11:30?

Not even a text from Cam could improve Kailani's mood this morning. Not when Mr. Martinez had just played his next move in a way she would never be able to match. Free nutrition guidance with every personal training contract? If Kailani wanted to do something like that, she would have to hire a nutritionist, and it wasn't like those grew on trees. That would cost money. Money she didn't have. Money she couldn't use even if she had it. How could Riptide afford something like that?

Letting out a sigh, Kailani looked out her office window at her little gym and wished she knew what she could do to make it thrive. If she could get some actual income instead of bleeding out money every day, she could start her after-school workout program for kids and teens who didn't have a great home life. She could get a better apartment than the tiny box that barely had enough space for her, let alone Isla too, but was the only thing the two of them could afford if they wanted to avoid moving back home. At least the protein shake thing had brought in more people, and the place was pretty full today. Enough so that Kailani wanted to be out there, actually working with her clients instead of watching from behind the glass like some zoo animal.

That was the whole point of this. She *loved* working with people. But she also had a business to run, and that side of things had been taking up all of her time since the moment she opened her doors. She had had to force herself to go out onto the floor a few times a day and interact with people so they at least recognized the face behind Horizon Gym, all the while knowing she had work to do.

Was this going to be her life? Sitting behind a desk and wishing she'd never chased her dream in the first place? This was awful.

Her phone buzzed with a call where it sat on the desk, making her jump. Guessing it was her mom with some sort of request, she answered without looking at the screen. "Hi."

"Oh good, so I didn't imagine you?"

Her stomach did a strange somersault at the sound of Cam's deep voice. She definitely hadn't expected *him* on the other end of the line, and heat pulsed through her as his crooked smile filled her mind's eye. "Cam! Hi. How—how are you?"

"Better now that I know you're real." He chuckled, and she imagined it rumbling through his chest. Though she'd tried not to dwell on it, she'd been revisiting his pectorals for weeks. Her up close and personal view as he'd cradled her had lodged itself in her brain, though she couldn't be too angry about it. As someone who prided herself on her own personal fitness, she'd appreciated feeling small and protected in his hold. Yes, she was strong enough to take care of herself. No, she didn't dislike the idea of someone being stronger if she needed it.

"You thought I wasn't real?" she asked, cursing the way she'd gone breathless. She hadn't seen the guy in weeks; how did he still affect her so much?

"Yeah, well, when all I've got is faceless texts, I was starting to think maybe someone was catfishing me. Why else would you cancel all of our plans?"

Because she was drowning, but she wasn't about to tell him that. Cam was the one good thing she had in her life. Taking a deep breath, she told herself that she couldn't mess things up with him before they even started. No matter how much she was struggling, she had to make this effort. "You canceled too," she reminded him. "But Thursday sounds great."

"I changed my mind."

Her heart sank. "What?"

Though he laughed, it wasn't enough to quell the fear that she'd already lost her chance. His next words, however... "Thursday is too far away. I've been wanting to see you since the moment I walked away at the race. Got anything going on today?"

Too much. But surely she could spare an hour, right? Her two trainers had been handling everything anyway, and Kailani could definitely use the caffeine boost if she was going to find a way to compete against Martinez's nutrition strategy. Brainstorming was easier with a little shot of energy. Maybe Cam would be able to offer up some ideas, seeing as he was a trainer as well.

Hoping she wasn't going to shoot herself in the foot by sharing her business issues, Kailani took another deep breath and took the plunge. "I've got some time. What part of the city are you in?"

"East side. What about you?" Cam's happiness was clear in his voice.

"Same. That makes this easier!"

"There's a smoothie shop on Hunter Ave."

"I know it." In fact, it was one of Kailani's favorite places to go when she wasn't being extra frugal. Their acai bowls were incredible, and their coffee even better. "Meet you there in half an hour?"

"Can you make it fifteen minutes? I'm feeling impatient."

Kailani laughed. How had she put this off for so long when Cam was such a breath of fresh, honest air? "I can make that happen. Let me just make sure my team is good, and I'll see you there."

"Your team, huh? You never did say what you do for work."

Hadn't she? They'd talked about so many things at the race and while texting over the last few weeks, but Kailani had intentionally strayed from anything too personal. Cam didn't know where she lived or what she did, and she definitely hadn't said anything about her family. But why? She'd lied to herself, telling herself it was for her own safety, until she knew Cam wouldn't serial killer murder her in her sleep, but she really doubted he had a dangerous bone in his body, despite his size.

She'd been protecting her heart, plain and simple.

Maybe that should change, but old habits died hard. "I'll tell you all about it at Blended Perfection," she said.

"Hearing you say those words is perfection." He cursed, and then he hung up.

Grinning, Kailani sat at her desk for a minute as she processed what had just happened. With one phone call, Cam had managed to convince her to get her away from her stress and do something for herself for once. Not that smoothies were all that indulgent, but every penny counted. Hopefully it would be worth it.

That was when she realized she only had fifteen minutes to make sure she looked cute and alert and not at all stressed. No big deal.

Twenty-three minutes later, she sprinted down the sidewalk and hoped Cam was like her and not super great about punctuality. She hadn't meant to take so long, but one of her clients had been squatting with terrible form, and the other trainers had been busy, so she'd spent ten minutes walking the woman through the exercise. Then she'd seen herself in the wall of mirrors and realized her hair was an absolute mess, and it took three different braids before it finally cooperated.

She also may have hunted down a Horizon Gym t-shirt to wear so she could impress Cam. He already seemed to like her, but a little power play couldn't hurt.

Finally reaching the smoothie shop, Blended Perfection, Kailani tugged the door and rushed inside.

Directly into a pair of strong, warm arms.

"I wasn't expecting this kind of greeting," Cam said with a rumbling laugh, "but I'll take it."

"Sorry!" She probably should have pulled away as soon as she recovered from the collision, but her feet refused to move. Probably because his hold seemed to chase away all of the lingering doubt she'd been harboring about this guy for the last few weeks. She shifted a little deeper into his arms, pressing herself up against his hard chest and wishing she wasn't so starved for attention that she could so easily ignore the strangeness of hugging someone she'd only known in person for a couple of hours. Hugging someone like this, in particular. Why did she turn into a touch-starved maniac whenever she was around him? She hadn't been this way before meeting him.

"Bad day?" he asked, and his warm breath tickled the loose little hairs by her ear.

He hadn't smelled this good at the race. Not that he'd smelled bad—apparently Cam was one of those rare breeds of men who still smelled pretty great when all sweaty. Those genes should have been illegal. But today, Cam didn't just smell okay. He smelled *amazing*. Whatever cologne or after-shave he used, it filled her nose like a wave curling over her toes on a sandy beach. That metaphor didn't even make sense, but it was how it made her feel, and she breathed him in without shame.

"Are you smelling me?" he asked.

Okay, maybe a little shame. Her face flaming, Kailani slowly pulled out of his hold and stepped back so she could give him a sheepish smile. "You smell good. Sorry for running into you. Literally."

His eyes sparkled, despite there being no twinkling lights anywhere nearby to make that happen. Eyes didn't just sparkle on their own, but apparently Cam's did. She hadn't paid much attention at the race, but his eyes were such a unique color of brown. Like cinnamon. She'd never seen eyes that color, and she loved them.

"I'm guessing you were excited to see me?" he said, one corner of his lips lifting to create that adorable half smile.

Kailani grinned right back. He said everything with such ease that it made it easy to be open and honest with him. On the rare occasions she dated, she felt like she had to hide pieces of herself and be strategic about when she pulled them out for display. A first date was almost like a job interview. But Cam had yet to give her any reason to think she couldn't be entirely herself, and it was utterly refreshing. Not that she'd really taken him up on it, but at least she felt like she could be more open with him than she'd ever been with anyone else.

"Well, when you kept rescheduling," she said.

He narrowed those fascinating eyes as his hand found hers, like holding her hand was the most natural thing in the world. "Excuse me, but *you* were the one who canceled more times than me. Now, I believe you owe me a smoothie."

Kailani loved that he gave her a gentle tug to pull her into the line with him. "You're really going to let me pay?" she asked, giving his hand a little squeeze.

He shifted an inch closer to her. "Only because this means I can pay for dinner the next time we get together."

He was impossible to look away from. She didn't know how he did it, but Cam was like a magnet, drawing her in with his open expression and big hand wrapped around hers and that delicious smell of his making her wonder if he would taste as good as he smelled. She was never one to kiss on the first date, but he seemed worth the exception. She'd almost kissed him at the race, after all, and all those text conversations over the last few weeks had definitely made this feel less like a first date and more like a reunion after a long time apart.

"What can I get you guys?"

Kailani flinched when she realized they'd reached the front of the line. Just how long had she been staring at the man?

Grinning as if he knew exactly how she felt, Cam gestured for Kailani to order first. "Just so I know how much you're willing to spoil me," he said with a wink.

He joked, but Kailani genuinely appreciated his thoughtfulness. By letting her order first, he could gauge her budget, something he proved when he ordered something slightly less expensive than the green smoothie she chose for herself.

Smoothies in hand and fingers laced together, they headed for the outdoor seating without saying a word. It was like they'd been on this date a million times already and knew the routine, and Kailani's heart kept beating faster with every minute that passed. Both with excitement and with fear. All of this felt so much like they were meant to be together, but there was no way Cam was *this* perfect. She could live in the fantasy of this moment for a little longer, but at some point the other shoe was going to drop and leave her dreams squished on the sidewalk.

As soon as they'd sat on some high stools at a round table outside, hands still clasped together, Cam shook his head as if clearing away a fog. "Can I say something?"

"Please." Kailani sipped her smoothie, intentionally drinking the smallest amount that she could to draw out this date as long as possible.

His expression held some measure of reverence beneath his easy smile as he took her in inch by inch. "I'm gonna sound crazy, but it feels like you and I..."

Like they what? Kailani might have asked if he hadn't lost his smile at the same time he lost his words. Following his eyes, she glanced down at her t-shirt with her gym's logo splashed across the front. "I'm actually a trainer too," she said warily. Maybe she had made a mistake in choosing to impress him. He had already admitted he was intimidated by her, so she probably should have eased him into the idea of her being in the same sphere as him.

"You work at Horizon Gym?" he asked. His voice had dropped almost to a whisper, his face turning slightly green.

Kailani wasn't sure if she wanted to answer that question with the way he was looking at her like she'd run over his dog. "I, um, own it."

"No, you don't."

What kind of response was that? "Yeah, I do?"

"No."

"You don't believe I can own a gym?"

He slid off the stool and started pacing, though he didn't have a whole lot of space to do it. Not only were the tables all packed closely together, but he was so big that he used up every square inch as he rubbed his palms along his thighs. "No," he said, making her heart sink. But then he kept talking. "No, I don't want you to own *that* gym."

What did he have against her gym? "Why not?"

He glanced at her and stopped pacing, nothing but pain in his expression as he stuffed his hands into his dark hair. "Because if you own Horizon, we can't be…"

As she gripped her smoothie cup, she wished she wasn't so entirely confused so she could make sense of this conversation. "What does that…" That was when she saw it. His jacket had covered it before, but with his arms up, she could see the wave logo printed on his shirt over his heart.

Riptide.

Kailani's heart dropped, and she was pretty sure it had left her body entirely instead of falling into her stomach. It wouldn't be enough for him to be an employee there. He wouldn't freak out this much. "Cam, what's your last name?"

She already knew the answer to that question, but she wanted to hear him say it.

He winced. "Martinez. And you're Adams." It wasn't a question.

Of all the gyms in Diamond Springs, why did Cam have to own *that* one? The only one that Kailani hated.

"We can't Romeo and Juliet our way out of this one," Cam muttered and clenched his jaw, moving his hands from his hair to under his arms, making his shoulders look even bigger.

"Romeo and Juliet die in the end," Kailani replied. Her smoothie suddenly tasted sour, and she regretted making the purchase. The fifteen dollars she'd dropped ten minutes ago could have been so much more useful somewhere else.

Cam looked miserable. "Exactly." And then his expression shifted, his eyebrows pulling together as his thoughts worked through his head. When his eyes snapped back to hers, something had changed. His entire body had gone stiff, muscles tensing as he gazed at her. "What's your next move?" he asked.

Kailani's eyes widened. *Seriously?* "As if I would tell you."

"You've got to be planning something after my nutrition play."

"Yeah, and if I tell you what it is, then you'll just do the same thing and be one step ahead of me again."

"No, I won't." He turned slightly green and pressed a hand to his mouth as he swallowed. "Fine. You don't have to tell me."

She narrowed her eyes as she stood. "Don't act like you get to tell me what to do. I just bought you a smoothie."

When he stepped closer, he seemed to grow in size. Instead of protective and safe, he looked almost scary. "I'll pay you back if going on a date with me is so repulsive to you."

Kailani rose up on her toes, trying to match his height as she closed the distance between them. "I wouldn't have gone out with you if I'd known—"

"Is that why you kept canceling on me?"

"What?"

"You flirt with me to throw me off my game and knock me off balance?"

"Are you insane? I didn't flirt with you!"

Eyes flashing, he leaned closer as if hoping to add power to his words. "You were totally into me."

She scoffed. "Ego, much?"

He let out a bark of a laugh that had no trace of humor. "You almost kissed me at the race. Admit it!"

"I wouldn't be caught *dead* kissing you." But as if they weren't paying any attention to what she was saying, her eyes slipped down to his mouth. She'd been dreaming about that mouth for weeks. *Rein it in, Lani.* "You could be the last man on earth, Cam Martinez. You could smell amazing, and you could have abs of steel, and you could have the most tempting lips I have ever seen, but I still wouldn't—"

For being so big, the guy moved fast. He grabbed her waist and pulled her against him, his mouth only an inch from hers, and he went so still that it was like he was made of stone.

"You sure about that?" he breathed.

Nope. She definitely wasn't sure. And despite her brain screaming at her to get out of there, her body decided it was a great idea to take the reins.

FOUR

Lips.

That was the only thing Cam could think about. Kailani's lips specifically, because his attempt to throw her off kilter had backfired the minute she closed the distance between them and locked her mouth onto his.

She was kissing him.

He wasn't stopping her.

In fact, he was enjoying it a little too much—the way she tasted like her peach smoothie and her hands splayed against his chest and every part of her seemed created to fit against him. He kept trying to pull her closer even though she was as close as she could get, like if he let go he would stop existing because every sensation would disappear as soon as the moment was over.

This wasn't going to end well.

Thankfully, a scream pulled him out of it before he got lost. Though, he probably shouldn't be thankful for someone screaming, and he didn't appreciate Kailani shoving him backward until he crashed into a table, nearly knocking it over.

Who had screamed?

Two young women stood just a few feet away, their phones pointed directly at Cam and Kailani with their mouths hanging open. Had something exploded behind him and he'd been so caught up in mapping out every tiny detail of Kailani's lips that he'd missed it? He glanced behind him, trying to catch his breath, but the only thing there was a one-footed pigeon on the low wall lining the property, staring at him with its head cocked to one side.

Unnerved, Cam turned back to the girls.

One of them lowered her phone and started typing away, but the other one went off on a monologue, gesticulating as she stared at her screen. "People, are you realizing what you just saw? That's right! That is Hot Body Cam in all his muscled glory making out with *the* Lovely Lani."

"What is happening?" Kailani whispered.

Cam noticed with pleasure she looked a little dazed as she touched her lips, maybe without even realizing she was doing it. He would never consider himself an expert when it came to kissing, but he was pretty sure he could do the job well. Her awed expression confirmed that.

That isn't important right now. The girl was still gabbing away to whatever followers she thought were watching her little livestream, and she and her friend had blocked his escape. He needed to get out of there before he did something else stupid.

"I wouldn't believe it if I didn't see it with my own eyes," the girl was saying, "but these two are *totally dating*." She squealed, jumping up and down. "Do you know what this means? It means #camlanilove has officially set sail! Our dreams are coming true!"

Cam cleared his throat, trying to find a way to set the record straight before things got out of hand. He'd seen too well how quickly a hashtag could—

His phone pinged, then pinged twice more, and he knew without looking that he was already too late. But he grabbed his phone anyway, dread churning in his stomach as his phone continued receiving notification after notification. He'd been tagged in a picture—so had his gym—and the photo was taking the internet by storm.

Over two hundred likes in less than a minute. Was that even possible?

His mind spinning while the girl continued to gush over the moment she'd just witnessed, Cam stared at the photo and felt like a stranger to his own life. Yes, he'd definitely been in the moment when he kissed Kailani, but this was… Based on the way the two of them were pressed together, limbs tangled and mouths locked, that had been more than just a kiss.

He swallowed, barely noticing that Kailani had pulled out her phone as well and seemed frozen in place.

This wasn't good.

"We need to go," he muttered, and when he took hold of Kailani's hand, both girls squealed again.

"Aren't they so cute?" the videographer asked her phone, while the other snapped several more photos.

This *definitely* wasn't good. Tugging Kailani with him, he muttered something that sort of resembled, "Excuse me," and pushed past the girls, picking up his pace as soon as he had an open path.

"Seriously, what was that?" Kailani asked. She'd gotten over the initial shock, apparently, but that would hardly make any of this easier.

Cam had been living in the public eye for several months now with the #hotbodycam thing that had started at his last job, but nothing had ever gone viral. He ignored all of it anyway, not really caring to see not-so-sneaky pictures of himself that other people had posted.

Based on the way his phone wouldn't stop buzzing, this was an entirely different ballgame. As they walked, he double checked his phone to make sure none of the notifications were important, and then he turned it off before it drove him crazy. It would all be waiting for him as soon as he really processed the last ten minutes.

Only when they'd gotten far enough away from Blended Perfection for Cam to feel confident about not being followed—he still double checked—did he pause and let go of Kailani's hand. It would hardly make a difference in terms of the actual problem, but not having anyone staring at him helped to calm him down. A bit.

"This is bad," he muttered, knowing that didn't answer her question. Honestly, he wasn't even sure *how* it was bad, but he knew it wasn't good. His whole body had been tense from the moment he broke away from the kiss, and he had learned to trust his body.

As she played with the end of her long braid—a braid Cam was fairly sure he'd gripped in his fingers just a few minutes ago—Kailani stared at him like he was her only link to reality.

He really hoped that wasn't true.

"There's a hashtag for us," he said and flinched, waiting for her angry response.

She just blinked. "A what?"

"A hashtag."

"What's a hashtag?"

"What are you, eighty?"

She folded her arms. "Well, excuse me for not spending all my time connected to my phone."

"I don't spend all my— It doesn't matter. This is a big problem."

"Why?"

He wished he had a good answer to that. But if she really didn't spend enough time on the internet to know what a hashtag was, he probably needed to explain a few things first. "A hashtag is a way to categorize social media posts and search them."

"Okay?"

This was going to be harder than he thought. Maybe if he started with just him… "I've had one attached to me for a while. #hotbodycam. Anytime people post pictures of me, they use…" He paused when one of her eyebrows rose high, realizing how he sounded. "I didn't start any of it. Someone at my old gym liked the way I looked, and…" He groaned, running his hands through his hair. "There's no way to make myself sound good."

"Wouldn't make a difference anyway," she replied with a roll of her eyes.

If that was the case… He folded his arms to match her. "Fine. A lot of people who came to my old gym would post pictures of me with the hashtag *hotbodycam*, and I've got a decent following. I've used it at my gym to get more clients to sign up for training."

Kailani huffed. "Typical."

"It's business, Lani."

"Don't call me that." She said that as her face lit up red.

Cam couldn't decide if that was because she was angry or because she liked the nickname. *Again, not important*, he told himself. "Anyway," he growled, "it sounds like you might have a hashtag too. And now there's one for both of us."

Oh, she didn't like that, her eyes going wide as she dropped her arms. "Was that the Cam Lani Love thing she was saying?"

Just how long had #camlanilove existed? Their gyms had been open for barely over a month. "I think so. Actually, give me your phone."

"Why?"

"Because I turned mine off."

"Wh—"

He grabbed her phone out of her hand, both glad that she didn't have a screen lock and miffed that she wouldn't protect herself with one. Though nervous about what he would find, he searched the hashtag and clenched his jaw as way more posts popped up than he was comfortable with, complete with fanart and bad photoshops of the two of them together. Did people not realize they were actual humans and not just bodies?

"What are you looking at?" Kailani asked, grabbing his arm and leaning in to look—right as Cam scrolled to a photoshopped picture with their faces pasted over a couple who were definitely *not* working out.

He cursed and dropped the phone.

Thankfully, Kailani caught it before it hit the cement. But then she was able to get a good look at the picture, and she closed out of the search as she turned a deep scarlet. "That's what hashtags are?" she whispered.

He swallowed, though his words seemed to have lodged in his throat. "Not usually," he croaked and took a step away from her in case she thought he might get some ideas from that photo. "Most of my tags, at least, are just when I'm training or working out. Fully clothed. By myself."

"But now it looks like people want us to be a thing," Kailani concluded, finally catching on. "But how would they even know about both of us?"

It was a good question, though it wasn't like their little rivalry had been much of a secret with their constant attempts at one-upping each other. But how did people take away a relationship when Cam and Kailani had definitely never interacted in public? The only time they could have been seen together before today was at that race, and no one except the volunteer had actually seen them together. No one except Oliver.

Oliver was a lot of things, but Cam highly doubted he would start a hashtag like that. Oliver didn't even know Kailani's name, and Cam hadn't known about her owning the gym until just a few minutes ago. So how would people have…?

"Hang on," he said, turning his phone back on. Impatient as it booted up, he started to pace again to give his energy somewhere to go. His theory was so unlikely, but it was the only thing that made sense.

Ignoring the million notifications that popped up as soon as his phone was on, Cam pulled up the original photo he'd been tagged in and clicked on the girl's account. Sure enough, she had posted multiple photos of both Cam *and* Lani from inside their gyms.

"They're members of both," he said, hardly believing it.

Kailani shifted close again, though she seemed wary about what she might find on his screen. "Both gyms? The girls at the smoothie shop?"

Cam resisted the urge to take a deep whiff of her hair and her tropical shampoo, but it was difficult to ignore when her head lingered right under his nose. That intoxicating smell of hers had contributed to the whole kiss fiasco in the first place, and he did not need to fan the flames of this unexpected fame. Knowing his luck, someone would find them mid-kiss again and record the whole thing.

Now he was remembering the feel of her lips on his, his focus slipping.

"Is that good or bad?" Kailani asked, stepping back.

Cam considered slapping himself to keep himself from reliving the kiss but thought better of the idea, shaking his head instead. He didn't want to come across as a lunatic, even if his chances with this woman were now at zero. "Based on the number of followers I've gotten in the last fifteen minutes, it's hard to say. This might bring in a lot of business."

Kailani looked at her own phone, squinting at it. "How do I see how many followers I have?"

"Seriously, do you live under a rock?"

"My sister set up my account. I've never had to look at it because I never use it."

Sighing, Cam took hold of her phone and pretended he didn't feel a weird spark when his finger brushed against hers. It was just static electricity. Not attraction.

His stomach roiled, apparently angry that he would try to lie to himself. That was new. Usually that only happened when he said something out loud, and he hoped that wasn't a new evolution in the insanity that was his gut. He liked being honest, especially with himself, but sometimes a guy needed to pretend the truth was wrong for the sake of his mental health.

"You have almost three thousand followers," he said, pulling up the list. Some of them weren't even in Diamond Springs, and he guessed his account would look pretty similar in that regard. He did have almost five times her followers, but that didn't mean much when he rarely posted anything.

Kailani's eyes went wide as she pulled her phone back to see for herself. "How is that possible? I'm pretty sure this morning I had, like, zero."

With the popularity of the *lovelylani* hashtag, Cam doubted that. She'd probably been gaining followers for a long time without even realizing it, and the fact that she had a good deal of content on her page had him wondering how she had no idea that her sister had done more than simply set up the account for her.

Though the photos and videos that had been posted weren't exactly useful for building Kailani's business, content was still content. She could probably start posting snippets of workout videos and link those to a website, and…

He stopped himself there. Helping Kailani would only hurt his own chances. And from the looks of things, her training style was a whole lot different from his. He wouldn't have the first idea how to help her unless he did some research, and he definitely didn't have the time to build up his own media presence let alone his enemy's.

"She's not the enemy," he muttered.

"What?"

Wincing, he scrambled for something that would save him from that slip. "The girl who took the video. She's not the enemy." It technically wasn't a lie, but his stomach still didn't like that response.

Kailani didn't like it either. "How is she not the enemy? Both those women just posted about us without our permission. All of these people did!"

"Unless you have it written into your policy, there's nothing to stop people from taking pictures of us and putting them wherever they want. And out in public? There are no laws against that." Not that he was a lawyer, but even if he was wrong, he was pretty sure there was nothing they could do unless actual harm came from the photo and video. Even then, it would probably be a pretty shoddy case.

Besides, he'd meant what he said about the girls not being their enemy. This publicity could potentially be really good for both of them. And it wouldn't cost them a thing.

"We should probably just ride this out," he said with some hesitation. "See where things go. This whole thing could blow over in a matter of hours, or…"

Kailani grimaced. "Or what?"

"Or it turns into a really big deal and could make or break us both."

"I liked that first option a lot better."

"Me too."

"So now we just go back to work and pretend nothing happened?"

Cam considered that, though he didn't like that he was the deciding voice for anyone but himself. Kailani had just given him a lot of power, and she seemed ready to follow his lead with whatever he did. He could easily use that to his advantage and tell her something that would kill her business, and then he would be free to thrive and make something great of his little gym.

He would never be able to live with himself if he did that, and his stomach twinged to remind him that he would never be able to lie to her in the first place.

Taking a slow and careful breath, he decided that, for now, he wouldn't decide at all. "I need to get back to Riptide," he said. "Make sure nothing has gone crazy in the last hour. I'll…" He glanced at her, hating that he had no idea where they stood now. In the space of a few minutes they'd gone from attraction to hatred to making out, and now? Now everything was weird. Complicated. He never would have thought a simple kiss could do so much damage.

"I'll text you," he muttered, and then he hurried off toward his gym. But when he gave her a backward glance and found her frowning at him with those delicious lips of hers, he knew he couldn't call what they'd shared *simple*.

Nothing about this was simple.

FIVE

THREE DAYS. THAT WAS HOW long it took Cam to send her a text. Three days of nonstop posts and tags and pins and sub-reddits and all the things Kailani had never heard of until the day of that stupid, mind-numbingly good kiss. It had been three days of fielding phone calls that had nothing to do with becoming a gym member. Three days of ignoring all of her siblings who had suddenly discovered posts they should definitely not be seeing. Three days of wondering if Cam was ignoring her because he had hated kissing her.

It shouldn't have mattered if he enjoyed their kiss, seeing as he was her nemesis, but it did. She'd dated in the past, of course, but never seriously, and the kisses she'd shared with people had been chaste and, honestly, boring. Bland.

Kissing Cam? Kissing Cam had turned into something that should have gone down in the history books as the most epic kiss ever, and it hadn't even lasted that long. It had definitely been outlived by the hashtag that had become ridiculously popular and probably confused a whole lot of people because the posts had nothing to do with a jumbotron: #kisscam.

That photo and video had been used so many times that they were permanently burned into Kailani's brain from all angles now. She'd lived through it, and now she got to relive it every day through the never-ending photos and videos. The memes. The drawings. The insatiable desire to *do it again*.

So when Cam's text finally came in, Kailani was just about at her wit's end.

Cam: We should talk.

Kailani groaned, glad that she had locked the gym doors for the night so she could be alone for this. There were no sentences more terrifying than that one, and she did not need her entire full-to-capacity gym watching her glare at her phone. She might not have been so annoyed with him if he had texted her sooner, but it had been a long three days.

Kailani: Who is this?
Cam: Nice try.
Cam: This isn't dying down like I thought it would.
Cam: When are you free to meet up?

This was way less fun than texting about a future date.

Kailani: How does a few days from now sound?

As soon as she sent that, her phone lit up with a call from the man.

"You're really mad at me for seeing if things fixed themselves?" he said by way of greeting.

"I had no idea what was happening," she argued. "And you knew that."

He let out a heavy sigh as if completely exhausted. "You could have texted me first, Lani."

A shiver ran through her at the nickname, just like it had the last time he'd used it. Her parents and siblings called her Lani, so it wasn't like there was anything new about it, but his deep voice speaking her name did strange things to her spine. It sounded so different from what she was used to, like it meant something to him.

She had to stay focused. "Well, when you say you're going to text, *Cameron*, I expect you to text."

He growled a little. "So you found out my full name. Good for you. Don't call me that. And I never said *when* I would text you."

That was interesting. Why wouldn't he like his full name?

"When can we talk?" he asked again.

"We're talking right now."

"This isn't—" He growled again. "I don't think this is the kind of conversation we should have over the phone. This might be a bigger deal than we want it to be."

Kailani didn't like the sound of that. She had hoped Cam would come up with a solution to the insanity that had been her life for the last three days, and now she felt stupid for not trying to fix this herself. She'd gone her whole life without ever relying on someone else, and a pretty face and rock-hard body shouldn't have been enough to change that part of her.

But trying to fix this when she had no clue what she was doing was like trying to fix her own shattered bone with duct tape.

"Fine," she said, though reluctantly. "Tomorrow night?"

"I've got something…never mind. I can make it work. We should meet in a neutral location."

What was this, an illegal money drop?

"Roger that," Kailani said. "Meet at oh-nine hundred hours?"

"That's nine in the morning."

"Whatever. Nine p.m.?"

"Why so late?"

With the way Cam grumbled that question, Kailani had a feeling he was not a night owl. Neither was she, but she'd had to keep her gym open longer because so many people had signed up for personal training. Technically that was a good thing, but she only had so much manpower to do it all. Only had so much energy to deal with the sudden fame and attention. And there was no telling if it would last.

"It's nine o'clock or nothing, Cam."

"Fine. Where are we meeting?"

It was nice of him to let her choose, though it wasn't like he was the kind of guy who would ever do anything terrible. Sure, he was her rival, but he had proven himself to be a decent man. The only thing she had to fear from him was the fate of her business.

But where could they meet and ensure they kept things civil? And rated PG...

Now Kailani was thinking about kissing the man again.

"You with me, Lani?"

Probably a little too much. "What about O'Reilly's?"

The sound that came out of Cam's mouth was something between a laugh and a cough. "The fun center?"

"It's a public place, and there will be plenty of people to—"

"Figure out exactly who we are?"

He made a good point, but Kailani's argument came quickly. "I don't know if you've ever been, but that place is always full of kids and preteens. If those people know who we are, we've got bigger problems. Or do you have a better idea?"

There was that sort-of laugh again. "No, that sounds great."

"Great."

"Great."

And now Kailani had no idea what to say. From the very beginning, things had always been so easy with Cam, but now that they'd become rivals and gotten into this whole hashtag mess, she had no idea what their relationship was anymore.

They hadn't had a relationship to begin with. Not really.

"So I'll see you tomorrow?" she ventured.

He let out a huge sigh.

"Wow, I'm sorry the idea of having a conversation with me is so repulsive to you."

Groaning in a way that shouldn't have been attractive but absolutely was, Cam took a second to answer. "That's not what... We just got tagged again."

"I've been getting tagged all week."

"Not like this."

Her heart pounding with dread, Kailani pulled her phone away from her ear, switched the call to speakerphone, and opened up the latest notification. It was the same photo of the kiss that she'd been seeing all week, but this time it had been inserted into a mock news story with the headline "Trouble in Paradise?" The second photo was a half-and-half picture of both of them, one on each side. Cam was looking off into the distance looking broody—in the hottest way possible—while the picture of Kailani had her frowning down at her phone in her office. She had been doing that a lot the last few days, so it wasn't all that surprising.

It was the caption that had her worried:

> *Diamond Springs' favorite athletic pair may have already called it quits, making this star-crossed love story a tragedy for the ages. Has #camlanilove died before it even had a chance to begin? Maybe it's time we start looking elsewhere for our romance fix. Or maybe we can convince these two to work things out so WE can keep working out.*

Kailani swore.

"Yeah," Cam breathed.

"This is going to kill me."

"You and me both, Princess."

"What do we do?" But even as she asked that question, she already knew the answer. It didn't matter how attracted she was to the guy; he was now her sworn enemy. There was no way it was going to work, but did they even have a choice? "We're going to have to pretend to date, aren't we?"

He groaned again, the sound low and thrumming with energy. "It's not going to work," he confirmed, but there was enough hesitation in his voice to tell Kailani that he was considering the idea.

"You don't think we can convince—"

"I can't lie, Kailani."

She sighed. "I know it isn't ideal. I don't like the idea any more than—"

"No, I mean I literally *can't*. If I try, I usually… We need to come up with a different plan."

Kailani didn't have a different plan. She liked to think she was pretty smart, and she knew in her gut that their perceived relationship was the only reason they'd had any real business over the last few days. With how many likes and comments that latest post was getting, even in the last few minutes, chances were high that those few sentences would spell the end of *both* their gyms if they didn't do something about it.

"Let's talk about it tomorrow," she suggested. If he was still against the idea after they had a chance to think about it, he would hopefully have a better suggestion that wouldn't involve lying out the wazoo. Trying to undermine the man's business had made her feel guilty enough, and lying to all of her clients would be even worse. But it could possibly be her only choice.

Cam grunted, his frustration with her answer clear. "Fine. Nine o'clock. Don't be late again."

He hung up before she could think of a clever response.

If dating that infuriating man was her only chance at saving her gym, Kailani was doomed.

"FITNESS COMPETITION?"

"Give out free towels or something."

"Every fifth month is free."

As his three friends shouted out suggestions for how to save his gym, Cam tried to stay focused on the game of laser tag happening around him. The four of them had been playing for almost an hour now—Oliver rented out the arena so they wouldn't be joined by any eight-year-olds—and the game had been a nice diversion. Or it would have been, if the guys hadn't insisted on turning the battle into a brainstorming session.

He'd suggested the game as a way to distract himself from his problems, but then he'd gone and opened his mouth, telling them—in detail—about everything that had happened with Kailani and their kiss.

For the most part, he had been ignoring their suggestions, letting them hash it out amongst themselves, and he'd kept his focus on racking up as many points as possible. One of these days he would surpass Oliver's high score, and then he could finally have bragging rights about something.

"What about doing a speed dating event with you as the only man?"

Cam stopped dead when he heard Oliver's words on the balcony overhead, and his vest lit up with three different shots almost immediately. He threw Oliver a glare before ducking behind a pillar. "That is the stupidest idea I've ever heard," he growled.

"Yeah, well, if everyone finds out you're not dating this girl, you need to capitalize on the attention. You've got women all over you, and they clearly want to see you happily settled. Just set a high entry fee, and you're golden."

As he hid from further attacks, Cam closed his eyes and tracked the sounds of his friends' footsteps. They'd been playing at the O'Reilly's laser arena for more than fifteen years now, and all four of them knew every nook and cranny of the place. He wouldn't be safe for long, but that was okay.

He knew Ben was likely in his corner on the top level, biding his time and taking sniper shots at every opportunity. As long as Cam kept to the tunnels, he'd be safe from overhead attacks. Oliver had moved to the lower level, and it sounded like Kit had joined him for a temporary truce, the two of them closing in from either side.

If he could attack first, he would get in some serious points.

He took a deep breath, adjusted his finger on the trigger, and started counting down as the acrid odor from the smoke curled around him and nearly made him sneeze. *Three... Two... One...*

His phone buzzed to life in his pocket with a call, his ringtone on full volume. Cursing, he fought to silence it, but it was too late. His vest lit up with sounds of explosion, and the arena lights turned on overhead at the same time the game ended.

While his friends cheered, Cam grabbed his phone and grimaced when he saw that it was Kailani calling. "Hey," he said when he answered the call.

"Where are you? I thought we were meeting at nine."

Kit threw an arm around his shoulders and pulled him toward the gear room so they could drop off their vests and see their scores. "Better luck next time, Luchador!" he shouted.

No one liked laser tag quite as much as Kit Morgan.

Pulling himself free, Cam cleared his throat. "I'm only a couple of minutes late. I got caught up with something."

"Wrestling?"

"What?"

"Luchador."

"Uh, laser tag."

She was quiet for a second. "Are you already at O'Reilly's? I thought you had a thing."

Was she seriously annoyed by the fact that he'd taken advantage of the location she picked? Shrugging out of his electronic vest, Cam carefully tucked his gear away and glanced at the high score board while the other guys horsed around on the other side of the room. They were in a good mood despite his currently sticky situation...

He was still too far behind Oliver on the top score board. He'd been trying for almost fifteen years to catch up, but he had a long way to go before he reached the god status Oliver had gained. Oliver would always be one step behind Kit, the two of them an inseparable pair—leaving Cam to trail behind and hope he didn't get left in the dust as they moved on to greater things.

"I did have a thing," Cam grunted, holding his phone a little tighter as he rubbed the tightness from his chest. Now was not a good time to start getting anxious about things beyond his control. "It just happened to be at the fun center. I'm on my way out."

"That her?" Oliver asked once Cam hung up. He glanced at his watch, lifting his eyebrows. "Either she's running late and apologizing, or she's as punctual as Kit and angry."

Kit shoved Oliver, nearly knocking him off his feet because he was still riding high from the game. Laser tag (or any other form of competition) was one of the few times Kit loosened up.

"Punctuality is a bad thing? Sorry for making you late, Cam. If Ben had shown up when he was supposed to…"

Ben immediately turned bright red. "I was only a few minutes late. And it was Allie's fault, anyway."

Oliver snickered. "Makeouts do make it pretty easy to lose track of time. They're dangerous in a lot of ways."

They stepped through the laser tag door into the main floor of the fun center, a wave of cold air blasting them. Cam hadn't realized how sweaty he'd gotten until he shivered in the sudden temperature change, but it made sense. He had been pushing himself pretty hard, like he always did when trying to escape a problem.

"I wasn't making—never mind." Ben tucked his hands into his pockets, eyes on the ground. He and his girlfriend had only officially been dating for a month and a half, but things seemed to be going well. Ben had been a lot more confident since meeting Allie. Happier. Most of the time, anyway. Cam imagined Ben still wasn't used to the extra attention he got nowadays, something Cam understood way too easily.

"We never came up with a plan to save your gym," Kit said as they entered the arcade.

"I told you," Oliver replied. "Our own version of *The Bachelor.*"

Cam groaned. "I literally can't think of anything worse. Can you imagine what the internet would say about Kailani if I did that?" Then he froze as he caught sight of Kailani standing near the front doors, her toned arms folded and a fire burning in her eyes as she took in the gang of guys surrounding Cam.

"Maybe it was a bad idea to bring you guys," he muttered.

Kit put his arm around Cam's shoulders again, making Cam realize he had been backing up when he came to a sudden stop against Kit's hold. "First of all," Kit said, "you're the one who scheduled this meeting on a Wonder Boy night. Bad form.

Second, you're gonna need an unbiased third party in all of this."

"There is no way any of you are unbiased. And I'm not positive you'd all be on my side."

Kit rolled his eyes. "Even so, you're going to need support tonight. So don't push us away."

Chest tightening further still, Cam forced himself to focus on the moment and not the thought of being completely on his own for all of this. Before Kit could pull away, Cam pulled him into a quick but tight hug. "Thanks," he murmured so only Kit could hear.

Kit nodded, saying nothing. He didn't have to. He was the only one who understood why Cam had fought so hard against becoming a part of the Wonder Boys back in junior high, and he was the only one who could recognize Cam slipping into a panic.

Though it took a little self-convincing, Cam finally worked up the courage to cross the last bit of distance between him and Kailani. "Sorry for the delay," he said, folding his arms to match hers. "I hope you don't mind, but I brought some witnesses."

Kailani eyed each guy in turn, her eyes lingering a little longer on Ben. "I know you," she said after a moment.

Ben turned scarlet again. "We met at the climbing gym a few months ago."

"No, that's not it. Have I seen you in Horizon Gym before?"

When Ben didn't deny it, Cam's jaw dropped. "Are you kidding me? Where's your loyalty, man?"

Shrugging, Ben looked like he wanted to be anywhere but next to Cam's glare. "It was Allie's idea. She wanted to go to a gym run by a woman because she thought it would be less, uh, *macho.*"

Cam might have argued that point, but he knew too well how people saw him. It was hard for some people to see past the muscle, but he would have thought Ben's girlfriend knew him better by now. Regardless, that wasn't going to change his current situation, so he figured he should let it go for now.

"Let's sit down," he suggested, gesturing with his head toward the tables. Thankfully, it was late enough on a school night that the bulk of people left in the fun center were teens and older, leaving the picnic tables free from birthday parties and overwhelmed parents.

Though she hesitated, Kailani nodded and followed the four of them to one of the plastic red-and-white tables and settled on the edge of the bench, next to Kit and across from Cam. "I'm assuming you've come up with a better solution than fake dating?"

Cam really wished he had a different answer to that question. "No."

"I suggested—"

Cam whacked Oliver in the gut, cutting him off. "No, I think that might be our best option, with the way comments have been going today."

He'd been trying not to pay attention to yesterday's #camlanilove post, but the internet was convinced the two of them were on the rocks. Fewer people had been inside his gym today. All signs pointed to their relationship, real or otherwise, being the only thing keeping him afloat.

He needed Kailani, and she needed him.

Watching Oliver warily, Kailani nodded. "What happened to that inability to lie?"

Cam swallowed, nausea already rising in his gut. "I'll be fine."

"Someone grab a bucket," Oliver said.

Cam whacked him again. "I'll make it work," he amended. He just hoped the Wonder Boys would have some magical solutions for *this* problem, one he'd had for half his life. If not, it was going to take a lot of cleverness to make something work without lying about everything.

Kailani didn't look convinced, but there wasn't much Cam could do about that. Not when she set her jaw with a determination that put him in awe. "Fine," she said. "So we fake this relationship, and then what? I don't think this will keep us in business forever."

"One of you is going to have to leave." Oliver flinched, probably expecting Cam to hit him again. He was right, though, as much as Cam didn't want to admit it.

"I can't afford to move," he muttered.

Kailani sighed. "Neither can I."

Which meant they were no closer to a solution than they'd been before.

Kit sat forward, his thinking face on as he fiddled with the leather bracelet he always wore. "If neither of you is willing to leave, you could do some sort of competition. The loser has to concede."

Kailani's expression probably matched Cam's, her disgust clear as she turned to Kit next to her. "We've tried that already with all our promos and things, and it got us into this mess." She gestured to Cam.

"Watch who you're calling a mess," he growled. She wasn't wrong about the competition, though, and they would never be able to pit their businesses against each other like they'd been doing. "Unless it's just us competing, not our gyms, that will only make things worse. But that still doesn't change the fact that neither of us can afford to lease anywhere else."

Oliver raised a hand. "I could always—"

"*No.*" Cam didn't even move his arm this time, but Oliver still flinched again. It was kind of him to offer, but Cam had already taken more of Oliver's money than he was comfortable with. Oliver was too loaded to understand why it was so hard for Cam to borrow from him, and that was never going to change.

"I suppose..." Kailani's eyes flitted between Cam and Oliver, as if trying to understand the relationship between them.

If she thought she could figure it out in a night, more power to her. The two of them had been in the same friend group for fifteen years at this point, and Cam was pretty sure neither would call the other an actual friend. Not a good one, anyway. The only reason they tolerated each other was because of Kit.

She cleared her throat and continued. "I suppose we should focus on the dating part of things while we try to come up with a real solution."

The dating part was the part Cam was going to hate more than anything. If he couldn't tell a trivial lie without almost vomiting, how was he supposed to fake an entire relationship when he would so much rather have it be real? "Maybe we should talk alone," he suggested.

Kailani didn't move. "I prefer witnesses."

"Fine."

"Fine."

As a headache started to form between his eyes, Cam pinched the bridge of his nose and told himself to remain calm. It wasn't working, so he rose to his feet and started to pace. "Okay, so, a relationship..." Where did they even start?

"Ground rules," Kailani said, rising as well, though she didn't pace. She probably just wanted to level out the playing field.

"Agreed," Cam replied. "No more kissing." As much as he wanted to...

"*More* kissing?" Oliver asked, his eyes wide. What, had he completely ignored their entire laser tag conversation?

Kailani ignored him; she was learning quickly. "Except when clients are watching us."

Valid. "But we still keep them to a minimum."

Kailani made a face of disgust, as if the very thought of kissing him made her sick. It passed quickly, and she laid out the next rule. "Each of us agrees to at least one social media post together or about the other person a week."

"Make it two," Cam argued. "The more we keep it in people's thoughts, the better it will work."

"Fine. When it comes to offering perks, we will—"

"Whoa, whoa, whoa. It's my turn."

"No one said we had to take turns."

"So you just decided to walk all over me? How is this deal supposed to work if we don't remain equal?"

"Fine." Kailani folded her arms. At some point, she'd come around the table and was only a foot away from him. "Your *turn*, you baby."

"No more free perks to try to outdo the other."

Kailani groaned and rubbed her temples. "I thought we'd already agreed on that, but yes, no more perks. We still have to make money, after all."

If it weren't for the whole money thing, Cam wouldn't care about any of this. If he could give everyone free training, he would do it, but that made for a terrible business model. He was barely in the black as it was, and he still had to pay rent on his tiny apartment above the gym. He never thought he would admit this, but he missed the apartment he had shared with Ben before all of this went down. At least that had been livable.

He let out a deep sigh. "Your turn."

"Going back to rule number one. We agree to stay out of the other's gym as much as possible."

"How are people supposed to know you're dating?" Ben asked, looking between them with an odd look in his eyes. "Social media isn't enough to sell it if you never see each other, and the people you're concerned about are the people at the gyms."

Yet another person who was right. Why did all his friends have to be so smart tonight? Cam folded his arms, meeting Kailani's gaze.

She thought about that for a moment. "Fine. You can come to my gym. But if you make one comment about how my training style is any less than yours, the truce is off."

Cam nodded, though he had no idea what her style was outside of being less *macho* than his; all he knew was it was different. That was as much as he'd gotten out of Sasha when he'd asked, since she walked past it every day. He would have to investigate to soothe his curiosity. And, of course, to be a dutiful boyfriend.

"You might want a routine," Kit suggested. "Every good couple has a routine."

"Says the perpetual bachelor," Oliver muttered with a grin.

Oliver meant it as a joke, but Cam glanced at Kit anyway. As always, when it came to the subject of his bachelorhood, Kit wore a mask of indifference.

Cam forced himself to stay focused instead of trying to figure out what Kit was really feeling. "How long do you think we'll have to keep this up?"

"You're the social media guru," she said with a shrug. "You tell me."

Oliver scoffed. "If you're not going to go with the bachelor idea, then I'm reiterating the idea of a fitness competition. Loser has to pack up and leave."

"That's a terrible idea," Cam groaned. "Besides, it wouldn't be fair."

That got a laugh out of Kailani. "Why? Because I would beat you in every event? Don't worry, I would go easy on you. Let you win at least a couple of events."

Tensing without meaning to, Cam growled as his competitive nature rose to meet his rising attraction for this woman.

His admiration of her gumption wasn't going to make this any easier. "Yeah, I don't think you would have to bother letting me win anything. I can hold my own."

She dropped her voice, leaning in a bit. "I'm sure you can, with all this muscle of yours." She ran her finger along his arm, her eyes so focused on her hand that it was almost like she had forgotten where they were. The finger turned into a hand, stroking his bicep down to his forearm in a careful examination.

Cam didn't breathe. He couldn't. But when her hand made its way back up his arm and over to his chest, he let out a grunt that made her eyes jump up to his like she'd been caught doing something she shouldn't. The victory he felt was small, but at least he knew he affected her at least half as much as she affected him.

He smiled. "I'm adding one more rule." It was taking everything in him not to kiss her like he had outside Blended Perfection. Would she taste the same way she had that morning? He was particularly fond of peaches.

Her face bright red, she took a wide step back. "No touching," she said, probably reading his thoughts. "Except when necessary. But I will have to touch you when you bring me a smoothie every other morning."

"When I what?" Cam shook his head, trying to stop the buzzing that had risen in his ears. Was she thinking about smoothies too? That smoothie in particular? Meaning the moment *after* the smoothie, when he'd tested the waters and she'd dived right in.

"And when I drop off dinner for you on those days you train late," Kailani said.

He caught on, though he rolled his eyes. "A routine?"

She snickered, her nose crinkling in the most infuriating way. It was adorable. "It's better than catching each other off guard, isn't it?"

His jaw tightened in response to the way she stepped close again. "Yes, it's better." Though, he wished he wouldn't have to see her so often. How was he supposed to reconcile between the strong and capable woman he'd met at the race and the one thing standing in his way of finally making something of his life?

Why did she have to be both his enemy and the most alluring, determined, fierce woman he had ever met?

It's better this way, he told himself. Given his track record with relationships, faking it would spare the disappointed expectations in the end.

"So…" She twisted her lips to the side, and Cam had to bite the inside of his cheeks to ignore the temptation that presented. Nothing with her would be real from this point on, but he hoped he could enjoy what time he got with her in the meantime. "I guess now we should post something so everyone knows we're still together?"

"Already done," Oliver said, slamming his phone on the table and looking way too pleased with himself.

Cam barely held his fist back as his heart rate skyrocketed. Oliver knew better than to scare him, and he was lucky Kailani was standing right there and holding a good portion of his focus, or his reflexes would have kicked in. He'd been so focused on her that he'd forgotten about the fun center entirely. Impressive—or maybe terrifying—considering the deafening sounds of the arcade around them. No one had ever had quite that effect on him before.

Taking a giant step to the side to distance himself from Kailani while he tried to calm his heart rate back down, he did his best to keep his voice even. "What, exactly, do you mean by that?" He kept his eyes on the phone in Oliver's hand, as if staring at it long enough would unlock the screen and show him what was on there.

It turned out he didn't need to see Oliver's phone. Not when his own pinged with a notification.

"I thought you didn't know about the kiss," Cam muttered as he watched the video Oliver had taken of his conversation with Kailani, complete with the #camlanilove tag. The words they were saying in the video were too quiet to hear, but if Cam hadn't known better, he would have thought the two of them were whispering sweet nothings while Kailani stroked his arm.

Oliver chuckled. "I've been here all night, you dingbat. I just didn't think it was all that spectacular until I looked it up a minute ago. Dang, Martinez; you've got more game than I thought!"

Heat flaring in his face, Cam stared at his phone as the comments started growing. While Oliver's caption had been vague—*Spotted at O'Reilly's and hoping for another epic smooch*—nearly every comment was one of celebration.

"Um." Kailani grabbed his arm, making him tense, but the way she was staring at the other end of the arcade pulled his attention away from the fire that spread through him from her touch.

Three teenagers were pointing their direction, phones out and eyes eager.

"Time to go," Cam said, grabbing her hand and tugging her toward the door before they got swarmed by fans.

They got about halfway across the fun center before someone stepped into their path of escape, but Kailani pivoted and dragged Cam around an arcade game, throwing off their admirer just long enough that they could slip through the door. She didn't stop until she'd reached an old Buick that looked like it had been built in the eighties.

Cam didn't tell her she was still holding his hand, even after they'd stopped their frantic dash.

"I don't think I'm ever going to get used to that," she said, a little out of breath. Her heart was probably racing just like Cam's.

Wishing he had a way to calm her down, Cam said the only thing that wouldn't be an outright lie. "It's probably going to get worse. We should keep to the gyms as much as possible, where we can better control who comes in and out."

That was when Kailani seemed to realize she still gripped his hand, and she frowned before prying her fingers free. Cam tried not to look disappointed.

"I think you're right," she said, "as much as it pains me to say it."

He took a step back, his chest tightening again. Having such an attractive rival was bad enough, but it was knowing what could have been under different circumstances that killed him. He'd never felt this way about anyone, and he wasn't ready to end it yet.

But maybe it was better that something had come between them. This way, no one would get their heart broken when the relationship ended in a month or two, because Cam wasn't sure he would have made it through intact if they'd gone on much longer the way they had been.

He'd never put his heart on the line before, and he was too scared to do that now. Even if he almost wanted to.

"I'll stop by tomorrow," he muttered, shoving his hands into his pockets. "For better or for worse, we'll make this work."

"Wait!" She rushed forward and planted a kiss on his cheek, lingering there long enough to send Cam's heart racing. "They're standing at the door watching us. See you in the morning."

She slipped into her car and drove off, leaving Cam wondering if it was already too late to make it out of this thing in one piece.

SEVEN

KAILANI WAS DOOMED. SHE'D BEEN open for all of three hours, and already she'd had six different people asking her about her relationship with Cam. And it wasn't just women coming up to her; a couple of men had fished for information, though she suspected that was because they wanted to ask her out but wouldn't do it if she really was taken by someone like Cam.

"One positive to all of this," she mumbled. She had a great reason to turn them all down.

A great reason that was also going to be the death of her with his crooked little smile and painfully fit body.

It didn't help that her heart beat a little faster every time the door opened, as if it was hoping it might be Cam. That was nothing short of ridiculous, but she still found herself glancing over with every tinkle of the doorbell.

She wasn't supposed to like him still. From the moment she realized he was the reason she dreaded her next utility bill, she should have forgotten everything that was appealing about him. *Should have* being the key words, because things had only gotten worse after their little pow-wow last night. Not only was he extra attractive when sweaty from his laser tag game, but the way he'd interacted with his friends—and the way they had had his back but still thought of Kailani's welfare—meant he was part of a group of excessively good guys. That meant *he* was also excessively good, something she'd suspected from the start.

Why couldn't he have been some crotchety old man with a beer gut and roving eyes? It would have been so much easier to hate him.

Kailani was in the middle of a training session when the door opened, and she would have known it was Cam even if the gym hadn't gone suddenly silent. Her whole body erupted into goosebumps, and she made a mental note to check the thermostat as she continued talking her client through beginner's squats.

"You should try having her wear a band below her knees for extra support." Cam's voice was deeper than Kailani remembered, which was stupid considering she'd seen him just last night. Maybe it was just because there weren't any other sounds in the building, so his voice resonated in her chest like she was tuned specifically to him.

Even her client had paused, her eyes wide as she glanced back and forth between Cam and Kailani and probably made herself dizzy.

Taking a deep breath, Kailani counted to five, then turned around. "Hi, *pumpkin*. What are you doing here?"

Cam slung an arm over her shoulder, which didn't help the goosebump situation even though he felt like a human space heater. "I brought you a smoothie, *darling*. Your favorite." He held the green smoothie in front of her face, giving her something to focus on that wasn't the muscle on his forearm pressing into her neck.

The smoothie really *was* her favorite, which meant he'd been paying enough attention on their started-out-as-a-date last week to remember. Seriously, why did he have to be so frustratingly cute? It was more than just his physical aspects that were attractive; everything about him from the moment she caught him at the race had checked all the boxes on the list she didn't know she had.

"It's really true?" the client whispered. Somehow her eyes had gotten wider over the last twenty seconds. "You guys are an item?"

Cam spoke before Kailani could. "We're together, yes."

Whatever happened to not being able to lie? Had *that* been a lie? Kailani supposed he hadn't said they were dating, just that they were *together*, which technically was true with him standing right next to her.

"You guys are soooo cute!"

Cam's chuckle rumbled through Kailani's ribcage, pressed up against him as she was. At some point she'd wrapped her arm around his trim waist, though she didn't remember doing it. Now that she was paying attention, though, she could feel every oblique muscle move beneath her fingers, and suddenly she couldn't concentrate on anything else until he spoke, leaning down close to murmur in her ear.

"You got a second, babe?"

I've got a lot of seconds.

Waving another trainer over, Kailani grabbed hold of the smoothie and took a long drink, ignoring the brain freeze that came from it because anything was better than getting lost in Cam's dark gaze. "Let's go talk in my office," she breathed, though she wished there was somewhere more private. But maybe the audience would help her keep a clear head.

She had to remind herself that all of this was fake. And Cameron Martinez was *the enemy*.

Though she liked to pretend it wasn't the case, given her age—twenty-seven—and level of independence, Kailani hadn't dated much. She hadn't had the time, too busy working at the rec center near her parents' house and looking after her younger siblings until one of them was old enough to babysit. She'd had crushes in high school, but she'd never been able to make the time to go to the fancy dances or even on most simple dates she got asked on. The few that had actually happened hadn't given her much hope in her dating abilities.

The one time she'd come close to dating someone, he had made a run for it the first time she tried to bring him home, breaking up with her before they'd even left her parents' house. Needless to say, she didn't tell anyone about her family anymore. She loved them, but they made the whole dating thing pretty much impossible.

By the time they made it back to Kailani's office and closed the door—a lot of good it did them, with the glass walls—she'd drunk half her smoothie and wasn't sure she was willing to set it down and have an actual conversation with the man who had so gently held her hand the whole walk back. For all his strength, that tender side of him was enough to make a girl swoon.

Kailani had never swooned in her life, unless she counted that time she ran too hard for too long and got so dizzy that she fell over. That was nothing like this.

It's fake, Kailani, she reminded herself. Which was exactly what she needed. She'd spent most of the night last night talking herself through her new reality, and the fake part of this relationship meant she could keep everything surface level. No reason to let Cam in deep enough that he stopped liking what he saw.

"So," she said and leaned against her desk while Cam settled on a chair. She was still thinking about falling, and she had to try really hard not to think about the time *Cam* ran too hard for too long and fell over. Onto her. Starting this whole mess. "How are things looking for you this morning?"

Cam glanced out into the gym behind him, a furrow forming between his eyebrows. "Better than last week. You?"

"Outside of everyone getting way too involved in my personal life, it almost feels like business is settling down comfortably."

"That's probably not going to last."

"I know."

Too many people were pretending to work out as they surreptitiously watched them, and Kailani knew they couldn't linger for long. They had to put on a show, and then she would have to kick Cam out before she forgot what the point of all of this was. She needed him to help her business. AKA the gym was her focus, not the way his jaw muscles strained as he clenched his teeth.

"I guess we need to look like we like each other," she said with a sigh.

That brought his dark eyes back to her. "I can do that. Can you do that?"

Maybe a little too well. She knew it was probably a bad idea, but she decided to run with it as soon as it popped into her head. Despite the tension in his giant shoulders, Kailani slowly slid onto Cam's lap and hooked her hands behind his neck.

"I'm sorry," she said. "Were you not at Blended Perfection the other day? Who kissed who?"

"Why *did* you kiss me?"

She hadn't expected that question, and she wished she was the one facing away from the gym. Right now, everyone had a great view of her expression, so she ducked her face into his neck and sneaked a deep breath of his soap or cologne or whatever it was that made him smell so good. Maybe it was just his natural scent.

Too bad she didn't really have an answer to his question, though. That kiss had been so out of character for her, just like when she'd given him her number. She seemed to do a lot of things she didn't understand when she was around this man. "Heat of the moment?" she said lamely.

Cam growled a little. "Do you end all arguments with a kiss like that?"

What was that supposed to mean? Sitting back up, Kailani did her best to keep her face hidden from the gym as she scowled at him. "Maybe I do. Why should you care?"

"Because if I'm going to pretend to be your loving boy-friend, I need to know you won't be off making out with the cop who gives you a speeding ticket." He leaned closer, his nose almost touching hers.

She smirked, her hands sliding down so she could stroke his pectorals and abs. Muscles like that should be outlawed. "I've never been pulled over."

"Of course you haven't."

Next thing she knew, he was kissing her.

Oh mama. Somehow, it was better than the first time, probably because he was really laying into it as part of the charade. That was what she kept telling herself, but the longer his lips explored hers, the less she understood her own thoughts and the more she never wanted to leave that spot. She wanted to be mouth to mouth for the rest of her life, his giant hands tucked around her waist while she threaded her fingers into his silky dark hair. So many things being said between them without either speaking a word. She was both elated and terrified of what those unspoken thoughts might be.

How was he so good at this? He must have kissed so many people and had plenty of practice.

That thought broke the spell.

"Well," she said, breaking away abruptly and hopping to her feet. "That should do it. Thanks for stopping by."

Though she felt a good deal of pleasure from the fact that Cam stared at her dumbstruck, as if as blown away by that kiss as she had been, she was lucky she managed to keep standing straight. There had definitely been a reason they'd set the no kissing rule. Cam had broken that rule, and now Kailani was going to have to deal with a gym full of people who had just gotten a front row seat to that indiscretion.

When Cam didn't move, still staring at her a little dazed, she moved for the door and pulled it open. "I think your gym is missing you," she muttered.

That seemed to wake him up, though he shook his head a couple of times as he rose to his feet. "I didn't know you taught calisthenics," he said, rather than responding to her comment.

Kailani scowled. "I thought we agreed to no judgment."

"I'm not judging." He stuffed his hands into the pockets of his sweatpants, his eyes roving the gym and lingering on one of the training videos that was playing. In the video, Kailani was demonstrating a trunk twist, and Cam watched it for a moment before his eyes jumped to Kailani and trailed from her head to her toes.

Had he been anyone else, his roving eyes would have prompted a slap in the face, but Cam seemed to study her with the eyes of an expert. Someone who could understand the time and dedication it took to do some of the things she did. Kailani was proud of her body, and she appreciated the acknowledgement of the sweat and tears that had gone into getting her to this point.

Her face still burned, though.

It felt like an hour before Cam finally pulled his hands from his pockets and took a step toward the door. "I'm working late on Friday," he told her, which was probably his way of saying it was her turn to return the smoothie favor. As she led him out onto the floor, he offered up one of his dazzling smiles, then he planted a whisper of a kiss on her cheek and wandered out the door.

Kailani really needed to check that thermostat; the whole building had just warmed ten degrees.

"Um, he is soooo much hotter in person."

Kailani jumped at the unexpected statement, spinning around to find her sister Isla bouncing lightly on an exercise ball. When had she appeared?

"What?" Kailani asked, though she knew it was a pointless question. Twenty-year-old Isla practically lived on her phone and had probably posted several memes with their kiss already. Kailani was so glad they had kept missing each other the last few days with their different schedules, though she'd known this conversation would happen eventually.

Isla hopped up, her blue eyes twinkling with mischief. But something caught her eye, and she leaned around Kailani as she put on a bright smile. "Yes, my leg is fake. You spotted it. Can we carry on now?"

The man she'd spoken to turned a deep red and returned to his jump rope, though he tangled his legs in the rope almost immediately.

Isla grabbed Kailani's arm. "Don't kick him out. People stare all the time."

"But he—"

"It's been more than a decade since I lost my leg," she said, tossing her blonde hair back over her shoulder. "I'm over it. It's not important. What is important is that beefcake that just walked out the door after kissing you senseless. You should have told me he was not very photogenic! Comparatively, I mean." She pulled out her phone as if Kailani needed to see what she meant, scrolling through her photo gallery. "Okay, well, that's not true either. Still super hot in pictures. I took a bunch of photos while the two of you were face sucking in there, and this is going to get you a bazillion more followers once I post them."

"No, don't—"

"Done! So." She grabbed Kailani's arm. "We need to talk about why you didn't tell me you started dating the Juliet to your Romeo."

Kailani felt dizzy, which happened more often than not when Isla was around. She was a human tornado, coming in a flash and leaving chaos in her wake. "Uh, why am I Romeo?"

"Because everyone is in love with Juliet, so it fits him better." But then she winced, looking up from her phone to give Kailani a sympathetic grimace. "Sorry. I didn't mean that how it sounded. I'm sure people are in love with you. *He* clearly is."

Oh, that definitely wasn't true, but Kailani wasn't about to argue. She'd had that argument too many times at this point, and Isla had yet to budge on her side. "I don't really want to talk about Cam," she said, hoping she could end this conversation before it got away from her. "I'm too busy to—"

"I quit school."

Kailani nearly stumbled backwards. "What?"

Isla shrugged, and then she reached for a bar over her head and gave a half-hearted attempt at a pull up despite wearing a mini skirt and heels. How did she even wear heels with her prosthetic? "You looked like you wanted a change in topic. So... I quit school this morning."

Yeah, Kailani had wanted to change the subject, but she hadn't been prepared for a bombshell like that. "But I thought you loved fashion."

"I do! I just thought it was time I ventured out on my own. I don't need old white men telling me I don't understand fashion when they're the ones who have no idea what's up."

"Do Mom and Dad know?"

"I'll tell them if they ask."

"Ah." Kailani would probably do the same thing in her shoes. Not that she would ever *wear* her shoes. Kailani had a strict no-heels policy. She was glad Isla was telling her about school, though. If nothing else, they had each other. "So what now?"

Isla gave her a wicked grin that did not at all make Kailani nervous. Not even a little bit. Okay, it was terrifying. "Now I get to help you capitalize on this little 'rivals to romance' thing you've got going with the Riptide stud muffin."

That sounded like a nightmare. "Nope," Kailani said, holding up a hand. "I don't need you to capitalize on anything."

As she dropped back to her feet, Isla let out a little laugh. She may have only been twenty, but losing her leg to cancer as a kid had always made her seem older. "Oh, honey, you don't think all these people are here because of fitness right? You're already capitalizing on the man-candy. I just want to help you take it to the next level. How did you go from sworn enemies to America's favorite couple, anyway?"

Kailani didn't know how to answer that without Isla taking full credit for all of this. Unless she straight-up lied, she was going to get an earful. Pinching the bridge of her nose, she braced for a squeal as she said, "We met at that race you—"

Isla's scream echoed throughout the room, pulling way more attention their way than Kailani would have liked. "I knew it! I knew going to that race was a good idea!"

"You knew nothing."

"I knew you'd been talking about that Healing Pond place for weeks, but finding yourself a red hot makeout buddy is way better." Her face twisted into confusion. "But I'm surprised you're okay with the whole rivals thing. I thought you hated the man behind Riptide."

There was really no good way to explain how everything had gone down. Kailani was still trying to figure it out herself. It didn't matter how much she liked Cam, because deep down she knew there were too many obstacles in their way for anything to really happen. Their gyms would never survive, no matter how much business a relationship drummed up, and Horizon was the only thing Kailani had that was her own. The only thing that made her feel like she was worth something.

She had put everything she had and then some into this gym, and if she lost it…

"Okay, there is way too much going on in that head of yours," Isla said, grabbing Kailani's hand and tugging her toward the front door. "You have to tell me everything. You're taking your lunch break."

"I can't take a—"

"I don't care what work you think you need to do. You have to take a break, Lani."

Kailani knew she couldn't really afford any time away from the gym, but she felt like she was drowning. If nothing else, Isla's energy would distract her for a few minutes and give her a chance to breathe. "Thanks," she said when they reached the sidewalk outside.

Isla gave her a soft smile before pulling her in for a hug. "We'll figure this thing out, okay? You deserve to be happy."

Kailani hoped she was right, but with the way things were going, she had no idea how she was supposed to get there.

EIGHT

Kit: Club meeting tonight at Oliver's house.

Oliver: Excuse me?

Ben: We meet on Thursdays all the time. Why are you confused?

Oliver: Since when do we meet anywhere that isn't Kit's?

Ben: Good point.

Ben: Kit, did something happen to your house?

Kit: My house is fine.

Oliver: ???

Ben: ????

Kit: Why are you guys freaking out so much?

Oliver: No reason. Usual time?

Kit: Obviously.

The text conversation had happened while Cam was in the middle of a training session, and he had no idea what it meant. They'd been having "club meetings" more regularly since Oliver and Madi's wedding, but outside of places like O'Reilly's Fun Center or their usual pizza hangout, they *always* went to Kit's townhouse.

Kit hated change and always had. Cam had never fully figured out why, but the older they got, the more he thought he understood some of the underlying reasoning. Cam had never had much stability in his life, and those few things that remained constant were the things he clung to as much as he could. It would only make sense that Kit might be the same way, even if pretty much everything in his life was stable.

The fear of losing something good was one Cam knew well. And Kit had a lot of good to lose.

Cam just wished Kit had waited to send that confusing text until later in the day, so he wouldn't be so distracted. He nearly told a seventy-five-year-old man to squat three hundred pounds, only noticing how much weight he'd put on the bar right as the man was about to take it on.

He admired the guy's gumption, but that could have turned into an expensive mistake. Disastrous.

It didn't help that half his brain was still thinking about that kiss yesterday. He hadn't meant to do it, but she'd been sitting so close. He'd felt the stares of her clients as if they were all begging for him to do it, and logic had given way to impulse. Impulse had given way to the best kiss of his life until she broke away, unaffected.

He had no idea how she could kiss like that and act like nothing had happened.

Cam's whole life had changed the moment he laid eyes on this girl, and he was never going to get to keep her.

"Can I ask you something, Martinez?"

Cam glanced up from the electrolyte drink he had been stirring for an indeterminate amount of time. It had probably been longer than he'd like to admit. Sasha was definitely staring at him like he'd been in a daze for at least ten minutes. "What's up?"

His trainer tucked her arms behind her back in the military stance she took whenever she was uncomfortable. "I don't usually pay attention to social media," she began.

Cam grimaced. He hadn't told his staff about the plan with Kailani, mostly because he was pretty sure it was doomed to fail. "And?"

Sasha narrowed her eyes. "And I'll just say I'm a little confused. Since when are you dating the Horizon chick?"

His stomach churning, Cam tried to come up with an answer that wouldn't be a lie. At least by technicality. "Everything started at the half-marathon. I didn't know about her connection with Horizon until last week."

"You guys must not be serious if you didn't even know she owned a gym until recently." Based on the look on Sasha's face, she clearly didn't approve of the pairing. She reaffirmed that when she said, "So now what? Trying to get close to the enemy?"

"I'm not—" Cam swallowed his words before he said something stupid. "I don't know what's going to happen, but she's not the enemy. We're trying to figure something out."

Sasha scoffed. "You're digging yourself deeper into a hole the longer you're with her. You know that, right?"

"I know."

"So why even bother? She can't be that great, if she's still pushing to win. We opened first, so if she actually liked you, she'd be surrendering and letting us do what we need to."

It wasn't that simple, but Cam had a feeling Sasha wouldn't understand, even if he tried to explain. He had convinced her to come work with him because she didn't take excuses. She knew how to push and get results. But when it came to connecting with people, she lacked a natural inclination and preferred to be alone.

She probably thought war with Horizon Gym was preferable to finding a solution that would work for both sides, and Cam would have to keep an eye on her. Make sure she didn't sabotage anything.

"Do I have any more sessions this afternoon?" he asked, already exhausted from the thought of dealing with Sasha on top of everything else.

"Why? Late for a date?"

As much as he didn't want to, Cam hardened his gaze and put a little more force into his words. "I don't appreciate that tone, Sasha, and I know you're better than stooping to pettiness. I'm asking because it's my job. *Your* job is laying out the schedule."

She blushed, probably the first time Cam had ever seen her embarrassed. "Sorry," she mumbled, grabbing her phone to pull up the schedule. "Henry has one more before he leaves, but you're clear unless we have a walk-in. The rest are mine."

Cam offered a brief smile. "Thanks. I've got a meeting with the Boys tonight. Are you good to close up on your own? I know it's been crazy this week."

Sasha rolled her eyes, though the expression was softer than usual. She was probably still recovering from Cam's censure. "It's only crazy when you're here. I knew you were popular on social back at the old gym, but I didn't realize you'd become a literal celebrity. Honestly, it kinda feels like you dating this girl has been good for business, but that doesn't make sense."

"It doesn't," he agreed, his gag reflex nearly kicking in on that one.

He hadn't texted Kailani at all today, hoping that would keep his mind off of her. But it had only succeeded in making him think of her even more, wondering how business was looking for her and if she was doing hands-on training or too busy to get out on the floor.

As much as Cam loved training more than anything, he'd had to cut way back on sessions just to keep things going.

"You know I'm just looking out for you, right?"

Cam met Sasha's gaze, grimacing when he realized she was still standing tense. He'd gotten lucky when she agreed to leave her stable job to come work with him, and he'd done a poor job of making sure she knew her value. "I know," he said, clenching his hands. "Thank you. I would have been dead in the water weeks ago without you, Sash. Why don't you hop on a treadmill and go for a run?"

She frowned. "But I've got—"

"You need it. Unwind for a few minutes. I've still got some time, so I'll take your next session before I head out."

Ducking her head, probably to hide a rare smile, Sasha nodded. "Thanks. Twenty minutes, and I'll be good."

"Twenty-five. Don't think I haven't seen you rolling your shoulders all day." Cam had worked with Sasha long enough to know when she was holding in tension and stress. She was one of those weirdos who actually found running relaxing, and they'd been so busy lately that she probably hadn't had the time or energy to do it much lately. "Make it a hard run."

This time she smiled big. "Is there any other kind? Thanks, Martinez."

"Yeah, whatever."

Though the training session with Sasha's client was a nice distraction for a little while, when he headed out to his car, all of his thoughts came crashing back. He probably needed to text Kailani and make sure everything was still good on her end, but first he had to figure out why Kit was acting so strangely and setting up Wonder Boy meetings in strange places.

By the time Cam made it to Oliver's house, he was contemplating making up a headache or something to get out of staying very long. He'd never be able to get away with it without throwing up on Oliver's carpet, but maybe that would be worth it.

Oliver answered the door without a word, looking Cam over for a second before he stepped aside to let him in. "Kit isn't here yet," he said once they were both sitting in the living room.

Cam nodded. Kit would be there any minute; he tended to stick to plans and schedules religiously. "Where's Madi?"

"Out in the guest house. Allie came over to hang out with her tonight, so Ben's probably a little distracted."

Nodding again, Cam rubbed his palms on his thighs and tried to think of something to say. Something about Allie turning Ben from a shy and hesitant guy to someone a lot more confident. Or maybe asking about Madi and her pregnancy. But all of his words settled thick in his mouth, stuck there.

After five minutes of sitting on the couch in silence, Oliver cleared his throat. "Is this as weird for you as it is for me?"

Cam grunted his agreement. The fact that Kit was late wasn't helping anything. Not only did Cam not get along with Oliver if the two of them were left alone for too long, but it wasn't like Kit to stray from routine. Either something was wrong, or Kit was up to something.

Cam's money was on that last option.

Kit Morgan was the most reliable and predictable man on the planet, but every once in a while it was like another side of him made an appearance, here and gone too quickly for Cam to ever figure out where the change came from.

"At least Ben has an excuse for being late," Oliver muttered. "Even if he lives in the backyard. That guy really needs to get married so he can spend even more time with Allie. They're clearly meant for each other."

"How's his book coming?"

Ben and Allie had written a graphic novel last fall that went viral after her ex sent it to a website for free downloads, and though they were still in a legal battle to get the rights back, they had been picked up by a publisher to make another one.

Oliver shrugged. "You know Ben. He says they have a lot of work to do, but from what I've seen of the second book, they're well on their way to becoming rich and famous."

"That's good." Drumming his fingers on the arm of the couch, Cam glanced at his phone and debated calling Kit to make sure something hadn't happened to him.

Oliver, on the other hand, sat forward and rested his elbows on his knees. "You know, I really could lend you—"

"Please don't." Cam clenched his hands into fists and felt rather proud of himself for keeping his cool right now. The last thing he needed was good-at-everything Oliver flaunting his money while they sat in his giant house. It wasn't that Cam wanted to be wealthy, though that would be nice. It was more than that. As much as he wished he wasn't jealous of Oliver Hamilton, he was.

Oliver had everything Cam had ever wanted. He was Kit's best friend, crazy smart, cheerful and carefree. He'd built up a business from his college dorm to the point where he could sell it for literal millions and never have to work again if he didn't want to. He had Madi…

Cam had never wanted to date Madi—she was too much like a little sister—but it was the idea of someone so perfectly suited to someone else that had him envying Oliver. Oliver lacked the trauma of a difficult childhood and had no problem letting someone else in. He had a kid on the way, and he would have the perfect family Cam had always wanted but would probably never have.

Oliver cleared his throat again, definitely more wary this time as he said, "How *is* business looking? Really?"

Cam might not have answered that question if he didn't know Oliver might be his best chance of surviving. He'd given him some useful advice before he'd started out, and as much as Cam hated the idea, Oliver knew what it took to make money. Cam would be stupid to turn that down, no matter how much it hurt his pride. It helped that Oliver seemed perfectly serious as he waited for an answer.

"The numbers are looking okay," Cam admitted. "But not sustainable if it's all dependent on this stupid relationship thing."

"How's that relationship thing going?" Oliver jumped right back to his usual self, wiggling his eyebrows.

Cam threw a half-hearted punch, not caring that Oliver easily dodged it. "She drives me crazy," he said with a groan. "It's like she was designed for me."

"Uh, that's a good thing."

"Not when she's the only woman I can't have," Cam argued.

"Is it really one or the other? Why can't you—"

"You know as well as I do that neither of us is going to survive if the other is around too." Cam ran a hand through his hair, suddenly aware of how long it had gotten. He could really use a haircut; he hadn't had any time for months. "And before you try again to tell me you could lend me the money to relocate, I looked into other spaces. Everywhere else has too many gyms nearby already, so it would be the same problem all over again without something to set me apart because the other places are established. Either I stay where I am, or I leave town."

His chest tightened at the thought, a bit of blackness playing at the edges of his vision as he tried to keep breathing normally. But now that the thought of leaving town was in his head, he couldn't get it to go away. It was sinking in deep, taking root, clouding everything else. The only family he had—Kit, Madi, Oliver, and Ben—were here. If he moved to a different city, he would have no one.

He would really be alone.

"Hey, are you okay?"

Cam jumped to his feet as soon as Oliver touched his shoulder, though dizziness nearly pulled him back down. "Fine," he said, barely holding back the nausea that pooled in his stomach.

He definitely wasn't fine.

"Cam?"

He made a beeline for the front door, reaching it at the same time it opened. Kit stood on the other side. Cam opened his mouth to give some excuse for why he couldn't stay, but no sound came out.

Kit grabbed his arm and pulled him outside, dragging him around the corner of the house until they were out of sight of the front door. "Look at me, Martinez."

Cam shook his head. Oliver was supposed to never see him like this. What would he think of him now?

"Cam!"

The slap that followed surprised him more than it hurt him. Kit wasn't scrawny by any means—he came to the gym twice a week to train—but he was too nice to really put much force into a hit like that. But it was enough to drag Cam back to the surface. He forced a stunted breath, trying to focus on the way the streetlight reflected off Kit's glasses.

"Smell that?" Kit asked.

Smelling required breathing, but Cam caught a whiff. "Barbecue."

"What kind?"

Cam frowned. How was he supposed to know that? Although, the longer he breathed it in, the more he recognized the smell. "Steak."

Kit nodded. "How about that wall behind you?"

Finally recognizing Kit's attempts at grounding him, Cam pressed his palms against the stone and let the roughness scrape against his palms. He'd had worse anxiety attacks, but it had been a while since he got this deep into one. He hated that Kit even had to guide him, and the anger from that wasn't helping anything.

Kit narrowed his eyes, taking a step back. "What did he do?"

For the first time in a long time, Cam chose to defend Oliver. "It wasn't his fault," he muttered, still running his hands across the stone. He could breathe again, but his heart still beat an erratic rhythm. "He was trying to help Riptide, and I started thinking about how I might have to pack up and leave town."

"You wouldn't actually do that, would you?" The concern in Kit's voice was subtle, which Cam appreciated. Making a big deal out of this would only make it worse.

"If I had to?" Cam shrugged. "Maybe. I don't know."

"But your family's here."

Cam dropped his head. "I don't have a family." He didn't mean that, and he knew that Kit knew it, but he still refused to see the hurt in his friend's eyes. Since they were fourteen, Kit and his parents, Duke and Lydia, had been a second family to Cam while he lived with his great aunt, his only remaining relative. When she died during Cam's freshman year of college, Duke had made all the funeral arrangements, and Lydia had told him he would always have a bed at their house if he needed it.

Kit had been a brother to him for fifteen years, and Cam hated that he would even pretend otherwise.

It hadn't been a lie, but that didn't mean it was true either.

"I'm sorry," Cam said weakly.

Kit shrugged, though his shoulders had gone tense. The comment must have hit him harder than he wanted Cam to know. "I know. You're not leaving town."

"What if I—"

"That's what we're meeting about tonight. Come on. Ben's probably in the house by now."

Cam wished he could stay out in the cold for another twenty minutes, but the longer he stayed outside, the more Oliver would wonder. It was a miracle Oliver had no idea about Cam's anxiety in the first place; Cam wanted it to stay that way as long as possible.

So he took a deep breath, stuffed his hands into the pocket of his hoodie, and followed Kit inside.

Sure enough, Ben had taken a seat on one end of the sectional, Oliver on the other, which left Cam to take Ben's side and Kit settling next to Oliver in the middle. The setup was similar to what they usually did, but being anywhere but Kit's living room still felt wrong.

Especially with the way Oliver was watching Cam while trying not to look like he was watching him.

Unwilling to remain the center of attention, Cam kicked Kit's foot.

Kit rolled his eyes but took the hint. "Okay, men. We're on a mission. We need to keep Cam's relationship intact until we can figure out a way to save both gyms."

So much for not being the center of attention.

"What if they just combine forces?" Ben asked.

As if Cam hadn't thought of that from the beginning. "We have totally different training styles. She's all about calisthenics, and I'm…not." Even if he was fascinated by that type of training. "Neither of our spaces has room for both of us, anyway."

"At least your little pretend relationship has bought some time to figure this out," Kit replied, though he made a face when he said *pretend*. He hadn't liked Oliver's fake relationship with Madi either, and he definitely hadn't liked learning that everything Ben had had with Allie had started out fake.

The fact that all three of them had been stupid enough to get into these messes in the first place was honestly pretty laughable at this point, even if Kit didn't see the irony of both Oliver and Ben ending up with their soulmates because of it.

The same wouldn't be true for Cam; he couldn't see a way they both could win. Besides, a future with Kailani—with anyone—had been doomed from the start.

As his phone buzzed with a social media message, Cam glanced down out of reflex. He'd been ignoring those as much as possible, checking only to make sure it wasn't a new tag or speculation. Most people sent messages hoping to get a free membership or training tips, so he ignored those.

Honestly, he wished that the media wasn't attached to his gym so he could ignore all of it.

"I need to figure out a way we can..." Cam paused, his eyes dropping back to his phone. Had he seen that right? "*No way.*"

"What?" all three guys said at once. Oliver even grabbed his own phone as if to try to see what Cam was looking at.

Scrambling to open up the message, Cam read it over twice, then clicked on the profile to make sure it was legit. It looked very real, and the message included very real contact information.

"Are you going to keep us in suspense?" Kit asked. "I can't tell if you're excited or about to throw up."

"Both," Oliver guessed, his eyebrows lifting high when Cam nodded.

"Breakout Brad," Cam breathed.

"Are we supposed to know who that is?"

Rising to his feet, Cam started to pace as his energy level kept climbing along with his heart rate. "Bradley Whitehall. He was one of the most well-known fitness gurus in the eighties. Revolutionized high intensity interval training, and his videos are the reason I went into personal training in the first place."

"I thought that was because you were too scared to go into boxing," Oliver said.

Kit punched him in the arm, but it didn't do much good.

Cam could already feel memories rising, his fingers curling into fists out of reflex. The lingering urge to hit something grew stronger with each second he thought about it, and Oliver wasn't wrong. Cam had been *terrified* of going into something like competitive boxing because he'd seen the damage a fist could do.

And his hands used to like to inflict that damage. Cam had managed to curb that old instinct for the most part, but every once in a while it creeped back up. Especially when Oliver was around.

Cam stuffed his hands back into his hoodie pocket and pushed his pace a little faster. He didn't need to slip up tonight just because Oliver had mentioned a generally taboo topic. He'd gone more than a decade without getting into a fight, and he wanted to keep it that way. This was something entirely different. "Brad just sent me a message saying he wants to meet tomorrow. Here in Diamond Springs."

"How does he know who you are?" Ben asked.

Breakout Brad had asked him to bring Kailani along, which could only mean one thing. "He knows about the hashtag."

"But that only started, like, a week ago," Oliver argued. "I know you went viral, but I thought it was a local kind of viral."

"I don't think that's a thing," Ben said. "When my novel leaked, it was worldwide in a matter of hours."

Oliver rolled his eyes. "Yeah, but that's because your graphic novel is bomb. Why would people care so much about a random guy from Diamond Springs? No offense."

"Offense definitely taken," Cam said.

"It's your classic *Romeo and Juliet* scenario," Kit threw in. "It's not every day that happens in real life."

Cam wished he had a jump rope or something to work out the anxiety building in his system. "Romeo and Juliet die in the end," he muttered. That argument was making even more sense than it had before. The similarities to the story had him concerned, particularly if he gave Sasha the role of Tybalt. Sure, that technically made Cam Juliet, but he would have to make sure Sasha didn't stir up trouble and do what she thought he wouldn't.

Well, that's just ridiculous, he thought, shaking his head. She was too good a person to stoop that low, but that didn't stop his mind from imagining the worst-case scenario in which Sasha enlisted Henry, the two of them sneaking over to Horizon Gym and putting itching powder in the vents.

Was itching powder even a real thing?

"I need to tell Kailani about Brad," he said, feeling sick to his stomach in a way that had nothing to do with lying. This had already been one of the longest days of his life after all the effort he'd gone through to avoid thinking of Kailani, and it was far from over. He had no idea why someone rich and famous would be interested in him, but if it had anything to do with the hashtag, something told him he wasn't going to like the reason.

NINE

AFTER AN ENTIRE DAY AT the gym doing everything she could to pretend Cam didn't exist—basically impossible—Kailani was ready to collapse onto her bed and sleep for hours. Who would have thought deflecting annoying questions from clients would be so exhausting? Unfortunately for her, Isla had brought home all of her leftover schoolwork after lunch yesterday, which meant the entire apartment, including her bed, was covered in clothing and fabric and what Kailani was pretty sure was a Bedazzler.

"Oh, you're home!" Isla waved Kailani over to where she was sprawled out on the floor, surrounded by swaths of Spandex. "I need your help picking a color."

Kailani groaned. "You know I'm not good at that stuff."

"Yeah, well, this is for your gym, so I need your input."

"I really don't like the sound of that."

Scoffing, Isla shook her head. "It's nothing crazy. And don't make me chase you down. I took my prosthetic off an hour ago."

Kailani scowled, but Isla had played her best card pretty quickly; she must have really been excited about whatever this was. "Fine, but I really need to get to bed soon. Today was exhausting."

"Too busy pretending your relationship with Hot Body Cam is fake?" Isla wiggled her perfect blonde eyebrows.

"I only told you the truth because I thought you would tease me less," Kailani complained as she plopped onto the couch. "We're not really dating."

"I saw that smooch yesterday. You're not fooling anyone except yourselves."

As memories of that "smooch" resurfaced, Kailani forced herself to stay focused on the fabric in front of her. "You know I hate Spandex, right?"

Isla snickered. "Okay, fine, I'll let you off the hook for now. But don't think I don't have more to say on the subject of Hottie McBody."

How she could possibly have more to say, Kailani had no idea. Their lunch had lasted more than an hour the day before, and Kailani had barely managed to get a word in.

"Spandex," she pressed.

"I'm not actually planning on making anything out of straight Spandex," Isla said, rolling her eyes.

"That's a relief."

"I just happened to be in the middle of a project at school that required maximum stretchiness, so I have a lot of it. Really, I'm just using it for color comparisons. I want to make you some leggings for Horizon."

As much as Kailani appreciated the enthusiasm… "I can't afford to stock any more apparel unless I start *selling* apparel. No one is buying anything, which is why the back room is full of boxes of t-shirts."

"I know that. But none of your merch has anything to do with Muscly Martinez."

"These names are getting a little ridiculous."

"Just pick a color, Lani!"

Kailani wrinkled her nose, looking at all the neon in front of her. "You're going to make my clients look like they belong in the eighties."

"Pick."

"Blue."

"Great!" Isla clapped her hands, a gleam in her eyes. That meant she would probably start making a mock-up right this minute, and Kailani would never be able to get an early bedtime with the sewing machine going.

If only they could afford a bigger apartment, one that had actual bedrooms instead of alcoves for their beds. At least Isla wouldn't be paying for school anymore, and if she started selling clothes or got a job, she could help with rent.

"I'm going to go sit outside for a bit," Kailani muttered, grabbing a blanket from her bed.

"It's like thirty degrees out there."

"Don't care."

Though they'd signed the lease over a year ago, Kailani hadn't bothered to spend any money on furniture for their little balcony, so anytime she needed to get some fresh air and think, she went out to a little bench on the grounds of the complex. It was more comfortable than it looked, and the only people who ever came over this way were people needing to give their dogs some privacy to do their business.

Most of the time, Kailani had the spot to herself. It wasn't glamorous, but the nearby flower beds were nice in the spring.

Her phone buzzed soon after she'd sat down, and she couldn't decide if she was happy or annoyed that Cam was texting her. She was supposed to be relaxing.

> Cam: Ever heard of Breakout Brad?

Kailani frowned. What kind of conversation starter was that?

> Kailani: Is that a trick question? I only wanted to be him when I was little.
> Cam: So the fact that he just messaged me and wants to meet for brunch tomorrow might be cause for celebration?

She nearly screamed when she read that one. "Why does he get all the fame and fortune?" she mourned out loud. Not only had he been popular on social media *before* the whole rivalry and dating thing, but now he had celebrities calling him up for hangouts? At this point, it almost made sense for Kailani to admit defeat and give up.

> Cam: You'll probably want to come over to Riptide first so we can head over together.

What?!

> Kailani: I can come???

Cam's name lit up her screen with a call, and she had to smile at that. Hardly anyone ever used phones for actual phone calls anymore, but Cam had proved more than once that he preferred talking over typing. Kailani rather liked that about him, and it offered up more opportunity for him to say things he wouldn't otherwise say. She'd seen his tongue get away from him more than once.

"Did I not mention that?" he said when she answered. "He wants to talk to both of us."

That was even better. Now it wasn't just Cam inviting her along to be nice; Bradley Whitehall had *requested* her. "Why?"

"I have my guesses, but I don't know for sure. He seems interested in our love story."

"We don't have a love story," Kailani argued, almost letting out a sigh.

"Maybe, but we probably shouldn't let Brad know that. Whatever this is, it could be big. So I'll see you tomorrow at ten?"

Kailani was about to agree, but her words caught in her throat. She hadn't seen Cam since their last kiss, and that made her feel...something. She wasn't sure what that something was, but it sat heavy in her gut.

Hoping she wasn't overstepping, she gripped her phone a little tighter and said, "Do you think you could stop by my apartment complex for a minute tonight? I'm not too far from the gyms."

"I'm not at… Never mind. Why?"

Why, indeed? She wanted to see him, like she needed the reassurance that he still existed. She couldn't tell him that without sounding ridiculous, though. They weren't actually dating. They had every reason to be enemies. But she ached to touch him again and see his crooked smile. She wanted the validation that someone found her worthwhile.

She cleared her throat. "We should really post a picture together. We haven't done that yet."

"We have several—"

"Other people have posted those. If we want people to think we're really dating, we need to do more than make out where people can see."

"I don't mind that part."

Kailani snorted a laugh, enjoying the warmth that spread over her from that admission. At least it wasn't just her who felt the chemistry between them. "I don't either," she said before Cam could try to backtrack like he often did. "But still…"

She could hear his smile as he replied, "You're probably right. Text me the address?"

As soon as she sent him the address, he told her he'd be there in twenty and arrived almost to the minute. He pulled up in a little white BMW that looked exactly like the kind of car a gym bro would drive, and that surprised her. He'd been so different from what she expected up until now that the stereotype surprised her.

"Fancy car," she said as he approached the bench.

Dang, he looked good. Kailani still hadn't figured out how anyone could make sweats look so attractive, though she had a feeling he would look delicious in pretty much anything.

Maybe it was the way his clothes were just baggy enough to hide the muscle beneath, as if he didn't want anyone to know how strong he was.

Kailani knew. She had those abs burned into her brain from the day of the race, and she'd felt a good number of his muscles with her own hands.

Not creepy at all.

Once he reached her, Cam leaned against a nearby tree, hands in his pockets, and glanced back at the parking lot. "I guess so."

Though it may have been the poor lighting coming from the apartment building, he looked exhausted.

Kailani tried to lighten the mood and see if she could get him to smile. "You know, you could have gotten something cheaper and had a little more money for your gym."

He hadn't actually looked at her yet, and now his gaze was on his tennis shoes. "I was eighteen when I bought it with the life insurance money from when my guardian died."

And now she felt like a jerk. "Oh. Sorry. I shouldn't have—"

"Should we take a picture?"

He was definitely exhausted. Everything about his bearing said so, as did the dark circles under his eyes, and there was probably something else going on with him too.

"I'm sorry," she said again. "You're having a bad day, and I shouldn't have made you come all the way over—"

"The distraction is nice, actually." He finally looked up, meeting her gaze with eyes that looked almost black in the dim light.

Kailani's heart ached for him, and she patted the seat next to her. "Wanna sit and talk about it? I've been told I have a great listening ear, though it was an eight-year-old who told me that at the time and it was probably more than a decade ago. So take that however you want to."

He managed a little smile—nothing close to the full one she'd come to love, but it was something. "I'm not sure you want to hear all my woes when I'm your nemesis."

She cocked her head, unsure what the answer to her next question might be. "Is that because you don't trust me or because you don't trust your own mouth to not say too much?"

There's that smile. It didn't get rid of the exhaustion in his eyes, but as his lips twisted up in that crooked grin she liked so much, he seemed to stand a little lighter.

"More of the second one," he said, slowly shuffling over and settling next to her. "Are you sure you want to hear my dark secrets?"

Though it technically went against the rules, Kailani shifted closer and leaned against him. Her thin blanket didn't keep out the winter chill, and he was just as warm as he'd been the last time. A human space heater. As if he knew her thoughts, Cam wrapped his arm around her and let her snuggle in deeper.

"I get the feeling you don't have a lot of secrets, Martinez," she said, perfectly content in her new spot.

He chuckled. "True. I've always been a bit of an over-sharer."

"Tell me about your guardian."

For a second, she worried she'd been too direct, but then Cam said, "My great aunt. My mom died when I was really little—too little to remember her—and my dad was a Marine. He was gone as much as he was around, and he was killed in action when I was in seventh grade."

Kailani snuggled closer, sympathetic tears pricking her eyes. "I'm so sorry," she whispered.

Cam sighed. "From what I remember about him, he was a good man, but he hadn't been meant for the single parent thing. My great aunt watched me whenever he was deployed. She hadn't ever gotten married or had kids, so she was about as ready for parenthood as Dad had been."

"Any other family?" Kailani asked.

"Nope."

"You were only eighteen when she died? So does that mean—"

"I've been on my own for the last eleven years." His voice broke on the last word, his whole body going tense beneath her.

Kailani had been five years old when her parents brought Chase home, after he'd been put up for adoption the minute his mom gave birth. Isla had come just a few years after that. Kailani had never been on her own in her life, so she had no idea how that loneliness would feel. But she knew how much it bothered Cam, based on the way every inch of him had turned solid.

"I really like your friends," she said, even if it didn't exactly make sense as a response. She wrapped an arm around his waist and squeezed, letting him know she was there. "Ben was at Horizon this morning with his girlfriend."

"Traitor," Cam grumbled.

"He only had good things to say about you."

In fact, Kailani had been trying to avoid Ben because she thought interacting with Cam's buddy would be some conflict of interest. But Ben had come back to her office, his face bright red, and told her that Cam might seem rough around the edges but had a big heart and would do whatever it took to make sure they both won. Ben seemed like a quiet sort of guy, but he spoke with so much conviction that it was impossible not to believe him.

Cam shifted a little, as if uncomfortable from the vague praise. "Ben's one of the best guys I know," he said quietly. "We used to be roommates, before I moved closer to Riptide. I didn't know him super well before that, which is crazy because we've been friends since junior high, but living with him gave me a chance to see the guy beneath the shy exterior. It was nice. Maybe if I…" He grunted, cutting himself off.

Kailani couldn't pretend to know everything about this guy, but she wanted to. She wanted to stay on that bench all night and talk until she knew every little part of Cam Martinez. So she guessed what he'd been about to say, hoping he didn't think she was too presumptuous.

"Do you think you and Oliver would get along better if you'd lived together at some point?"

He tensed again, though he relaxed as soon as she started stroking his ribcage with her thumb. His own fingers found her hair and began running through it. "Maybe," he admitted. "But probably not. Oliver is too…"

From what Kailani had seen at the fun center, Oliver and Cam were incredibly similar. Sure, Cam was stronger and Oliver more fashion-forward, but they both had an outward confidence that, honestly, was incredibly attractive. Kailani had watched the pair of them with interest—she'd been watching all four, incredibly fascinated by such close friends at their age—but the way Cam had interacted with Oliver, and vice versa, had given her a lot of information she hadn't known what to do with until now.

There was clearly some sort of power struggle between those two, but not a struggle for the top. That position had been held by Kit, clear as day, even if Kit had been more of an observer that night at O'Reilly's. Kailani was pretty sure Cam and Oliver both wanted to be the favorite, and they'd been battling for years.

With that on top of all of this stuff with their gyms, it was no wonder Cam was exhausted.

Cam sighed. "I think Kit tried to get me and Oliver to bond tonight. He was late for the meeting, and Kit's never late."

Kailani knew better than to question a relationship she knew next to nothing about, but she wanted to help, if she could. "Why now? If you guys have known each other for years?"

"Almost fifteen years," he confirmed. "And Kit never does anything out of the ordinary like this, so it has me worried. Why's he trying to change things all of a sudden? The man literally hates change. Hates it! And he thinks leaving me in a room with Oliver is going to fix years of—"

Kailani sat up, shutting Cam up immediately, and he stared at her with his expression frozen in anxiety. "You're overthinking things," she said gently. She would have to break the rules again, but maybe this counted as necessary touching. Moving slowly, she reached up and ran her thumb between his eyebrows, smoothing out the crease that had formed there. Then she brushed his eyes closed, touching the delicate skin beneath them and wishing she could help him get a decent night's sleep.

Don't think about sleep and Cam, Lani.

She shivered, glad that Cam's eyes were still closed so he couldn't see any signs of the heat that flooded her face. Why did this man have to be her enemy? Why couldn't he have just been a guy she met at a race and fell in love with over time?

Because that would leave you heartbroken when he gives up on you, she reminded herself.

"Just take one day at a time," she said, speaking as much to herself as to Cam. "If I know anything, I know you can't do anything about other people's actions, so don't stress yourself out about things out of your control."

Though he kept his eyes closed, Cam pulled her closer, one hand finding her cheek. "I can't control you," he murmured. "And you stress me out like nothing else ever has. Want me to stop thinking about you?"

Yes was the answer she should have given. This thing between them could never go anywhere without one of them being resentful of the other. She *knew* that. But she also knew she had never met anyone like Cam and never would again, and she really didn't want to let go of that.

So she whispered, "No," and crossed the space between them.

Cam gave her two seconds. Two seconds of a closed-mouth kiss that was still full of fireworks before he pushed her away with a chuckle. He met her gaze, eyes sparkling, and grinned as he shook his head. "You are trouble, Lani."

"And you have a lot more self-control than I do," she grumbled.

In answer, he held up a fist that he was clenching so hard that his knuckles had turned white. "I'm trying to be a gentleman here, but you're not making it easy."

"No one asked you to be a gentleman."

"*Kailani.*"

She huffed a sigh and settled back against him, unwilling to let him go just yet. "I know," she whined. "But if you knew how close I've come to shutting the doors of Horizon for good so I can—"

"Don't." Cam wrapped both arms around her this time, holding her tight. "I know things… I don't see a way for this to end well, but… We'll find a way to make this work. Maybe."

Kailani didn't exactly like the lack of confidence, but he was right. No matter what they did, it was hard to see a way their relationship could last if one of their gyms failed because of the other. But it sounded like he wanted that inevitable failure as little as she did. "But does that make this a fake relationship or a real one?" she asked, as if it could make a difference in the outcome. But she didn't want to dive into this without knowing where his headspace was. She wanted to match his investment.

He sighed. "I don't know. I just know I don't want to hate you."

"Me neither."

But that still didn't answer her question about their relationship. It certainly felt real. Kailani had never felt more at home than she did in his arms. She felt safe, and warm, and wanted, and she couldn't imagine a relationship being better than this. Cam had trusted her with vulnerability tonight, and she wanted to be that person for him always. The one who listened and calmed and distracted.

Her family always needed her and always had. But this was different. *Everything* about Cam was different. His need didn't have her dreading what that meant for her, and as terrifying as it was to imagine laying her whole heart on the line, she wanted to do whatever it took to make sure he was happy. No matter what that meant for her. That sensation was as thrilling as it was new, and she clung to the hope that the outcome would be worth it in the end.

"Cam?"

He pressed a kiss to the top of her head. "Hmm?"

"Thanks for coming over tonight. I was…" Did she want to tell him how overwhelmed she felt? She did, but she had just relieved some of his burden—she hoped she had, at least—and she couldn't very well give him some of hers. Maybe someday, when he wasn't already weighed down by so much. "Thanks," she repeated lamely.

"You were right about needing to post something," he said, an edge to his voice.

Right. They needed to take a picture so people would keep believing they were dating. Kailani started to sit up, but Cam held her down.

"You can stay there," he explained, pulling his phone out of his pocket. "Close your eyes."

Kailani complied, focusing on how it felt to be cuddled against his warm body. If she memorized this moment, maybe it could hold her over until all of this was over. Hopefully Cam really could find a way for them both to keep their gyms, but if he couldn't…

She pulled herself even closer, hating that she even had to think about this. But if she had to lose something, Kailani didn't want it to be him.

After Cam had walked her to her door, complete with a lingering forehead kiss that nearly destroyed her, Kailani settled in her bed—Isla had crashed and was snoring in her own bed—and pulled up Cam's social media account. He'd posted a picture with the caption, "Dreaming of warm summer nights—but I'm not complaining in the meantime." And the picture… He'd cut off half his face and kept the focus on her, but his crooked smile was on full display. Kailani looked asleep curled up against him, her own smile subtle but definitely there.

They looked made for each other, and Kailani drifted off to dreams of never having to leave his arms.

TEN

CAM WAS NERVOUS. HE *HATED* being nervous. He'd already made one client cry—Sasha had been glaring at him all morning for that—and he'd nearly broken one of the weight machines by doing so many reps that his arms gave out and made him drop the weight. (Sasha had been glaring at him for that too.)

She'd relegated him to the front desk, where he was so fidgety that he'd already broken three pens by playing with them until they snapped in half.

At least he'd slept last night. Every night since finding out Kailani owned Horizon had gotten worse than the last. Some nights, he had almost considered pulling an all-nighter and researching grants that could help him get his charity side under way. But last night he'd fallen asleep almost as soon as his head hit the pillow, not moving an inch until his alarm jolted him out of a dream.

That dream had turned into a daydream, so when he wasn't stressing over what Breakout Brad might want to talk about, he was imagining a life where he didn't have to say goodnight to Kailani Adams.

"She didn't trust you enough to tell you what's bothering her," he reminded himself out loud. Thankfully, no one was near the front desk; everyone was actually working out today. That would change as soon as Kailani showed up, but for now, Riptide felt like it was functioning how it should.

He supposed he couldn't blame Kailani for not trusting him yet. They still barely knew each other.

He snapped another pen, just to give himself something to do while he waited for ten o'clock. He'd wanted her to tell him why she'd been so eager for him to meet her so late at night. Based on the fact that she'd forgotten about taking a picture until he'd reminded her, he knew that hadn't been the reason.

He'd asked her why she was sitting out in the cold, and she'd mumbled something about her sister and sewing. Just like at the race, she clammed up when talking about anything that had to do with her family. Cam liked to think he could make a good impression on family members, but he'd never been in a relationship long enough to meet any.

He usually ended things before that point. Meeting the family meant things were serious, and Cam didn't do serious. He never let himself get so deep that he would wind up wounded when things inevitably ended.

Everything ended. It wasn't a matter of *if* but *when*.

So why was he picturing thirty years down the road with Kailani? That was a dangerous line of thinking, because history had taught him that he didn't get to keep people longer than a few years. He didn't get the happy endings.

Kailani deserved better than that.

But when she stepped through the door of Riptide, the whole building lit up at the same time as Cam's soul. He was doomed. How was he supposed to let her go once they figured out how to save both gyms? Did he *have* to let her go? She was the brightest part of his life, but if he let himself think he could avoid heartbreak, everything was only going to hurt worse.

With a huge grin on her face, she bounced over to him. "Ready to meet the greatest trainer in history?"

He narrowed his eyes. "I take offense to that."

"You can be third greatest."

"Who's second?"

"Me. Obviously."

Half because they were being watched and half because he just wanted to, Cam leaned over the counter and pulled her in for a kiss. Thankfully, she was smiling too wide for him to make it good, so they broke apart before he revisited some of last night's dreams in reality.

"I suppose I can accept third place," he said, rolling his eyes. "You ready?"

"Born ready. Are *you* ready?" Her eyes almost literally sparkled. Apparently he had underestimated her comment about wanting to be Breakout Brad, and she was even more of a fan than he was.

Ignoring the stares of everyone in the gym—Sasha's was still a glare—Cam planted a hand on the counter and leapt, swinging his legs over rather than walking around.

Kailani pursed her lips when he landed right next to her. "Trying to impress me?" She looked like she was trying not to laugh.

Cam raised an eyebrow. "Is it working?"

Her lips twisted into a tempting smile that Cam couldn't resist. "Maybe."

"Guess I'll have to try harder." He leaned in.

"You're going to be late," Sasha grumbled from a few feet away, stopping Cam from kissing Kailani again.

"Saved by the trainer," he muttered, touching a kiss to her cheek instead. "She's right, though. We don't want to be late."

Nodding to Sasha, he grabbed Kailani's hand and led her out into the sunshine. The early February day was teasing spring with its almost-warm temperature, and he couldn't help but grin up at the sunny sky as they started walking.

"You're in a good mood today," Kailani said.

"I wasn't until you showed up."

He loved how much that made her smile.

Kailani nudged her shoulder into his. "Have you been having a bad morning? You don't look as tired as you did yesterday."

She'd noticed that? Cam squeezed her hand. "I'm just nervous," he admitted. "I have no idea why Brad wants to talk to us or what it might mean for our gyms. And for…" He glanced at their hands linked between them, his eyebrows pulling low.

This relationship had caught the attention of someone much bigger than them. Either they would have to keep it going despite the impending doom, or it could spell the end of everything before Cam was ready to let go.

"Let's just see what he wants and not overthink it," she suggested.

"As you discovered last night, I'm great at overthinking."

"Guess it's a good thing you have me, isn't it?"

Cam paused, tugging Kailani to a stop. They were still on the verge of being late, but he wanted to make sure she believed what he was about to tell her. "It's a good thing. Really. I know all of this has been crazy, and we don't know how it's going to end, but…" He took a deep breath. "I'm glad you caught me at that race."

Her smile soft and warm, Kailani reached up and brushed her fingers through his hair. "Technically, you caught me first."

Cam might have pulled her into a kiss if a boisterous voice didn't choose that moment to interrupt. "Well, aren't you two the cutest thing?"

Reluctantly, Cam pulled his gaze away from Kailani to address whatever fan had gotten in his way. Then he froze. Breakout Brad stood there in all his neon Spandex glory, watching them as if he'd never seen anything more enthralling. He looked just like he had on TV when Cam was a kid, if a bit older, dressed head to toe in wildly vivid colors.

"I was just about to message you," Brad said, bouncing on the balls of his feet. "I decided last minute to change locations. This is where it started, after all."

Cam followed his waving arm to the sign on the door Brad had just stepped through. *Blended Perfection.*

"Y'all like smoothies, right?" Without waiting for an answer, Brad grabbed hold of Kailani's hand and shook it with enough enthusiasm that it shook her whole arm. Then he held his hand out to Cam.

Cam swallowed. "Sorry, I don't… I don't shake hands. I had a bad experience."

Brad raised an eyebrow. "What happened?"

"A bad experience."

At least Brad laughed, clapping Cam on the shoulder with impressive strength for a guy in his sixties. He really hadn't changed much from his eighties glory days, still packed with muscle and full of energy. The only difference was the long gray beard that hung down to his chest to match the length of his ponytailed hair.

"Let's grab seats, shall we? I need to have a quick chat with the staff so we aren't bothered. I'll let you lovebirds pick a spot."

The only reason Cam even moved was because Kailani tugged his arm. He was almost convinced this whole morning was a dream, her soft hand the only thing keeping him grounded in reality. They followed Brad inside, and Kailani picked a table in the corner while Brad went to the register.

As soon as they were alone, Kailani leaned in close. "Am I allowed to know why you don't shake hands?"

Cam grimaced. "It might involve breaking Dirk Hansen's hand when I met him several years ago."

"Wait, the Dirk Hansen who was one of the first men to ever run more than three hundred miles?"

"The very same."

"How did you break his hand?"

Cam suddenly wished he hadn't told her. "I got excited. I didn't mean to, but his bones were, uh, brittle."

Kailani snorted a laugh, though she almost held it in as she looked around to make sure no one was paying attention to them. "I guess he is pretty old now…"

"I don't think the guy drank his milk as a kid." Cam winced. "Imagine little dry twigs just…snapping in your hand. That's what it felt like."

"Gross."

"You're telling me."

"So!" Brad returned, rubbing his hands together as he settled in his seat. "Let's talk business."

Cam frowned. "Business?"

"That's why I'm here."

"What kind of business?" Kailani asked.

Brad flashed a wide smile that looked far more genuine than Cam would be able to produce right now. "First off, I ordered you that green smoothie you're so clearly fond of. They've changed the name to the 'Lani Lean and Green', did you know?"

Kailani glanced at the menu, her eyes going wide. "It's only been in two pictures," she said weakly.

Cam gripped her hand a little tighter, though he had no idea if she needed support or congratulations. He wondered if he had a smoothie named after him too, but he didn't care to check. His whole focus was on Brad, whose crystal blue eyes were wide and excited.

Cam cleared his throat. "We need to get back to our gyms soon, so what—"

"Right! Right, right. So…" Clasping his hands together, Brad rested his elbows on the table and leaned forward, suddenly all business. "Those two photos, Miss Adams, have reached more than five million people in the last week. Internet searches for at-home workouts have tripled in the last three days alone, and sales for exercise equipment have maxed out capacity of some manufacturers. And do you know which question has been floating around the fitness world more than anything this week?"

Cam didn't want to know. All he'd wanted to do was start up a little gym and offer health and fitness training to people who otherwise couldn't afford it. He'd never wanted to become a viral sensation, and he certainly didn't want the whole world to know who he was.

But that ship had already sailed, and even if things died down as quickly as they'd sparked to life, Cam was realizing there was no going backward from here. He gripped the edge of the linoleum table to avoid squeezing Kailani's hand, his anxiety skyrocketing from all the unknowns in front of him.

Brad flashed another grin, though he remained silent for a moment as if adding suspense. "The question on everyone's mind is 'How do I learn from Cam Lani Love?'."

"What exactly are you saying?" Cam asked warily.

"I'm saying I want you two on my TV show."

The corner of the table snapped beneath Cam's fingers, leaving him with a hunk of linoleum in his hand.

Kailani spoke for him, though her words stuttered as she stared at the broken table. Maybe she was just glad that hadn't been her hand. "TV show? I didn't realize you were still—"

"Oh, it's nothing like it used to be," Brad said, waving a hand. He, too, seemed fixated on the piece in Cam's frozen hand. "It's more like a talk show. Or a cooking show? Whatever the fitness equivalent of that would be. I'm constantly bringing on new instructors and experts and, uh, entertain—was that table cracked already?"

Cam shook his head, his face on fire because it was like Dirk Hansen's hand all over again. At least this time it was just a table, but he would still have to pay for it. And Breakout Brad was always going to remember him as the guy who panicked so much that he turned destructive.

"Wow, that's quite a grip, son."

Knowing it wouldn't work, Cam still tried to force the two pieces back together as he croaked, "Why do you want us on your show? And what would we gain from it?" More importantly, how could he get out of it?

"We evidently don't need the publicity," Kailani added helpfully.

Cam nodded his agreement.

Brad chuckled but didn't say anything until the Blended Perfection staff handed out their smoothies. The last thing Cam wanted was a smoothie, but he took a sip anyway to show his gratitude.

"I can see you need some incentive," Brad said with a nod. "Perfectly understandable when you have businesses to run. Not only would your appearance on the show expand your credibility, but I'm prepared to offer you both full coverage of overhead for the next month."

Cam choked on his smoothie. "The full month?" he gasped, glad to see Kailani's eyes were as wide as his. He was barely making it by each month, and not having to worry about costs for thirty days would give him a small cushion of extra cash. Maybe even get him to relax a bit.

Brad grinned. "I thought that might sweeten the deal. But there's more. I've got a whole multi-episode series all planned out over the course of a week that'll give you both a chance to show what you're made of. Gain yourself a real following."

"But wh—"

"I know what you're thinking," he said, raising a hand before Kailani could finish the word that came out of her mouth. "You can't possibly leave your gyms to film multiple episodes. You can if I fly out some of my trainers to cover your gyms for you. And yes, they know calisthenics."

"But—"

"Everything was all planned out already, but the trainers who were originally going to be on the show both got injured in a skiing accident. We were set up to film in Sun City, which is—what? Two hours from here?—so it should be easy to move everything here so you can sleep in your own beds each night. Lucky for you, eh?"

"How are injuries lucky?" Cam breathed. Brad seemed to think every word coming out of his mouth was supposed to be making them more interested, but he was only succeeding in making Cam's heart rate keep climbing.

Brad waved a hand, ignoring his question. "Happening upon you two was practically fate! Rival gym owners each trying to beat the other business until your romance could no longer be denied? That's a story that sells itself."

Kailani gripped Cam's hand tighter. "I don't understand why you would—"

"Oh, I love a good love story as much as the next person," Brad said, stroking his beard. "You'd be surprised how compelling a story like this would be."

With the number of likes and comments and shares they'd gotten over the last several days, Cam wouldn't be all that surprised. But Brad's reasoning still didn't make any sense. "How…" He took a breath. "How does that help your business? How does it help *ours*? Our relationship doesn't have anything to do with—"

"Your story makes you human," Brad said with a shrug. "It makes people want to be you. It makes them want to do whatever it is you're doing on the off chance they'll find what you've found." He gestured to the pair of them, his smile somehow growing wider. It hadn't dropped even a little bit since the moment they sat down. "Besides, I'm a philanthropist at heart. When I heard about your little businesses struggling, I had to jump at the chance to step in."

"So you want us on your show so we can get more follow-ers?" Kailani asked, her eyebrows pulled low.

Brad shook his head. "I want you on my show so the two of you can take your little competition to the next level."

As the world started to spin around him, Cam tried to take deep breaths and stay focused. He needed his wits about him to deal with everything Brad was throwing his way, and he most certainly didn't want one of his idols to think he couldn't perform under pressure. How was he supposed to run a business if he couldn't even have a conversation with someone important?

"Competition?" he finally choked out, glad Kailani held his hand a little tighter. "What do you mean next level?"

"I mean the episodes will feature challenges where you go head-to-head against each other," Brad replied with a wide grin. Stroking his beard, he sipped his smoothie as he thought about that. "I may change up some of the planned challenges now that I've met you, but it'll be something entertaining to watch, for sure. Something for your fans to root for. I would imagine you're both pretty competitive. It's part of a trainer's nature, and you can't run a business without being willing to push beyond comfort zones. So, what do you think? Want to be a part of my show?"

Most of the time, Cam couldn't stop words from coming out of his mouth. It was a curse and a blessing, and he'd always considered it a part of who he was. But sitting at a broken table inside his favorite smoothie shop, staring down one of the biggest names in the fitness world, he was entirely speechless.

He didn't like it.

None of this made any sense.

He couldn't breathe.

"Can you give us a second?" Kailani asked, already rising to her feet and pulling Cam with her.

Thankfully, Brad seemed more than willing to give them a chance to talk things through, even if Cam wasn't sure he would be able to talk in the first place. Everything was still spinning, leaving him dizzy as he leaned against the empty countertop next to the barstools on the other side of the shop.

Kailani still held onto his hand, for which he was grateful, but she was looking at him like he might fall apart. "You good?"

He shrugged, unwilling to risk a lie in case he couldn't hold in the bit of smoothie he'd drunk.

Reaching up, Kailani pressed her palm to his cheek, her eyes so fixed on him that he felt exposed. "Look at me, Cam."

"I'm looking at you," he said breathlessly, though he only held her gaze for a second. He needed to pace. To scream. To run outside and try to get a full breath before he fell apart.

"You're okay," she said and grabbed his other hand, holding them both tight. "Just breathe." She demonstrated, exaggerating her own breath. "How can I help?"

She couldn't. He just needed to ground himself, and he'd be fine. He'd talked himself out of anxiety attacks plenty of times over the years, and he just needed to focus on what was around him. Pick out details. The smell of oranges. The feel of her warm hands. The way her eyes were such a deep brown but carried a hint of greenish gray around the edges.

But there was also the way she was looking at him and still exaggerating her breaths so he could match. The longer he focused on her and her thumb brushing his cheek, the more he realized how focused she was on him. Like she was trying to feel what he was feeling and ride it out with him.

"I'm okay," he said, matching her words even though he felt like his heart was trying to pound out of his chest. It was slowing, though. The idea of a TV show shouldn't have freaked him out this much—he was used to being watched— but a gym full of people or a full set of bleachers at the high school was not the same thing as hundreds of thousands of people.

Maybe that was exaggerating, but Brad Whitehall was far from unknown. He was one of the biggest names in the fitness world, and some of the episodes of his show online had millions of views. If what he said about their story being compelling was true, this proposal of his could turn out to be something bigger than Cam was ready to handle.

"You don't look okay," Kailani said, smiling a little. "It's not like we haven't talked about doing a competition, right?"

"That was an idiotic idea from a man who I thought was smart enough to know not to suggest it in the first place. This is so much different," he argued, wishing the Wonder Boys had had some viable options the other night. The problem was the guys didn't know just how much was at stake if Cam lost his gym because he hadn't told them how close he was to straight-up bankruptcy. He'd put everything he had into this gym.

He focused on Kailani again, staring at the little smile on her lips. How was she *not* panicking? She'd freaked out about the viral kiss video way more than he had, and this was so much bigger.

"Yeah," she agreed, "but I haven't found a way to save my gym, and this would give us an extra month to find some sort of solution. Have you come up with any new ideas between last night and this morning?"

No, he hadn't, and Cam forced a deep breath as he thought about Riptide. His little gym was barely hanging on, and Kailani was right. This was probably the only way to save it. That thirty days of money meant thirty more days to figure out how to make enough to keep him from having to close his doors.

"Okay," he said. Not really as an agreement but more because he didn't know what else to say.

At least Kailani seemed to know him well enough to rec-ognize his intention behind the word. Frowning, she pulled her hands free and started fidgeting with her hair. It was back in a long ponytail today, looking extra silky and soft. Under different circumstances, Cam might have reached out to touch it like he had last night.

Right now, he was lucky to still be upright.

"How did you know how to talk me down?" he asked. She hadn't done much, but she'd clearly recognized he was panicking.

She shrugged, her eyes on her feet. "I've been around, uh, someone…who has panic attacks."

Something told him it was someone in her family, and he didn't bother asking. Most likely she would only deflect his question. Instead, he ran a hand through his hair and said, "You really want to do this?"

Laughing a little, she folded her arms around herself and shook her head. "No. But do I have a choice? That money would mean so much. A whole month to figure out…" She swallowed, looking up at him with so much vulnerability in her eyes that it made Cam's heart ache for her. "I've been so focused on saving *my* gym that I never really stopped to think about yours. What if this can save both of them? What if it can save…"

Though she trailed off, Cam was pretty sure he could read the rest of her sentence in her expression. She didn't want this relationship to fail any more than she wanted their gyms to die.

"Did I mention there's a sponsorship involved?" Brad said, appearing at their side.

Cam jumped so badly he knocked a stool over. Cursing, he took a deep breath as he picked the stool up and situated himself away from anything else he might damage. He really needed to get a hold of himself. "Sponsorship?" Why couldn't Brad have led with that?

"Picture this." Grinning, Brad held up his splayed hands as if they could see what was in his head. "Brand new equipment, a bigger space with rent paid up for a full year, all the top technology and marketing money can buy. That's what's in store for whoever wins my little tournament."

With his heart pounding for a new reason, Cam tried not to picture it like Brad suggested. It all sounded too good to be true, and he wasn't ready to have his heart broken by letting a stranger get his hopes up. It was already well on its way to being shattered by his growing feelings for Kailani when she left him. Maybe beyond repair. Cam should have backed off by this point to save himself the misery, but Kailani was like a magnet, constantly pulling him in closer.

"And what happens to the loser?" Kailani asked. "Do you really expect us to go up against each other?"

Brad took a long sip of his smoothie, his expression difficult to read. "All of this started with a rivalry, didn't it?"

"Yeah, but—"

"It's what the people want. They want tension. Angst. Something to root for. This little cutesy thing you've started will work for a while, but unless you've got a reason for people to keep paying attention, they'll write you off as a normal Joe."

"What if we want to be a normal Joe?" Cam's fingers were starting to go numb from clenching his fists too hard, and he wasn't sure how much longer he would last in this conversation without something to work out his anxiety. He wished he had Kit here, or even Ben. Someone who knew him better than the girl who somehow simultaneously stressed him out and helped him relax. They could talk him into doing it.

Not that he really needed that. If Kailani said she wanted to do it, Cam would do it with her. And he would hate every minute of it outside of the fact that he got to spend some real time with her. He didn't like the idea of leaving his gym for a full week, but a month without having to worry about rent and paychecks? A week with Kailani at his side? That was sounding a little too tempting.

Brad wrapped an arm around Cam's shoulders, pulling him in way too close. "Son, no one wants to be normal. And you've already proven you're not. Just look at that little table over there."

That little table was currently the subject of concern for the Blended Perfection staff, both of whom were examining the broken corner with worried expressions.

"The two of you are something special," Brad continued. "And the world is going to agree with me. This could mean success beyond your wildest dreams. A chance to do whatever it is you set out to do. Something tells me you both have more planned for yourselves than helping people get strong."

Still caught in Brad's hold, Cam met Kailani's gaze. She looked right on back, both of them trying to read the other. He wasn't sure what she saw, but he could tell there was something pushing Kailani to accept. She had a fire burning in her eyes that seemed to match his.

Getting a sponsorship from Breakout Brad would make Cam's charity possible. A full year of profits? He could really use that to help people master their bodies to master their minds. Give the weak a chance to feel strong. Make sure kids like him never felt like they had no control. He couldn't give up on that chance, which meant he couldn't afford to lose.

"I'll do it," Cam said before he could chicken out. It wasn't like he had much of a choice.

Kailani's eyes went wide, her expression unreadable. "Me too," she said after a moment.

Brad finally released Cam so he could applaud them both. "Excellent! I'll have my people contact you, and we'll start filming in three days."

Cam nearly swallowed his tongue. "Th-three days? Don't you need time to prepare, or—"

"Fame waits for no one, son. I told you we were all set up to film in Sun City, didn't I? No point in delaying when it will only take a few hours to move everything here."

This was ridiculous. "But *we're* not prepared," Cam tried, his anxiety rising again. "You haven't told us anything about the competitions."

Brad waved that one away, pulling out a couple hundred-dollar bills—Cam didn't know where he'd been keeping those, seeing as Brad didn't have any pockets—and tossing them on the table. "That's the point," he said, as if it should be obvious. "I can't have either of you practicing something to get an edge. Blind competitions are so much more thrilling. So!" He clapped his hands, making Cam flinch, then held out a couple of business cards for them to take. "If you have any questions, you can direct them to my assistant, and she'll be sending over contracts and all the info you'll need. I'll see you both in three days!" Brad did a little gleeful dance and then slipped out of the store.

When something touched his hand, Cam flinched into defense mode, fists at the ready to block an attack before he remembered where he was and forced himself to relax. "Sorry," he gasped. "I'm a little on edge."

"I noticed." She lifted one eyebrow. "If you don't want to do this, we don't—"

"I'll do it. I just… I need a second to process."

Kailani was still holding onto his hand, even if that hand was a fist. "You really don't like the spotlight, do you? I wouldn't have thought anything could scare you."

"A lot of things scare me." Cam grimaced, though he generally tried to be okay with vulnerability. At least when Oliver wasn't around.

"What would make this easier? Something to distract you?"

Tempting as that was—a little too tempting, given Cam was now thinking about kissing her as the ultimate distraction—it would probably be better if they parted ways until filming started so he could focus on making sure Riptide wouldn't fall apart while he was gone. But what he should do didn't mean much when his heart so often took the reins. "I don't want to go," he said out loud.

"To film the show? But you told Brad you—"

"I don't want to leave this spot." Cam could feel the emptiness of the room around them—the staff hadn't let any new customers in since Brad's arrival—and he had a feeling it would be a long time before they could be alone like this again. "I'll do the show, Lani, but I need you to know that I'm terrified of what's going to happen."

She smiled a little. "Don't worry. I'll let you win a few rounds, but—"

"No. I'm worried about what happens *after* all of this. What happens to you and me?" Cam wanted to take her hand, but he was still too tense to relax his fists. He probably needed to go a few rounds with the punching bag at Riptide before the tension left his body and let him breathe again. So he just stood there, hoping she understood what he meant.

She asked last night if this relationship was fake.

He still didn't have an answer.

Either way, it wasn't going to change the outcome.

"One of us is going to lose," he said when she kept her mouth shut. "One of us was always going to lose; it just looks different now. And if I wasn't..." He didn't even know how to put it into words. Even if he lost to Kailani, she would have the chance to move her gym to a new space, giving him an opportunity to really try to make it with the space he was in. But he doubted he would have enough money to offer free training for clients in need anytime soon. That dream would be within reach with Brad's money behind him, and he would be able to help so many people. Could he really put that all on hold when he had this chance? "I would let you win if I could. But I can't."

"And I can't afford to lose," she replied, her expression miserable. "Why did I agree to televise our relationship burning to the ground?"

Did that mean they *had* a relationship? Fake or not, Cam knew his life had changed the day he ran up to Kailani, and he was never again going to be the same person he'd been before that race began. That terrified him.

Swallowing, he forced his hand open and brushed her cheek with a trembling thumb. "I don't want to look at it that way. Even if it's true. Whatever happens after all of this, I don't want to waste the time I have with you. I wish I could just put reality on pause for a while and pretend all of this could stay."

She took his hand and pressed his palm to her cheek. "Why can't we?" she asked, her dark eyes wide and pleading. "What if we do exactly that while we're doing the show?"

As his heart beat a little stronger, Cam stepped half an inch closer. "Meaning what?"

She smiled. "Meaning the next week while we're with Brad, we pretend our lives are fine. We don't have worries or failing gyms or a f—people—who need us. It's just you and me making the best of a crappy situation and having fun while we do it. We make this thing real."

Nothing had ever sounded better, and Cam couldn't believe he had found someone who could turn the absolute worst thing in his life into a positive. Kit had always done his best, but even Kit Morgan wouldn't have been able to come up with a way to make reality bearable in this moment.

Smiling for the first time since meeting Breakout Brad, Cam leaned in and brushed his nose against hers. As much as he wanted to kiss her, he figured now probably wasn't the time. Plus, he was all too aware of the camera pointed in their direction by one of the smoothie staff. There had been enough kissing shared across the internet, and the next time Cam kissed Kailani Adams, he wanted it to be just for them.

"I think I can handle your plan," he said. "As long as you promise not to let me win anything. If we're doing this competition, we're doing it for real too."

Kailani smiled wide, looking immensely beautiful. "Deal. Now, I'd better get back to my gym before I decide to do something I probably shouldn't do. No matter how much I want to."

Cam groaned. "You're right."

"I'm always right."

"I believe you."

"Are we going to move at some point, or…?"

Cam shook his head as a realization hit him, one he almost didn't want to voice because it was seriously going to hurt. "Oliver," he moaned.

She raised an eyebrow. "What about him?"

"When he finds out we really are having a competition, he's never going to let me hear the end of it."

Kailani burst into laughter, though she tried valiantly to fight it. Honestly, he would have preferred the laughter because her attempt at holding it back only made her expression look like one of pity. "Sorry," she whispered, squeezing his hand a little tighter. "I wish I had a way to soften the blow, but I don't."

"I'll live," he said with a sigh. "For now…" He wouldn't let go of her hand until he absolutely had to. "I don't know if I'm going to be able to concentrate on anything next week if you're competing right next to me," he admitted. "How is that fair?"

Though she freed herself and headed for the door, Kailani kept her eyes on Cam as she walked backward. "Because I have a feeling that at some point during this thing, you're going to lose your shirt. And I'm not sure I'll survive that."

Cam made a mental note to remove his shirt as often as possible. If he was going to have to deal with watching Kailani perform feats of strength, he was going to do whatever he could to be equally disarming.

After all, it had to be a fair fight.

ELEVEN

AT SOME POINT DURING THE conversation with Brad, Kailani had lost her mind. That was the only explanation for how she had ended up in a hair and makeup tent in the middle of Frostwick Park, less than an hour away from filming a worldwide television show to try to save her gym.

"Why did I agree to this?" she asked as soon as the team of highly specialized hair and makeup stylists had left her alone for more than two seconds.

"Because it's going to be awesome." Isla didn't even look up from her phone, sitting in the corner and typing away. Whatever was on there, it must have been either important or far more interesting than a man trying to figure out how to get Kailani's hair to cooperate.

Good luck, buddy, but I've been fighting that losing battle for twenty-six years.

Why had Isla even come if she wasn't going to pay any attention to what was going on?

Kailani sighed. "Could you at least pretend to be supportive? I was nice enough to let you come with me."

Isla snorted, finally looking up. "You mean you begged me for twenty minutes until I agreed. Shouldn't your support dog be your tasty manfriend instead of me? Where is he, anyway?"

Kailani had been wondering the same thing for the last half an hour. She'd made a point of being on time, knowing Cam would comment on it like he had before, but he still hadn't shown up. Nor had he answered his phone. He should have been there almost an hour ago, and he had Kailani worried.

As if brought into the tent by her nerves, Cam suddenly stumbled inside. Had he tripped? But then a second man followed him inside—Kit, the one friend Kailani knew the least about even though he was Cam's favorite—and grabbed him by the shoulders.

"Will you stop trying to run away?" Kit grunted. "If I went through the effort of making sub plans and finding a substitute who won't ruin my class, you're going to see this through. You're fine."

Kailani grinned. Kit didn't look like an intimidating guy by any stretch of the imagination, but Cam looked genuinely afraid of his friend. The two of them were clearly close. She wondered what that would feel like, having a best friend.

She'd never had time for friends. If she thought about it, she'd gotten closer to Cam in the last couple of weeks than she'd been to anyone except for Isla and their brother Chase.

"Oo, who's the cute professor-looking one?" Isla had forgotten about her phone, her eyes on Kit while the two men had a heated but whispered conversation.

Kailani knew next to nothing about the guy, so she had no idea if he was even worth Isla's time. Had it been Oliver, Kailani would have steered her sister clear without hesitation, but Cam had only had good things to say about Kit when he'd briefly mentioned him at the race.

It had been one of the few personal things Cam had talked about while they walked back to the start. Kit was his best friend, and Cam considered him one of the best men he knew.

"His name is Kit," Kailani said, wincing when both men immediately stopped talking. She must have spoken louder than she thought.

Kit was the first to turn, his face reddening when he realized they weren't alone in the tent. He waved a little, one arm still wrapped around Cam's massive shoulders. He was probably only able to get a good hold on him because he was so tall, though he had a decent bit of muscle on him as well. Probably a perk of being friends with Cam.

When Cam finally turned, he looked just as nervous as he had at Blended Perfection the other day. Maybe even more so, and Kailani felt bad for convincing him to do this. He hadn't been kidding when he said he was afraid of the spotlight.

Kailani probably should have been more nervous than she was. The last three days had been full of getting Brad's trainers up to speed on the process at Horizon and pretending she had no idea what her siblings were talking about when they asked about her sudden social media fame. Isla was the only one who really had any details, and she'd been ridiculously excited about the whole prospect of the TV show. Kailani was excited too, which made her guilt over Cam's anxiety grow stronger.

He'd agreed to do this with her, and she didn't want him to regret that decision.

Honestly, Kailani hadn't been able to come up with many downsides to the whole thing outside of potentially humiliating herself for the internet to see. The contract she'd signed two days ago said she could request certain footage to be edited out, but there was no guarantee that Brad wouldn't override her wishes. Failure tended to make for good views.

Even with that possibility, Kailani figured her gym would benefit from this, no matter what. Either she got the sponsorship and moved into a bigger space with more resources, or Cam would leave the block and give her gym a chance to thrive in its current space. Regardless, the next month of her gym costs were paid for, which was a benefit all on its own.

The only real downfall she could see, one harder to stomach than humiliation, came from either scenario; she had no idea what would happen between her and Cam. She'd liked the idea of making their relationship real until she thought about the likely end of it. At some point, reality was going to come crashing back and Cam was going to realize Kailani wasn't worth the effort.

She hated that thought the instant it entered her head. Cam had never given her any reasons to think he would do that.

But neither had the last guy she dated.

"Hey," she said, meeting Cam's gaze, "can I talk to you for a sec? Before the stylists attack you?"

His eyes went wide. "Before the who does what?"

Grinning, Kailani reached out her hand and was glad when Cam stepped forward without hesitation. Once they'd retreated to the far side of the tent, giving Isla and Kit an opportunity to meet—whether that was good or bad, Kailani wasn't sure—she grabbed hold of Cam's other hand to tell him that she would be right by his side the whole time.

Though he stood tense and his fingers trembled, Cam's expression had relaxed at the contact. "Is that why you look prettier than normal?" he asked, looking her over. "I mean, you're always pretty, but… But I'm going to stop talking before I stick my foot in my mouth."

"No, go ahead and keep going."

"Ha. What did you want to talk about?"

"Us."

Cam took a step back, though Kailani was pretty sure it was just reflex because it seemed to confuse him. He pulled his eyebrows down low and moved back in, taking a deep breath that seemed to give him some confidence.

Taking a breath to match, Kailani tried to put her own fears into words. "I don't want this competition to get between us. I don't want to keep thinking this—you and I—will end when the competition does. We already agreed to have fun with it, but I worry about what happens afterward. I couldn't stop thinking about it last night."

"Now who's overthinking things?" Something shifted in Cam. He stood a little taller, his hands steadier and his gaze strong before he closed his eyes and pressed his forehead to hers. "You said it the other day; let's just focus on right now. There's nothing I want more than to stay on this path we're on."

Interesting. He suddenly sounded so confident. Apparently Cam's nerves went away if he was looking after someone else. Kailani could take care of herself, and she would never let that change. But from the beginning, Cam had made her feel like she didn't *have* to take care of herself, and that was something she'd never experienced before.

When she was so busy taking care of everyone else, she tended to be the first one to fall by the wayside.

He hadn't flat-out promised he would stick around after the competition—it would be crazy to ask him to promise something like that—but neither did he seem like the type of guy to run away when something got hard. At least, she hoped he wasn't. He was here, after all, even when he was clearly anxious. But she hadn't told him anything about her family yet, and that wasn't exactly something she could avoid forever.

"You sure you're up for this?" she asked, squeezing his hand. "We might still be able to get out of our contracts."

He smiled. "Backing out already, Princess? I had my heart set on some real competition for once."

Kailani shook her head. "You really need to come up with a better nickname."

"I know."

"Is he finally here?" One of the stylists flew into the tent, her blue eyes wide in panic, but then she stopped dead as soon as she saw Cam and Kailani holding each other close. "Oh. My. Gosh. You guys are so *cute* together! I mean, I saw the pictures, but it's even better in—Serena! You have to come see these guys! Go get Felipe. He's gonna die."

Next thing she knew, Kailani and Cam were both being shuffled back to the chairs where Kailani had spent the last half an hour even though she was already all made up. Cam looked like a deer in headlights as three beauticians came at him with brushes and powders, and he kept a firm grip on Kailani's hand as if expecting her to abandon him in his time of need.

Kailani had no interest in letting go.

"Don't even think about it," Cam growled, startling the man about to touch his hair. But Cam was glaring at Kit, who had his phone out.

Kit hardly seemed to care as he snapped several photos of Cam with a makeup brush in his face. "You never know when this might be useful," he said gleefully.

"Love a man who's willing to blackmail his friend," Isla said just behind him. "I like you, Clark."

"It's Kit."

"I know Superman's alter-ego when I see him."

The two of them shared a look that seemed to indicate they'd bonded in the short time after Kit's arrival. Kailani still wasn't sure how to feel about that, particularly if the two of them ended up getting close. And when Kit grinned at Isla, making her blush a perfect pink, Kailani's stomach twisted.

She wasn't ready for Isla to grow up yet.

"Does it look like they're flirting?" Cam asked, leaning closer and lowering his voice so only Kailani and the beauticians would hear. "Because I'm not sure I like them flirting."

As much as she was glad to know it wasn't just her, Kailani still felt a twinge in her stomach. "Because she's not good enough for your best friend?"

"Ha! No. Kit doesn't date. Usually. He's the most consistent man I've ever known, and..." He frowned when Isla swung her leg up, practically forcing Kit to catch it as she explained the prosthetic he now held. Though it definitely seemed to catch Kit off guard—likely Isla's plan in the first place—his smile returned quickly as the two of them continued talking despite Isla's strange position with her leg in the air. "I just don't know how much change I can handle right now."

Kailani could understand that, but she was glad to know Kit hadn't batted an eye at Isla's missing leg. "You don't even know my sister. They could be good for each other."

"That's your sister?"

She shouldn't have said anything. Now she would have to explain why they looked nothing alike. Not that adoption was anything crazy, but... "She was the second kid my parents adopted," she said quietly. "It definitely shows the power behind nature versus nurture. She and I are nothing alike." Except when it came to familial expectations, in which case they'd both endured feeling like they weren't enough.

Cam furrowed his eyebrows a bit as he studied Isla, though one of the stylists snapped at him and told him to relax. "What happened to her—"

"Bone cancer when she was nine." Kailani's heart ached just thinking about it. "She had several surgeries to try to remove the cancer, but eventually they had to go for the leg. She's never let it stop her, though."

"Maybe she should be on the show with you instead of me."

Kailani squeezed his hand tight, half out of appreciation for that comment and half out of fear that he would actually try to get out of it. "You worried I'm going to beat you in every event?"

"Of course not." His expression said otherwise. He looked completely sick, which had Kailani wondering if that was a lie. She wasn't positive if this was the case, but she was pretty sure the man hadn't been exaggerating when he said he couldn't lie.

His stomach wouldn't let him.

"Have you seen Brad yet this morning?" Cam asked, probably trying to change the subject before he lost his breakfast.

Kailani had been too excited (or maybe nervous) to eat breakfast this morning, though she knew she was going to regret that eventually. Her body was going to get angry with her for the lack of good fuel.

"I saw him for maybe five minutes before these guys got to me," she said, forcing a smile as the three beauticians glanced at her. "I still have no idea what today's competition will be. I also have no idea why we have to look so perfect," she added under her breath.

Cam's hand tightened around hers, which meant he must have heard her grumble. "You always look perfect," he argued.

If anyone looked perfect all the time, *he* did. "That is definitely not true. Most of the time I look sweaty and tired."

"You look confident and strong."

She turned to him, even though Felipe practically had him in a headlock to work on his hair. "How do you do that?"

Cam's eyes shifted in her direction. "Do what?"

"How do you say things like that so easily? Like, I'm sitting here hoping whatever we do today will give me a chance to admire that rocking bod of yours, but it's not like I can say that out loud."

His deliciously crooked grin made its appearance, warming her to her core. "You just did."

"But only because you said something first. There's no way I would be able to do that with anyone else, but it seems like the words come so easily for you."

"You do remember how many times I stuck my foot in my mouth when we met, right? It's not always a good thing."

"Yeah, but you've barely done that since then. You've just been honest. I don't think I've ever met anyone as open and honest as you. How do you do it?"

Jerking his head free of Felipe's hold, Cam glared at the beauticians until all three of them backed away. He gave them a look that seemed to say, "Are you done?" and they must have agreed, because they muttered unintelligible things and then shuffled from the tent.

Now that he was free and they were relatively alone, Kit and Isla deep in conversation several feet away, Cam shifted in his seat to face her with a curious expression on his face. "Can I tell you a secret? I mean, a secret that my three closest friends already know so it's not all that secret?"

Kailani nodded eagerly, scooting to the edge of her chair to get as close as she could.

Cam shot a glance at Kit, who was still busy talking to Isla, and then he lowered his voice as he said, "I didn't used to be this way. Honest, I mean. When I was a kid, I got into a lot of trouble. A lot of…fights." His eyebrows shifted down, his eyes going distant. "I was so angry. For a lot of reasons. Then, in seventh grade…"

He tensed up, throwing another look at Kit before he leaned in close and dropped his voice. "The day after I found out my dad died, I lied to my teacher so I could skip class and go find something to make the hurt go away. Kit found me in the hall—we didn't know each other yet—and told me to go back to class. I ignored the skinny white kid and carried on my way. I came back for the last class of the day because I knew my aunt would be picking me up, but after school, Kit came up to me and started lecturing me about attendance and how it's important. No fear at all of the angry Hispanic twice his size with bottled up aggression."

He smiled a little as he glanced at the tent door, as if remembering the two of them as kids. "I beat the crap out of him," he said, wincing. "And we ended up in detention after school for three weeks. I refused to talk to him at first, but the guy's persistent. He could tell I was really struggling, and Kit is not one to let suffering go unnoticed. Once I realized he had only been looking out for me, we started getting to know each other. He helped me realize that being angry wasn't going to change my situation. And when he invited me to his house to meet his family, something changed in me."

Kailani was afraid to even breathe in case Cam stopped talking. She hadn't meant for her question to turn into a life story, but she wasn't complaining about this insight to the man who was turning out to be so much more than his exterior appearance.

"Seeing how easily Duke and Lydia accepted me into their home made me wonder if there was more to family than blood," he said, with so much emotion in his face that it brought tears to Kailani's eyes. "And I went from being alone to having not just one brother but three, and a cute little sister who saw the world through such innocent eyes. I became a Wonder Boy, and none of them cared that I had a shady past. Even Oliver… They made me want to be better. I didn't want to hide, or fight, or lie anymore. Especially not lie.

"The night I became a part of Kit's family was the night I made a vow to be honest in everything I did. To let myself feel all the emotions, good and bad, because they showed me that it was okay to feel things. And…" He blinked and bit his lip. "And I just told you way more than you probably wanted to hear. I'm sorry. I tend to overshare when I'm nervous. Or excited. Or anytime, really."

When he brushed a tear from her lashes, Kailani shuddered. She'd never met anyone like this man, and she was worried she'd just crossed a threshold and would never be able to go back.

I want you to tell me everything about you, she wanted to say. But if she was going to expect that of him, she would have to do the same thing, and she wasn't sure if she was ready for something like that. She hadn't made a vow as a teen to be open and honest, and there were some things better left un-said. She wanted to explore this thing with Cam. She really did. But he deserved better than someone who wasn't worth the love he was clearly capable of giving.

So instead of being honest and telling him that she was really starting to fall for him, she smiled and squeezed his hand. "I don't mind. Like I said, I'm a good listener."

"Ah, my lovebirds are ready!" Brad hopped into the tent, his megawatt grin filling the place with light as much as his neon spandex did. "Sharing sweet nothings, are we?" He winked at Kailani, who had no idea how to respond to that. "And I see you've brought friends. Welcome! I've got special seats for you in the audience."

"Audience?" Kailani and Cam said in unison.

Chuckling, Brad rubbed his hands together with excite-ment. "I was amazed by how many people volunteered! But then again, you two have caused quite a stir in this town, so maybe I shouldn't have been surprised at all! Are you ready for your first challenge?"

Kailani definitely wished she had eaten breakfast as her stomach churned with sudden nerves, though maybe it was a good thing she had nothing to throw up. She'd been prepared for people to see her in action *after* the fact. Not during. No one had said anything about a live audience, and now she won-dered if she should have spent a little more time reading the contract she had signed yesterday.

"What if…" Cam paused halfway through his sentence and scowled.

Kailani followed his gaze to find Kit glaring at him, though it wasn't all that potent of a glare. Still, it seemed to be doing the trick, because Cam let out a sigh and stood, pulling Kailani with him.

"Great!" Brad said. "Follow me!"

"I'm gonna make you pay for this," Cam growled as they passed Kit.

Kit merely grinned, while Isla had her phone out and gleefully filmed their walk of shame behind Brad.

There was definitely something Kailani was missing. "What—"

"Kit bet that I would back out of this thing," Cam said roughly. "Not that I was planning on doing that, but it's the principle of the thing. If I lose, I have to spend a month at Oliver's house after his wife has her baby."

"That doesn't sound so horrible," Kailani replied. They were passing several other tents and trailers, heading toward the soccer fields where the noise of a thundering crowd made her fingers start to shake. "Oliver is annoying, but—"

"If you think he's annoying now, he's going to be so much worse when he's got a kid. He'll be that guy who takes a million photos that all look the same and uses a ridiculous baby voice without caring that other people can hear him."

That actually sounded adorable, but Kailani kept that to herself. Her nerves were building, and as they followed Brad the last little bit, she latched on to the first thought that came up to distract her. How was Cam with kids? Did he want any? She almost couldn't picture him with anyone who couldn't lift fifty pounds, and that made her sadder than she wanted to admit. Not that she was thinking about that kind of future with him…

Her stomach did a somersault, and for a horrifying moment she wondered if Cam's anti-lying mechanism was contagious.

Then Brad came to a halt and turned to face them. "Welcome to the beginning of your futures," he said with a huge grin. "I'm going to go out there and do all the introductions, and when I say your names, that's when you'll run out onto the field. We'll be right in the middle. I usually like to practice this sort of thing, but the surprise will be far more entertaining than having everything go according to plan. Any questions?"

"Only a million," Cam grumbled, too quiet for Brad to hear.

Kailani had no idea how to answer.

"Great!" Brad clapped his hands. "Let's get this competition rolling!"

TWELVE

CAM HAD A LOT OF regrets in his life. That was never going to change, and it often kept him up at night if he thought too long about things he'd done in his past. But nothing was ever going to come close to his decision to tell Kit about the TV show.

Calling it a decision wasn't exactly accurate. Kit had shown up at the gym for his training session, and everything had been going fine until he asked about his meeting with Breakout Brad. Cam had tried—oh, how he tried—to keep his mouth shut, but it was either throw up in the middle of the gym or admit to being part of the show.

That had led to several clients freaking out about Breakout Brad being in Diamond Springs, and before he knew it, Cam was surrounded by people asking him questions he was terrified to answer.

Thank goodness for Sasha, who pulled Cam away to answer a "very important phone call" that was just a confused telemarketer who didn't understand why Cam would want to buy makeup. Cam had grumbled something about how men could wear makeup if they wanted, accidentally ordered a sample case that he very much hoped was free because he had no intention of using it, and then he'd rushed back to the steam room to try to catch his breath for a second.

That was where Kit had cornered him and figured out exactly what was happening with Brad, and then he forced

Cam to stay at his house that night so he couldn't chicken out. He'd fully planned on following through with his agreement, even without the contract binding him to it, but things had gone from okay to awful pretty quickly. This morning had started off decent until his anxiety skyrocketed ten minutes before he had to leave. Only when Kit made the bet had Cam been able to calm down enough—partially out of fear—to get in Kit's car and show up, but that didn't mean he was happy to be here.

You'll be fine, he told himself as he paced underneath the bleachers while Brad spoke excitedly into a microphone. By some miracle, his self-talk didn't make him sick, so maybe it would actually be true. Well, it didn't make him any sicker than he already was after telling Kailani about when he met Kit.

He'd tried to stop himself. She didn't need to know all of that, and she'd been looking at him differently ever since. With a sort of pity in her dark eyes. Why couldn't he have just stuck with a simple explanation?

Because that wasn't how he worked, that's why.

He paused his pacing just long enough to try to read her expression again as they waited for their first competition. Nope. Nothing. She was a blank slate, completely guarded. What had happened to the expressive woman he'd met at the race? It felt like the longer he knew her, the more she pretended there was nothing more to know. Particularly when it came to her family. Cam didn't need to know every little detail about her right this minute, but he wanted to know *something*. He hadn't even known her sister was adopted until he saw her in the tent. Not that that mattered, but Cam had been imagining someone entirely different, and now he was wondering what else he might be wrong about.

"We're almost ready for you guys," a bearded man said, appearing from around the corner with a tablet in his hands and a headset making him look all official. He nodded to

Kailani, but when he met Cam's gaze, he frowned a little. "Can I get some water back here?" he said into the headset with some measure of urgency.

Cam swallowed. Did he look that bad?

Kailani turned to him and smiled, for the first time showing some nerves as she tugged on the hem of her athletic tank top. "Are we crazy?" she asked, a little breathless.

The closest Cam got to a smile was a little twitch of his lips. "Probably," he croaked.

That made her frown. "You okay?"

He wasn't even going to try to lie with that one, so he said nothing.

"Don't think of this as a competition," she said, reaching for his hand and pressing it between both of hers. "We're just here to have fun, remember? That's what I keep telling myself."

"Fun," he repeated. They'd decided that in the beginning, but that was before he knew half of Diamond Springs would be there watching. "That depends entirely on what we're about to do." Just how creative was Brad going to get? And why couldn't he have just told them ahead of time what the competition was? Cam probably would have been too anxious to practice anything even if he had.

This whole thing was a nightmare.

A nightmare that was two seconds away from pushing Cam into an anxiety attack.

"Cam? Stay with me."

One second away.

"Hey!" Kailani grabbed his t-shirt collar and pulled him down until their lips collided.

Yeah, okay. Cam tugged her body against his even though he knew this definitely wasn't the time for a makeout session. She just fit so well against him that he couldn't help it, and if anything was going to distract him, this was. Her kisses were the kind of thing that shut out the world, and he dove in.

"Everyone welcome Kailani Adams and Cameron Martinez!"

Kailani broke away, her eyes wide, and then she grinned. "May the best woman win."

Cam stood there for two seconds as she broke into a jog and disappeared, completely stunned because somehow that kiss had been better than the last one. Was it because they'd gone from pretending to real?

Then he saw the camera just behind him. He had no idea how long the camera man had been standing there filming their exchange, but his heart sank when he realized Kailani had just been playing up the relationship because she knew they were being filmed.

Shaking his head clear, he forced himself forward and plastered on a smile that he hoped would look real enough from a distance. Though Kailani had prevented him from losing the battle against his anxiety, she'd also knocked the wind right out of his sails.

How much of this was real to her?

Stop looking for reasons to think she'll leave you, he scolded himself as he picked up his pace. True, he knew they couldn't *actually* stay a couple forever—Cam knew better than to argue the fact that everyone left eventually—but he had no actual proof that she was pulling away from him already. They'd agreed to pretend everything was well and good while they were doing the show.

He was overthinking again.

The cheering crowd grew louder when he finally rounded the corner and entered the field. He could see the platform where Brad was waiting—Kailani had just reached it—but his eyes caught on the volleyball net surrounded by cameras.

Beneath the net was a whole lot of mud.

"He may be a little slow when it comes to running," Brad said as Cam climbed the steps to the platform, "but don't let that fool you! Cam played four different sports in high school—you heard that right, *four*—and may have some state championships under his belt."

Cam peeled his eyes away from the field to look at Brad. How did he know all that?

As Brad started talking about their respective gyms, Kailani leaned over and muttered, "Four sports?"

Cam cleared his throat, though it still felt like something was stuck in there. He had no idea how he was supposed to feel right now. Kailani was as attractive as ever, her kisses earth-shattering, but reality was crashing down hard. The winner of this competition would have all their dreams come true, and the loser would be left behind.

With his past being the way it was, it would probably be him.

"Swimming," he grunted. "Water polo. Basketball. Baseball."

She smiled. "I swam too, though I never did water polo. I bet you look amazing in a baseball uniform, don't you?"

Cam didn't get a chance to react to the wink she sent him.

"Are we ready to see who today's champion will be?" Brad shouted into the microphone. The crowd went crazy.

"Are we just playing solo volleyball?" Kailani asked.

Cam shrugged. Everything was happening too fast for him to process. But volleyball? He could play volleyball. The problem was Kailani also looked like she could play volleyball.

He frowned as the two of them headed toward the muddy court. "Did you also play volleyball in high school?"

Her smirk sent a jolt of electricity through him, though he had no idea if that was good or bad. Mostly, he felt pretty numb right now.

Slipping out of his shoes when he reached the edge of the court, Cam tried to remind himself that they'd agreed to have fun with these competitions. The *competition* part wouldn't get out of his head, however. The winner of these challenges would get a lot of financial backing, AKA the chance to actually succeed. Cam clearly couldn't do it on his own—at least, not with Kailani's gym right next to his—so he needed to win as many of these things as he could.

The problem was if he won, that would mean Kailani lost. He didn't like that part. Watching her lose would feel the same as losing himself.

Was there any way for him to actually win in this scenario?

His toes squelched through the mud as he stepped onto his side of the field, the mud slimy and cool. It would probably get fairly slippery, so he would have to keep his guard up. Kailani was given the opportunity to call heads or tails to see who would serve first, and within moments he was standing at the back with the ball, wondering why in the world he needed makeup and a hair stylist for this but ready to start the game.

He *hoped* he was ready to start. This wasn't exactly how he had envisioned feeling when he woke up this morning. Plus, it had been a while since he played a good game of volleyball, and he'd never played on his own before.

And certainly not in front of a roaring crowd.

It's just like your high school basketball games, he reminded himself. Only, back then he'd shared the court with four other guys, Kit among them most of the time. He could see Kit in the audience, but his face quickly blurred into a mass of faces on the bleachers. Not helpful.

Focus on the game, Cam.

His first serve was mainly to get a feel for the ball and the distance of the smaller-than-normal court, not necessarily in an attempt to get a point. Kailani easily saved the ball and set it over the net after a light bump, apparently choosing to do the same thing and get a feel for everything first. As long as she really started playing when he did, he wouldn't feel too bad if he ended up beating her.

After several volleys back and forth, Cam set himself up for a spike that Kailani only missed because her foot stuck a bit in the mud. She gave him a playful glare as he returned to the back of the court to serve again, and it almost brought a smile out of him.

"Okay," he breathed, telling himself once again that they were supposed to be having fun. This time, when he served, he hit it to the back corner of her side to give her a little challenge.

She managed to save the ball again, though she couldn't get herself any good power in a spike as she scrambled back to the center of the court. At least, that was what Cam thought until the ball sailed over his head with impressive speed and skidded through the mud behind him.

"You sure you're ready for this?" Kailani asked with a grin.

Cam bit his lip as he tossed the ball over for her to serve. "Why don't you play the game and see?" he said instead of trying to give her an answer. It saved him the risk of telling a lie and also counted as decent banter.

He could do banter.

Kailani served the ball with the confidence of someone who had done it many times. Cam had to dive to save it, hitting it back over with that single hit to give himself a chance to climb out of the mud that coated his body. The ball was back before he was ready, but he caught it with a fist and managed to get it over the net once more. Kailani hit it back but at the expense of her balance as she slid and nearly fell.

After several slides and multiple volleys, Kailani got the point.

The longer they played, the muddier they got, and when he slipped onto his side at one point right after Kailani did the same and lost the ball to his serve, Cam couldn't help but laugh. This game was getting ridiculous, and it was probably only going to get worse. They were fairly evenly matched, though Kailani was ahead by two points, and one of them would have to win eventually.

Maybe it was time to *really* have some fun. What was the point in being so serious, anyway? Though Cam wanted his gym to succeed, he didn't want to have to beat Kailani for that to happen. Instead of being so focused on winning, he just needed to play. Have fun. Exactly like they'd agreed.

As he got up to serve, Cam's shirt flapped against his belly, hanging heavy with mud, and he spun the ball a few times as he considered his next move. She'd admitted to one of her weaknesses the other day, but he wouldn't be showing off just for her if he exploited that.

The whole country would be getting a show.

Kailani narrowed her eyes as she waited for him to serve the ball, a challenge in her smug smile.

"Whatever," he muttered and set the ball in the mud at his feet. The crowd stilled, confused, and Cam fingered the hem of his shirt just long enough for Kailani to figure out what he was about to do.

Her eyes went wide at the same time he grabbed the back of his collar and tugged his shirt over his head.

The audience went wild, but Cam did his best to ignore them as he rolled his shoulders. He took his time stretching one arm over his head, then the other, all the while pretending he wasn't keenly aware of the way Kailani had gone slack jawed.

He had the ball in hand and up in the air a second later, and though Kailani made a valiant effort to save it, she ended up sprawled in the mud and glaring.

The glare turned into admiration only a second later.

"Cheater," she said as she got to her feet, eyes locked on Cam's chest.

He flexed. She'd seen his body before, but not this much of it. "I don't know what you're talking about."

He served the ball again. This time she was ready, and they volleyed back and forth several times until Cam's foot slid and he lost the ball.

His distraction had worked, but not as well as he'd wanted, and he made a quick circuit of his side of the court to shake out the disappointment. If nothing else, at least the audience seemed to be having a good time, and he could imagine a good number of posts with *#hotbodycam* would be making the rounds for the next few days.

He turned just as the ref blew her whistle for the next volley, but then he froze.

Kailani had lost her tank top and was now in only a sports bra.

He didn't even try to get the ball she served to him, not when he had a full view of just how strong she really was. It landed with a splat behind him. If any of these competitions involved core strength, she would beat him. Hands down.

"No fair," he squeaked, his mouth dry.

Kailani winked. "All's fair in love and war," she said. "And you did it first. Give me the ball."

He did, though reluctantly. Now he would have to watch the way she moved as she served, every inch of her lithe and limber. He'd known she was strong, but...

He managed to volley the ball back over the net three times, each time getting closer to the net, before the mud proved to be his downfall again. Kailani hit the ball over his head, and as he turned to dive for it, his feet slipped out from under him, sending him under the net and directly into Kailani's legs.

Next thing he knew, she was on top of him, solid and warm and with way too much skin to skin for him to have any chance of breathing like a normal human.

"Sorry," he groaned, shutting his eyes. He hadn't realized how cold the mud was until feeling her warmth, and now he couldn't concentrate on anything else. It took everything in him not to wrap his fingers around her bare waist and feel that muscle for himself while pulling her against him and never letting go.

Kailani snorted a laugh, apparently unaware of how much he desperately wanted her to move. "Is this your new tactic? Take out your opponent?"

If she wasn't going to free him, he might as well play along. Opening his eyes and finding himself face to face with a mud-streaked Kailani, he smiled at her and scooped up a handful of mud. "Is it working?" he asked.

Then he plopped his goopy handful on top of her head, splattering his own face in the process.

She gasped, but her shock led immediately to a literal armful of mud directly into his face.

He reacted instinctively, rolling to the side and taking her with him until their positions were reversed, Cam up on his knees. But his advantage lasted only long enough for Kailani to wrap one leg around his and grab hold of his arm. With one good tug, he crumpled, and she rolled back the way they'd come and had him pinned.

She had never been more attractive than she was right then, covered in mud and fully in control. Cam had never met anyone who could match him in strength, and he had no idea what to do about that.

"That look in your eyes is dangerous," she warned, her own eyes alight with something intense.

"And what look is that?" Cam asked. More than ever, he wanted to know what made this woman tick. He wanted to see beneath the armor she wore.

Figuratively. Right now, she wore next to nothing, all of her strength on display. Maybe she could actually be the person that stuck around.

Maybe she wouldn't leave him like everyone else had.

He lifted his head, not necessarily with the intent to kiss her—not that he would hate that outcome—but because he wanted to get closer. He wanted to see into her soul and find out if she could break his curse. But in order to know for sure, she would have to let him in.

Can you do that? he silently asked her. *Can you trust me enough to be vulnerable with all of you?*

Kailani's lips parted, as if she was about to answer his unspoken question.

"Looks like our players have gotten a little distracted. I guess we have a winner! Give it up for Kailani Adams!"

As the noise of the crowd reached alarming decibels—Cam had forgotten anyone was even there—Kailani slowly got to her feet and held out her hand to help Cam up. They both slipped several times trying to get off the field and back to the platform where Brad was beaming, but they made it eventually.

As Brad thanked everyone for attending the first event and explained that there would be plenty more to come, Cam kept his eyes on Kailani. She'd closed off again, standing with her arms folded across her bare stomach, and she had her eyes focused on something in the crowd.

Her grinning sister. And next to Isla sat Kit, who was looking at Cam with his eyebrows low and his lips pursed. His signature worried expression.

Was he worried about Cam losing? This was only the first competition, and Cam had been outmatched from the beginning. But he wouldn't be that way all the time, and at some point he would start with the advantage.

Kailani's arm brushed against his, and Cam realized she was shivering. It was only February, after all, and now that they weren't moving, a chill had settled around them. Though he had no idea how she would react, Cam wrapped his arms around her from behind and pulled her against his bare chest.

She relaxed into him immediately, and the crowd *awwed* as if they'd never seen anything sweeter.

"Thanks," she whispered. "I have no idea how you're this warm, but... Thanks."

"It's not like it's much of a sacrifice," he replied, biting his tongue because that sounded ridiculous. "I just mean I... I'm not going to finish that sentence. You're welcome." *I mean I have never felt more whole than when I'm holding you in my arms.* That was what he wanted to say.

Finally, Brad ended his spiel, and all of the camera men lowered their cameras. He clapped his hands, clearly pleased, and beamed at both of them. "We've got hot showers waiting," he said. "And food in the catering tent. I would imagine the two of you worked up quite an appetite."

Cam had an appetite, all right, but not for food. For the first time in his life, he wanted more than something casual with someone.

For the first time, he wanted a future.

THIRTEEN

DESPITE SPENDING MOST OF HER childhood on a tropical island where the temperature rarely dropped below sixty degrees, Kailani almost never got cold. It was a nice trait, considering her low body fat percentage, and something she hadn't truly appreciated until this moment, when it utterly failed her.

Even the sweatshirt she'd requested after her shower had only done her so much good inside the heated catering tent. After her shower, in which she'd drained the portable hot water tank, she had put on every stitch of clothing she had brought with her. For some reason, this chill sat too deep for the propane heater above her to penetrate it, and it was driving her crazy.

It was too bad Isla had left to grab lunch with Kit. The two of them seemed to be hitting it off really well—pros and cons there—and it meant Isla couldn't go to the apartment and grab her favorite oversized fleece for her. Maybe something familiar would have warmed her up.

Kailani just hoped she would be able to leave soon. Being away from her gym was already making her antsy, even though Brad had assured them their gyms would be in good hands. She'd put her heart and soul into that place and hadn't been away for longer than—

"Cheese and crackers, why am I so cold?" She growled the words out loud, angrily pulling her feet onto the bench where she sat so she could hug her legs and hope they brought some extra warmth to her body.

A deep chuckle made her jump. "Maybe if you hadn't done your little strip tease," Cam said in the tent doorway.

Kailani glared at him. "Winning the game is not a strip tease."

How was the man in only a t-shirt and joggers? It didn't help that his gray shirt looked a size too small so it hugged every inch of him, reminding her of what exactly was underneath. Not that she'd forgotten. Seeing everything on display earlier had sent her heart racing in an erratic rhythm, and it had taken everything in her not to dwell on the memory since leaving the field.

She hadn't really succeeded at that part.

He folded his arms, his expression teasing. "You only won because we stopped the game early so you could gaze into my eyes."

"I wasn't—" She stopped herself. She had definitely been gazing into his eyes, and she shivered just thinking about the way he'd looked at her down in the mud. He was always expressive, but that had been something entirely new. It was like he'd been trying to learn everything about her by looking at her. And she wanted him to know it all.

That didn't mean she wasn't terrified of telling him about her complicated family. The last time she'd done that, the guy had almost literally run away. What guarantee did she have that Cam wouldn't do the same?

Grin still intact, Cam glanced at the several caterers Kailani had been ignoring despite the gnawing sensation in her gut, and then he sidled over to her little bench and grabbed her feet. "Stop hogging the heater, Tease."

"You *are* the heater," she complained, though she didn't stop him from swiveling her where she sat. "You don't need it."

"I know. Come here."

Kailani didn't have to be told twice. The second he opened his arms, she practically tackled him as she slid into his embrace. Then she let out a sigh of contentment. "That's better."

"For you, maybe. Your nose feels like ice."

She tucked her legs over his, nearly sitting in his lap now, and pressed her nose even deeper into his neck. Unless he'd brought his soap with him, that delicious smell of his was just his natural scent, and that made her furious. She definitely didn't smell that good without assistance.

That wasn't important, though. Maybe it was time to test the waters. Give him a little insight into her life. "I have to tell you something," she said.

"Oh?" His arms tightened around her, as if he knew how hard this was for her. As if he'd been hoping for this moment.

She nodded, though that was partially to help warm her icy nose. "I did play volleyball in high school."

He held his breath for several seconds, waiting, but then he let it all out with a deep sigh. "I guessed as much, with the way you played."

She hated how disappointed he sounded, like he had just resigned himself to never learning anything else about her. Swallowing, she clung to him a little tighter, afraid he might leave her behind because she was too scared to open up. *Be brave, Lani.* "I played until halfway through my junior season, but then my parents took in a couple of foster kids and needed help around the house. Dad picked up a second job, and Mom put me on homework duty so she could make dinner every night. I didn't have time for practice after school anymore."

It was her turn to hold her breath as she waited for him to react to that.

"How many kids are in your family?" he asked, though nothing in his tone clued her in to what he was thinking.

What would he, an only child, think of her parents and their obsessive need to keep adding to the family? They'd started fostering when they moved from Hawaii, and that had quickly turned into adopting. "There are ten of us now."

"You're the oldest?"

"Yep."

"And how many are—"

"Adopted? Everyone except me. Mom hated that she couldn't have any more biological kids, but it had been hard enough to get me. Technically, I wasn't supposed to make it past six months."

Cam stiffened, but Kailani kept talking. Apparently, once she opened up, it was difficult to stop.

"I was born early, and my lungs were underdeveloped. They didn't think I was ever going to breathe on my own. Even then, I guess I wanted to prove people wrong."

Though he still sat tense, Cam's voice had gotten gentler when he said, "I'm glad you defied the odds." He shifted, his nose brushing her cheek, and if she just turned ever so slightly…

"I see we're all fresh and clean!" Brad said, making them both jump.

What was it with this guy and interrupting their best moments? Kailani shouldn't have been so disappointed, given their precarious dating situation, but she was. After their last kiss, Cam had been somewhat grumpy, and Kailani still didn't know what to make of that. Either he'd been angry about the interruption, or he hadn't wanted her to kiss him.

Technically, it was against their rules, and their moment in the mud might have been for show for all she knew.

Stupid rules. Stupid competition. Stupid games of pretend.

He'd agreed to make their relationship real, but could they really go from fake to real at the flip of a switch? They'd done the opposite, after they realized who the other person was, but Brad and his show had made everything way more complicated than it had been before.

As he came up beside them, Brad stroked his beard and seemed to be examining the pair of them huddled together. Whatever he saw, it made him grin. "I may have to start having a camera follow you around wherever you go," he said brightly. "So much intriguing behind-the-scenes could really boost views and sympathize viewers to your cause."

Kailani felt Cam gulp behind her. "Is that necessary?" she asked. "We'd be happy to—"

"Oh, I think it's necessary. Your good luck kiss this morning was so much better than anything scripted might have been."

Kailani's stomach dropped. "Our what? You were filming us?" Her whole body seemed to catch fire from the embarrassment of that, and she dropped her face into Cam's neck. "Please tell me it wasn't completely humiliating."

"You didn't know about the camera?" Cam asked. There was a strange edge to his question, almost like it carried a hint of hope.

Kailani shook her head. "I definitely wouldn't have thrown myself at you like that if I'd known we were being filmed," she breathed. "And admitting that is almost as embarrassing. I'm sorry. I shouldn't have—"

"Don't be sorry," he murmured, his breath brushing her ear as he pulled her closer to his warm chest. "Never be sorry for a kiss like that."

Kailani thought maybe she was floating, every inch of her on fire with happiness. For a guy who had bumbled through their first meeting, he had really dialed in the flirting thing now that he didn't seem so anxious.

"See what I mean?" Brad said, interrupting yet again. "This is gold! I suppose phone footage will have to do for now." Sure enough, he had his phone out, his eyes glittering with excitement. "Now, let's get you kids fed before our next event!"

As soon as he skipped away, Kailani and Cam both burst into laughter.

"He's going to be the death of us," Cam decided out loud.

Kailani wholeheartedly agreed, and though she slid from Cam's lap so they could make their way to the delicious-smelling food, she grabbed hold of his hand with no intention of letting go. "Sounds like we're going to be watched a lot," she said.

Cam's eyes smoldered. "As long as I don't have to pretend with you anymore, I don't care. You said the other day that we should make this real, which means there's nothing stopping me from doing this." He pressed a kiss to her forehead. "And this." He kissed her nose. "And—"

"We have just about anything your heart may desire," Brad said. "And if we don't have it, all you need to do is ask. You kids are worth the expense."

Kailani bit her lip when Cam growled low in his throat. Though she didn't say it out loud—that was a little too terrifying—right now, her heart desired the man in front of her.

The man who hadn't batted an eye when he learned more about her complicated life.

FOURTEEN

"YOU WANT US TO WHAT?" Kailani was fully convinced she had heard the afternoon's challenge wrong, but Brad had brought them into a fancy, temporary kitchen full of ingredients. What else could he have said?

"Make a pizza," he confirmed, laughter in his words. "You didn't think all my competitions would be physical, did you?"

Cam, who had taken a nap after lunch and still looked half-asleep despite being attacked by the beauticians again, blinked several times as he took in the scene in front of them. "Uh, we sort of did," he said. "You're sponsoring one of our gyms, so…"

Brad chuckled, folding his arms. "Exactly. My competition needs to be about more than strength. It's acting under pressure. Being flexible. Adapting."

"What does pizza have to do with adapting?" Kailani asked weakly. Had Brad done some spying and realized she didn't cook? At all? Was this his way of keeping things balanced at the beginning of the competition so no one pulled ahead too quickly?

Her only hope was that Cam was as poor a cook as she was. If his skills extended to the kitchen, that would make him a little too perfect.

"Pizza has everything to do with everything," Brad replied, apparently unaware of how strange that sounded to someone who wasn't a big fan of pizza to begin with.

After someone spends several months in a row buying a pizza at least once a week, she loses her taste for it. The curse of not being able to cook anything more than boxed pasta. And Isla hated cooking with a passion, so she had never been much help either.

Cam let out a yawn, running a hand through his carefully made-up hair. Felipe was probably somewhere in the distance, cursing that big hand for ruining his painstakingly crafted masterpiece.

Kailani didn't mind the change; Cam looked more human this way. Plus, there was the benefit of watching his muscles shift and bulge with each movement of his arm.

"Who's going to judge the pizza?" he asked at the tail end of his yawn.

Kailani hid her sympathetic yawn that easily followed. She'd tried to follow his example and take a nap in the little trailer they told her she could use, but her brain had refused to turn off. She'd spent the last two hours thinking about all the things she wanted to tell Cam about herself but wasn't sure she was brave enough to. Not yet, anyway.

He had seemed to appreciate her confession before lunch, but that had been the easy one. How could she know how he would respond to anything deeper than that?

What if he met her chaotic family and ran for the hills? Talking about the number was a whole lot different from actually being around all of them, and Kailani's family was non-negotiable. Despite everything they made her feel—or didn't feel—she loved them and would always be there to help them when they needed it. But if Kailani herself didn't scare Cam off, they likely would.

Brad wrapped an arm around each of them, taking a deep breath as if gearing up for something. "I've got a panel all lined up," he said brightly. He really had endless enthusiasm and cheerfulness, something Kailani had always thought he saved for his training videos. But no, that was just how he was. "And they'll be tasting blind, so you don't have to worry about the judging being biased."

That wasn't going to change anything if Cam had any portion of skill. She was still holding out hope that his unconventional childhood had not given him much of an opportunity to learn.

"We'll be ready to start in just a few," Brad continued. "So hang tight, and choose which side you want to work on." He bounded off toward the many cameras set up on the other side of the tent.

The kitchen wasn't all that large, so they would be working side by side. That was a relief, knowing if nothing else Kailani could follow Cam's example.

"Someone looks nervous."

Kailani glanced at Cam, trying to fix her expression so she seemed more carefree. "I'm just trying to decide what sort of toppings I'm going to use. So I'm guessing you're talking about yourself?"

He chuckled, entirely at ease. Maybe it helped that they didn't have an audience for this one beyond the filming crew? Or maybe he had finally figured out the whole "have fun and don't worry" thing she'd been trying to nail down since their first meeting with Brad. "Nice try, Tease. You do remember that I give my clients nutrition advice, right?"

Kailani's heart skittered, both from that revelation and from the new nickname. "Wait, *you* are the nutritionist at Riptide?"

Grinning, he cracked his knuckles and started looking over the ingredients laid out on the counter. "I got my bachelor's in nutrition," he said with a shrug. "I couldn't afford to go into dietetics, but I considered it. I got certified as a nutritionist instead."

"That doesn't necessarily mean you can cook." She hated how hopeful she sounded.

Cam merely grinned.

So the night was to be a disaster, was it? Kailani reminded herself that this morning's competition had been a lot more fun when she stopped trying to be serious about it, and she would simply have to do the same with this.

"Don't be surprised if I accidentally spill tomato sauce all over my shirt," Cam said after a moment. Though he kept his eyes on the kitchen, his smirk was easy to see. "And with the ovens on, things may get a little…hot."

Heaven help her. If Cam decided to remove his shirt when she was only a few steps away from him, she would have even less of a chance. "Cameron Martinez, if you even think of—"

"They should probably make you use a hair net," he continued. This time he looked over, his eyes running from the top of her head to where her braid ended in the middle of her back. She felt his eyes in every inch of her body. "Unfortunately, no one has ever been able to make a hair net look sexy. Maybe you could be the first?"

Kailani narrowed her eyes, desperately searching for some kind of taunting she might use to counteract his well-aimed blows. Why, of all times, did she have to come up blank tonight? It was his fault, with that hungry look in his eyes. Where was the bumbling Cam when she needed him most?

"I hate you," she snapped instead of coming up with some clever response.

Cam chuckled. "Someone missed her nap today, didn't she? And you know you love me."

Did she know that? The answer terrified her, so she refused to even wonder.

"I'm taking the right side," she mumbled.

"Fine by me."

Ten minutes later, they were both in ridiculously tall chef hats and cutesy aprons, and Brad was calling action on the cameras.

To save some time, they'd each been given a bowl of pizza dough already made up, for which Kailani was immensely grateful. If she'd had to make her own, she definitely would have ended up with something inedible. At least this way she could only mess it up so badly.

Cam dove right into chopping vegetables, so Kailani followed suit, though she had no idea what vegetables would be good on a pizza outside of the usuals—peppers, olives, definitely *not* mushrooms…

"How do you even eat those?" she asked, eyeing the fungus in Cam's obviously capable hands.

He chopped without hesitation, veggies flying beneath the sharp knife he held. "Mushrooms are a great low-calorie food, and they're full of antioxidants and—"

"I didn't ask *why* you eat them. I asked *how*."

Cam laughed, glancing at her mushroom-free countertop. "I take it you're not a fan. You're going to want to remove the seeds from that pepper."

Kailani scoffed. "I was getting to that next," she said, even if it was a total lie. "For the record, I know how to eat well. I just don't know how to…" Maybe it was a bad idea to admit that part.

"You're not much of a cook," Cam finished for her. "I could always help you." He rinsed his hands and then tossed the towel over his shoulder like he'd done it a million times. That wasn't supposed to be a sexy move, but it totally was.

And it distracted Kailani from what he'd said for a whole five seconds before it clicked. "Uh, thanks, but no thanks. I'm in this to win, Martinez, and I don't need your help to do it."

"Whatever you say, Tease."

Since she had no clue what she was doing, Kailani opted for a classic supreme pizza. It may not have been all that healthy, but she hoped it would taste good. She had no clue what type of judges Brad had hired, and for all she knew they could be college frat boys. At this point, nothing Brad did would surprise her.

With her minimal veggies prepped, Kailani figured she should start rolling out her dough. She'd seen enough movies to know she would probably need some flour on her counter-top, but her know-how ended there. She started with dumping her dough onto the sprinkle of flour she'd laid out, and she considered her next move. Most pizza places spun their dough in the air to get a nice, thin circle.

There was no way she was going to attempt that while being filmed.

Instead, she began spreading the dough with her fingers and hoping she could get it at least semi-round.

"Ahem." Cam nudged what looked like a miniature rolling pin with his pinky just before he dumped out his own dough.

Much as she hated the hint, Kailani grabbed the roller and stabbed at her dough with it. It was definitely easier than using her hands, that was for sure.

Cam, on the other hand, picked up his dough and began working it through his fingers, letting gravity do half the work as he turned it in a circle with confidence. Kailani tried to stay focused on her own side—she needed all the focus she could muster—but the moment his dough flew into the air, she froze.

"You've got to be kidding me."

Grinning, Cam tossed the dough again and caught it with ease. "You stole my rolling pin," he said with a shrug, though it was clear he preferred the method he was using.

Kailani huffed. "Okay, Martinelli. Are you secretly Italian and I never knew it?"

"Nope."

"But you've worked in a pizza place before?"

He nodded, giving his dough one last toss before dropping it back on the counter and spreading it out into a perfect circle.

"The one on Harrison Street. I worked there all during high school, and it became a favorite place for the Wonder Boys to hang out. Just like O'Reilly's."

Kailani had forgotten that he called his group of friends the Wonder Boys. He'd told her that while they walked back to the start of the race. Though she had no idea where the name had come from, Kailani loved that it had stuck even years later. "Wait," she said, something clicking in her head. "Didn't you do a million sports? How did you have time for anything else?"

His energy dimmed at that question. "I didn't have time," he said with a frown, his focus fully on his pizza even though he wasn't moving. "But I also didn't have a choice. At that point, my aunt was retired and living off of social security, and what was left of the death gratuity I got when my dad died was only going to cover some of my college expenses. If I wanted to graduate with more than an associate degree, I had to work."

"That kinda sucks," Kailani said, which was the understatement of the century. And she thought *she'd* had it bad. She'd never had to pay for school because she hadn't *gone* to school. She'd picked a profession she could do without student loans because she'd known she would be on her own.

Cam glanced over. "You're going to put sauce on that first, right Tease?"

His change of subject felt a bit like the closing of a door, but Kailani knew they probably needed to focus. Brad's show wasn't a therapy session, nor was it a great time to get to know each other. Not unless they wanted the rest of the country to get to know them too.

Grabbing the sauce in question, Kailani dipped her fingers in the jar and flicked it at Cam. "Yes, I'm going to put sauce on it! I was going for a cheese-infused crust." That was a complete lie—again—but it actually sounded pretty good, so she smashed her palms into the cheese she'd been sprinkling without thinking until it sank deep into her uneven dough. She really needed to start paying attention to what she was doing, or the internet was going to think she'd never seen a pizza before.

Something thunked against her head, and an olive landed on the counter and rolled a few inches.

Kailani glared at Cam's falsely innocent expression. "Oh, I don't think you want to go there, Martinelli."

"You're not going to stop calling me that, are you?"

"Not as long as you keep calling me Tease." She tossed a little handful of cheese to add weight to her retort.

Cam laughed. "You're still going to want to put sauce—"

She groaned, this time taking an entire spoonful of sauce and throwing it at him. The way it splattered against his giant tricep was oddly satisfying, even if it had probably stained his t-shirt. "I told you I don't need help," she snapped, though her smile probably didn't give her complaint much effectiveness.

Cam took his time looking down at his shoulder, his eyes burning when they rose slowly to meet hers. "And I'm pretty sure I told you what would happen if I got sauce on my shirt," he replied, his voice deep and velvety.

Yes, please. The temperature of the tent had risen by a million degrees, so he would probably be more comfortable without that layer of fabric. Kailani would definitely be enjoying herself more. Her pizza resembled a lump of soggy dough with some cheese clumped about, and with the way Cam was looking at her, she didn't care. Even if she lost this battle, one measly shirt stood in her way of actually winning tonight.

Cam leaned in, his tongue brushing his lower lip. "Are you sure you want to go there?"

Kailani's heart was racing like she'd just run a full marathon, only instead of limping on bruised and bleeding toes, she had never felt more whole. She knew there were cameras trained on them, and she knew this distraction was not exactly what Brad had had in mind when he planned this little competition. But knowing that did nothing to change the way Cam had made her feel from the moment he'd woken up in her arms at that race.

What if she really, truly let him into her life? What if she told him everything? About her family, about her fears and insecurities, about the way she'd never met anyone like him and never would again? What if she let herself be brave? She could see herself building a life with this man, one where she never had to wonder if she meant something to him because he was the sort of person who never held anything back.

"You've got a little something right there," Cam said when they were only inches apart. He brushed his finger down her nose, leaving a trail of tomato sauce in its wake.

Kailani gasped, and not just because of the sudden food on her skin. The hold this man had over her… It was terrifying.

Thankfully, two could play at his game.

Snatching another handful of cheese, she threw it in his face and shrieked when he immediately grabbed her around the waist and lifted her off her feet. Her chef's hat tumbled to the ground as her arm knocked his from his head, and though she struggled to free herself, Kailani suddenly found herself flung over his shoulder like the towel.

With one of his arms wrapped around her legs to keep her in place, he turned back to his countertop without a word.

"Are you…are you making your pizza?" she asked in bewilderment.

Cam's laugh rumbled through his whole body. "I'm here to win, Tease."

"So are you going to put me down so I can make *my* pizza?" Not that she was complaining about her view. Her hands rested against the corded muscles in his back, all of them shifting with every movement. She ran her hands lower and explored since she was stuck there anyway. Even his lower back was straight muscle, and she'd never seen—let alone felt—a body like his.

A shudder ran through him, and he tensed when her hands hit the base of his spine. "Careful there," he murmured. "Or I might start getting the wrong idea."

"I wasn't going to go any lower," she complained, trying to lift herself back up so she could wiggle free.

Cam only tightened his hold on her legs. "I'm not so sure about that. Will you stop squirming? I'm trying to cut these tomatoes."

"Excuse me, but did you just say you have a *knife* in your hands?"

"Just the one hand."

She squirmed despite his request, suddenly afraid for the safety of her feet.

"You should really stop moving," Cam said, grunting a little as he tried to keep his hold on her. "I'll definitely end up cutting you if you keep kicking like that!"

"Put me down!"

"I don't trust you."

"I promise I won't throw any more food at you!"

"That's not good enough."

Kailani huffed, straightening her torso so the blood would stop rushing to her head. Apparently making pizza would turn into a moderate core workout, depending on how long he kept her on his shoulder. "What will it take for you to put me back on my feet, Martinelli? I may not have the same kitchen skills as you, but I'm determined to do my best so I don't have to blame you when I inevitably lose. I have my dignity, after all." That was rich, considering her rear end was not only right next to Cam's face but pointed directly at the cameras.

At least she could say she was proud of the way her rear end looked.

"Hmm."

Cam's arms both wrapped around Kailani's legs, and with a little tug from him and an *oof* from her, she was suddenly cradled in his arms and staring up into his cinnamon eyes. In the lights of the tent, they were even more of a rich brown than they usually were, and she was transfixed.

"How about this?" he said, gaze smoldering. "You promise me that you'll answer a specific question for me, and I'll let you finish your, uh, *pizza*." He wrinkled his nose at her little blob of dough, laughter in his expression.

That wasn't so bad, assuming he didn't ask anything outrageous. "What's the question?" She needed to know if it would be a worthy tradeoff. She was going to lose anyway, but her curiosity had her frozen in place.

He shook his head. "Nope. You can't know ahead of time, and I'm not sure when I'll ask it. But I'll be sure to tell you when it is The Question."

Okay, so maybe it *was* that bad. Kailani folded her arms, even if she probably didn't look all that intimidating nestled in his arms like that. "You're telling me that you're going to ask me some big, unknown question at some point in my life, and I have to answer no matter what just because you want me to?"

"That about sums it up."

"Why in the world would I agree to that?"

His lips twisted up in that crooked grin of his. "Because you don't really have a choice."

She probably could escape his arms if she really tried. Cam was strong, but so was she, and if she limp-fished him and then went straight as a board, she would probably knock him off balance enough to get back on her feet. But where would be the fun in that?

"I suppose you're right," she said, putting on a thinking face. "So I guess I have to agree to your ridiculous terms."

"If you want to bake your pizza, yes. Though, I'm not sure why you would want to…"

She swatted him. "Be nice. Not all of us have a nutrition degree."

"Pizza has nothing to do with nutrition."

Based on the sheer number of veggies already on his pizza, that was debatable.

"So," she said, taking a deep breath and letting it out slowly. "Are you going to put me down, or…?"

Eyes sparkling with amusement, Cam lifted her closer so their faces were only a few inches apart. "You didn't actually agree to answer the question."

Kailani lifted her hand and brushed it across his smooth jaw, marveling at the sharp edges and the way everything about him was strong, down to his features. She hadn't really taken the time to admire him this close, and as long as he held her like this, she would take advantage of it.

He seemed more than willing to let her do it, his eyes locked on hers and his expression open and vulnerable. As always. How was he so unafraid of people seeing everything about him? Knowing that about him, his mystery question was almost more terrifying than it might have been with someone else. But if she was going to let anyone see into her soul, she wanted it to be him.

"Okay," she said, daring to be brave. "I promise I will answer your question."

"Honestly?"

"Honestly."

His grin stretched across his face, somehow still crooked even at its widest. "Thank you," he murmured and then placed a lingering kiss on her forehead that made her insides melt. How could such a big, strong man be so tender at the same time? Everything he did made her feel protected and safe, and that was a feeling she had scarcely had enough of in her life when she had always had to take care of herself. "That really means a lot to me."

Once she was back on her feet—feeling a tad unsteady after being in the man's arms for so long—Kailani cleared her throat and tried to refocus her attention on the task at hand. She didn't know how long they'd stalled for their little conversation, but she had to wonder if Brad was fed up with them yet. So far, they'd barely managed to participate in the competitions let alone finish them. At least Brad had told them their relationship was part of the reason he'd wanted them, so he couldn't be too angry with them if it was a crucial factor of the show.

"Don't forget your sauce, Tease," Cam said, and his smile spoke volumes as he continued to dress up his pizza to perfection.

If it was really going to be that easy to make the guy happy, maybe things could actually work out in the end.

Maybe being the key word, though. Kailani refused to put all of her eggs in one basket. If life had taught her anything, it was to remember that not everything was as good as it seemed. Inevitably, disappointment always followed happiness, and sooner or later, he was going to realize she wasn't worth the effort it would take to love her. The same thing everyone else already knew.

FIFTEEN

FOR THE FIRST TIME SINCE moving in, Cam hated the sight of his apartment. The place was tiny and unfinished, wedged in above his gym space like an afterthought to the building. He'd always thought it cool that he only had to go downstairs to get to work, and it had definitely made things easier while he got the space ready before opening day.

But as he stood in the doorway, only the hallway light illuminating the small space, he realized how little his apartment resembled a home. Exposed brick lined three walls, with the fourth existing only of framing and insulation because he hadn't gotten to the drywall yet. A toilet sat in the corner with a hanging sheet blocking it from the rest of the room. There were only two windows that barely gave him a view of the street below, and the kitchen consisted of a hot plate on a rickety folding table that doubled as his dining table next to the sink. He didn't even have a shower—he used the one in the gym downstairs—and his mini fridge only held enough space for a few meals at a time.

How had this not bothered him before?

Because he'd only been thinking of himself before.

A shiver ran through him as he slowly made his way inside and flipped on the fluorescent light that always burned his eyes. Was he really thinking about a future with someone else in it? He'd never done that before.

As he tossed his keys onto the table, he let out a heavy sigh before sinking onto the mattress that sat on the floor. He had been living here for more than two months now, and somehow he had managed to ignore the abundance of dust. The strange smell that definitely wasn't a normal toilet smell. The way it never warmed beyond sixty-five degrees. This wasn't the sort of place anyone would want to live, and it wasn't anywhere close to a permanent situation.

It wasn't the kind of place he could bring Kailani and know she was safe and comfortable, but he would never be able to afford anything better if things didn't work out with the competition and with his gym. He could barely afford *this*.

His chest growing tight, Cam pulled his phone out of his pocket and dialed Kit's number, hoping he could stave off another anxiety attack.

"How was your evening?" Kit asked brightly.

"You sound a lot more alert than someone who's usually in bed by now," Cam muttered.

"Isla and I got talking and lost track of time."

That was surprising. Kit was friendly and could talk to pretty much anyone, but he didn't usually put this much energy into one person at a time.

"I was not expecting that," Cam admitted. "She doesn't seem very…"

Kit laughed. "Oh, there's definitely nothing going to happen between us. She's way more enthusiastic than I could ever handle, and definitely too young. But she had a lot to say about your *pretend* girlfriend."

Cam swallowed. He hadn't told anyone about their decision to make their relationship real, and he wasn't sure he wanted to. Still, Kit was far too observant, and with the way he said the word pretend, it seemed like he had decided the relationship was real after watching the morning's events.

"It's…" He swallowed. "It's not so pretend."

"I could have told you that," Kit replied easily. "But you want the gang to think it is?"

"It's easier."

"How?"

Cam rubbed his chest. "This way, they won't start getting their hopes up."

Sighing, Kit didn't reply to that for a long few seconds. "You really like her, don't you?"

"Is it crazy if I say yes?"

"Why would that be crazy?"

Cam flopped down onto his pillow, realizing how uncomfortable his mattress was when his sore shoulders complained. Who would have thought volleyball would be so strenuous? It hadn't been just the game, though. He'd held Kailani in his arms for way longer than was reasonable. She wasn't heavy, but the weight of the impossibility of their relationship seemed to pull him down. He was trying so hard to convince himself that things didn't have to end, but the wall around his heart was thick and sturdy.

He couldn't ignore the fact that so many people had left him throughout his life, and his heart had always been so much safer when he didn't let anyone reach it. He *wanted* to trust that Kailani would stick around. He *wanted* to believe there was a real chance for the two of them.

But wanting and believing were two different things.

"Because I'm me," he said, shutting his eyes tight. "Kit, you know how hard it is for me to keep people in my life. And I don't know if I'll survive losing her if this goes on much longer."

Kit was quiet for a second, which meant he was thinking. "You don't know she's going to leave, Cam."

"*Everyone* leaves."

"I haven't."

Despite lying perfectly still, Cam felt like the room was spinning, and he took a slow, deliberate breath. "Not yet," he mumbled. It was bound to happen eventually, and every day that passed with his friends still around was a day that surprised him to no end. It had been more than fifteen years, which was about ten years longer than he'd expected them to stick with him.

"Have you thought any more about going to therapy?" Kit asked.

Cam groaned. Of course he'd thought about it. That didn't mean it would ever go beyond that. "I can't afford therapy, Kit. You know that. I can barely afford—"

"I told you I'll pay for it. Besides, I think you'd like my therapist."

Letting Kit pay for it was as bad as taking money from Oliver. Worse, because Kit didn't have much to spare. "Kit."

Kit sighed again. "Fine. Just know the offer still stands. So, did you call me just to talk about how much you like Kailani? Because I already knew that part. Pretty sure the whole world knows at this point, with the way you two gaze longingly into each other's eyes."

"We don't gaze—"

"You do, and you know it. Save yourself a trip to the toilet."

Cam really needed to get some sleep, considering he had a couple of training sessions first thing in the morning before he headed to Frostwick Park for their next competition. He hadn't been able to give them *all* up to Brad's people, as much as that would have helped make this week a little easier. A few clients had refused, and Cam didn't want to lose their business if he didn't keep them happy, something he couldn't afford. So he needed to get as much sleep as he could before he faced another long day.

But talking to his best friend always had a calming effect, and no one knew him better than Kit. Only Kit would know that this conversation meant more than a crush.

"I'm scared," he admitted, running a hand down his face. "I've never felt this way about anyone, and I mean it when I say I'm not sure I'll survive if she leaves. I'm too far gone." It was ridiculous to think he could feel this way, but all signs were pointing to the fact that Cam was hopelessly in love with Kailani.

If only he knew why she was so scared to let him in.

"I never thought I'd see the day when Cam Martinez fell in love," Kit said, sounding almost reverent. "This is big for you, man."

It was terrifying.

"So, quick question."

Cam didn't like the sound of that. "What?"

"What's stopping you from telling her how you feel? And I know it's not because of the whole fake-but-not relationship thing, so don't even try to lie."

Who needed therapy when Kit Morgan was around? The man was more perceptive than most people realized, and he always had good advice. Swapping his phone to speaker, Cam rolled over onto his stomach and cradled his pillow in his arms. "I mean, you already know my issues."

"I know that." Kit's voice was slightly muffled, and Cam could easily picture him lying in his own bed, half his face pressed into the pillow. He really was up past his bedtime, and Kit never functioned well outside of his usual routine. "But I'm pretty sure it still helps for you to talk about it. But if I'm pushing too far, let me know. You're dealing with a lot right now, so I don't want to make it worse."

"You're a good friend."

"I know. Now talk."

Cam sighed. "I let people in too easily. And then they leave. And every time I get my hopes up even though I know I shouldn't, I'm crushed. I'm tired of getting hurt, Kit."

Kit was quiet for a long few seconds, either thinking hard or falling asleep. "When was the last time someone left you, Cam?"

That was easy. "Halley. Last year."

"You mean the girl you dumped when she told you she loved you?"

Huffing a humorless laugh, Cam tightened his hold on his pillow. "*She* broke up with *me*."

"After you told her you didn't see things going anywhere."

"What's your point?"

"You pushed her away, Cam. Just like you pushed away Sydney and Gina before that. You've never let anyone get close enough to you for them to want to stick around, so you can't blame their leaving on anyone but yourself."

"That's not making me feel better."

"It's not supposed to. When are you going to push Kailani away?"

"I don't want to push her away."

"So tell her how you feel."

"I can't."

"Why not?"

"Because I don't think she'll ever feel the same way." Cam tensed as soon as those words left his mouth. They were the truth, but they weren't exactly something he wanted Kit to know.

Yet again, Kit was silent for an uncomfortably long time. "Why do you think that?"

Don't say it, Cam. He doesn't need to know how idiotic you are. "Because I'm not..." He bit the words back, hating that he couldn't keep himself from saying them. But apparently his body didn't distinguish between telling a lie and not telling the truth, because his stomach heaved. "I'm not worth loving," he growled out. *There.* Let Kit try to fix that one.

Kit spoke slowly, as if he wanted to say something else but wasn't sure he could. "Why do you think that?" he said again.

"Why else would she refuse to tell me anything about herself?"

"Wait, are we talking about Kailani specifically, or everyone?"

"Ev—just—I don't know." Cam groaned. He hadn't meant to say that either.

"Let's focus on Kailani for now. You don't think she tells you anything?"

"That's not… She tells me about herself. But it's all surface level stuff. It's like she's afraid to tell me all the real stuff. The stuff that makes her *her*. You know?"

This time when Kit spoke, he sounded wary. "Yeah… Isla didn't really say anything like that. She said Kailani's an open book and the best older sister ever. She kind of couldn't stop gushing about her, actually."

"So she just doesn't want to tell *me* anything," Cam surmised, his chest tightening again. He rubbed his sternum, pushing his focus back to breathing. Kailani *had* told him about having to quit volleyball to help her family. That was something. But it wasn't enough. There was so much she was holding back, like she knew things weren't going to last anyway. Was she feeling the same way about him? He was trying to be open. Was she?

Cam groaned again. "It's because I'm—"

"You're not cursed, Cam. I promise you're not." Kit sighed, probably because he was tired of having this same argument year after year. Cam didn't blame him. "How did tonight's competition go?"

Sighing, Cam rolled over onto his back again. "I know you're trying to change the subject so I don't start panicking."

"Is it working?"

Cam's mind flashed back to the moment when he'd held Kailani in his arms. Heat blossomed in his chest, sparking a smile. "Yeah, it's working. It was a cooking competition."

"Oh, that's...different. Who won?"

Cam barked out a laugh. "I did. I'm not even sure Kailani had a chance. Her pizza looked more like a calzone, and not on purpose. I think there were about three bites that weren't raw or burned, and I'm not sure how she managed that. I'm pretty sure *Madi* could have beaten her, and that's saying something." Kit's sister, Madi, was a terrible cook.

"I still don't know why you let Oliver believe you can't cook and that your bachelor's degree is in personal training," Kit said, clear disapproval in his voice. "That's not even a real degree."

Kit would never understand the relationship between Cam and Oliver. Kit got along with literally everyone, and he probably had no idea that his three best friends would never have tolerated each other without him. Cam and Oliver were fundamentally different people in a lot of ways, but they had too many things in common to not see each other as rivals.

"He made an assumption," Cam said with a shrug. "I didn't bother correcting him."

"But you have a minor in culinary—"

"If we're going to keep talking about Oliver, I'm going to hang up. I'm still mad at you for forcing us together the other night." Granted, his stress levels had been rising for days, but that moment with Oliver had led to one of the more severe anxiety attacks Cam had experienced in recent years. Cam had refused to interact with Oliver since. There was no telling what Oliver would do now that he knew Cam wasn't as strong as he pretended to be.

"You can't blame me for trying," Kit grumbled. "Okay, so back to Kailani. How do you think this week is going to play out?"

"I don't know if I want to think about that. I'm taking things minute by minute."

"Have you figured out what's going to happen when it's all over? With the two of you, I mean."

Before the competition started, Cam had had a long talk with Kit about his pact to keep things light and fun with Kailani while they were doing the competition. So far, he hadn't done very well. At least in the light department. He was working on it, but that didn't stop him from imagining the day he had to say goodbye to Kailani.

"No," he mourned. "And I don't think we'll know anything until it happens. I just wish…"

Kit spoke through a massive yawn; it was definitely time for the conversation to be over. "What?"

"I just wish she would open up to me. Trust me." He had gotten her to agree to answer one question, but he wanted more than one piece of her. He wanted to know it all. "I like to think I've given her plenty of reasons to believe that I won't run away from the hard stuff."

"So why are you so afraid that she'll do that to you? Look." Kit yawned again. "I know the future scares you, so you have to stop thinking about the future. Think about right now. Focus on one day at a time, and keep being honest with Kailani. Keep giving her reasons to trust you, and eventually she will. Maybe she's just as scared as you are that things are going to end, and she doesn't know what to do with that."

"Did Isla tell you that?"

Kit chuckled. "No. But we're all human, Cam. Kailani may look like she's afraid of nothing, and she may be the most confident person you've ever met. But that doesn't mean she's not as vulnerable as you. Don't push things, don't push *her*, and maybe it'll all work out. One day at a time. Show her the man that you are, and you'll have done everything you can."

If it had been anyone else, Cam wouldn't have listened to that advice. Especially from someone very much single. But this was Kit, and if anyone knew how to navigate this kind of thing, it was him. Besides, *he* was the most confident person Cam knew. If Kit thought this was the way to go, he was probably right.

"I'll do my best. Thanks, Kit. As always."

"You know I've got your back, no matter what happens. And Cam?"

"Yeah?"

"I'm not leaving. The Wonder Boys aren't either. I can't make any promises about Kailani, but you're allowed to believe people will stick around."

Cam fell asleep with a warm feeling in his gut he'd scarcely allowed himself before: hope.

SIXTEEN

"HOW ARE MY FAVORITE LOVEBIRDS this fine morning?"

Brad was extra chipper today when he greeted them in the makeup tent, something Kailani didn't particularly appreciate. Not when she'd been kept up half the night by Isla, who had been waiting for her at the apartment so they could talk boys. Apparently, Isla had found herself a unicorn in Kit Morgan.

"Not only is he handsome and has a stable job," she'd said more than once, "but he's adorkably awkward and the sweetest person I've ever met in my life, but, like, super confident at the same time. There's no way he's single when he's this perfect, but I couldn't find any trace of a wife or girlfriend anywhere on social media."

Kailani was pretty sure Kit was single, so at least he was available. Isla didn't always care about that part, though she'd never gotten in the middle of anyone's relationship. No, she just fell hard and fast and got her heart broken a million times over when it never worked out.

Kailani stifled a yawn, receiving glares from the makeup artists for scrunching up their canvas. "Are you going to tell us what today's challenge is, or are we going in blind again?"

Brad chuckled without looking up from the tablet screen he'd been glued to since the beauticians started. "You'll know soon enough. The surprise is the best part!"

"For you," Cam said. He wasn't nearly as on edge as he'd been yesterday morning, sitting casually in his chair and typing away on his phone. He was either writing a novel, or he had been texting someone all morning.

Kailani didn't like the little jealous feeling that burned inside her like a hot coal. She had only just started dating Cam, so she had no right to be jealous. He could be texting Kit, for all she knew, and she was being ridiculous for thinking that little smile of his was meant for someone other than her.

"You're staring at me, Tease."

Kailani flinched, her gaze jumping from Cam's mouth to his eyes. "I wasn't staring," she said too quickly.

Literally everyone in the tent laughed at that, making Kailani's face burn. She didn't often get embarrassed, but when she did, it hit her hard.

Nudging Felipe away from his hair, Cam reached out and took Kailani's hand so he could brush a kiss to her knuckles. "You can stare at me anytime you'd like," he said, his smile growing.

"You two aren't going to have any fans left if you keep up like that," Brad said. He finally handed his tablet off to the assistant who waited behind him.

Kailani's stomach dropped. "What do you mean? What did we do wrong?"

Thankfully, Brad laughed again. "No, that's not... I mean you're going to kill them all with your cuteness. How do the kids put it nowadays? They'll be *deceased*."

Cam cringed. "I'm not sure how I feel about you using modern slang."

"I'm not that old," Brad complained cheerfully. His gray beard begged to differ, though his energy was definitely that of a younger man. "Anyway, our first episode is almost ready to air thanks to my intrepid editors, and we're going to have people eating out of the palms of our hands."

Kailani was suddenly very aware of her own palm, which was still pressed against Cam's. It wasn't like they hadn't held hands before, but she'd never been so aware of how his hand was just big enough that it fit around hers perfectly, the same way she felt whenever he wrapped her up in his arms.

Just before Isla finally let Kailani go to sleep, she'd said something about Cam that Kailani hadn't really processed until just this moment, when she was gazing into Cam's cinnamon eyes. He tightened his hold on her hand as if he'd realized the same thing she had about their hands.

"There's something special about him, Lani," Isla had said. "And the way he looks at you… It's like he would capture the moon for you if you asked him to. If I could find someone who looked at me like that, I'd never let him go. Don't mess this up."

Kailani didn't want to mess it up, but it still wouldn't change the fact that one of them was going to lose this competition. She could talk the talk all she wanted, but would she really be capable of looking past the resentment she would inevitably feel if Cam won? Even with his gym gone, it would probably take a long time for her to make enough money to start her after-school program that she really didn't have much space for anyway.

There were so many unknowns and complications, and Kailani's life was chaotic enough. Unless she knew Cam wouldn't run for the hills when he realized how much she came up short, she wasn't sure she could risk losing her heart to him.

Cam was better than anyone she'd ever known, but no one could be perfect.

"Well!" Brad clapped his hands, making Kailani jump. "Are you two ready for today's first competition?"

"First?" Cam and Kailani said at the same time. It was to be another long day, then. Kailani had expected it, but she'd also hoped for the chance to go to bed extra early tonight.

Somehow, Cam looked fully refreshed for the first time since this whole thing started. He leaned in close to her, his crooked grin doing strange things to her nervous system. "Guess you're stuck with me all day, Tease."

"There are worse things," she replied, which, according to Cam's smile doubling in size, was the right thing to say.

"Follow me, then!" Brad said and led the way out of the tent. "Hope neither of you are afraid of heights."

Sharing a glance with Cam, Kailani picked up her pace. Knowing Brad, their challenge could be pretty much anything, but if it was what she thought it was... Sure enough, the climbing wall came into view only a moment later, and her own lips twisted into a smile to match Cam's. Rock climbing was how they'd first met, however briefly, and she'd seen how skilled he was at scaling the wall back then. For a guy who shouldn't have had a great range of motion because of his bulk, he'd been impressively speedy.

This would be a real competition, and the excitement of that made her practically skip after Brad.

Cam, apparently, noticed that skip, and he let out a burst of laughter as he stuffed his hands into his pockets and followed lazily. "This could get interesting," he said.

Kailani bumped into him. "You didn't see me climb back then," she pointed out. "You have no idea—"

"Oh, I saw you. I nearly dropped Ben at one point because my eyes were on you instead of paying attention to the belay."

"Wait, really?"

"Would I lie to you?"

"I thought you couldn't lie."

"I can't."

Brad paused to speak to the several cameramen waiting near the wall, giving Kailani a chance to face Cam and try to read his expression.

"I'm curious about that, actually," she said. "Like, I know you don't *like* lying, but—"

"I get sick when I lie." He cringed. "Which you don't really need to know, but… It's not like you haven't seen it, right?"

So it *was* true! "Do you always throw up when you lie?"

Cam narrowed his eyes. "I'm a little afraid to answer that question."

"I promised to answer one of *your* questions," she pointed out.

But that only made him grin. "If you're going to use your one special question on whether or not I vomit on a regular basis, then—"

"Okay, fine. Don't tell me. But you also just admitted to possibly lying all the time, which doesn't really put you in a good light."

He acknowledged that with a dip of his head, his lips in what seemed like a permanent grin now. "Yes," he said at the same time someone handed each of them a climbing harness. "It doesn't really matter how small of a lie; it always makes me sick. I think I took my honesty vow to an extreme level when I changed my ways."

"So, if I asked you to tell a lie right now?" Kailani knew she should probably stay focused on the competition looming overhead, but these moments when she and Cam pretended no one else was around were her favorite. When they could get to know each other and pretend this was just a normal date and they had a normal relationship.

As he cinched up his harness, Cam groaned. "You're going to make me do it, aren't you? Is this your way of sabotaging the event so you can win?"

Kailani grinned. Her smile would probably become just as permanent as Cam's if they carried on like this. No one had ever treated her like an equal. She was either too strong for them or not smart enough, but Cam didn't seem to care about either. He just liked her the way she was.

"Oh, I don't have to sabotage anything," she said. Her cheeks were going to hurt if she kept smiling like this, but she didn't care. "And it's okay if you're still nervous around me. I know how intimidating I can be."

"I'm not nervous around…" He clamped his mouth shut, shaking his head as he turned the slightest bit green.

Wow, he wasn't kidding. Biting back laughter, Kailani patted his arm reassuringly. Well, it started as a pat but quickly turned into a stroke, as if she'd forgotten just how strong this guy was. It didn't hurt that he *was* nervous; it meant he wasn't perfectly confident and therefore closer to Kailani's level. "Please don't throw up," she said. "I want to beat you on this climb without giving you any excuses."

"You sure know the way to a guy's heart," he replied.

"Okay, lovebirds!" Brad skipped back over to them, shuffling them closer to the wall. "This competition is two-fold because I'm wildly curious."

What in the world was that supposed to mean? "Curious about what?" Kailani asked.

Brad winked. "So many things, Miss Adams. In this instance, I suspect the two of you will be evenly matched, so the first half of the competition will be speed. Hector and Ronnie here will belay." He nodded toward a couple of burly guys dressed all in black, a stark contrast to Brad's multi-colored neon.

"And the second half?" Cam asked. He had one eye on Ronnie, who had shifted closer to Kailani, and he definitely seemed to be flexing.

As much as Kailani hated when men felt the need to show their own machismo when encountering fellow men, she didn't particularly mind the protective glare in Cam's gaze.

Brad, on the other hand, didn't seem to notice the exchange as he grinned up at the rock wall. "The other half will be a test of your budding relationship."

"Excuse me?" Cam and Kailani said together.

"After last night's adorable pizza adventure, I want to see how the two of you work *together* under pressure."

"Why?" they both asked.

Brad shrugged, clearly enjoying their synchrony. "It sounds like fun. And the viewers will love it; your fans have been rooting for you since before you even got together, remember? Don't forget; this is a business venture for me. Not just an opportunity for one of you."

"Can't forget about the viewers," Cam mumbled. "So what will we be—"

"That can wait until after the race. Speaking of, I believe we're ready to go?" He glanced around, seemed to get all of the nods he needed, and then wrapped his arms around both their shoulders. He waited until a camera was directly in front of them, and then he put on a smile.

"Welcome to day two of my Lovers' Quarrel challenge!"

"Is that what you're calling it?" Cam asked before turning rather red and muttering, "I did not mean to say that out loud. Sorry."

Brad chuckled. "I have a feeling today's first competition is going to be one of my favorites, and you'll want to start putting in your bets right now, folks, because this is going to get exciting."

At a signal from Ronnie, Kailani slipped away from Brad and began tying herself into the rope while Brad explained the rules. She only half-listened, busy watching Cam expertly work the knot onto his own harness. She was pretty sure she could beat him, but she'd also been sure she would cream him in volleyball. She didn't spend a year and a half on the varsity team because she was bad at the game.

He'd surprised her then by holding his own, and maybe he would surprise her now. No, she *knew* he would. Cam had been nothing but surprises since day one.

"Are you even listening, Tease? Or are you too busy ogling me?"

Kailani smirked at Cam as Hector examined his knot to make sure it was safe. "I'm listening. We have to stick with a single route, and any rocks outside that route will lose us points. First one to ring the bell wins bonus points."

Cam gave her a silent applause. "Did you also hear the part where he said most of these routes are rated 5.10 and above? Because I did." He glanced up the rock wall, trying to see holds closer to the top. "5.10 is the edge of my comfort zone."

Kailani forced back the slight tinge of fear that settled in her gut. Not fear, necessarily, but worry. She bouldered more than she climbed, and she generally kept to the 5.9s or under so she could climb more for the fun of it and less for the challenge.

She spotted a 5.8 rated route on her side of the wall, but it would give her fewer points than one of the more difficult routes. But if it would give her speed, maybe the trade-off would be worth it.

"Can I ask you a question?"

Kailani glanced at Cam, digging her hands into the chalk bag attached to her harness. "Is this your oh-so-special question?"

"Of course not."

"Ready, climbers?" Brad jumped between the two of them, a black-and-white checkered flag in hand.

"Ready," Kailani replied, even if she was wildly curious about his question. He could ask it after she beat him in the climb.

"Martinez?"

Cam grinned. "Always."

"Go!"

It took Kailani three holds into her 5.9 climb to realize Cam had picked the route that brought him as close to her half of the wall as he could get. That was going to be distracting, but she tried to stay focused on getting her right foot anchored so she could rise to the next red hold above her head.

"Why'd you pick calisthenics?"

Kailani leapt for the hold right as Cam spoke. Her fingers slipped off the rock, though thankfully she maintained her grip with her left hand. "Can't this wait?"

"This seems like a great time to get to know you, don't you think?" With a wink, Cam moved onward and climbed five feet in no time at all before he seemed to get stuck on a particularly difficult section.

Kailani used his pause to scramble as high as she could, working her way to just above him. Then *she* got stuck, unsure of how to reach the next solid hold without using the tiny rock to her left. She'd never been great at those little finger holds since breaking her thumb a couple of years ago.

"I like the idea of relying on the body," she said as she examined the rock face, leaning into the rope to save her arms and shake blood back to her hands. "Besides, it saved me from having to buy a bunch of bulky equipment."

"You've got a hold right there." Cam pointed to the tiny red rock she'd been avoiding, then practically leapt to his next hold.

Kailani would not let him be "helpful" like he had with the pizza. "I'm well aware of that," she growled, and then she pushed herself up with both hands to get high enough to wedge her foot on top of a lower hold. Before gravity changed its mind about letting her rise, she jumped up and grabbed the rock above the little hold.

Cam chuckled, resting against his rope just like she had and grabbing more chalk. They'd made it about a third of the way up the rock wall, and neither seemed in a big hurry.

"I have a hunch there's a reason for your hesitation," he said, lifting an eyebrow. "Care to share?"

"Is *that* your big question?"

Instead of answering, Cam moved up two more holds.

Kailani quickly followed, even if she knew she was climbing right into embarrassment. "I broke my hand a few years ago," she admitted once she surpassed him. "The base of my thumb. Those little holds are just right for putting me in a lot of pain."

"How did you—"

"I got into a fight."

Cam's hand slipped, and he fell a couple of feet before Hector caught him. He resituated himself quickly, somehow managing to catch up to Kailani despite her best efforts to keep some distance between them.

"A fight?" he gasped. Either he was completely shocked, or the climb had finally started to get to him. Though he had more muscle, that meant he had a lot more weight to carry than she did. "What kind of fight?"

Kailani sighed, stretching one arm and then the other before moving onward. "I mean, technically it wasn't my fight. I was *breaking up* a fight."

"That makes way more sense."

Glancing down at him, she snickered. "You don't think I'm the fighting type?"

Cam had definitely slowed down, though he was putting up a good effort as he fought to keep up with her. For some reason, the conversation was making the climb easier, like she wasn't so in her head about everything anymore.

"You seem more like the 'make sure everyone gets along' type," he huffed.

Wasn't that the truth… Kailani had dealt with far too many of her siblings' petty disputes, being the one her parents relied on when they weren't able to step in.

That had happened far more often than she'd liked.

"How do you break your thumb in a fight?" Cam was suddenly so close that Kailani lost her grip.

How long had she been sitting there? It had only felt like a second, but Cam was right next to her instead of several feet below, looking at her with furrowed brow as he sat back against his rope.

"I'm guessing this topic is bigger than a broken thumb," he said slowly.

Kailani gave him a tight-lipped smile and was just about to keep moving when Isla's voice popped into her head. Something she had said last night.

"I'm so glad someone has finally seen the amazing woman you are," she'd said. "It's about time!"

But Cam hadn't seen her. Not really. She'd kept herself close to the vest, protecting her heart so Cam wouldn't break it when he told her she was too much for him. Or too little.

Maybe it was finally time to test that. See if he really was as good as he seemed.

"My parents always wanted a big family," she said, even though it had nothing to do with her thumb. This conversation felt too big, though, so she reached for the next hold to pull herself out of it.

Cam grabbed her hand to stop her, his gaze eager but wary. Did he really want this? Did he really want to know the messy stuff?

She took a deep breath. She would never know if she could trust him if she didn't try. "My siblings haven't always gotten along, and I'm more than four years older than the oldest. It doesn't feel like much now, but when we were younger... I had to keep the peace. Mom and Dad both worked, so I babysat, and especially Chase..."

She frowned. "My brother has always been wild. But there was a while, after he graduated high school, that he kind of went off the deep end. I don't know why. I lost track of how many fights he got into, always coming home bruised and bloodied. And one day he got into it with the next-door neighbor. I happened to be around, and I tried to break them up before Chase put the kid in the hospital. I got knocked down, and *bam*. Broken thumb."

She waved the offending hand around. "Pretty stupid reason, right?"

Cam didn't answer. He seemed frozen in place, eyes locked on hers and an unreadable expression on his face. This was usually the part where people lost interest, and she hadn't even mentioned any of the other siblings and their many issues, or the way they thought about her. Maybe it was because he had nowhere to go, but he wasn't running. In fact, he'd tightened his hold on her hand and seemed unwilling to let go.

Kailani didn't know what to do with that. "Cam?"

He blinked, as if waking from a trance. And then the most beautiful smile spread across his face. "You're talking to the guy who spent half his life getting into fights he didn't need to be in. I think you broke your hand for the best reason. Wanna finish this climb and move forward with things?"

Most definitely. A ball of light had burst into life inside of Kailani's chest, and she was desperate to get back down to the ground to figure out what had just happened. She'd let someone into her fortress. Maybe not to see the cluttered kitchen or the weird carpet stain in the spare bedroom, but she'd let him come into the entryway and look around.

As far as she could tell, he liked what he saw. And maybe he would even like the rest.

SEVENTEEN

KAILANI WON THE CLIMB. CAM had given it his best effort, but he really couldn't be mad that she'd sped off for the last quarter of the wall, leaving him in a cloud of chalk dust. Honestly, he was almost glad. They had barely started Breakout Brad's competition, but Cam was about ready to surrender and let Kailani have whatever she wanted.

She'd told him something real up on that wall, and he was never going to forget how it felt to be that trusted. Now, if he could just get her to open up the rest of the way and stop hiding things from him, maybe he could get over his stupid fear that she would leave.

Maybe he could convince her that their relationship didn't have to end when all of this was over.

Ever since his conversation with Kit last night, something had felt different. He'd felt lighter, and that hope still thudded in his chest with every heartbeat. And Kailani actually talking to him had only added to that hope, to the point where he was willing to do just about anything Brad asked so the day could be over with sooner.

He was desperate to have an actual conversation with Kailani. Maybe even tell her how he felt about her. Terrifying as that was, he wanted to find out what would happen. Maybe, if she knew how hard he was falling, she would trust him with more of the difficult stuff.

"Since you're our winner," Brad said to Kailani when both of them were back on the ground, "you get to choose. Climb or belay?"

Kailani glanced at Cam, her eyes sweeping over him with appreciation, then grinned. "If he's going to be on the other end, I'd rather climb. Not sure I can handle all that weight." She winked, and it took everything in him not to scoop her up into his arms and kiss her till her head spun.

He reminded himself that they were still on Brad's dime. He couldn't just kiss her whenever he wanted to. He folded his arms, clenching his jaw and repeating that fact over and over while Brad explained their next task.

This was the relationship tester, and it might actually be a good indication of how well they would work as a real couple, depending on what they were supposed to do. They hadn't had a chance to really put a relationship to the test at all since their decision to stop pretending; they'd been too busy with the competition.

Which meant Cam should probably pay attention instead of staring at Kailani's shoulders while she adjusted her ponytail.

"Here's your blindfold," Brad said, handing it to her.

Cam tensed. Blindfold? What had he missed?

Kailani didn't look particularly thrilled, but she handed the other end of her rope to Cam anyway and pulled the blindfold onto her head, resting it just above her eyes. Was she seriously going to climb without seeing where she was going?

"You'd better not let me fall, Martinelli," she warned.

Brad laughed at the growl in her voice. "One thing I forgot to mention," he said cheerfully. How was he always so chipper? "This challenge has its own prize, independent of the end prize. The faster you get her up the wall, Cameron, the bigger the apartments I rent for the two of you."

Cam's fingers slipped on the rope he'd been stuffing into his belay device. "Wait, what? Apartments?"

Kailani looked just as dumbfounded.

Brad grinned like a maniac, and Cam was starting to wonder if he'd had too many energy drink endorsements and had given himself permanent brain damage somehow. "I've been doing my homework and asking around, and neither of you can say you live in anything resembling a decent home. Don't try to deny it."

Cam had no intention of making himself sick, so he kept his mouth shut. But he had to wonder what Kailani's place looked like if Brad was wrinkling his nose at it. Why wouldn't she stay with her parents if it was so bad?

Folding her arms, as if protecting herself, Kailani cocked her head to one side. "We've both had to make sacrifices to get our gyms up and running," she defended. "But why would you do something like this? We're already dumbfounded that you would sponsor one of us to begin with."

"But grateful," Cam threw in.

Thankfully, Brad's smile softened as he looked between them. "My friends, I have more money than I know what to do with. And each of you has a noble vision and good intentions, so it only makes sense that I would want to get behind that. Besides, as I've been making my plans for the winner's gym, my people have been in contact with other local businesses and members of the community, and I'm not the only one who sees your potential. One benefactor in particular was eager to give back so the two of you could benefit this city like you plan."

Cam glanced at Kailani again. Was there more to her gym than a business? Like his?

"I've also been where you are," Brad continued. "I've made the sacrifices and given up my basic human rights for the greater good. No one should have to live like that. But…" His eyes jumped to the wall, dancing with amusement. "I also want this show to succeed and maybe even expand to other entrepreneurs like you, so I want to keep things interesting.

Therefore, the faster the climb, the higher the square footage. Six months' rent and utilities all paid for. Ready?"

Cam scrambled to finish getting the rope ready.

"Go!"

Kailani slipped the blindfold on and grabbed the two nearest handholds. Apparently, she didn't need to follow a certain route, which was helpful. "Where am I going, Martinez?"

Finally getting himself hooked in, Cam tugged the rope until only a little slack remained. "Up?" he said, knowing that wasn't helpful but still too flustered to think properly.

Sighing heavily, Kailani reached up and felt around until she located another hold. "I like to think I'm not a material person," she grumbled as she struggled to find a foothold, "but I'm not going to ignore the opportunity for free rent. Even if it's temporary. And I'm sure Isla would love to have a little more space for her Spandex."

Cam very much wanted her to expand on that sentence, but what came out of his mouth was, "Now you've got me thinking about you in Spandex."

Kailani missed her next hold and slipped, landing awkwardly back on the ground. "Oh. Um."

"Sorry. Shouldn't have said anything."

"You can…" But she shook her head. "Nope. Never mind. You're literally never going to see me in straight Spandex, so I'm going to move on and focus on that whole apartment thing. Even if I don't like it."

"Why wouldn't you like it?"

Brad was right, and Cam couldn't keep living in a crawl space with poor circulation and no AC. Just the thought of trying to sleep up there in the heat of summer made him shudder, despite the fact that it was only February. And he couldn't say he knew Isla well—or at all—but she seemed different enough from Kailani that he couldn't picture them sharing a space without getting on each other's nerves sometimes.

As outlandish as Brad's offering was, Cam was going to take it without hesitation.

"It just seems like a lot. I don't think I…we…deserve it. I can take care of myself, anyway." Kailani scrambled back onto the wall, but her hands shook as she started her climb. The confidence she'd shown earlier was gone, blocked out by that stupid blindfold. Or maybe by whatever insecurity she'd just let slip.

"I'm not going to let you fall, Tease," Cam said, wishing he knew what to ask her to get her to admit to the real reason she was hesitating.

"You already did," she argued.

"You were three feet in the air. You're already higher than you were before."

"Not helping," she growled. She was clinging to the rock in front of her face with both hands, and she was never going to reach the next hold if she didn't start taking some risks.

"Above you about four feet and off to the right by three feet," Cam said. "It's your best hold."

"I was going to go straight up. It'll be faster."

"There's nothing good up there."

She tried anyway, her hand scraping against the fake rock surface of the wall.

"To the right," Cam said again.

"I know there's one up here. I studied the wall while you were busy checking me out."

Cam groaned. "Will you just trust me?"

Kailani seemed to freeze, which wasn't exactly promising. It was already hard enough to get her to open up and tell him about herself, but if she didn't trust him even with this? He could only do so much on his end.

He held his breath, that bit of hope growing dimmer with each second that passed.

Then, to his complete surprise, Kailani said, "Where do I put my foot?"

She was still low enough that Cam could reach her. Stepping forward, he gently touched her ankle before wrapping his fingers around her foot. He lifted her leg, resisting the temptation to kiss the smooth skin above her ankle exposed by her leggings, and placed it on her next foothold.

"Thanks," she breathed.

"Anytime," he replied, just as breathless. Before he could stop himself, he slid his hand up her leg and to the back of her knee, relishing in the way she trembled under his touch. He'd known from the start she felt attraction, but he hoped she felt the same way he did. He would find out when he finally got a chance to talk to her in private. "Are you ready?"

She nodded and reached for her chalk bag, finding the side of his head instead. Her fingers traced his ear for a second, leaving him a little weak in the knees, before moving on to the chalk. "Let's do this."

Cam backed up, taking a second to admire her lithe body and the way she regained her confidence so quickly, and then he mapped out a path for her to go. "Okay, next hold…"

It took almost twenty minutes to get Kailani up the wall, especially when she got high enough that he had to shout and couldn't see the holds as well. But when she finally rang the bell at the top, Cam felt so much closer to her than he had before the climb started.

She'd been tentative at first, reaching for each new hold with hesitation. But after the third time she fell and Cam caught her before she went anywhere, she seemed to finally trust him. Her hesitation turned to confidence, and the last half of the wall went a lot faster than the first.

Now that she was done, Cam lowered her slowly, letting her glide down smoothly so she didn't have to walk down the wall to avoid running into it. He was feeling pretty good about things, so when she got near the bottom, he stood directly beneath her and let her drop right into his arms.

She had the biggest smile on her face. "We did it," she said, wrapping her arms around his neck.

He shook his head. "*You* did it."

Brushing her fingers through the hair on his forehead, she leaned closer. "I couldn't have done it without you, Cam."

"Kailani, I—"

"That was fantastic!" Brad bounded over to them, smile as wide as ever. "I've got lunch waiting, and then we'll move onto our afternoon challenge. And if you trust my people with your keys, we could have you moved into your new places tonight! You can watch the first episode on your new TVs."

Never let it be said that Breakout Brad wasn't efficient in everything he did.

Glancing at Kailani to try to judge her opinion on the matter, Cam was about to decline—he could move his own stuff. But all words failed him when he found her still gazing at him with a smile that sent electricity coursing through him.

He never wanted to put her down.

"My keys are in the makeup tent," he said, his voice strained. He didn't even care.

"Same," Kailani replied.

"Hungry?"

"Starving."

Putting her down so they could slip out of their harnesses, Cam kept his eyes on Kailani as if she might close off again if he blinked too many times. As soon as they were free, he scooped her back up again and headed for the catering tent, feeling more hopeful than ever that he might actually have a future with this girl.

EIGHTEEN

"I'M NOT SURE I'M COMFORTABLE with this."

Cam's response to Kailani's whispered comment was a grunt, which she guessed meant something similar.

After Cam beat Kailani in an arm-wrestling competition after lunch—she gave it her best but was outmatched from the beginning—one of Brad's employees had given them the address to their new apartment building and told them the codes for the keypads. Because yes, it was one of those fancy buildings where they didn't have actual keys. The fact that there was an elevator and a door attendant should have been the first clues that the place was beyond expensive, but Kailani had tried to give Brad the benefit of the doubt.

But as soon as they opened the doors—which were right next to each other—both of them had stopped dead.

The apartment was as big as her parents' house. That may have been a slight exaggeration, but not by much, and Kailani had no idea how one person would even need this much space. The front room alone was at least half the size of her little gym, with a massive kitchen with state-of-the-art stainless-steel appliances and white cabinets. Granite countertops, vaulted ceilings, real hardwood flooring, a full wall of windows... Every new thing made Kailani more uneasy.

She couldn't accept this level of kindness from a practical stranger. If what Brad said about a benefactor was right, she would probably never find out who had paid for the place, and she hated that.

"Nope," she said, shutting the door as if not seeing the apartment would make it cease to exist. She was especially glad she had begged Brad not to film their homecomings, knowing she was already on the fence about this whole thing. Brad had fought her on it, wanting to add a little magic to the show, but Kailani had told him she didn't want anyone else knowing how much she was struggling to pay for things.

Cam had added his voice to that part, and Brad had reluctantly agreed to keep the apartments out of the show.

Though Kailani was ready to start loading everything back up into her car, Cam grabbed her shoulder before she could return to the elevator. "The anonymous donor paid for the six months up front. Non-refundable." His eyes were locked on the open kitchen in his place, and Kailani was pretty sure the only reason he hadn't gone to inspect the room was because he was in awe.

Maybe he *didn't* have the same thoughts as she did.

"Cam, this is way too much. We don't deserve—"

"Sure we do." Pulling her in with him, Cam headed straight for the kitchen, opening the fridge—it was full to the brim with food—and several cabinets—all of them stocked with dishes and small appliances. "Sweet mother of ravioli," he breathed, running a hand along his jaw.

Kailani would never admit out loud how much she wanted to see him hard at work in that kitchen, with a towel over his shoulder and his large hands working a knife with precision.

His eyes strayed to the hallway that had to lead to the bedroom. "You can't tell me you're not at least curious," he said, throwing her a grin.

She groaned. "Fine. But I still think we can't accept these. And who said I was okay with living right next to you? You're probably a terrible neighbor."

Cam rolled his eyes. "I'm a great neighbor. Just you wait."

Kailani didn't want to wait. She wanted to know he would always be right next to her. She wanted to jump all in before she was ready, even knowing she would probably end up heartbroken when he decided he couldn't love her.

Following Cam down the hall, Kailani tried to convince herself that all of this was fine until she ran smack into his glorious shoulders.

He snickered before stepping aside and letting her see into the first room.

"Oh," she said in surprise, admiring the little home gym Brad had set up. Complete with treadmill, free weights, plyo boxes, and a long pull up bar, it was exactly the kind of thing she would put in her own house if she had one. Hopefully she had the same thing over on her side.

Cam grabbed a note that had been taped to the treadmill. "'To avoid unnecessary attention from your fans'," he read. "That's actually really smart. I haven't been able to get a proper workout in for weeks."

"You'd never guess it," Kailani assured him, giving him another tricep pat-slash-stroke. If this was him slacking on workouts, how big was he on a good day?

Cam snorted. "I don't know why you're trying to butter me up, but it's working. I do seem to recall a rule about unnecessary touching, though…"

Kailani pulled her hand back in alarm. Had she misread everything?

Laughing, Cam grabbed her hand and pressed a slow kiss to her palm. "But that was before we started dating for real," he said, his voice low.

Where was the thermostat in this place? Kailani needed to turn the temperature down thirty degrees. *Stat.*

"Come on." Cam tugged her to the next door and kept his hold on her as he opened it.

This time it was a bedroom, decorated in masculine blues and grays. The windows filled the whole wall again, though navy blackout curtains hung on either side so the world could be shut out. Several pairs of name brand shoes sat on a shoe rack by the walk-in closet, which was full of Cam's rather small collection of clothing. A desk with a laptop sat against one wall next to a door that must have led to an *en suite* bathroom.

Cam cocked his head at the king-sized bed. "Do you ever not realize how little you own until it's all put in a large space?" he muttered.

"Hang on," Kailani said, taking a step inside. "Is that *more* shoes in the closet? How many do you have?"

"We don't need to talk about it." Despite her laughing protest, Cam grabbed her around the waist and pulled her from the room, closing the door behind him. "Let's go see *your* apartment!"

Suddenly Kailani was afraid of what she might find, but Cam held her firm as he walked out into the hall and held her in front of the door so she could type in the code. Sure enough, she found a matching workout room, though her apartment mirrored Cam's instead of being exactly the same layout.

Her bedroom had been decorated in cream and beige, which wouldn't have been her first choice, but she could appreciate the clean look to it. Anything was better than the cheap purple spread she'd bought at the thrift store, with its mismatched pillowcases. This room sat at the corner of the building, so along with the wall of windows, she had two more high above the bed that would probably let in a lot of afternoon sunlight. A large photo of one of the Kama'ole beaches in Maui hung between the bathroom and closet, and the sight of it broke Kailani's resolve to decline Brad's gift.

That photo felt like a reminder of happier times and a promise of happy times to come.

"I don't know about you," Cam said quietly, "but I could use a shower. Are you hungry?"

Kailani started to say she was fine, but a hand squeeze from Cam made her shut her mouth. Trust. She was trying to trust him, and that meant letting herself be human. She was allowed to be tired and hungry and let someone help *her* for a change. "Very," she said. "We could order in?"

That made him burst into laughter, and he shook his head as he backed up toward the hallway. "Good one. But no. What kind of boyfriend would I be if I didn't make dinner for my gorgeous girlfriend?"

"You don't have to—"

"I've missed cooking," he admitted, placing a hand on either side of the door frame. "Living above Riptide didn't exactly give me much opportunity. And I want to cook for you. Please?"

Kailani frowned. "Are you sure you're real, Cam Martinez?"

"See you in a bit. I'll text you my code." He flashed his crooked grin and disappeared.

Almost an hour later, Kailani emerged from her steam shower—Who knew how nice those were?—feeling better than she had in weeks. She was still exhausted, but the longer she was there, the more at ease she felt.

Even with the knowledge that a specimen like Cam was somewhere on the other side of the bedroom wall they shared.

Forcing herself not to think about the kinds of things she might stumble across—thank goodness they had their own apartments—Kailani located a pair of soft leggings and a loose sweatshirt. Might as well get comfortable. She wasn't one for dressing up to begin with, but she sort of wanted to put Cam to the test. He'd really only seen her in workout clothes, and while his eyes had done plenty of admiring and making her feel desirable if not beautiful, he had told her more than once that he was attracted to her.

She was curious to see how he would respond to something less flattering. To Kailani, plain and simple.

After pulling her wet hair into a braid, Kailani tentatively stepped out into the hallway and was hit with a wave of music and a strong aroma coming from behind his door.

Amazing aroma. The whole hall smelled of basil and something she couldn't place, and her mouth watered as she tiptoed toward the door and typed in the code. She wasn't sure why she was being so cautious until she peeked her head through the open door and got her first glimpse of Hot Body Cam fully uninhibited.

Dancing.

And as it turned out, Cam could *not* dance.

Kailani clapped a hand over her mouth as Cam flailed around the kitchen, so far off the beat that she had to wonder if he could even *hear* the beat. "Born This Way" by Lady Gaga blared from the walls—apparently there were speakers installed—and Cam was using a whisk as a microphone while he lip synced and "danced." She didn't even want to call the weird arm wiggle he was doing dancing.

She poked her head in a little farther, and that was when he saw her.

The whisk went flying at the same time he skidded to a stop, though momentum kept him sliding in his socks until he was flat on his back.

Kailani couldn't hold her laughter back anymore, and while he groaned, she hurried inside and dropped to his side, pressing her hands to his chest. "Sorry," she squeaked. "I should have warned you I was coming."

Though he winced, he grabbed hold of her hands so she was trapped. "Please tell me you weren't standing there for very long."

She bit her lip. "Have you always been a dancer?"

He groaned again, dropping his head to the floor. "I'm terrible. I know. Kit likes to say my hips are the only parts of me that *do* lie."

Kailani snorted. "At least there's one thing you can't do. I was starting to think you really were perfect."

"You smell really good."

As heat surged through her face, Kailani adjusted her grip on his hands and pulled him up to a sitting position. "It's that fancy shampoo Brad's people put in there. I usually go with the cheap stuff, and I don't know if my hair is going to let me go back."

Cam pulled one hand free to tuck some loose hair behind her ear. "I'll be sure to thank Brad when I see him tomorrow."

Something in his gaze held her captive, though she had no idea what it meant. All she knew was she had never been happier sitting on a floor, and she didn't want the moment to end. She could stay right there forever, lost in his cinnamon gaze and imagining a future where she could be in this spot every night. If she took the plunge and let Cam in for real, could this be her life?

Just as Kailani was about to kiss the man without inhibition, the music switched to the most horrendous thing Kailani had ever heard, breaking the spell.

Cam's eyes went wide as "Axel F" by Crazy Frog started blasting throughout the apartment.

Kailani lost it, falling to the ground in a fit of laughter while he scrambled to grab his phone and stop the music. "Please tell me that was your personal playlist."

Cam stuffed his phone into the pocket of his sweatpants with a scoff. "Of course it wasn't." Then he turned to the sink and heaved.

Though nothing came out, Kailani was sure the experience wasn't pleasant for him, and she hopped up to put her arm around him. "Sorry, I kinda set you up for that one. Who would have thought a person could be their own lie detector?"

Cam leaned his elbows on the edge of the sink, shaking a little. "I'd be okay if I didn't have it," he admitted. "It wouldn't change me telling the truth, but I could avoid, uh, this."

Be brave, Lani. "This isn't so bad, is it?" she asked, tightening her hold on him.

Wrapping an arm around her waist, he lifted his head until their noses brushed. "Not terrible," he murmured. "Not at all."

Curse the oven timer for choosing that moment to go off.

Laughing softly, Cam lingered for a moment longer before he grabbed an oven mitt and pulled out the source of the divine smell, setting it atop the stove for Kailani to admire.

And admire it, she did. It looked amazing, whatever it was, chicken breasts topped with tomatoes, cheese, and basil. She watched eagerly as he transferred the chicken to two plates, and when he drizzled balsamic vinegar over the top and added a few fresh rolls of basil leaves, she nearly got down on one knee.

It wasn't just the food, though it did look incredible. Something in the way he worked had her transfixed. In the confidence he displayed and the crooked grin that remained despite the interruption. Combined with the dance show earlier, Kailani felt like she was seeing a side of Cam few people got to see, and she treasured the fact that he felt no fear in being himself around her.

She wanted so badly to be the same, but she wasn't sure wishing it would be enough. She wasn't sure *she* would be enough.

"Let's sit on the couch," she suggested when Cam handed her a plate.

He grimaced, his eyes flicking toward the mahogany dining table. "The table is easier to clean."

"Are you expecting to make a mess?" Kailani never would have pegged him for a clean freak, but she'd just noticed the lack of dishes. He'd already cleaned everything he had used to make the food.

He let out a weak laugh. "No, but—"

"So you're expecting *me* to make a mess?"

"That's not—" He cut himself off before he got sick again.

Kailani smirked, grabbing his free hand and pulling him toward the large sitting room and its plush couch. "I'm not saying I never make a mess, but there are few things I love more than eating anywhere that isn't the dining table. I think you'll survive, Nelli."

He pressed a hand to his heart as if wounded. "I'm not even Martinelli anymore? I don't know how to feel about that."

"Anything is better than Tease," she replied, even though she'd secretly started to adore that nickname. Or maybe she just adored the man who had given it to her.

As Cam carefully settled on the couch, his food perched on his knees, he seemed to take several breaths before he really relaxed and began eating. Slowly. With utter caution.

Kailani giggled. "You're terrified, aren't you?"

He nodded as he painstakingly sliced his knife through the chicken on his plate. "It doesn't help that I'm not the one paying for this apartment. And that I don't *know* who is paying for it."

Kailani cut her own bite as she watched him move with such deliberation. She was about to say whoever had enough money lying around to pay for two luxury apartments could probably afford to get the rug professionally cleaned if they needed to, but the moment the food touched her tongue, she melted.

"Oh," she moaned, closing her eyes. "This is the most amazing thing I've ever tasted."

"Thanks. I don't appreciate the exaggeration, but—"

Kailani grabbed his arm. "I mean it. I'm already a sucker for balsamic, and something about the way you cooked this… It's perfection, Cam. Just like you."

His crooked smile came out in full force. "Pot and kettle," he chuckled.

Was he trying to say *she* was perfect? There was no way, but she couldn't fathom any other meaning for his words, and her heart did a happy sort of wiggle in her chest.

After a few quiet minutes while they ate, Cam nibbled his last bit of tomato, then said, "Can I ask you something?"

As she neared a blissful food-coma, Kailani wanted to tell him everything. "Is this—"

"No, it's not The Question. I'm just curious. Why do you like eating away from the table?"

She shouldn't have been surprised that he would catch that subtle hint at her life, but she was. Anyone else she'd known would have moved on by now. But not Cam.

Setting aside her empty plate, Kailani told herself to be brave. To trust this man who had given her no reason to do otherwise. "I have nine siblings, remember? And the youngest is four. Any time we had family dinner, I always spent most of it helping the younger ones cut their food and figure out how to use a spoon. It wasn't until I moved away that I finally experienced an uninterrupted meal. And kitchen tables always make me feel like someone is going to ask me to cut the crusts off their grilled cheese."

She peeked up, not sure what to expect. But she definitely hadn't expected to see anger in Cam's eyes. Was he mad at her for ruining the moment? Bringing down the mood?

Setting his plate on the coffee table, he worked his jaw around as if he'd been clenching it. "How old were you when you moved away from home?"

She winced. Would he think her pathetic for staying as long as she had? "It was last year. Right before I started planning my gym."

"So you've spent the majority of your life being a third parent?"

Not to that extent. "Sort of, but—"

"That really sucks, Lani."

Until this moment, Kailani hadn't known how she wanted someone to respond to her childhood. But Cam—of course—had hit it right on the head.

"It does suck," she agreed. "I love my family, and I'm glad I could be there to help, but…"

"Is that why you want your gym to do well?" He didn't even wait for her response before he growled a little. "You're still bailing them out, aren't you? You may have moved out, but your family still relies on you. And…" He pulled his eyebrows together and seemed to wait for her to finish his thoughts for him.

She sighed, playing with the end of her braid. It was only the partial truth, but it was easier than admitting the fact that she'd never been able to do enough for her family to treat her like she mattered to them. She'd never felt important. It was why she wanted to start her after-school program, so kids would have a place to go when home didn't feel like a safe space. Not that she'd felt that way, exactly, but she knew how difficult things could get. "Money has always been tight. Adoption is expensive, and some of my siblings have health problems that require surgeries. As much as I wish I could focus on me and my goals, I can't just abandon my family."

Cam grabbed her hands, his eyes boring into hers when she looked at him. "That shouldn't come at the expense of your own life. Why do they deserve to enjoy their existence any more than you do?"

She didn't have an answer for that. The only thing that came to mind was, *I haven't done anything to make me worthy of more*, but she had a feeling she knew how Cam would take that. He had it so much easier, not having any family to look after or prove himself to.

Cam's expression shifted, as if he could hear her thoughts, and he dropped her hands as he retreated to the corner of the couch and stretched his legs out with a sigh. "Sorry," he muttered. "I shouldn't push for personal things if you don't want to share them."

He looked so miserable that Kailani's heart broke for him. Maybe he didn't understand her struggles, but that didn't mean he was free of his own. No, he didn't have a family to take care of, but that only meant he was alone. Without Kit and his other friends, he would have nothing.

Swallowing her lingering fears, Kailani crawled closer to Cam with a smile. Though he watched with some confusion, it didn't take him long to understand what she wanted.

"You know there's a fireplace, right?" he grunted, but he dutifully slid down the couch so she could settle on top of him and soak in his warmth.

"This is so much better," she said, breathing him in. He smelled of fancy shampoo and roasted tomato, and there really was nothing that compared to the heat that radiated off his body. She wasn't even cold, not really, but she pressed herself into him anyway. Why was it so hard to trust him? She didn't want it to be, and there in his hold, she felt just safe enough to share more.

"That's not the only reason I want my gym to succeed," she said quietly.

Cam stiffened beneath her, no longer breathing. It was as if he was too scared to take a breath because it would scare her into silence.

She was doing that perfectly well on her own, but she swallowed the fear and said, "I want to make an after-school program for kids who don't want to go home yet. Somewhere they can go to get strong and feel like they can do hard things. Like they're important."

Cam finally took a breath, his heart beating faster in Kailani's ear. "Really?"

"Yeah. That's why I need the sponsorship. So I can afford to run the program without charging the kids."

"I want to offer free training and nutrition guidance to low-income people who don't have easy access to getting healthy."

Kailani lifted her head, meeting his eyes as she finally understood why he was so eager to win. "Oh," she said, really wishing he had told her he wanted to get rich so he could buy a winter home in Florida. "That's a really good reason."

"So is yours."

"Now what?"

He shrugged, reaching up and tucking some hair behind her ear. "I guess now we wait and see who wins? Either way, I'll make sure you get your program up and running."

Well, that turned her to mush, and she snuggled back into him, tucking her head under his chin. "And I'll make sure you get yours. We can do this."

"We can do this," he repeated.

They lay there in silence for a little bit, Kailani listening to Cam's heartbeat while he stroked the top of her head or rubbed her back in soothing circles. It was the kind of simple existence together that she'd always craved in a relationship.

After a while, Cam's heart slowed, as did his breathing, and Kailani felt herself slipping into sleep right along with him.

NINETEEN

Cam didn't dream often, but when he did, it was always vivid and bizarre, to the point where sometimes he genuinely wondered about his sanity. Dreams like being a part of the elephant secret service (the head of which was a kangaroo) and experiencing the end of the world through a core implosion couldn't be normal, and he usually woke up wondering if maybe Kit was right about that whole therapy thing. Maybe all of his strange imaginings were a result of his childhood trauma trying to rear its ugly head.

No matter the reason, he woke this morning with Kailani gently snoring on his chest and his back aching in protest, and the only thing he could think about was the tail end of his dream.

His dream where he'd been standing at an altar on a Hawaiian beach, a white-dressed Kailani beside him.

We can do this.

His chest had never felt tighter, but it wasn't in a panicked sort of way. It was probably because of the person on top of it, but he was sure there was more to it than that. When his aunt died, Cam had made a vow to himself to never let anyone in too deep. The Wonder Boys and Madi had already affixed themselves to his life, so they didn't count, but he'd refused to feel the pain of that loss again.

He'd dated, of course. He never liked being alone, so the last decade had been filled with one girlfriend after another, each staying only as long as it took for them to want more than a casual relationship. Then he'd pull the cord and make his escape. He'd always thought he was protecting himself, but...

He brushed a finger against Kailani's soft cheek. She had wiggled her way into his heart, all the while keeping her own locked up in a chest with no key, and he was suddenly on the other end of his own scheme.

It sucked, and he sent a silent apology to all of his past girlfriends who hadn't deserved to be treated like coping mechanisms.

His stomach rumbled, and he let out a deep sigh. As much as he wished he could stay in that spot forever, he needed food. Kailani would too, and their next competition was in a couple of hours.

Rolling carefully to the side, Cam resituated Kailani on the couch and crept away to take a quick shower.

While the cool water ran over his skin, he made a game plan. He didn't want to spend the rest of his life tiptoeing around the truth when it came to Kailani. He wanted things to be lasting, and he had made some progress yesterday. Especially when she told him about her reasons for wanting the sponsorship. Kit had been right when he said he needed to give Kailani opportunities to open up.

He also didn't want to push her too far too fast. She'd still clammed up a bit last night when he prodded too much, and Kailani didn't seem the sort to take kindly to people telling her what to do. This was a delicate situation, and there had to be a way to convince her to trust him with everything else. With whatever family issues she was keeping to herself.

By the time his burning limbs had calmed down—Kailani was a whole lot warmer than a blanket, which he rarely used to begin with—he had a game plan. He had no idea how much he could execute with Brad's stupid challenges getting in the way—at this point, he was tempted to tell Brad to just give it to Kailani—but he had to try to show her that he was good for her.

That he hadn't just been repeating her words when he said they could do this. He'd been talking about their gyms, yes, but he'd also been talking about their relationship. About making things last.

First: it was time to pull out the big guns. Literally.

When Cam returned to the kitchen, Kailani was awake, stretching and yawning. But as her gaze focused on him, she went as still as a statue, her eyes growing wider by the second.

Cam didn't usually cook shirtless—too many chances for injury—but he was going to use every tool he had. Every. Single. One. He may have done a few dozen crunches before coming back to the front room, just to emphasize certain assets. And maybe he was wearing his sweats just a bit lower on his hips than he usually did to highlight his Adonis belt.

Those pesky transversus abs took enough upkeep that of course he was going to show them off.

"Morning," Kailani squeaked.

Cam tried not to smile as he grabbed ingredients for omelets. "Sleep well?"

She didn't answer, probably because her jaw was hanging open. It wasn't like she hadn't seen him shirtless before, but now there wasn't any mud to hide the hard work he'd put in.

Step one seemed to be doing the trick nicely.

Step two involved food, so Cam shifted his focus to the task at hand, chopping up ham and vegetables as quickly as he could so he could get to step three: make Kailani feel like the most valued person in the world.

Sure, that step was pretty vague, but it would probably be the easiest one to accomplish. All Cam had to do was look at her mess of bed head and that oversized sweatshirt to remind himself that he was head over heels for her. That feeling could only grow stronger the more he got to know her.

"Here's your phone," Kailani said, settling herself on one of the barstools at the kitchen counter. "You got a couple of texts while you were, uh…" She blinked, shaking her head before lifting her eyes to Cam's face. "You got a couple of texts."

Had she just been thinking about him in the shower? Even Cam felt the heat of that one, and he cleared his throat before grabbing the phone to make sure none of it was important.

The fact that he had a couple of missed calls from Madi and twelve texts in the Wonder Boys group chat had him mildly concerned, so he stopped whipping the eggs and opened up the thread to make sure nothing bad had happened.

Kit's sister had been the one to start the conversation, but it had been late last night, and the conversation continued into this morning, probably when Kit woke up for school.

Madi: Are you guys watching this Breakout show?

Ben: Not yet. Is it up?

Madi: Cam, you have some explaining to do. Are you sure this relationship is fake?

Oliver: Maybe he's a moonlight reality TV star and we had no idea until now. Or maybe soap operas. Telenovelas, anyone?

Ben: I'm pretty sure acting is technically lying.

Oliver: Good point. So Madi's question still stands.

Oliver: Do you think he's not answering because he doesn't want to lie about it?

Kit: I think he didn't answer because he just moved in with Kailani.

Oliver: Excuse me?

Ben: He did what?

Madi: WHAT?!

Madi: Cam, you'd better start answering your phone.

Cam was going to kill Kit. He knew he shouldn't have told him, but when Kit texted yesterday afternoon to ask how the competition was going, the apartment had just slipped out. He made a vow right then and there to stop using voice-to-text, and then he stuffed his phone into his pocket. He would have to respond eventually and figure out how Kit had misunderstood so completely, but everything was so gray right now.

Kailani admiring his body was not the same as her having deeper feelings for him. She could admire him just as easily as a trainer as she could as a girlfriend, so step one was only the start. He had a long way to go before he could start wondering about her affection lasting longer than a few weeks.

"Everything okay?" Kailani asked, eyes on his hidden phone. Or maybe she was just staring at his abs again.

Cam grunted as he dropped some coconut oil into a pan on the stove. "I'm just questioning why I keep my friends around." He swallowed the nausea that rose into his throat. It was mostly a lie, but it felt too close to the truth for comfort. Sometimes he was convinced the only reason he hadn't pushed them away was because Kit hadn't let him.

Kailani snickered. "The Wonder Boys? Why do you call them that, anyway?"

"Madi. She was obsessed with Wonder Woman when we were younger, and she thought it sounded cool. We didn't have the heart to tell her that it sounded like we needed bowl cuts and guitars." He poured half the egg into the heated pan, letting the sizzle calm his nerves. He had no idea why this conversation was making his anxiety rise, but it was.

Maybe he just really wanted Kailani to like his friends. They were essentially part of the package. His family.

"Do you sing as well as you dance?"

He groaned. "You're never going to forget what you saw last night, are you?"

"Never. Answer the question."

Cam thought for a moment, deciding how he wanted to answer that. "I'm a better singer than I am a dancer," he said. "You?"

"Singing is a definite no. My mom taught me hula, but that's pretty much the only dancing I do. And I don't do it in front of people, generally."

"Would you do it for me?" Something told Cam he would wildly enjoy watching her dance, regardless of her skill.

Kailani's smile crept wider. "Maaaaybe," she said, drawing the word out. "If you earn it."

Cam leaned his elbows on the counter in front of her. "How do I earn it? You're beautiful, by the way."

She wrinkled her nose. "You're lying. I never look good in the morning."

"Do you see me throwing up?" That question made *him* wrinkle his nose. "That was about the least attractive thing I could have said, wasn't it?"

"Surprisingly, no." Her eyes glittered, and unless he was mistaken, she had leaned closer. "It was sweet."

Apparently step three was underway, and Cam hoped he could do it justice. Leaning even closer—why was this stupid counter so wide?—he touched his nose to hers and mentally fist pumped when she didn't retreat. Maybe "Operation make Lani fall in love" wouldn't be as difficult as he'd thought.

"You're the most beautiful thing I've ever seen," he said.

"Your eggs are burning," she replied.

He cursed and grabbed the pan. Thankfully, it wasn't so overcooked that it wouldn't be edible. "I'll eat this one, and you can have the next. I promise I won't burn it."

"You're making me breakfast?"

Cam grinned at the surprise in her words. "I'll happily cook every meal for you."

Sliding from the stool, Kailani made her way around the counter and slid her arms around his waist with zero hesitation. Even with him being half naked. "Thank you. I was always busy helping with homework, so Mom never taught me to cook."

It was another piece of the Kailani puzzle, and Cam treasured the knowledge. He treasured *her*, and he wrapped his arms around her, pulling her in tight and resting his head on top of hers.

"I can teach you, if you want," he said, though some hesitation leaked into his voice without his say-so. It was probably going to take more than a few days to get his fear to go away entirely.

But Kailani tightened her hold. "I'd like that. As long as you promise to keep Shirtless Breakfast a thing."

The laugh that escaped out of him felt like it put several significant cracks in the wall that had been his shield for the last decade. Of course, he was working on breaking down that wall on his own, but he wouldn't say no to a little help. And any little sign that Kailani was willing to match his effort and make this relationship stronger was worth its weight in gold.

TWENTY

"CAN I ASK YOU A question?"

Kailani glanced up from the picture she was coloring. After a morning of losing to Cam in a game of ping pong, the change of pace was quite nice, even if she had no idea how someone was supposed to judge a children's coloring page.

That hadn't stopped her from trying to do some fancy shading and blending.

"Question?" she asked.

Cam smirked. "Not that question. Will you tell me about your siblings?"

Hearing that set off a chain reaction inside Kailani's heart that started with her wanting to go throw up, followed by her heart picking up so much speed that she thought it might stop functioning, and then nearly ended with her leaping across the table and kissing the crooked smile right off his face because no matter how many times she had deflected when it came to her family, he was still asking. And that had her overwhelmed with hope. She remained composed, however. At least on the outside.

Cam had been different since last night. He always perked up when she told him something about herself, but after she was extra vulnerable last night, he was treating her like… Well, like he wanted this relationship to be a forever kind of thing.

Like she was important to him. She'd never felt important to anyone. Not like that.

First a delicious omelet, then he offered to drive and opened her door for her, and he'd touched her hand far more often than a game of ping pong required by handing her the ball rather than tossing it every time it was her turn to serve and looking at her like she held the answers to the universe.

And his smiles…

Kailani could get used to that crooked smile being a permanent fixture in her life. It was more than just his attractiveness, which couldn't be denied. There was something in the way he lived so open and vulnerable that made her feel trusted. His smile seemed to warm her to her core, telling her that she was special, that he admired her inside and out, that he would do anything it took to make her happy.

She never would have thought someone could say so much with a smile until she met Cam.

Despite all of that, however, fear still sat heavy in her stomach as she considered his question. "Are you sure you want to hear about *all* of them?" she asked quietly.

Cam's smile didn't falter in the slightest. "I asked, didn't I? Keep in mind Ben is the fourth of seven kids, so it's not like I haven't been around big families before."

"Oh."

He'd said that so casually, not knowing that Kailani had been stressing about her giant family since the day she met him. The number of them was only half the battle, though. Someday he might actually *meet* them, unless Kailani could delay that moment forever, and then everything would change.

Trying to cover her growing nerves, she opted for some levity to the moment. "If I tell you, will you show me your picture?"

Cam had used his hand to block his page since the second he started, and at her question he slid his arm forward to cover the paper even more. "Absolutely not. I won't have you cheating."

"How can you cheat at coloring?"

"I'm pretty sure my color choices are way better than yours."

Kailani laughed, relaxing a little. "I highly doubt that." Cam was coloring a picture of farm animals, and he'd been using an awful lot of blue and purple.

Still, Cam didn't move as he grabbed a seafoam green pencil and continued scribbling away. "You said the youngest is four?"

"Carter," she said with a nod. "He's deaf, and somehow he has the whole family wrapped around his little finger even though he's only been with the family for about eighteen months."

"Do you know sign language?"

"Enough. But I'm not great."

Cam grinned. "You know more than me, so I think that makes you pretty great. Who's the next youngest?"

Kailani went through every single one of the Adams kids, expecting Cam to lose attention with each one. But he didn't. He remained riveted, asking questions when he was curious about something she said.

"Chase is the oldest, after me," she finished.

"Why did you say his name like that?"

Kailani blinked and looked up. "Like what?"

The furrow in Cam's brow couldn't be just from concentration, especially because he seemed to have abandoned his coloring page for the time being. At some point, he had flipped it over and written several things on the back of the paper.

He swallowed hard, as if afraid to clarify this question. "Why did you say it with, I don't know, longing? What's Chase's deal? He's the one who got into fights, right?"

Kailani really hoped this wouldn't be some sort of trigger for him, though it wasn't like she could skirt around the subject forever. Especially if they continued together after the show. "He's a Marine," she said warily, thinking of Cam's dad. "I haven't seen him in almost two years. He's supposed to come home sometime soon, but we don't know when. And Chase is notoriously bad at communicating. He and I have always been really close, though."

Though he reached out for her hand, Cam moved rather stiffly. His eyes weren't fully focused on her, and his grip was tighter than usual as he asked, "Where's he stationed?"

"Hawaii. I kind of hate him for it, but not really. He says it's like being home again."

"So he was born in Hawaii like you?" Cam asked as he wrote another line on his paper. He'd relaxed again, thankfully. "Okay, so we've got Carter, then Baxter and Sylvia, followed by the twins, Marcus and Jesse, and then it's Felicia, Bryce, Isla, Chase, and you?" He ran his finger down his paper as he went.

"Wait, are you writing all of this down?" Leaning forward, Kailani strained to see the notes he'd taken. Sure enough, he'd written down every name with one or two attributes next to each.

Cam raised an eyebrow. "How else am I going to remember who's who?"

Be still her beating heart. "It's not like I was going to quiz you."

"No, but *they* might. Assuming you let me meet them."

"You *want* to meet them?"

"Why wouldn't I?"

Because they probably don't care about meeting you. Kailani shrugged as she settled back in her seat. "I don't know. It just seems like it would be a lot of effort for people who just started precariously dating."

"You're right. But this doesn't feel new to me. Or precarious."

What was that supposed to mean? Kailani didn't get a chance to ask, because Brad bounded toward them with a delighted, "Time's up!" and grabbed their pictures before they could do anything else. "I'll just bring these to our judges…"

Kailani's eyes followed him to the other end of the tent where all the cameras were ready and waiting, and as soon as she saw the panel of judges, her jaw dropped. "They're kids!"

Cam burst into laughter and wrapped an arm around Kailani's shoulders as he led her over to the filming spot. "I'm so going to win this."

If the way the kids were frowning at her picture was any indication, Cam was probably right. The judges couldn't have been older than five or six, and all four of them definitely seemed to focus more on Cam's page.

"As you can see," Brad said into one of the cameras, "it looks like Adams went with a more traditional approach, while Martinez chose to be a little more flashy. So far, the judges seem to be enjoying the flair."

"Typical," Kailani grumbled, staring at Cam's multi-colored page. "You do know that sheep aren't supposed to be rainbow, right?"

Cam's response came with an unexpected kiss to the top of her head. "One thing I always tell my clients is that they can't let limiting beliefs hold them back. They're so much stronger than they think they are. If a sheep wants to be iridescent, it can be iridescent, just like how a person can make any transformation if they break through those mental barriers telling them they can't. Why limit your possibilities when you deserve the world you want?"

Kailani gaped at him, her face flushed and her heart racing in the strangest way. "Where in the world did you come from, Cam?" she whispered, unable to resist leaning in close. "That was the sexiest thing I've ever heard."

"Pretty sure you shouldn't say *sexy* in front of five-year-olds," he whispered back.

"I said that one only for you."

Her lips had just brushed against his when a chorus of childish *ewwws* filled the tent.

Though he snorted a laugh, Cam didn't move, holding Kailani against him as he pressed his forehead to hers. "New rule," he said under his breath. "The next time I kiss you, it'll be when we can't get interrupted. And *that* will be only for you. No cameras. No timers. Just you and me. Deal?"

"Deal." Kailani was pretty sure she was about to melt into a puddle, and the only thing that kept her upright as they turned to face Brad and find out who won was Cam's hand wrapped securely around hers.

Something had changed in Cam, and Kailani was *absolutely* here for it.

TWENTY-ONE

THERE WAS NOTHING QUITE SO terrifying as facing down an angry Madi Hamilton. This was something Cam had known from the first day he met Kit's little sister, and he had made sure he never got on her bad side. The last time had been when Cam didn't realize just how distracted Oliver was during a training session, which led to Oliver fracturing his foot.

For the record, Oliver breaking his foot had given him and Madi a chance to realize they were madly in love with each other, something they'd been denying at the time. So in a way, Madi should have been *thanking* Cam, not glaring at him.

Not that Madi was glaring tonight. She'd actually been quite calm, though maybe that was because Oliver had been giving her foot rubs for the last twenty minutes. Her presence had kept Oliver's attention mostly off of Cam, which was nice. This was their first time being around each other since his anxiety attack, and that event was not something he wanted to explain.

"For the last time," Cam muttered, "I don't know how to define our relationship."

As much as he wished he could keep pretending every-thing was fake, he couldn't perpetuate the lie now that the Wonder Gang were asking about it. Having to stick to truths had made things difficult, but he wasn't ready to commit to anything until he told Kailani exactly how he felt. Cam might have tried tonight, if Madi hadn't called an emergency Wonder Boys meeting. When Madi called a meeting, the Boys had no choice but to attend. Cam had almost brought Kailani along—every minute away from her seemed to pull him apart at the seams—but he was glad he hadn't.

Not when this had turned into a Madi interrogation.

Madi narrowed her eyes, stroking her rounded belly with one thumb. She was only halfway through her pregnancy, but she'd taken to being pregnant like a gym rat to protein supplements. She made it look so natural and easy. "Your relationship looked pretty defined to me, Cameron."

Cam winced. Madi only used his full name when he was in trouble because she knew how much he hated the reminder of his dad. Dad was the only one who had ever called him Cameron. "You've only seen a highly edited and sensationalized—"

"Episode Two dropped this afternoon," she interrupted. "There's a pattern now."

Oliver chuckled without looking away from his wife's toes. "You carried her to a tent," he pointed out. "Pretty sure Kailani's fully capable of walking on her own, even if she trounced you in rock climbing."

Cam didn't have a response to that one. It would probably be a good idea for the two of them to know what they were up against when it came to the show and the responses that would come from it. Thankfully, part of Brad's contract had required them to stay off of social media while they were filming, something Cam hadn't been sad about. Taking a step away from the madness had given him a better chance of getting to know Kailani better.

Of falling in love with her.

"Ha!" Madi pointed at Cam before raising both fists in the air. "Kit, you owe me twenty bucks."

Kit, who was at the wet bar with Ben while Ben made hot chocolate for the group, growled a little. "Says who?"

"Says the look on Cam's face."

"That's not an admission of love, Mads."

"Hang on," Cam said, holding up a hand. "Did you two make bets on whether or not I would fall in love with Kailani?" And why had Kit bet *against* him when he knew how Cam felt? Technically, Madi was right and definitely deserved the twenty bucks. Not that Cam would tell her that.

Madi, however, brushed Cam's question away. "We're getting off topic."

"Except we're not?" Ben said, raising an eyebrow. "We literally haven't strayed from the topic of Cam's love life since he got here."

Cam hoped Ben was as annoyed as he was, though two against three wasn't going to help him much. At least Ben had already sort of been through this during the first few months he was dating Allie.

Speaking of… "Where's Allie tonight?" Cam asked.

Ben grimaced as he poured warm milk into a mug. Of all of them, he was by far the most easygoing, so whatever it was that got him all ruffled, it had to be big. "She's with her mom." When all eyes turned to him, he turned bright red. "Apparently, her mom is determined to start making, uh, wedding… plans…"

Cam and Oliver were on their feet in an instant, Madi right behind them (with a little more difficulty). "Benjamin Nakamura," Oliver said accusatively, "did you forget to tell us that you got engaged?"

"No!" Ben's hands slipped, spilling milk all over the counter. "No, we're not… I mean, maybe someday. But we've only been officially dating since Christmas!"

"Your relationship was about as fake as Cam's." Madi rolled her eyes. "You've been dating since October."

Cam pretended he hadn't been brought back into the conversation, keeping his focus on his old roommate. "So if you're not engaged," he said, "why in the world would her mom be planning a wedding?"

Ben heaved a deep sigh. "Because she hopes that if everything is planned, we won't have a reason not to do it."

"*Is* there any reason not to?" Oliver asked.

"Yeah. Because we've only been dating for four months! Besides, we're in the middle of the legal battle with *Menace Unknown*." He and Allie were trying to get royalties from their book that had been posted online for download without their permission, though Cam wasn't sure where things were at with that. Apparently in the messy middle.

Scoffing, Oliver waved a hand and settled back into his seat. "You're going to win that thing, Ben, and soon you'll be rolling in cash. Besides, four months is tons of time when it comes to being in a relationship."

"Don't listen to the guy who proposed after less than twenty-four hours of dating someone," Cam growled, rolling his eyes. He still thought Oliver was lucky Kit hadn't killed him for pulling that stunt, even if he and Madi had basically been designed for each other. Asking Madi to marry him before they'd even really been in a relationship had been risky for so many reasons, but it was such an Oliver thing to do. He never questioned things; he dove in headfirst, and somehow things always worked out for him.

"Don't listen to the guy who hasn't been able to commit until now, either," Kit added as he nudged Ben's arm, though he threw Cam a smile to let him know he was joking. "I know you're a people pleaser, Ben, but this is one decision you have to make for yourself. If you want to marry Allie, then that's great! If you don't, that's fine. And if you want to wait three years before you tie the knot, that's your choice. Just make sure you're both on the same page with this."

"Sound advice from the perpetually single Kit Morgan," Oliver said, tugging Madi back to the couch so he could resume rubbing her feet.

"He ha—" Cam got halfway through the word before he stopped himself and clenched his jaw shut, something Kit definitely noticed because he narrowed his eyes while looking terrified at the same time. Cam cleared his throat. "As much as I love these club meetings," he said, hoping no one else noticed his almost slip-up, "can I go back home? I have an early—"

"Oh right!" Madi smacked Oliver on the arm. "I was going to ask about that too. What's this about you *moving in* with Kailani? And you're still going to tell me you don't have a firm grip on where you two stand?"

Cam sighed. "I didn't move in with her. Some benefactor rented us a couple of apartments. As in plural. Brad thinks we've both sacrificed too much and deserve decent places to live."

"Did you not already have a decent place to live?" Kit asked in alarm.

Another sigh eased out of Cam, and he berated himself for letting his mouth get away from him. As always. He'd done a surprisingly decent job of skirting around the subject of his above-the-gym apartment for the last few months, somehow managing to avoid both lying and admitting the truth about where he was staying. Mostly because he didn't want Kit to try to fix it. "Um, not exactly."

Kit folded his arms, moving closer to the couches to stare Cam down. "Not exactly? Where have you been living, Cameron?"

"Not you too. You don't have to call me—"

"Answer the question," Madi said.

"He's been living above the gym," Oliver said, suddenly going very still, as if he hadn't meant to say that.

Cam narrowed his eyes. "How did you know that?"

Shrugging, Oliver became fixated on Madi's feet as he rubbed his thumbs into her arches, though he glanced up and met Kit's gaze for a split second, the two of them sharing a look

Cam didn't understand. It seemed significant, though. "Because I happened to be running past when you came down the stairs to open the gym one morning."

"You were running," Cam repeated with a hefty amount of skepticism. "Past Bank Street."

"Yeah."

Oliver lived twenty minutes by car from Riptide, and there was no way he could have run that far. "Why would you—"

"This isn't important!" Madi said, shoving her foot into Oliver's chest to give herself some space. "Cam, start telling us about your apartment."

And now he was stuck. Madi had been like a little sister to him since he was fourteen, and he couldn't say no to her. "Okay, yes, I live above the gym," he began, sparking a thirty-minute conversation about the necessities of life and how great the anonymous donor was for rescuing Cam from squalor and, for some reason, the pros and cons of butter versus margarine.

By the time he finally made it out to his car and found a text from Kailani, inviting him over for a movie, Cam was more than ready to get back to his fancy new apartment building and his gorgeous new neighbor. He'd missed the chance to make her dinner again, and he was not about to waste his evening on oil and fat—something he regretted thinking as soon as he opened her apartment door and was hit with a wave of salt and butter, like he'd just stepped into a movie theater.

"Finally!"

It took Cam a second to locate Kailani in the dim room. She sat curled up in a ball on the couch, burritoed in a fuzzy white blanket that blended into the cushions. The only reason he could tell she was there was that fact that her bronze skin stood out from the mass of white.

He smiled at the sight of her, already breathing easier. "Sorry I'm late, sugar plum. Save any popcorn for me?"

"That's a terrible pet name you're never going to use again." She held the popcorn bowl toward him as she stuffed a handful into her mouth. "I know I shouldn't eat this stuff, but sometimes I think the reason I work out is so I can eat whatever I want."

"Solid reasoning. What are we watching?"

Despite wanting to take a shower after Kailani beat him in a plank competition—she lasted five minutes longer than he did, only giving up because she was bored—Cam settled next to Kailani. He left a few inches of space between them, choosing to let her close the gap if she wanted to.

After Shirtless Breakfast and his declaration after the coloring contest, it was her turn to make a move. Show him she was as invested as him.

"We're watching Brad's show," she said once he'd settled. She had it queued up already, and the first episode had way more views than Cam had expected.

The freeze frame that served as the cover shot was the pair of them covered in mud and gazing into each other's eyes.

Longingly, according to Kit.

"No," Cam said.

Kailani turned to him. "No, what?"

"No, we're not watching this."

"Why not?"

"Because I don't want to watch myself lose at volleyball." He immediately heaved, pressing his fist to his mouth. Curse his stomach.

Shaking herself loose from her blanket, Kailani shifted so she sat facing him. Instead of a baggy sweatshirt, today she wore a loose pink tank top and gray cotton shorts. Shorts that showed a bit too much leg for Cam's comfort, sitting high up on her thighs with the way she was folded up. Though she often wore leggings that didn't hide much of her muscle, he hadn't seen this much bare skin before. And it was taking everything in him to keep his eyes on hers.

"What's the real reason?" she asked.

He shouldn't have said anything. He should have just ducked his head and watched the stupid show. But keeping his mouth shut never happened when he wanted it to, and now he had to deal with the consequences of his runaway mouth. "I'm terrified of what I'm going to see. What *you're* going to see."

Pulling her eyebrows together, Kailani glanced at the giant TV screen. "What do you think I'm going to see?" she asked. "I was there for all of it, remember? I mostly want to revisit my favorite part of the game, though I have to admit the breakfast version is even better." Her eyes wandered his torso as if mapping it out in preparation.

It was a testament to his nerves that his body barely reacted to her compliment. Nerves, not anxiety. Which was a nice change.

"How about this?" he said, taking hold of her hands and drawing them to his lips. "You and I will watch the show *after* it's done filming. You can check me out all you want, and I'll keep my laughing about your disaster of a pizza to a minimum. Just... Don't watch it yet, okay? Trust me."

He wasn't ready to tell her how he felt about her, and he absolutely didn't want her to find out when she realized how much time he spent smiling at her. If Madi was right about his expression, he'd probably been silently telling Kailani he was in love with her for the last few days without even knowing it.

And knowing Brad, he probably played up those moments when the two of them got lost in each other's eyes during the editing. Cam couldn't lie with his words, and neither could he keep his expressions to himself.

Cam wanted her to know he was in love with her, but he wanted to be the one to tell her. When the timing was right. When he was feeling braver than he was now.

"I do trust you," Kailani said quietly, pulling her hand free to brush his hair from his forehead. "We can watch something else tonight."

"Thank you. It will—I hope it will be worth the wait."

They picked an adventure movie neither of them had seen yet because they'd been too busy, and Cam settled low into the couch with his legs stretched out on the ottoman and the popcorn on his lap. And though the movie started playing, his focus was entirely on the girl next to him.

She seemed to be debating something, sitting cross-legged and straight-backed while still facing him. Her eyes were fixated somewhere near his ribcage, and though he could guess fairly easily what the debate was about, curiosity kept his mouth shut.

The only thing he did to help the situation was stretch one arm across the back of the couch, an open invitation to share his space.

Kailani hummed a bit, her fingers rubbing against the fuzzy blanket that waited bunched up around her hips. While it did look soft and warm, it couldn't possibly compare to a good cuddle.

"Is there any particular reason you're over there?"

She pursed her lips, clearly nervous about something as she glanced behind him. "Yes."

"And are you going to tell me what that reason is?"

The voice that answered was not Kailani's. "Oh my goodness, Lani, just ask him!"

Flinching, Cam twisted toward the hallway and found Kailani's sister standing there, one hip jutted out and her arms folded. "Uh, hi," he said. "Isla, right?"

"You got that right, Beefcake."

Kailani grabbed Cam's hand. "I couldn't let her stay in our awful old apartment, so she moved in this afternoon. We can go over to your place if you don't want her to—"

"Hey, don't answer the question for him," Isla complained, coming into the room and leaning over the couch between them. "What my dear sister is too scared to ask is if you're okay with me joining you two for a little movie night. I've been dying to get to know my sister's hunky manfriend, and your Clark Kent buddy didn't have a lot to say about you."

Kit hadn't said much about him? Cam couldn't decide if he was grateful or offended.

As if she could read his thoughts, Isla rolled her eyes. "He said I shouldn't form my opinion on someone's secondhand account. So here I am!"

"Like I said," Kailani said with a grimace, "you can say no. I can banish her to her bedroom for the night. Which, by the way, I'm going to be borrowing your home gym now that I have a fashionista living in mine."

Isla attacked Kailani with a hug from behind. "Aww, you called me a fashionista! I didn't think you knew what that word was!"

Grinning, Cam felt like most of his stress was melting away as he watched the two of them interact. Kailani had spoken of her other siblings with a nonchalance he hadn't bought for a second, but she always smiled when it came to Isla. He wished he could see her interact with everyone from her family, and though it was possibly the most terrifying thought he'd ever had, he wanted to see Kailani with her parents. He wanted to know why her family had her so spooked when it came to this relationship.

"Join us," he said, fighting a grin when both women stared at him in shock, their eyes matching in size despite the contrasting colors of brown and blue.

"Really?" they both said at the same time.

"Sure. I'd like to get to know you better, Isla."

"Cam wins," Isla said as she scurried around the couch and plopped herself down on Kailani's other side. She busied herself with removing her prosthetic as she kept talking. "Except maybe next time don't take so long to get home. Lani needs her beauty sleep."

Home. That word pierced his chest like an arrow and sank in deep, embedding itself in his heart. Tearing it out would only lead to heartbreak, so he opted to break the shaft and leave it exactly where it was.

"Come here," he said, holding his arm out to Kailani.

She snuggled in so quickly and easily that for a second Cam forgot how to breathe. Probably because he'd been struck by that *home* arrow, but her lack of hesitation didn't help anything. If anything, it pushed the arrow deeper.

Maybe he shouldn't have picked a movie with an archer for a hero. He was getting all sorts of strange mental images now.

"No making out during the movie," Isla said, bundling herself up in so many blankets that Cam wasn't sure how she could even see the TV. She and her sister seemed to share the same burrito tendencies.

Cam snorted. "I keep my promises," he said, only loud enough for Kailani to hear. He wouldn't kiss her unless they were alone, when he could make it memorable and make sure she knew that it was only for her.

"I don't know if this is ever going to get old," Kailani murmured against his chest. "Not just the warmth, but..."

Cam could fill in the blanks with so many things. His strength, the apartments, their promising relationship... Whatever Kailani valued, she kept it to herself, but he wanted to make sure she was able to keep it forever if it would make her happy.

TWENTY-TWO

As it turned out, the bed Brad had bought for Kailani was insanely comfortable. She woke feeling more refreshed than she had in years, even if she didn't remember moving to her bedroom after the movie ended. Neither did she remember most of the movie. She'd been so focused on Cam's strong and steady heartbeat, and the way his thumb stroked hers while they held hands against his chest. She must have fallen asleep in his arms, and unless she had suddenly developed sleep walking, he'd carried her to her bed.

Vague memories of a kiss to the forehead as he tucked a blanket around her seemed to confirm that idea, and Kailani squealed a little into her pillow. Was it too much to hope for a happily ever after?

As much as she wanted to take this opportunity to sleep in as long as she could, the prospect of seeing Cam again pulled her up and into the shower. She moved quickly, washing her hair in record time and putting on the first clothes she found.

By the time she scurried out of her apartment, she was positively vibrating with excitement. She'd never been this excited to see someone before, and at this point she couldn't reason away the feelings that burned hot inside her.

She was in love with Cam Martinez.

Who had apparently left something for her at her door. A plastic container sat in the hallway with a note taped to it.

Sorry I had to miss seeing your beautiful face this morning! I had some needy clients who refused to work with Brad's trainers, so I had to head into the gym before filming. I'll meet you at the park? I made you and Isla some protein-packed muffins. Can't wait to see you later! - C

Honestly, could the man get any more perfect? Kailani grabbed one of the muffins from the plastic container and tore off a piece as she gazed at the note. Cam had impeccably neat handwriting, which surprised her. Most guys didn't. And when had he had the time to make muffins? It was barely after six, which meant he'd either stayed up late or gotten up crazy early.

"One of these days," she muttered through a mouthful of delicious muffin, "I'm going to wake up from this dream and realize you're just a figment of my imagination." But until that moment, she was going to enjoy every minute of her time with Cam the well-named Wonder Boy.

She got to Frostwick Park almost half an hour earlier than she was supposed to be there, partly because she was bored but mostly because she hoped Cam would also be early. Not knowing how many clients he had or when he'd started, it was impossible for her to say what his plans were. But she hoped.

To her dismay, the only person in the makeup tent was Breakout Brad himself, who was usually already done up by the time they got there. Surprisingly, he wore not an inch of neon, dressed in black and gray sweats while he scrolled through his phone. All in all, with how calmly he sat there, he looked like a different person entirely.

He glanced up before Kailani could back out of the tent to kill some time in her car. "Ah, Miss Adams," he said with a smile. "Up early today?"

She shrugged. "A bit. I didn't have much to do at home, so I figured I would come here."

"Cam won't be here until call time."

"Oh."

Brad's smile grew, and he patted the chair next to his. "I can't say I know you very well, Kailani, but it does seem like something has changed for you over the last few days."

"Is that good or bad?"

"Definitely good. You were always confident—it's one of the reasons your gym caught my attention—but you seem more at peace than you did when I met you." Setting his phone on the vanity, Brad spun his chair to face her. "You've technically answered this question already, but I'm curious to see if anything has changed. Why do you want this sponsorship?"

For some reason, that question settled heavy in her gut even though she had a ready answer. When she'd signed the contract before the beginning of the competition, they had asked her that question on camera. She had jumped right into a spiel about empowering people to take charge of their bodies and use them to their full advantage. *It doesn't take huge weights or fancy machines to get the body you want.* She'd spoken of her after-school program without going into details about what had sparked that dream. But as she sat there looking at a very human, very normal Brad, she wanted to give a different answer.

"I don't want to worry anymore," she said quietly. "About my employees, my clients, my family. I spend so much of my time making sure the money is good that I've forgotten what it feels like to get to a client's level and watch them improve. I'm a trainer, not a businesswoman. That's never been me."

Nodding, Brad studied her for a moment before he spoke again. "But?"

She swallowed. "But I think Cam deserves it more than I do."

"Why is that?"

"I'm guessing he told you about his low-income thing?" When Brad nodded, Kailani smiled. "How could I get in the way of that? He's already lost so much, and he would do so much good with that program."

"More than you could do with the kids in yours?"

"I don't have any plans to not make my program happen. It just might take me a little longer. I'm okay with that."

Brad grinned. "I knew you were meant to be the first time I saw you two together." He was always so happy, even when not full of energy. Suddenly, Kailani wanted to know what his life had looked like outside of his training videos and other projects. Did he have a family? Or had he always given his full attention to the work?

She wasn't brave enough to ask.

"You think we're meant to be?" she said instead, warmth spreading through her limbs at the thought of spending her whole life with someone like Cam by her side. No, not *someone like*. Just Cam. It may not have always been in the best of lights, but she hadn't stopped thinking about him since the day they met in the climbing gym almost four months ago.

"You seem like the type to strive for perfection," Brad said, rising to his feet and putting a hand on Kailani's shoulder. "It's a commendable attribute, but you have to remember there are more important things than flawlessness, and your worth is more than what others think of you. Sometimes it's good to embrace your flaws and accept that your rough edges are what make you easier to hold onto. Just something to think about."

He headed for the door but paused at the entrance and glanced back. "Good luck with the competition today. You might want to brush up on your pull-up technique." He left with a wink, leaving Kailani feeling more hopeful than she'd been yet.

Who would have thought an eccentric guy like Brad would have been capable of divvying out such worthwhile nuggets of wisdom?

Much to the beautician Felipe's dismay, Cam showed up only a few minutes before they were supposed to meet Brad. He looked sweaty and out of breath, but the smile he gave Kailani as he slid into his chair made him more handsome than she'd ever seen him.

"Hey," he said just before Felipe smothered him with a towel and a few grumbled curses.

Kailani sipped a bottle of water as she lounged in her own chair. She'd spent the last half an hour talking to Serena about how different her hair was here versus when she'd lived in Hawaii, though she was young enough when her parents moved to Diamond Springs that she didn't remember much of a difference. It had been a nice conversation, though, and it made the time go by more quickly while she waited for Cam.

"Busy morning?" she asked. "You weren't working out with your clients, were you?" Though, that would give her an advantage for sure.

Cam snickered as Felipe rubbed down his hair with the towel, and when he was freed again, his crooked grin was wide. "Great news! The AC broke at Riptide. You'd think with it being February, it wouldn't matter, but oh…it does. I've been trying to make it work all morning, but my clients are having a grand smelly time today."

Kailani raised an eyebrow. "You seem oddly happy about something important breaking."

"Oh, it totally sucks. I'm happy that I was finally able to get away and come here once Brad's people showed up. I haven't seen you since yesterday."

He couldn't possibly get more adorable than that, and Kailani squealed internally. "Thanks for the muffins. I feel terrible that I can't make you anything to return the favor."

"You made some great popcorn last night."

"It was the microwave kind."

"And it was delicious."

He must have meant that because he showed no signs of nausea. Kailani still wondered if that was a real thing, but she doubted he would throw up on command just to prove a point. Like at the race when they first met, when his lies had prevented them from kissing. She couldn't help but wonder if things might have been different if they'd had more time together at that race.

"Can I ask you a question?" Kailani said.

He seemed to light up like a road flare, his excitement palpable even with Felipe grumpily trying to tame his dark hair into something presentable. "Always."

She was taking a risk with asking this question, but Brad's words were still resonating inside her, as if he'd flipped a switch and turned off her perfectionism. The risk was bound to be worth it when Cam was on the other side. "Do you ever regret things going the way they have? With us, I mean."

Cam chewed on that question for a second, seeming to search her face for any sign of why she was asking something like that. "So far?" He shrugged. "Not really. It's been chaotic, yeah, but I don't have much to complain about. Not when it comes to you."

That was such a good answer that Kailani pressed her palms to her cheeks to cool them down. "You don't wish we would have gotten together sooner?" Though they hadn't spent too much time hating each other, what might have happened if they hadn't gone through the viral kiss and the fake part of their relationship before they got to the good stuff with Brad? Would they have ever made things real, or would their gyms have kept them apart?

Cam pressed his lips together, his expression a mix between disappointment and curiosity. "Would you have trusted me sooner?" he asked eventually.

Kailani's breath caught. Had he really known that she hadn't trusted that he would stick around? "Is this—"

"No. This is just a question."

She didn't have to answer if she didn't want to. She could even lie to him and tell him that she'd trusted him from the beginning. But how could she match his honesty with dishonesty? He deserved better than that. "Probably not," she said quietly. Feeling small.

Cam, however, smiled again and reached out for her hand. "Then no. I don't wish we would have gotten together sooner. I'm glad you're starting to trust me now."

His cinnamon eyes pierced hers with the intensity of someone who desperately wanted something. Kailani could only guess what that something was—could only hope—but she desperately wanted to give it to him. She wanted to give him everything, including her heart.

"I've done what I can," Felipe said with a resigned sigh. "Hopefully everyone will be focused elsewhere and not look at your disaster of a hairstyle today."

Cam raised an eyebrow at Kailani, who thought his hair looked pretty great, as always. He had such long, thick hair that curled around his ears and looked perfect for running fingers through. The mahogany brown matched his eyebrows, which pulled lower the longer he looked at her.

"Do you know something I don't?" he asked. "What's today's challenge?"

"I don't know," she replied honestly. "Brad said something about pull-up form, though."

That made him smirk and curl his free arm up as he stood, showing off his incredible bicep. "Pull-ups? I think I can handle that."

"I'm sure you can."

"Maybe I'll have to lose my tank for this one."

Kailani glanced at him from the side as they left the tent. Flashbacks of yesterday's breakfast flitted through her head, and she let out a little sigh. "Maybe not," she breathed.

Cam laughed. "Definitely doing that. As long as you don't…"

She was already pulling off her t-shirt, stretching her arms overhead and matching the smirk that had disappeared from his face. "Great idea, Nelli." She hoped she looked as good as she usually did, though she hadn't gotten in a good workout in more than a week outside of Brad's competitions.

Groaning, Cam stuffed his hands into the pockets of his shorts and took a wide step to the left, distancing himself from her. "I hate when you play dirty, Tease." Though he tried to hide it, he heaved a little and swallowed hard to keep from throwing up.

As they stepped into the tent where they would be filming, Kailani made a pact with herself. She was going to make it through today's challenges, and then she was going to tell Cam exactly how she felt. Terrifying as the admission would be, she was tired of looking for reasons to play it safe and not go all in.

TWENTY-THREE

CAM HAD ALWAYS THOUGHT HIMSELF fairly focused, but Kailani had pushed him to the limit and was testing every ounce of patience he had. Seeing so much skin up close had electrified his nervous system and sent his heart thundering, but that he could handle.

It was her strength that got him.

Brad's competition had turned into a true challenge, the pair of them so evenly matched that they were going to be there all day if they weren't careful. He and Kailani were hanging from a bar, their knees pulled up to a ninety-degree angle as they passed a ten-pound weight back and forth to each other's laps. While Cam had started at a disadvantage, heart racing and hands shaking as he tried to keep his eyes away from Kailani's strong and lean body, he'd pulled his shirt off just before the challenge began and enjoyed Kailani's wide eyes before hopping up onto the bar.

Now, however, they were arm to arm, both of them breathing heavily as they passed the weight back and forth. Cam's left arm was screaming at him along with his abdominals every time he had to use his right arm to move the weight. Kailani hadn't said anything since the start of the challenge, but sweat dripped down her temples as she gritted her teeth.

He'd never met anyone as strong as her. Not just in body but in determination. She hadn't let losses embarrass her, nor had she shied away from his flirting, and she met Cam's every challenge with her own grit and confidence.

He had already decided he would tell her outright how he felt about her tonight when they got home, but with every passing second on that bar, his patience was waning thinner.

It wasn't exactly romantic to declare one's love in the middle of a competition like this, especially not while being filmed, but maybe Kailani would understand. But... It would be a good idea to avoid that if he could, just in case she didn't appreciate the public declaration.

He wasn't sure he had that kind of patience, though.

"Getting tired yet?" he asked as he handed her the weight plate. He only sounded moderately breathless, which was nice.

Kailani laughed, returning the weight with ease. "Of course not. You?"

Unlike Cam, she sounded entirely unaffected, and that sent a shock of fear through him. Not that he really cared about the outcome anymore, but his pride still governed a good deal of his surface-level happiness.

"Oh, I'm having the time of my life right now," he said. It wasn't entirely a lie, considering any minute he got to spend with Kailani was a great minute. But he would probably need to be careful if he wanted his muscles to stay assigned to the current task rather than launching his protein muffin breakfast out of his stomach.

His left arm trembled a bit when he handed Kailani the weight this time. Hopefully it was only because of his half-truth and not because he was getting tired.

"This actually feels really good," Kailani said. Once she returned the weight, she let go of the bar with her right hand to shake it out a bit. "It's been too long since I did a good workout."

"I don't know about that," Cam said, glancing at her ridged abdomen and regretting it as soon as fire shot through his limbs. Hers was the most beautiful body he'd ever seen, every inch of it perfection. Just like the woman inside it.

"Are you going to give it back?" Kailani asked, nodding toward the weight. "Or are you ready to give up?"

"Do I look ready to give up?" The question was a nice way to dodge a potential lie. He could keep going, but he wasn't sure for how long. "Just making sure you get a break." He mostly said that to himself, though he would never admit that out loud.

"You know what sounds really great right now?" Kailani asked.

Cam handed her the weight. "A giant cheeseburger?"

"The hot tub I found on my balcony this morning."

Cam's left hand slipped, and he barely managed to hang on with his right before he readjusted his grips. "Oh?" He tried to force away mental images of being in that hot tub with Kailani in a bikini. He failed. "I…didn't know you had a balcony."

The little smirk Kailani gave him was enough to give him a heart spasm. He might never recover. "Doesn't that sound nice, Nelli?"

As he returned the weight again, Cam's voice came out in a growl. "Living up to your name, I see."

"Oh? How so?" Kailani's falsely innocent voice wasn't helping anything as she rested the weight on his knees. "Oh, do you mean talking about spending the evening with you in the hot tub? That's a tease?"

He couldn't do it anymore. With the combination of his angry core muscles and Kailani's far-from-subtle flirting, Cam's body gave out, and he landed on the mat below with a crash. The weight rolled from his lap right to where Brad was sitting in silent laughter, and Cam didn't move.

He had died. Most definitely. And he didn't even care.

"And it looks like we have our winner," Brad said after a long moment.

Kailani hadn't moved either, still hanging with her knees up and her eyes dancing. Eventually, though it took her way longer than Cam's ego would have liked, she slowly lowered her feet to the ground and then sat herself down next to him.

"Sorry," she said, sounding anything but. "But I figured since you like it when I play dirty..." She ran her fingers through his sweaty hair.

Cam groaned, loving and hating this moment. "You're going to be the death of me," he muttered, clenching his hands into fists before he did anything he might regret. No matter how much he wanted to kiss her, he'd promised he wouldn't do it in front of the cameras.

That had been the stupidest promise he'd ever made.

TWENTY-FOUR

AFTER BEATING CAM IN A dancing video game—at this point, she was starting to think Brad was going solely for entertainment—Kailani found herself lingering at the tent door instead of going home. Cam was deep in conversation with Brad, probably talking about the AC in Riptide, and Kailani didn't want to leave him behind. They would inevitably end up next door regardless of when she left the park, and Cam had promised to make her dinner, but she still waited.

She hated being apart from him.

She had to tell him. She had to tell him tonight how deeply she'd fallen, and she had to tell him why she'd been so closed off about her family. If she wanted things to work with Cam, she had to go all in.

As she stood there watching the way Brad seemed delighted by whatever Cam was saying to him, Kailani tried to keep her heart from racing, but she wasn't doing a particularly good job. There was still the chance, however small, that Cam would take her explanation and suddenly realize all of her fears were valid, and that would be the end. But she liked to think he was better than that, and he'd spent the last two days proving to her how much he cared about her.

As her phone buzzed in her hand, Kailani swallowed the fear that kept trying to rear its ugly head and thanked whoever texted her for the distraction.

Isla: When are you coming home?

Frowning, Kailani considered that question. Isla didn't usually care where she was, always so focused on her own thing.

Kailani: Hopefully soon, but I'm not sure.

That depended entirely on the conversation she wanted to have with Cam. They should probably have it somewhere private, like his apartment, and Kailani didn't want to get distracted by her sister before she could confess her feelings.

Isla: You should make it sooner than later.
Kailani: Why?
Isla: No reason.
Kailani: Why??

When Isla didn't answer, Kailani groaned and hit the dial button. Whatever Isla was cooking up, she had to make sure it didn't get in the way of her plans. Kailani was feeling brave, but that didn't mean she would feel that way for long.

When the phone connected, Kailani jumped right into her complaint. "Isla, you know I hate it when you—"

"Hey, Lani."

At the sound of a familiar male voice on the other end, Kailani dropped her phone. She barely managed to catch it, scrambling to bring it back up to her ear. "Chase?" she gasped, not sure if she was going crazy.

Her brother laughed, one of the most beautiful sounds in the world. "Glad to see you haven't forgotten me."

"But when did you—"

"This afternoon. I went to your apartment only to find it empty, and I figured you were working so I called Isla. You have some explaining to do, Lani." He whistled low.

She could imagine him walking around her fancy new apartment and taking it all in. Isla could have told him just about anything, and Kailani hurried out the tent door toward her car. She would text Cam and explain where she'd gone, and hopefully he would understand. She hadn't seen her brother in two years!

"I'm on my way back," she breathed, her heart racing with excitement. "Why didn't you tell me you were coming home this week?" She'd known it would be sometime early in the year, but that could have meant anything with Chase.

He laughed. "Because the surprise is so much more fun. I was going to jump out and scare you, but this place is so big you probably wouldn't find me for days. So, what's this Isla is saying about a boy toy?"

Kailani groaned as she fumbled to unlock her car door. "Don't listen to anything she's telling you. I'll explain everything when I get there. Be there soon."

She hung up so she could free both hands, finally managing to turn the key in the lock and open the door. But then, as she stuffed the key into the ignition and twisted, the car did absolutely nothing. The engine didn't even turn over. "No," she moaned, dropping her head onto the steering wheel. Of all the times for her car to die, it had to be now? "Come on!"

A knock on her window made her jump, and she pressed a hand to her pounding heart as she turned to find Cam standing there looking worried.

Kailani pushed the door open. "Hey."

"You okay? You ran out of there pretty quick."

She loved that he was so concerned, but his furrowed brow wouldn't start her car. "My car is dead," she said as tears pricked at her eyes.

Cam crouched down and took hold of her hand, his eyebrows pulling even lower. "What's really going on? Why are you...?" He brushed a tear from her cheek.

Oh, he thought she was sad. She was, but only because this stupid car was keeping her from seeing her brother.

"Chase is home. I didn't know he was coming home today, and I have to get home and see him, but my stupid car won't start and I haven't seen him in two years and I—"

"Hey." Cam stood and then pulled Kailani from the car, kissing her forehead before giving her his crooked smile. "I'll give you a ride. We're going to the same place anyway, and I'm sure Brad could have your car towed to a mechanic. Or, you know, you can just keep getting rides from me."

Kailani threw her arms around his neck, loving the way he held her back so tightly. If Chase weren't waiting for her back at her apartment, she would tell Cam everything right now and then kiss him until morning because he was the best thing she'd ever had in her life. But first things first.

"Thank you," she said into his neck.

"I'm here for you, Lani. No matter what."

She believed him.

They were halfway to the apartment building when Isla texted again, and Kailani stared at the message for a full block before she really comprehended it. That didn't mean she liked it. "Oh."

Cam glanced over. "What?"

"I guess they…" She swallowed. She'd been prepared to *tell* Cam why she had such a hard time with her family, not *show* him. "They're heading over to my parents' house."

The car swerved a little, though Cam cleared his throat and pretended he wasn't gripping the steering wheel extra tight. "Okay. Do you want me to drop you off, or…?"

She could hear the question he wasn't asking, but she didn't know how to answer it. Did she want him to meet her parents? The whole family? If she wanted this relationship to last, he would have to meet them eventually, but was she ready for the chance that he would see what everyone else did and give up on her? She had hoped to have a stronger relationship built up with him before she rocked the boat.

Cam grabbed her hand, glancing at her every few seconds as he drove. "This is up to you, Lani," he said eventually, "but it'll take more than your family to scare me off. They can't be that bad."

"That's not..." Her words stuck in her throat, but she forced them out anyway. "I'm not worried what you'll think of them. I'm worried what you'll think of *me*."

He frowned. "What does that mean?"

How could she explain? "Turn left here."

Cam took each of her directions in silence, as if he was unwilling to say anything else until she confided in him. But Kailani wasn't sure what to say. She had a lifetime of issues, and she couldn't exactly sum it all up in a few minutes. He already knew she was like a third parent, but it all went so much deeper than that. She was like a third parent who never got any recognition. Who was only missed when someone needed something from her. Who had never been enough for her parents.

When they finally pulled up outside her family home, Cam had gone tense, all of his muscles flexing as he held onto the steering wheel for dear life even though he'd turned the car off. Kailani couldn't let him keep making conjectures and thinking the worst, even if he was right.

"I wish I was better at this kind of thing," she said quietly, feeling his eyes on her but refusing to look up from her knees. "I've never been good at expressing emotion, you know? And my family... Chase and Isla are different. The three of us are older, and we had to raise each other when more kids started coming. I know *they* love me."

Cam dropped his hands from the steering wheel. "You don't think the rest of your family loves you?" he asked, his voice strained but quiet.

Kailani shrugged. "They need me. But that's not the same thing. Just...you'll see. My mom will make the same meatloaf dinner she makes every time I come over even though I hate it. The twins will attack me. My dad will only talk about surfing. It's always the same when I come over because they don't even know what to do with me."

Cam didn't say anything, but he didn't have to. He probably didn't know what to say, and that was fine. Kailani had come to terms with her family's opinion of her long ago, and she hoped she was smart enough to know her family's lack of love didn't mean it would be the same story for everyone else.

She hoped she wasn't wrong in thinking Cam might love her.

"You don't have to come in," she said, giving him one last chance to avoid this potential catastrophe.

But Cam clenched his jaw and shook his head, putting on a tense smile. "It's a good thing I've already taken the crash course on the Adams family, right? Just…maybe don't expect me to remember names. One of the kid judges kept my coloring page cheat sheet."

Kailani climbed out of the car before she could chicken out, Cam right behind her. "Deal. And we don't have to stay for long. Chase and Isla feel pretty similar to the way I do, so I doubt they'll want to stay long either."

Cam simply grunted and took her hand, his expression difficult to read as he gazed at the house ahead.

Kailani gritted her teeth and led the way. This was going to be an interesting evening, but as long as Cam stuck with her, everything would be okay. It had to be okay.

As she opened the door, Carter was the first to greet her as he played with a little train set in the front room. The little four-year-old looked up when he saw movement, his eyes lingering on Cam before he held up a small plastic tree that had broken in half. He didn't have to sign anything for Kailani to know he wanted her to fix it.

Sighing, she took the tree and signed that she would find some glue—she hoped she did, anyway—and then she continued deeper into the house to the kitchen and dining room. "Mom?"

Instead, she found Chase leaning against the counter talking to fourteen-year-old Bryce. Unable to stop the squeal that came out of her, she dropped Cam's hand and jumped into Chase's arms, wrapping her limbs around him like a monkey in a tree. "You're really here!"

He laughed. He'd gotten big over the last two years, losing the last of his baby fat and replacing it with a good deal of muscle. "What, did you think I would lie to you? How would I have had Isla's phone? Incoming!"

Hearing the approaching yells, Kailani barely managed to get back on her feet in time to brace herself for dual ten-year-old tackles. The twins—Kailani had never really been able to tell them apart until she got a good look at them—had already grown taller than the last time she'd seen them, and Chase had to grab her arm to keep her from crashing to the ground.

"Every time," she grumbled as the twins scurried back the way they'd come, like trying to take her out was a perfectly normal way to greet her.

Chase laughed again, shaking his head a little. "They didn't even look at me, if it makes you feel any better."

"They don't remember you," Bryce said, rolling his eyes before disappearing down the hall opposite where the twins had gone.

Frowning, Chase watched him go before meeting Kailani's eyes again. "Has he always been that moody?"

Kailani scoffed. "Uh, yeah. He stole a car last year." And she'd had to cancel a loan interview to watch the younger kids while her parents dealt with the court date from that whole thing.

"Wait, I thought that was Marcus," Chase said.

"Marcus is ten."

"Right. And what's this Isla was saying about her quitting school?"

Kailani shrugged. "You can't honestly expect me to understand why she does what she does, can you? She seems happy."

"So do you." And that was when Chase's eyes flicked to the hall leading to the front room, where Cam was standing with his hands in his pockets and looking inordinately uncomfortable. She hadn't exactly forgotten he was there, but…she'd forgotten he was there, and her stomach twisted as Chase stood a little straighter, taking him in. "So this is the stud muffin?"

Kailani cringed. "Please don't start using Isla's terms. They're horrendous. Chase, this is Cam. Cam, my brother Chase."

Cam finally stepped into the kitchen, and though Chase held out his hand, Cam kept his safely tucked away in his pockets. Kailani had forgotten about his aversion to handshakes until now, though she doubted Cam could do any harm in this circumstance. If anyone could withstand his grip, it was Chase, and hopefully Cam didn't have any reason to be nervous.

Ha! Kailani was terrified, so maybe Cam was just as anxious. He certainly stood tense, acknowledging Chase's hand with a nod. "It's nice to finally meet you," he said, his voice low and gruff.

Chase narrowed his eyes, apparently unsure of what to make of Cam. "So who are you, Cam?" he asked. "Can't say that Lani has mentioned you in any of her emails, and I know better than to trust Isla without some hesitation."

Kailani swallowed when Cam looked over at her. They'd never put an actual title to it, even though they'd decided to make this a real relationship. It felt like a lot to put a word to it after they'd spent so many days in the Breakout Brad bubble.

Cam cleared his throat, taking a step closer to her. "I'm her boyfriend," he said with enough confidence to make Kailani melt a little.

"What?" Mom's shout startled Kailani enough to make her flinch right into Cam. Mom appeared from the family room, her dark eyes wide. "Boyfriend? Since when?"

That was when the chaos began.

As Mom hurried forward to greet Cam, kids filed in after her, like they'd heard her shout and felt like they needed to be a part of the welcoming committee. They'd done the exact same thing with Kailani's last date she brought home, and flashbacks of his overwhelmed expression—terror, really—sent her heart pounding as she got lost in the shuffle, essentially pushed to the side so all attention could be placed on Cam.

She reminded herself that Cam had been around big families before, and he was still smiling as they swarmed him, though she could see the tension in his shoulders. At what point should she rescue him? At what point *could* she?

"He'll be fine," Chase said, twisting around a couple of kids to get to her.

Kailani wasn't so sure. "You weren't here for the last guy I brought home."

"Maybe not, but Isla told me all about it on the drive over here."

"Why?"

"Because she had a feeling you would be bringing your behemoth with you and probably start freaking out."

Kailani did not like the idea of Isla being able to predict her actions so easily, but it wasn't like she was wrong. She *had* brought Cam with her—against her will, but still—and she *was* freaking out.

"Where is Isla, anyway?" she asked, grimacing when the terror twins grabbed Cam's hands and dragged him toward the back door. "Wait."

Taking hold of her arm, Chase pulled her into the front room where Carter was still puttering around with his trains, oblivious to the commotion in the kitchen.

"Will you stop worrying?" he said, forcing her onto the couch and then sitting next to her. "If you like this guy as much as Isla says, he's going to have to go through the hazing at some point or another. She's out in the garage with Dad, by the way."

Kailani pulled her eyebrows low. "She hates it out there. She thinks it smells like old oil and sadness."

Chase laughed. "That's because it does. Dad keeps working on that motorcycle thinking he'll get it to run one day, and he keeps being disappointed. Even I know that, and I haven't been here in two years. You know he's never going to change."

Settling a little heavier into the couch, Kailani tried to force herself to relax. The goal tonight was to lay herself bare and let Cam really see her, and she couldn't do that if she kept fighting the emotions that came up every time she came home. She needed to at least acknowledge what she was feeling. "Remember how we used to spend hours out there pretending to help while we watched surfing videos?"

Chase chuckled. "I *was* helping. *You* were the one watching the surf comps." He ran a hand through his hair, which was so much shorter than she'd ever seen it. Now that she was really getting a chance to look at him, he looked so much different from the twenty-year-old she'd said goodbye to two years ago. Everything about him was sharper and harder, and his smile wasn't as carefree. He may have only been twenty-two, but he looked older.

At the same time, he looked far more at home here than he ever had, which didn't make any sense. When they were younger, he'd done everything in his power to avoid being at home. Sometimes Kailani had wondered if that was why he signed up for the Marines in the first place. But he actually looked *happy* to be home.

Running his hand through his hair again, Chase looked around the little living room as if seeing it for the first time, and then his gaze landed on Carter, who hadn't even noticed them because he was so fixated on his train. "I don't even know him," he said with a frown. "How weird is that? I've only seen pictures."

Kailani hadn't realized. "I forgot they adopted him after you left."

Chase nodded, now staring at the hallway where plenty of noise was still echoing from the kitchen. Mom had probably started making dinner, and the teens were begrudgingly helping. Kailani would have been so happy to be in their position, but Mom had never wanted her in the kitchen.

"It feels so different," Chase said, shaking his head. "But also the same. It's like I'm seeing everything as an outsider now that I've been away for a while, and I'm realizing…"

Kailani tensed. "What?"

He let out a little laugh. "I'm realizing we were so wrong."

"Wrong about what?"

Before Chase could say anything, thirteen-year-old Felicia burst into the room, her eyes wide. "Lani, Mom's doing that thing again, and Baxter's throwing dirt at Sylvia, and Bryce won't help me with my homework because he says—"

"Okay," Kailani said, reluctantly getting to her feet. *This* was why she didn't like coming home. Everything always descended into chaos whenever she was here, and poor Cam was going to regret agreeing to come with her. Wherever he was…

"I'll get Baxter," Chase said. "And I can talk to Bryce. You take care of Mom."

Kailani blinked back tears. "Thanks," she choked, feeling like she'd been so vulnerable over this week that she wasn't sure if she would be able to control her emotions like she used to.

Chase gave her a little smile. "You're not alone, Lani. And you never have been."

When Kailani made it to the kitchen, she found her mom stirring a pitcher of punch with enough vigor to send it swirling over the sides if she kept going much longer. "Mom," she said gently, putting her hand on her arm. "Mom, it's all mixed up."

Mom blinked, thankfully letting go of the wooden spoon and watching it spin in the purple liquid for a second. "We need rolls with the meatloaf," she said eventually, scurrying over to the pantry and digging through the cluttered shelves. "I swear I had some green beans in here somewhere. We should have green beans. And there's no time to make rolls! I should have made rolls. Why didn't I make rolls?"

"Mom!"

She finally looked over at Kailani as her panic attack reached its peak, sending her sinking to the floor in a heap. "Rolls," she gasped.

Kailani crouched in front of her, taking hold of her hands. At least this seemed like a small one, already calming. "Just breathe, okay? Everything's okay. We don't need rolls." She really hoped she was right about everything being okay, but the night was far from over.

TWENTY-FIVE

CAM LIKED TO THINK HE was rather good at handling chaos. Gyms were often pretty chaotic, everyone doing something different, and when the Wonder Boys all got together, things could easily get pretty crazy. Then there were all the sports he'd done in school, juggling his job and homework, all of the fights and brawls he'd been in when he was younger.

The Adams family was something different.

By the time he'd managed to get away from the twins, who had decided he was a football player and wanted him to play with them out in the yard, he'd lost track of Kailani. Instead of wandering the house to find her, he agreed to help a teenage girl with her math after helping Chase break up a dirt fight in which the girl was completely trouncing her brother.

When he realized the trigonometry homework was beyond his skill set and he was getting as frustrated as Felicia, he was more than glad to see Isla come into the family room followed by a graying man who had to be Kailani's dad—he looked like the iconic blond California surfer gone to seed. Well, Cam was as glad as he could be knowing he was about to meet the father of the woman he loved. The woman who was who knew where.

"Dad, this is Kailani's manfriend, Cam," Isla said with a wide smile.

"Sean," her dad said, holding out his hand.

Cam grimaced, wishing he was brave enough to try a handshake again. But he wasn't. So, even though it made him look incredibly rude, Cam settled for a nod like he'd done with Chase. This would be a lot less terrifying if he'd done this "meet the parent" thing before, but he'd never let himself fall in love before. This was entirely unfamiliar territory. "It's good to meet you, sir."

Sean cocked his head to one side as he studied him. "You ever been surfing, Cam?"

"Uh, no, sir." He'd never even seen the ocean, though he wasn't interested in saying that part out loud when Sean was clearly still holding on to the old days. Kailani had been right about that part, at least. And the twins attacking her. He couldn't verify the dinner part, but he had yet to see any evidence of her claim that her family didn't love her.

He still hadn't recovered from that admission. If that was the reason she had been so hesitant to let him in, a lot of things were starting to make sense about her. He hated that she felt that way, but from what he'd seen so far, Kailani was pretty far off the mark. He just hoped he would be able to help her see it.

"Lani loves surfing," Sean said with a content smile. "We used to spend hours out on the waves together. I could never get Chase to get into it, and Isla here was too little."

"And I hate the ocean anyway," Isla said with a shrug. "It's so overrated." She flashed a wide smile that made Cam inordinately nervous. "So, Bigfoot, what's the deal with your hot friend?"

Cam felt as confused as Sean looked. "Are you talking about Kit?"

If Isla had been a cartoon, her eyes would have turned to hearts. "Mm, yes. He's single, right?"

"Only because—"

"You're not old enough to be talking about boys," Sean complained, and Cam was glad for the interruption. Yes, Kit was single, and Cam had been about to say why.

Isla scoffed. "I'm almost twenty-one."

"No, there's no way you're that old!"

Cam honestly couldn't tell if Sean was seriously confused or just really bad at telling dad jokes. And from the looks of things, Isla couldn't either, though she didn't seem surprised by the argument as she rolled her eyes and reached forward, grabbing Cam's hand.

"Come on," she said as they walked. "Dinner's probably ready. Mom likely made meatloaf even though Kailani stopped liking it when she was fifteen."

To Cam's relief, Kailani was in the kitchen, already cutting up meatloaf for the younger kids. He took his first full breath in a while as soon as he saw her, relaxing a bit even as the twins begged him to sit next to them.

"As long as I also get to sit next to your sister," he told them, which they didn't seem to understand until Kailani slipped onto the bench next to him and took his hand.

"I'm so sorry," she whispered, enough fear in her eyes to tell him that she was waiting for him to run away.

Despite the loud and large audience, Cam touched his forehead to hers. "It'll take more than that to scare me," he whispered, amazed when his stomach didn't twitch even a little bit.

Dinner passed in a whirlwind, the whole family shooting so many random questions toward Cam that he barely had a chance to eat. "What's your favorite color? Where did you go to college? Are you really a football player? Do you like turtles?" When he did manage to get a bite in, he couldn't figure out why Kailani wouldn't like her mom's meatloaf when it was absolutely delicious.

"This is the best meatloaf I've ever had," he told Kailani's mom—U'ilani—when there was a break between questions.

Her eyes went wide. "Oh?" she asked breathlessly. She'd barely touched her food, and when she fidgeted with the flower she wore in her hair—deep brown hair that matched Kailani's, only longer—her fingers trembled. "Th-thank you." Then she shook her head minutely at Sean, who watched her with concern.

Cam was concerned too. He could recognize anxiety when he saw it, and he knew he was at least partially to blame for her nerves. Now he also knew why Kailani had recognized his own anxiety at the smoothie shop. "I'm sorry to have shown up unannounced, Mrs. Adams. I hope I didn't cause any extra stress."

U'ilani waved her hand. "Oh, no, not at all! We're so glad to have you. How did you meet Lani? Do you know her through her gym?"

Cam felt Kailani tense, and though he had a million questions for her, mostly about why she apparently hadn't told her parents about the TV show, he tried to stay focused on what he said so he didn't say anything she didn't want him to.

"We met at a race about a month ago," he said, and when his stomach twisted a little, he held back a groan. That hadn't been a lie, though his stomach apparently thought so. "Well, technically we first met at the climbing gym back in October, but I was…" Nope. No need to tell them how much of an idiot he'd been. "We mostly connected at the race."

"How sweet."

"He's never been surfing," Sean said, as if he couldn't imagine anything worse.

U'ilani, however, smiled. "Well, we won't hold that against him. And what about your parents? Are they here in town?"

As Kailani grabbed his forearm and squeezed, Cam waited for the familiar anxiety to tighten his chest. Usually, when someone caught him off guard when it came to his parents, he started thinking about a future with no one left. His vision would tunnel, his breathing would grow shallow, some-times a full anxiety attack taking form if he wasn't feeling steady that day.

But sitting there in the packed Adams dining room full of children who had found a home despite unfathomable loss, with Kailani by his side, Cam found himself smiling. "I lost them a long time ago," he said. "But I've got family in Diamond Springs. In a manner of speaking."

U'ilani reached across the table to pat his hand. "I'm so sorry for your loss, but I'm glad you're not alone."

As if they were pulled together, he looked at Kailani right as she looked at him, his heart beating a little faster as he took in her expression. They hadn't said any specific words about it yet, but the look in her eyes told him she felt the same way he did. That, or he had crossed so far into hopeful that now he was deluding himself into thinking a future with this girl was not only possible but guaranteed.

Cam shifted his hand so it wrapped around Kailani's, hoping she understood what he was trying to tell her with his eyes. He would say it out loud as soon as they were alone, but for now…

"Well!" U'ilani said loudly, breaking Cam's concentration. "I think we need cookies. Who wants to help?"

The younger kids' hands flew into the air with excitement, and Kailani deflated in her seat. If Cam had to guess, she'd never had the chance to make cookies with her mom, just like she hadn't learned to cook. Another piece to the puzzle.

"Bryce, Felicia, you're on dish duty," Sean said before the teens could disappear. "Lani, could you—"

"Yeah," Kailani said with a sigh. Giving Cam's hand one last squeeze, she followed her siblings into the kitchen.

Cam would have gone to help her if Chase and Isla didn't slide in on either side of him and begin a conversation around him. Why they felt the need to do that, he had no idea, but it left him stuck to watch the chaos of the kitchen that seemed to temper every time Kailani opened her mouth, whether it was to direct the dish washing or explain a measurement to one of the younger kids. Cam was pretty sure those kids would do anything Kailani said, and her mom relaxed more with every directive as things calmed.

After several minutes of arguing with Isla about Diamond Springs versus Hawaii, Chase cleared his throat. "Hey, Cam, would you mind helping me bring my stuff in from Isla's car?"

Cam wasn't all that inclined to leave Kailani at the moment, with the way tension was building in her shoulders as her siblings kept asking her for things, but he could recognize the look in Chase's eyes. It was the same look Kit had whenever he had some sort of plan to help one of the Wonder Boys with something they didn't want to admit they needed help with.

"Sure," he said, following Chase out the front door.

Surprisingly, Chase actually did have a couple of bags in the trunk of the car in the driveway, though he could have easily carried them in himself. He handed the duffel bag to Cam, swinging the camouflage rucksack over his shoulder, and then he turned to face Cam.

"What has she told you?" he asked, his gaze focused.

Cam tried not to feel intimidated by the staredown, something he'd never had to *try* before. But Chase had the Marine intensity locked in, and for the first time in his life Cam's instinct was to back down instead of rising up to meet the challenge. That usually had to be a conscious choice, but tonight he put his hands into his pockets and ducked his head to keep himself calm.

"She hasn't told me much," he admitted. "Tonight was the first time she said anything about her family not…"

"Not loving her," Chase finished for him. "Yeah, I usually keep that part to myself too, so I can't say that I blame her."

But that made it sound like Kailani's belief was true. Cam furrowed his brow. "Do they really not—"

"They do." Chase shrugged his free shoulder. "They just don't know how to show it. It took me a while to figure that part out. Growing up, Lani, Isla, and I were kind of on our own. Lani more than anyone, being the oldest. Our mom gets overwhelmed pretty easily, though you'll never see her admit it, and Lani stepped up. She filled in all the gaps while our parents tried to figure out this adopting a million kids thing. She's…"

Chase cupped his hands together, blowing into them to warm them up as they stood there in the dim light of the front porch. "We all felt a little neglected at times, but Kailani has always thought if she could do just enough, be a little bit more, she would be able to find that appreciation she hasn't really gotten over the years. It wasn't until I spent some time on the base that I realized my home life was actually pretty great, even if it didn't look how I thought it was supposed to look. You know?"

Cam nodded, though his thoughts were swirling as he tried to fit everything together and make sense of it all. All throughout dinner, while he was answering question after question, Kailani had sat in silence. But the younger kids had gone to her to cut more little pieces of meatloaf. To blow on their food when it was too hot. The twins had been the first to greet her, even if their greeting was a little rough, and they'd had huge smiles on their faces the moment they saw her.

"She's looking at everything through the wrong lens," Cam muttered, mostly to himself.

But Chase nodded. "I think Isla has figured it out by this point too—she's way smarter than us—but she never really cared for their approval to begin with. It meant she could sympathize with Kailani without feeling the same hurt. And the way my mom cried when I showed up, I know she missed me. Even if she kept cleaning the playroom instead of catching up. I used to think that meant she didn't care, but now I know she's just overwhelmed. But Lani? She's never had a chance to really take a step back and see the way Mom relaxes every time she comes home. She thinks Dad is stuck in the glory days of his past surfing life when I really think he just misses all the time he used to spend with Lani. She's their only kid by blood, and I think the older she gets, the more desperate they are to hang on to her. They just don't know how to tell her that."

"Why are you telling me this?" Cam asked. It wasn't that he didn't want to know, but this was the kind of thing he'd hoped *Kailani* would tell him. Not her brother.

Pursing his lips, Chase seemed to debate his answer for a moment. "Because I've known Kailani my entire life, and I know she wouldn't have brought you here if she didn't trust you. And I want to see her happy, but she'll never get there on her own. If you're the person who's going to make her happy, I figure you could use all the help you can get. Just don't give up on her, okay?"

"I don't plan to."

"Good. Because if you hurt her, I'll have to hunt you down. You may be a giant, but you don't scare me."

Cam chuckled. "I'm scared enough of your sister. You don't have anything to worry about."

That made Chase laugh, and the two of them headed back into the house that had grown quieter in the few minutes they'd been outside.

Though he knew the night was far from over, Cam still felt more optimistic than he'd ever allowed himself as he followed Chase down the hall to the bedrooms. He still had the same fears running through him, but they were muted. White noise in the background that he could easily ignore if he kept focusing on the hope that glowed so much brighter.

Before he reached the end of the hall where Chase had disappeared, a familiar voice pulled Cam's attention to a room on the left. He paused, not sure if he really wanted to be nosy, but how was he supposed to resist Kailani reading a bedtime story to a couple of first graders?

Tucked in the corner of a little bed, Kailani held Baxter and Sylvia in either arm, a book stretched out between them. Kailani was reading the story with different voices for each character, and the two kids were eating it up. They were barely paying attention to the actual book because they kept looking up at Kailani, wide smiles on their faces.

Cam had never been brave enough to dream about a future that included something like kids, but the longer he watched Kailani talk of dragons and princess knights, the more easily he could picture it. The more he desperately wanted it. The more convinced he was that he would never love anything as much as he loved her.

A hand landed on his shoulder, and Cam was so dreamily relaxed from watching the bedtime story unfold that he didn't even flinch from the unexpected touch. He simply looked back at Chase, who grabbed his duffel off his shoulder with a smile.

"See what I mean?" Chase nodded toward the kids. "She can't see their faces like we can. Sylvia and Bax are shy and almost never ask for things, so Mom always asks Lani to read to them when she's here because they love it. Lani has complained in her emails about Mom passing off bedtime duty, but she has no idea what she means to these kids."

Did she know what she meant to Cam? Because he was ready to throw all caution to the wind and offer up his heart on a silver platter. She could do whatever she wanted with it, and as long as she was happy, he'd be okay.

"You sure you guys only started dating a couple of weeks ago?" Chase asked with a chuckle. "Because you're not looking at her like this is a new thing."

"I know it's crazy," Cam agreed.

"I didn't say that. Hey, Lani?"

Kailani looked up, turning red at the sight of them both standing in the doorway. "Yeah?"

Chase clapped Cam on the shoulder again. "Good luck tomorrow with the whole show thing. Isla and I will be in the audience hoping you faceplant."

She scowled and probably would have looked pretty intimidating if she wasn't cuddling a couple of kids. "I don't care if you've done a few pushups, Chase Mitchell Adams. I can still..." She paused, glancing down at the kids. "You don't need me to finish that sentence, right?"

Chase laughed as he headed down the hall. "Nope. Good luck with this one, Cam. You're gonna need it."

That was probably true. "Speaking of the show," Cam said, pulling out his phone to check the time. "We should probably go. I know we don't have any more challenges, but we should get as much sleep as we can."

"You hear that?" Kailani said to the kids. "We all need to go to bed!"

Though both kids complained, Baxter slid off the bed and grumbled the whole way to the bed on the other side. Kailani tucked Sylvia into her covers, doing the same thing with Baxter, and then she slid into Cam's waiting arms after closing the door on her way out.

Cam gladly pulled her in close, tucking his chin over her head. "And here I was thinking you couldn't get more attractive," he murmured into her hair.

"Funny. I was about to say the same thing about you."

"Ready to go home?" There was that word again. The one he had never really thought had anything special attached to it. Not until he met Kailani.

She breathed in deeply, her arms tight around him, before she said, "Yes," and pulled away. She seemed to relax when she gazed up at him, a little smile sprouting on her face. It was like she could breathe again now that she was in his arms, and Cam loved that he did that for her. He loved less how tense this house made her to begin with. Chase was right, and she needed someone to show her what she wasn't seeing.

Hopefully she trusted Cam enough by now to let that someone be him.

Taking his hand, Kailani led Cam back through the house and to the kitchen, where her mom was rolling cookies with Isla while her dad squinted at something on his phone, the light reflecting off his reading glasses.

"These look really…fashionable," Sean muttered as he scrolled.

Isla laughed, placing cookies on a baking sheet. "I don't expect you to like them. I just wanted you to see what I've been working on even without school."

"I still think it would have made sense for you to keep learning," he replied with a little shake of his head. "But you know best, I suppose."

"She'll do great things on her own," Kailani threw in, making everyone look up. "Isla has always learned best by doing, anyway."

As Isla beamed from the kitchen, U'ilani's eyes slipped down to Cam and Kailani's hands clasped together. She smiled, but her eyes also filled with tears that she brushed away with the back of her floury hand. "It was so nice to meet you, Cam," she said with a wavering voice. "You're welcome to come back anytime."

He planned to, if Kailani let him. "Thank you for letting me crash your dinner. It was delicious. I should probably be getting Lani home; we've got an early morning tomorrow."

"But the cookies aren't—"

"We need to go, Mom," Kailani said. She slipped from Cam's hand to give her mom a quick hug, patting her dad's shoulder on her way back to Cam's side. "I'll get some cookies next time."

U'ilani wilted, nodding as she looked down at the cookies she had probably been making specifically for Kailani because they were in the shape of a barbell. "Okay. Well, don't work yourself too hard. I know that gym is keeping you busy, and it's always so nice to have you around more. Are you sure you don't want to wait for cookies? You love these."

Though Kailani smiled, it was a tight sort of smile, like she was holding back frustration at the same time. Cam didn't know how he was going to convince her she was entirely wrong about her family, but he had to try. Her mom clearly missed her, and not just because she was helpful.

"Bye, Mom. Dad. I'll see you at home, Isla." She pulled Cam out to the car without a word and slipped into her seat as soon as he unlocked the door.

Cam paused for a second before opening his own door, looking back at the house.

He still didn't know what he could say to her, and he wished he hadn't spent his whole life running away from deeper, lasting connections. He didn't know how to translate everything he'd seen and felt tonight into words. Maybe if he hadn't been so broken inside, he would know how to help her.

But he didn't know, and if she was so convinced her family didn't love her when they so obviously did, what did that mean for him? Was she questioning *his* feelings as well?

Just as he was about to slip into the car, the front door opened and U'ilani poked her head out. "Cam?"

"Yeah?"

"Thank you."

His heart, which was already straining thanks to his doubts, picked up speed, partially because he didn't like having a conversation without Kailani being a part of it when it most likely involved her. But a quick glance into the car told him she'd closed her eyes and was waiting with folded arms. She probably thought he was stalling, delaying the inevitable conversation about her "unloving" family because she was smart enough to know he wasn't going to drop the subject.

Swallowing, Cam met U'ilani's gaze again. "For what?"

"Giving her a reason to smile. Isla showed us some of that show you're taping—not a lot of it, just some clips and pictures—and I haven't seen her that happy since..." She folded her arms around herself. "I don't even remember. So, thank you."

Cam didn't know what to say, something he truly hated, so he nodded and slipped into his seat.

Kailani didn't even open her eyes. "Did you get lost out there?" she asked, clearly trying to sound light-hearted but without a lot of success.

"I'm never lost when I'm with you," he replied. "I was just...thinking." Thinking of how he could convince Kailani she was wrong. He *needed* to convince her; otherwise, he would forever worry she didn't believe his love any more than she believed that of her parents.

By the time Cam pulled into the parking garage of their building, the tension had been expanding for several minutes, making the air around them thick with unspoken thoughts. He turned the car off, leaving them in an even deeper silence that was making him fidgety.

When Kailani finally spoke, he was all too ready to give his growing energy somewhere to go. "Now do you see?" she said, her voice small. "Every time I go home, everyone always needs something from me, and it's like they only see what I can do for them. But it's never enough."

"You're wrong." Cam's voice croaked out of his throat, and he gripped the steering wheel a little tighter. "I didn't see a family who doesn't love you. I saw a family who completely adores you and desperately wants you around."

"Because they *need* me."

"*Yes*. That's the point. Families need each other." He turned to her, feeling like he was starting to lose control but with no way to rein himself in because everything was bubbling to the surface all at once. He was used to letting himself feel whatever came at him, but he'd never had to deal with so many different emotions at once. He had no idea what to do with them all.

"Do you have any idea how lucky you are?" he asked. "I would have been thrilled to have siblings so excited to see me that they tackled me. To have a mother who made my favorite…" The words caught in his throat, and he swallowed, shaking his head. This was not the time to start panicking. Not when he was already making a mess of this whole conversation. *Stop thinking about your lack of family.*

"I'm not trying to invalidate what you're feeling," he said as he tried to keep breathing normally. "I'm just saying you might be seeing everything from the wrong angle."

Kailani shifted in her seat so she was facing him. "What is that supposed to mean?"

"It means…" But he had to stop as his heart raced even faster. Why? Why was his anxiety choosing *now* to remind him of the fears he'd been trying so hard to get rid of? After everything he'd experienced the last few weeks, he couldn't seriously still think everyone was going to leave him. The Wonder Boys disproved that. But that didn't stop him from panicking as he fought to keep talking. "I'm just trying to say…"

He was trying to say he didn't want her to end up like him, so scared of losing love that he had never let himself have it in the first place, but the words weren't coming. As his emotion kept building, he stumbled out of the car to try to get a deep breath in before he hyperventilated.

This anxiety hadn't been the plan, and it was going to mess everything up. He needed to keep going while he still could.

As soon as Kailani was out of the car, he kept talking, leaning his elbows on the roof and stuffing his hands into his hair. "Your mom clearly spends all her energy on her children, and the way she lit up when she saw you tonight… It was like she was so glad to have all her family back together again. She was terrified to meet me as soon as she realized who I was but did her best to make a good impression because she could see I'm important to you. And your dad. He probably misses surfing with you and brings it up because it was something the two of you shared. Felicia talked nonstop about how you used to help her with her homework, and it was obvious how much she treasured that one-on-one time with you because she kept talking about how P.E. is her favorite class and she wants to play volleyball. Baxter and Sylv…"

He shut his eyes, his heart beating way too fast and making him dizzy. He had to help her understand that her pain didn't have to exist before she let it talk her out of believing his love too, but there was too much happening inside him. This felt different. It didn't feel like his usual fears. This was something new. "They looked…looked at you like you were the moon and…stars." He needed to sit down. Take a deep breath. *Something*.

"Cam?" She hurried to his side and put her hands on his face. "Hey, it's okay. You're okay."

He shook his head, tears pricking his eyes. He wouldn't be okay until *she* was okay. That's what he was afraid of. That she wouldn't make it through this and be happy. Maybe if she understood all the thoughts and feelings rushing through him she would better understand what he was trying to say. "Everyone I've ever known has left me," he said, his voice raw. "My mom, my dad, my aunt. Every friend I had as a kid either died or went to jail. Teachers retired. Bosses moved on. Girlfriends left. Hell, even the stray cat I liked got hit by a car."

"Why are you telling—"

"You think your family doesn't love you," he said, hating how blunt that sounded. But how else could he put it? "I've been too scared to let myself love before now because almost everyone I've loved has left me behind. So I get it. Being scared sucks. But you can't let that fear keep you from being happy. Does the way you feel about your family mean you think I don't love you either?"

Only when Kailani's eyes went wide did he realize what he'd just said.

Running his hands through his hair, Cam shook his head. "That wasn't what I... I didn't mean to say—" He heaved, throwing himself to the side so he didn't throw up on Kailani's feet. Well, that was going to complicate things. Now she was going to think...

As he straightened up, Cam forced in a deep breath. Thankfully, the vomiting seemed to have broken him out of his panic, though his lungs were still working extra hard to keep him from passing out. Biting his lip and wishing he had some water, he turned to Kailani and waited for her to accuse him of lying to get her to believe him.

Instead, she seemed to be fighting a smile as she said, "You love me, Martinez?" Before he could say anything, she added, "Maybe take your time with this one. There's a whole lot going on in there right now." She waved her hand over his body, raising one eyebrow.

Leaning against the car, Cam smiled a little as he shook his head. "I planned for that admission to be a little more romantic. And not in the middle of...whatever that was."

Kailani approached cautiously, like she was worried he might slip back into the anxiety if she moved too quickly. "Why were you panicking?"

He shook his head, not even completely sure of the real reason. He didn't know what he could say that wouldn't lead to more intestinal distress. "You have no idea what you've done to me," he said in a whisper.

"Clearly a lot of damage," she replied, her smile growing.

Cam let out a little laugh. "Damage in a good way. You've broken through every barrier I have, Tease. You've left me defenseless."

When he reached out to her, she took his hand and let him pull her against him. "You're making me sound like a barbarian," she muttered into his chest. Then her arms tightened around his torso as she burrowed deeper into his hold. "I do believe you, you know."

His heart skipped a beat, but he couldn't get his hopes up too high until he knew for sure. "About which part?"

She took a long time to answer, which didn't bode well. "I believe you when you say you love me."

"Is that all you believe?" He held his breath.

"I… I trust you, Cam."

"But?"

She sighed. "But it's not exactly easy to ignore years of feeling otherwise. Maybe you're right about my family. Maybe you're not. Maybe…"

At some point he was going to need to breathe again, but he couldn't do it. Not yet. It felt like she was on the verge of something, and as someone who had a tendency to forget his own strength and push too hard, he refused to knock her down when she was so close—hopefully—to finding some peace with her family.

"I need some time," Kailani said, and when she pulled away, he nearly fell apart until he saw her warm smile. "Not time away from you—I'll never want that. But time to process what you said. To process how different Chase and Isla were tonight."

"So, you don't want to leave me?" Those words left his mouth before he could stop them, and he clenched his jaw, feeling pathetic. But the question was out there, and he'd never wanted an answer more than he did now.

Lifting her hand to his jaw, her soft touch making him relax, Kailani studied his face for a long moment before she spoke. "I'm not going anywhere. I'm in love with you, Cameron Martinez."

As those words washed over him, Cam felt like his heart was beating properly for the first time. It wasn't like she was the first woman to say those words to him, but... It was the first time he'd ever believed it. The first time he'd ever felt those words pierce his heart with life-giving hope.

Or maybe he felt himself coming to life because it was the first time in sixteen years that the sound of his full name hadn't made him mentally wince with pain. He'd actually *liked* the sound of his name, like he had never really heard it before he heard it on her lips.

"You are?" he whispered, staring into her warm brown eyes. He didn't exactly need clarification, but he hadn't expected her to say that now, standing in a dim parking garage next to his partially digested dinner. Cam glanced at said dinner, wrinkling his nose. "Did you just tell me you were in love with me next to a pile of—"

"Gross. But yes? You did it first."

He cringed. "I said it before that happened. I meant it, though. Regardless of what came after."

Laughing, she took his hand and pulled him toward the elevator. "So did I."

They were both quiet until they reached their apartments, each of them standing at their doors as if neither was ready to let the night end. Cam certainly wasn't, and the only reason he wasn't kissing Kailani was because he badly needed to rinse out his mouth and brush his teeth. And maybe look into seeing a doctor about his lying mechanism. His ridiculous reaction to lying couldn't have been normal.

"So," Kailani said, fiddling with her door handle. "Tomorrow's the big day."

"When we find out who won the competition," Cam finished. "I'm trying not to think about it."

"Me too. Except I can't stop thinking about how we're perfectly tied."

"I know." Cam was fairly sure Brad had done that on purpose, though it was hard to believe he could know who would win each competition. It seemed Brad did a lot of things that didn't make sense, like he was some neon-clad fairy godmother who had come out of nowhere to make all their dreams come true.

"You're going to win," Cam said, shaking away the image of Brad in a sparkly dress.

Kailani frowned. "You're *definitely* going to win."

"*When* you win," Cam argued, "I'll be right behind you. No matter what happens to me."

"Horizon will be just fine where and how it is while you're off building a place for all kinds of people." She narrowed her eyes, and her voice had gone sharper with her growing stubbornness.

He growled a little. They were going to be standing there arguing all night if they didn't stop now. "You are infuriating, Tease."

"You drive me crazy, Nelli." Then she smiled. "I love you."

"I love you too." Before he gave in and gave her the nastiest kiss a person could ever get, Cam punched in his lock code and slipped inside his apartment, shutting the door behind him a little more forcefully than necessary.

And as he slowly made his way back to his bedroom to try to get some sleep, Cam knew they had crossed a threshold and could never go back. He wasn't a praying man in general, but as he slipped off to sleep, he sent a thousand prayers to every deity in the world that Kailani would have the strength to see her family's love as well as his.

It was a good thing she was the strongest person he'd ever met.

TWENTY-SIX

By some miracle, Kailani managed to sleep for a couple of hours. She spent the rest of the night staring at the vaulted ceiling, thinking about Cam and the things he'd said to her in the parking garage. Mostly about Cam. And about the fact that he told her he loved her, and she didn't even give him a hug goodnight.

What was *wrong* with her?

At least she'd finally admitted how she felt about him in return, and it felt so good to have that out in the open now.

But the rest of the stuff from last night made the good parts feel less good. Like this big step in their relationship was tainted by the fact that Kailani couldn't easily accept the fact that Cam might be right about her family. Isla and Chase? She knew they loved her because they told her all the time. The three of them had shared the same feelings of inadequacy and unimportance.

But last night, Isla told Mom and Dad she quit school, and Dad still supported her even if he didn't understand it. Chase willingly chose to stay at home instead of crashing with a friend or even at Kailani's giant new apartment. Kailani sat dumbstruck next to Cam as he outlined things she'd never considered before.

After that whole conversation, which had her reeling, she checked her phone and found several texts from Chase and Isla.

> Chase: Don't be mad at me.
> Chase: I told Cam that we've been wrong about Mom and Dad.
> Isla: I know what you're thinking and no they didn't ask me about school. I chose to tell them. Seeing you so happy made me realize I didn't want to live with a cloud over my head and now I want to read into love languages after talking to Chase.
> Chase: By the way I've never gotten the chance to play the protective brother before and it was kind of fun. Too bad your boyfriend wasn't actually scared of me.
> Chase: I think Cam is really good for you Lani.
> Isla: I know tomorrow is going to be crazy but make sure you show that hunky stud of yours that you are glad he made it through the Adams crazy without flinching. I wasn't sure if that was possible.
> Chase: We'll be at the taping early in case you need to talk.
> Isla: I maybe told Mom and Dad about the show. Sorry not sorry.

When morning came around, Kailani wasn't sure if she wanted to talk to her siblings or if she wanted to hide in a supply tent somewhere until the last possible minute. She couldn't avoid Cam, since her car was still at the park so she needed a ride, but when she met him in the hallway between their doors, she didn't know what to say to him.

Apparently he was just as tongue-tied as her because he didn't say a word, gesturing with his head toward the elevator.

By the time they finished up with the stylists in the makeup tent, the silence was killing her, and she breathed a sigh of relief when Chase and Isla stepped inside. She still had a few minutes before call time, so she grabbed a jacket, mumbled something about going for a quick walk, and then headed out into the brisk morning air.

"That looked nice and awkward," Isla said before she'd even fully left the tent. "What in the world happened last night between you two?"

Chase snickered. "Did you two—"

Kailani elbowed him in the gut, glad to see she could still take him on even though he'd gotten bigger.

"You don't even know what I was going to say," he wheezed, though his smile said it all.

"Don't be gross," Isla said, smacking his arm for good measure. "Did you guys at least talk?"

Kailani picked up her pace, just in case someone was following her around with a camera. She'd been so glad Brad had never tried to film anything with her family, but she doubted she would get lucky here at the park full of film crews. "We talked," she said once she was sure there was no one within audio distance.

"About what?" Chase asked.

Reaching the final trailer that surrounded Brad's entourage, Kailani stopped moving, grabbing her ankle behind her and stretching her quad even though she was only going to be sitting for the day's filming. It was the only way she could work out some of her nerves without needing the stylists to make her look pretty again. "We talked about a lot of things," she said with a shrug.

Chase folded his arms. "Lani, I'm pretty sure you don't have all morning to stall. You talked about the family, didn't you?"

Kailani nodded.

"And?" Isla grabbed her arm, eyes wide. "What did he have to say about the family?"

Groaning, Kailani was regretting her decision to walk with these two more and more. "Do we have to do this now? I really should get back to—"

"We need to do this now," Chase said. "I'm sure Cam is going out of his mind in there. Whatever you two talked about, he's clearly waiting for something."

"He's waiting for me to believe him." Kailani dropped her head, clenching her hands into fists. "He said I—we—have been wrong this whole time."

Isla snorted. "Duh! Why do you think I sent that thing about love languages? Mom was telling me the whole time we were making cookies—which I hated, by the way—she couldn't stop talking about how she wishes she could keep making you dinners and she's looking into how hard it would be to make freezer meals for you to take home with you. She made those cookies because you haven't told her you don't like really sugary things anymore, but you used to love those. Doesn't that sound a bit like love?"

Kailani folded her arms. That sounded a lot like the things Cam was telling her last night. "Why couldn't she just say—"

"You know how much she hates when things get emotional," Chase said, raising an eyebrow. "She already feels vulnerable enough with her panic attacks, and you and Dad are the only ones who can talk her down."

Kailani hadn't thought of that, which was dumb because *she* hated emotional things too. Telling Cam she loved him last night had felt like jumping off a hundred-foot cliff, and thankfully the landing had been soft. Right into Cam's arms.

"Did you know Dad's been teaching driver's ed after school so he can help pay for your gym?" Chase said.

Kailani's face went slack. "What?"

He nodded. "He told me this morning. Said it would be worth the risk of death by teenage stupidity if it meant you could keep doing what you love. He didn't even know you were struggling so much. He just wanted to help."

He didn't know because Kailani hadn't wanted to tell him. When she already thought they saw her as someone to use when convenient, she hadn't wanted to give her parents any reason to think she couldn't be useful to them anymore. Even when she didn't think she had it, she'd always been desperate for any ounce of their love she could get.

"Why am I just finding out about all this now?" she gasped, wishing she had something solid to hold onto as her entire worldview collapsed. She wished she had *Cam* to hold onto. There was nothing more solid than him, in all ways.

Isla shrugged. "Because we didn't know about any of this until last night when we asked."

"You're just a few minutes from finding out about the fate of your future," Chase said, patting her shoulder. "It made sense to make sure you knew you had a bigger support system than you thought in case things don't go the way you want."

"Cam was right?" Kailani whispered, and she pressed her palm over her heart in case it tried to beat out of her chest. She couldn't believe she was actually considering what they were saying to her, but if she couldn't trust the people she loved, who could she trust?

Grinning, Isla pulled her into a hug that Kailani was too overwhelmed to return. "You really love Cam, don't you?"

"So much."

"Have you told him?" Chase asked.

When she was free again, Kailani nodded. "Last night. When we were talking about…"

A grin spread across Chase's face, like he had suddenly understood something. "Maybe you should tell him again," he said with another pat on the shoulder. "It might hit a little differently this time."

He was probably right, and Kailani wrapped both her siblings in a hug before hurrying back to find Cam.

It was a good thing Cam had gotten used to getting very little sleep over the last few months because he'd basically spent the whole night replaying the parking garage conversation over and over, wishing he could do it differently now that he was on the other side. For one, he wouldn't let himself get stupidly anxious over something that was entirely out of his control. He could try to help Kailani find ways to be happy, but he could never *make* her happy.

She hadn't really given him much this morning as they drove to the park, so he had no idea how she was feeling about last night's conversation. Conversation being a loose term. Kailani had barely said a word; it had been Cam spilling his guts for no reason—figuratively *and* literally. Nothing like a romantic splash of vomit to liven up a confession of adoration.

Not just adoration. *Love.*

Last night may have been a bit of a mystery, but Cam had no question as to why he was feeling anxious this morning. Kailani told him she was in love with him, but that meant nothing when she hadn't come to a conclusion about her family. Until she accepted she was capable of being loved, their whole relationship seemed fragile.

Great timing with the conclusion of the TV show…

Cam needed a distraction before he fell into another anxiety attack right before he had to meet Brad, so he grabbed his phone to call Kit and hoped school hadn't started yet.

Speaking of Kit… The man himself stepped into the makeup tent where Cam had been attacked by poor Felipe, who seemed more than ready to move on to a new canvas once the show was done. Kailani had gone on a walk with Chase and Isla just a minute ago, leaving Cam on his own with his thoughts. His thoughts and Felipe. The man seemed to be on the verge of a breakdown as he tried to control Cam's hair.

Kit, upon finding the tent empty except for Felipe, settled himself in Kailani's abandoned chair and pulled off his glasses to clean them.

Cam pulled his hair away from Felipe's hands. "Are you done?"

Felipe sighed. "Yes. Forever, *graças a Deus*." Giving Cam a flourished little bow, he gathered up his things and disappeared.

Though Kit smiled a little as Felipe left, his expression quickly turned to worry. "You look terrible."

"Thanks. What are you doing here?"

"I came to wish you luck and make sure you were okay. I haven't heard from you since our Wonder Boy meeting." He narrowed his eyes, as if he could see the reason Cam was so exhausted. "What happened?"

Cam knew better than to lie, but he was still tempted. Throwing up would probably be more pleasant than this conversation. Sighing, he spun his chair in a circle as he decided where to begin. Maybe it would be easiest to lay it all out at once. "I told her everything."

Kit's eyebrows shot high. "Everything?"

"Everything. I cried. It was great." Though he used a sarcastic tone, Cam's stomach remained settled. *Huh.* Maybe he really was glad he so often let down his guard around Kailani.

"I've never seen you cry." For some reason, Kit didn't seem to like that realization, frowning at his shoes. "Like, I can't remember *ever* seeing you cry. In fifteen years. What the crap, man?"

Cam stared at him. "You *want* me to cry?"

"Yes!"

"Why?"

"Because it means you're human. I don't know. Because it means you trust me."

Groaning, Cam checked his phone to see if he could use the excuse of needing to be somewhere, but he still had fifteen minutes to spare. He wasn't sure he had the energy for another heart-to-heart.

"I trust you, Kit," he said. "You know I do."

Kit glanced toward the door. "The Boys should be here any minute, by the way. We came to support."

Cam huffed a laugh. "I'm not sure 'Oliver' and 'support' go in the same sentence."

That made Kit sigh as he dropped his gaze to the floor. "What is it with you two? You say you trust me, but why won't you trust me when I tell you that you and Oliver have a lot more in common than you think?"

Why in the world would he keep talking about Oliver right now? Cam did not need the added stress. "Because he doesn't care about anyone but himself."

"Rude." The word came from the tent door.

Cam shot to his feet, feeling dizzy when he found the other two Wonder Boys standing there, Madi and Allie next to them. He cursed, his anxiety spiking because despite the lightness in Oliver's voice, he looked anything but amused.

Cam swallowed. "I didn't mean..." Nausea rumbled through his stomach, forcing him to stop.

Oliver noticed, narrowing his eyes. "Don't bother lying to spare my feelings. I've had enough throwing up in my life lately."

Kit jumped up at the same time Madi smacked Oliver. "Hey," he said. "Don't talk about my sister like that."

"Um." Ben waved, while Allie seemed to be deeply examining the structural integrity of the tent to avoid the awkwardness in the room. "We came to watch your last day of filming," he mumbled.

"What did you have to promise Oliver to force him to come?" Cam snapped.

"He wanted to come," Madi tried, but Oliver had already pulled away from her to get in Cam's face.

"Don't talk about me like I'm not here," he growled. "You do that often enough already."

Cam was suddenly wishing he'd gone on that walk with Kailani. Facing the possibility of her telling him she needed more time—or worse, time away from him despite what she'd said last night—was better than this idiocy; his hands were going numb from clenching them hard at his sides. "The world doesn't revolve around you, Hamilton. Even if you think it does."

"You know nothing about me."

"Oh, I'm sorry your life has been so perfect."

"Guys," Kit said, "stop—"

"Has Kailani gotten sick of you already?"

Cam threw the punch before he could stop himself. It was a reflex, triggered by fear, and he felt like he was watching himself in slow motion as his fist collided with Oliver's nose, cracking it beneath his knuckles.

Madi and Allie both screamed as Oliver went down hard, and Cam didn't resist when Kit pushed him back several feet. He was too shaky to do anything, anyway, knowing that he'd just severed what little ties he'd had to Oliver to begin with.

Oliver was going to leave.

Cam didn't blame him.

"S-sorry," he whispered, trying to keep his breathing even.

Kit seemed torn between helping Cam and checking on Oliver, his eyes wide as his head whipped back and forth between them. When Madi and Ben helped Oliver sit up, he turned his focus to Cam.

"You okay?"

Cam shook his head. "Doesn't matter," he gasped. Oliver was bleeding, his nose soaking his sleeve. That was Cam's fault. "I didn't mean…"

"I know," Kit replied, eyebrows low.

Oliver, on the other hand, spit out a mouthful of blood and glared at Cam. "Why are you defending him? He's just being typical Cam and using his fists instead of his head."

"Just keep breathing," Kit said to Cam. "Focus on—"

"You're always going to take his side," Oliver growled, his voice distorted from his swelling nose.

Kit frowned in frustration. "This isn't about sides, Ollie."

Oliver let out a humorless laugh. "Sure it isn't. You're just going to pretend—like always—that he can't do any wrong. Never mind the many times he nearly got suspended for mindless fighting."

"That was years ago," Kit argued.

"Clearly he's not over it."

Groaning, Kit gripped Cam's arm as he tried to look at both him and Oliver at the same time. There wasn't a way he could fix this, but Cam knew that wouldn't stop him from trying. "Give him some slack, Oliver. Both of his parents died before he hit fourteen. You think you wouldn't have some anger about something like that? He hasn't gotten into—"

Oliver scoffed. "That excuse doesn't work forever, Kit. What about that football game senior year? That had nothing to do with—"

"He was defending *you!*"

Oliver froze, his face going slack despite the blood still dribbling from his nose. "What?"

Kit glanced at Cam, as if asking for permission.

As reluctant as Cam was to have Oliver know the truth about that game, he was so done with secrets. "Just tell him," he muttered.

"Drew Beckett was talking crap about you," Kit said, speaking quietly as if he didn't want anyone to hear. Even though there was no one around but the Wonder Boys. "He was talking about how you were probably only valedictorian because your parents paid the school off, not because you're a literal genius. So Cam asked him to keep his mouth shut about things he knew nothing about."

"But he kept talking," Cam croaked, grateful for the distraction from his anxiety. "And it got worse." He didn't even want to remember some of the things Beckett had said about Oliver. "So I decked him to shut him up."

After that, instinct had kicked in, and the fight had continued until Oliver and Kit pulled him off of Beckett. Cam hadn't wanted to stop, only seeing red, and they'd had to literally tie him down to get him home.

He hadn't been in a fight since, but punching Oliver today had happened way too easily. All of his stress had been building for so long, and he hadn't had a chance to get in any good workouts to relieve the pressure for weeks. Oliver had always been able to push his buttons just right. The second he mentioned Kailani in relation to all of the fears Cam had been fighting to get rid of, Cam had felt like a wounded dog being kicked. Lashing out had been the only way he knew how to react. Maybe Kit's offer of therapy wasn't such a bad idea after all; he could use a few more tools for dealing with things.

When Oliver met his gaze, eyebrows low, Cam couldn't help but wonder if he'd ever seen that expression before. He wasn't sure what it meant, but he did know something had just shifted in Oliver. Something had shifted between them.

"Why would you do that?" Oliver asked, his voice breathless. "You don't even like me."

A weight settled in Cam's stomach. "At the time I thought you were one of my best friends."

The whole tent was silent, not even a breeze ruffling the tent walls. After a long few seconds, Oliver clambered to his feet and slowly approached Cam as if seeing him for the first time. Though Kit stood in between them, Oliver only had eyes for Cam.

"You were having a panic attack the other day, weren't you?"

Not wanting to throw up, Cam nodded even though he hated admitting that weakness to Oliver. It wasn't like he could hide the truth anymore anyway; his hands were still shaking.

Oliver's lips twitched, and he glanced down at the ground. "Before I sold my company, I worked myself so hard that I ended up in the hospital for three days because of stress and exhaustion."

"What?!" Cam and Kit shouted together.

Madi sniffled, but Cam kept his eyes on Oliver. He'd always thought Oliver was lazy and entitled, but suddenly he was realizing he might have been wrong.

"That's why you sold," Ben guessed, leaving Allie with Madi and approaching slowly. He looked far calmer than Kit, his eyes taking in the scene in that gentle way of his. None of this seemed to surprise him, which had Cam wondering how much he knew about all of their secrets without ever telling anyone. There was a reason they called him Watchdog in laser tag, and he had always lived up to his name. "You were trying to get away from the pressure."

Nodding, Oliver dabbed at his nose, but the bleeding seemed to have stopped for the most part. "Yeah," he said, his voice scraping out of his throat. "I spent so much energy trying to be the man who had it all that I didn't realize what I was doing to myself until it was almost too late. I've never been…" He shook his head, his eyes locked on the ground and his words coming out strained. "I don't know what to do when things get hard, and you…" He looked up, meeting Cam's gaze. "You've had a crazy hard life, and you keep pushing through no matter what comes at you. And I'm over here scared out of my mind because I'm terrified that I'm going to burn out as a dad just like I did with my business. I can't sell my kid and start over if I'm bad at parenting."

"Ollie," Madi whispered. She was standing in Allie's arms as the two women cried together. Maybe Madi hadn't known that last part about Oliver's fear of fatherhood.

Kit looked as solid as his sister, holding onto Cam's arm for dear life. "Why didn't you tell me?" he asked, clearly hurt by all these secrets coming out. Kit was supposed to be the glue, the one that knew everything.

Oliver looked just as miserable. "Maybe we should talk after the show. I should…probably go get cleaned up." He glanced at his blood-soaked shirt before he looked at Cam. "I'm sorry. Truly. I didn't realize…"

Cam shook his head. Kit was right about the two of them being similar, and they'd both been too stubborn to see it. "Me too. Friends?"

"Friends."

Oliver made it one step toward the door when Kit said, "Where do you think you're going?"

That stopped Oliver in his tracks, and he glanced back. "Something wrong, Captain?"

Kit narrowed his eyes. "Oliver Hamilton, you agreed."

"That was before he broke my nose. I don't want a black eye to go with it, thank you very much."

But Kit didn't move, folding his arms and clenching his jaw in a show of confidence Cam hadn't seen in a few years. He used to be the most confident person Cam knew, and it was nice to see him stepping into his own shoes after several years of rolling with the punches. Even if Cam had no idea what they were talking about.

"A bet is a bet, Ollie," Kit said. "You have to tell him. And you know what'll happen if *I* have to be the one to tell him."

Madi looked just as confused as Cam felt, glancing between her brother and her husband as they glared at each other. "I have no idea what is going on," she said, "but now I *have* to know what'll happen if you lose the bet, Ollie. You never make bets."

"For good reason," Oliver grumbled. "If I chicken out, I have to do a dramatic reading of Ben's book and put it on the internet." He glanced at Cam, a contemplative expression on his face as if he was considering that the better option.

Cam didn't have time for this. "Talk, Hamilton."

Though he clenched his jaw, Oliver sighed, likely knowing his best option would be to come clean before Kit did it for him. "I'm the one who paid for your apartment." He winced, probably expecting to get punched again.

If this had happened a week ago, when he was overwhelmed with stress, Cam probably would have done it. But this morning, he wasn't sure how to feel. It was like the stubbornness had been knocked out of him. Or maybe he just really liked that apartment. Besides, punching someone in the face clearly wasn't the best response to anger and frustration.

"You paid for my apartment?" he repeated, not sure if he really believed that. *Brad* had paid for the apartment. A mysterious old billionaire had paid for it. Anyone but the guy who had always made Cam feel like second best just by existing.

Oliver shrugged. "Brad talked to all of us before the show started, trying to learn more about you. And when he asked about your living situation… I didn't just run past your place above the gym the other day. I got curious, so I went up there and, uh, broke in."

"You *broke in?*" Cam growled and took a step forward, rethinking that whole not punching him again thing.

But Kit grabbed his arm, holding him back. "He paid for Kailani's too."

That got Cam's attention. "You paid for… Why?"

Shaking his head, Oliver smiled as he said, "Because I thought helping her would be the only way I could help *you.* We've all got our pride, man, but I have way too much money for my own good. Just let me use it."

What was Cam supposed to say? *No thanks* and move back into his crawl space? Not only did he *not* want to do that, but he was sick and tired of pretending he didn't need help. So he said, "Thank you," and wished those two words didn't leave everyone else in stunned silence. He knew his friendship with Oliver—if he could really call it that—had always been strained, but was it really so shocking for him to show some gratitude?

Cam knew the answer to that question without needing to ask it, and he glanced down at his fist, knowing he probably owed Oliver more than a few words. So he stretched his fingers out straight and held out his hand.

Everyone gasped, and Oliver's wide eyes meant he knew exactly why a handshake was a big deal. Cam hadn't shaken anyone's hand in almost a decade.

Oliver quirked a smile. "You're not going to break my fingers, are you?"

The answering smile that cracked through Cam's tense body seemed to break away years of stress and anxiety, like he'd been holding onto something he could have let go years ago if he had just talked to Oliver for once. The wall around his heart was just a pile of rubble now. He could *breathe*.

His smile grew. "Not this time."

When Oliver grasped his hand, Cam tugged him off balance and pulled him into a hug. He figured if he was going to offer an olive branch, he might as well go the whole way. Thankfully, Oliver matched his enthusiasm with a back slap that left Kit with his jaw hanging open once they broke apart.

Shaking his head, as if he couldn't believe what had just happened either, Oliver wiped beneath his eyes and turned without a word, wrapping his arm around Madi and pulling her against his side.

"We'll save you a seat, Kit," Ben said, and he seemed just as emotional as he took Allie's hand and followed Oliver out of the tent.

Cam immediately turned on Kit. "You planned all that."

His hands in his pockets now, Kit shrugged with false calmness, definitely holding back a grin. "I didn't want you to break his nose."

"But you wanted us to fight?"

"I wanted you to *talk*. But I'll take what I can get." He smiled when Cam shook his head, like he knew exactly how ridiculous his plan had been. Then again, his best plans always were. No one knew how to help people as well as Kit Morgan, and no one else could have gotten them to a point where a hug was the most natural conclusion. "How are you feeling? You've got a big day ahead of you."

Honestly, Cam still had no idea how to feel. The last twenty-four hours had put him through the wringer, and he was amazed he hadn't fallen apart yet. His body could handle just about anything, but he had apparently neglected to strengthen his heart over the years.

"I think I'm okay," he said, and the lack of queasiness in his gut told him that might actually be true. "I'm less worried about today's outcome than I thought I would be. After last night…" He ran his hands through his hair, then hoped Felipe wouldn't see it.

Kit raised an eyebrow. "Anything you need to tell me about last night?"

Frowning, Cam shook his head. "What's that question supposed to mean?"

"I don't know, you had a look."

"What kind of a look?"

"Forget I asked."

"She told me she loves me."

This time both of Kit's eyebrows flew high, his eyes wide. "Whoa. That's big."

"I know."

"No, I mean, you haven't run away."

Cam actually smiled, which felt like a sign unto itself. His anxiety had entirely melted away for what felt like the first time in years. "I know. I told her I was in love with her too."

Kit sank back into the chair he'd vacated earlier, as if he couldn't believe what he'd just heard. "Cam Martinez is in love," he said.

"You already knew that, genius."

"I know, but..." Kit shrugged. "I wasn't sure you'd ever be brave enough to say it out loud."

"I guess I've finally grown up. One of us should."

Snorting a laugh, Kit rose back to his feet and looked around, as if making sure he hadn't forgotten anything. It was classic Kit avoidance, which meant something was bothering him.

Cam folded his arms. "You know what this means, don't you?"

Kit grimaced, even though he asked, "What what means?"

Cam had definitely guessed right, and he grinned as he stepped in between his friend and the tent door. If Kit was going to get away with forcing difficult conversations, Cam was going to take a crack at it as well. "Are you really going to be the last man standing for the rest of your life?"

"I'm fine on my own."

"You may have the rest of them fooled, but I'm not buying that bull crap for a second. It's been long enough, man."

Kit looked sick to his stomach as he shook his head, eyes locked on the ground. When he spoke, his voice had gone small. "I can't go through that again."

Cam wished he could do more for the guy, but this wasn't the sort of thing he could fix for him. "You have to tell the Boys, Kit. Sooner or later, you know I'm going to spill your secret, and I don't think Madi wants to hear it from me."

Kit laughed a little, finally looking up at Cam as he fiddled with the leather bracelet he always wore. Cam had never been brave enough to ask about the bracelet—Kit had been wearing it since before they met as teens—but now he wanted to.

"I don't know why I thought it was a good idea to tell you," Kit muttered.

"Because your secret fiancée cheated on you, and you were hurting," Cam replied, enjoying the relief from finally being able to say it out loud—even if it was just back to Kit— rather than hold it in like he'd been doing for the last four years. That was way too long for him to have to hold onto something. "And I was just the person who happened to be close by."

Kit shook his head, his eyes gleaming. "You're like a brother to me, Cam. You're one of my best friends, so please don't downplay your importance. Please."

Though Cam warmed at that, he leveled Kit with a strong look. "At least tell your sister, okay? It's been four years since Angela broke your heart, and Madi deserves to know."

Four years since Cam showed up at Kit's brand-new house and found him staring at the wall as if dead. It had taken a good deal of pushing, but when Kit finally told him he'd been secretly dating someone for over a year before walking in on her with another guy, right after they got engaged, Cam had nearly gone on a manhunt for the idiot woman who thought anyone would be better than Kit Morgan. He wanted to shout at her until he went hoarse.

The look on Kit's face had been the only thing that kept Cam from leaving. He'd been completely broken, and Cam still had no idea how no one else had discovered the truth. Then again, Kit was better at hiding than anyone, so maybe it made perfect sense.

"One of these days," Cam said, heading for the door, "you're going to have to let us look out for you for once. I'll keep your secret as long as I can, but you know it's going to come out eventually. Until it does, Madi is probably going to start trying to set you up with anyone she meets so you're not the only one alone, and that's not going to end well for you unless you want to start dating Isla."

Kit's look of terror was the last thing Cam saw before he slipped out of the tent and nearly walked right into Kailani.

She blinked up at him, studying him for a moment. "You look happy."

Cam grinned. "I think I am." That alone was strange, but the lack of pressure sitting on his chest was even stranger. "I broke Oliver's nose."

"Really?"

He laughed and threw his arm around her shoulders, glad when she leaned into him while they walked. Now that they were talking again, all of his returning fears that she would leave felt so stupid. Their relationship was fine. "I'll tell you about it later, but it's a good thing. At least, I think it is. You look happy too." She seemed more at peace than he'd ever seen her, her expression open and relaxed as she smiled at him, and that felt like a good sign.

"You clearly don't know me very well. I'm terrified." But she smiled and bounced up to kiss his cheek.

Cam raised an eyebrow. "What was that for?" Not that he was complaining.

"I'm working on recognizing all the love from the people around me because someone told me I might have a lot more love in my life than I thought. And I'm inclined to believe him."

More beautiful words had never been spoken.

"Well, in that case." Pulling her to a stop, Cam bent and brushed his lips against hers. With his walls broken down, hers coming down as well, there was next to nothing stopping him from making this a part of every day. From making *her* a part of his life. "Maybe I should learn from you," he whispered. "You're definitely on to something."

"We're going to be late."

"I don't care. I love you."

"I love you too." And when Kailani wrapped her arms around his neck and deepened the kiss, he was pretty sure she didn't care either.

TWENTY-SEVEN

Brad's question sounded so simple, but Kailani had no idea how to respond. *Giddy* probably wasn't a good answer, even if it was true. How else would she be feeling after spending five minutes hiding around the corner of the filming tent with Cam, enjoying the best kiss of her life? She had never kissed a man she was in love with, knowing she was worthy of being loved back. That kiss had meant everything—love and trust and, if she was right, a future.

But she was also nervous, and with the cameras rolling she didn't want to admit as much.

Cam, on the other hand, wrapped his hand around hers and spoke with confidence. "We're falling apart, Brad."

The audience laughed right along with Brad, and Kailani hoped she didn't start sweating. With so many lights shining down on their little stage, she was more grateful than ever for the makeup team that had loaded a bunch of powder on her face to keep her looking polished and perfect. She was lucky she hadn't messed it all up, though Cam *had* had to help her fix her hair before they entered the tent, as well as send one of Brad's staff on an urgent search for lipstick.

Cam's hair had been a lost cause before she met up with him, but her hands hadn't done much to fix it. Even now, it was sticking up a bit on one side, and poor Felipe was probably off sobbing somewhere.

"There's no need to be nervous," Brad said, grinning wide.

"Are you saying that because I won?" Cam asked, sparking more laughter.

Brad clicked his tongue. "I like your enthusiasm, but you'll have to be patient a little longer."

"But I still won, right?"

"I think you've overestimated your skills," Kailani muttered, rolling her eyes.

Cam grinned, that crooked smile of his raising the temperature of the room. He seemed so completely *happy*. And with the way he looked at her, she would be crazy to think that wasn't because of her. Who would have thought she could be that for someone? She certainly hadn't.

Or maybe she had been as wrong about herself as she'd been about her family.

"What else is new?" Cam said. "It's not like I beat you in the arm wrestle three times in a row or anything."

"Because your arms are huge!" Kailani wrapped her fingers around his bicep, though she hardly needed to demonstrate. She couldn't even get her hands all the way around. "Your core is nothing to write home about, though."

His eyes narrowed just enough for Kailani to know he was fully prepared to counter that. "You mean this core?" he asked, lifting the hem of his shirt to the crowd's delight. "I seem to recall you enjoying a few aspects of this," he added, quietly enough that only she would hear him over the screams and whistles from the audience.

"Now who's a tease?" she replied.

Cam responded by leaning over the arm of his chair and planting a delicious kiss on her mouth, sending the crowd wild right along with Kailani's heart.

"Well, this leads right into my next question," Brad said with a chuckle once the noise level died down. "I know it seems strange to pit two people against each other when they're united in everything else, but I like to think I knew what I was doing. With your relationship being fairly new, how have things changed?"

"Well," Kailani said, since Brad was looking right at her, "we came into this thing with no expectations. We were already up against each other with our gyms, so it wasn't too hard to keep up the rivalry."

"Lani and I have had to learn to trust each other," Cam added, looking at her instead of Brad. His eyes burned with an intensity that made her shiver. "We could have easily gone in the other direction, but having this chance to focus on each other, knowing that whatever the outcome ends up being we'll still be in this together, has made me believe that what we have is something special."

The audience *awwed* while Kailani nearly broke into tears. "You mean that?" she whispered.

He held out his arms, giving her a look that seemed to say, "Does it look like I'm throwing up?"

Kailani wanted to crawl into those arms and never leave. "I love you," she mouthed, sending the audience into another fit because she'd forgotten she was on camera even if she didn't say anything out loud.

Brad watched them as if he couldn't have planned anything better, his smile so wide that it looked like it might fly right off his face. "Before we announce the winner, I want to go back and revisit the interviews we did before filming. Let's watch those."

"Why do you want this sponsorship?" Brad asked on the video that played on the screen behind them.

It was Cam that showed up first, his crooked grin firmly in place because he'd just won the cooking competition. He was still wearing his apron. Apparently he hadn't answered that question when he signed the contract, like she had. "Because everyone deserves to be healthy," he said. "There's such a big emphasis on looking good in today's society, but I'm more about *feeling* good. The way a person feels can directly impact every part of their life, and if someone feels strong and confident physically, that's going to translate to their mental and emotional sides as well. I started my gym so I could give that to people who can't afford to get training. Who are too afraid of being judged for what they can't control. Who don't know where to start. But I've got a long way to go before I can really start to help people, and this would help a ton."

Kailani grabbed his hand as the video paused on his face, and he looked at her with a question in his eyes. "You can't give that up for me," she whispered. "You deserve this so much more than I do."

Before he could respond, the video moved onto Kailani's response.

"The human body is an incredible thing," she said in the recording, not nearly as confidently as Cam had done. She blamed the uncertainty of not knowing what was coming. "I've seen so many people overcome so many hard things because they trusted their body and relied on their own strength to get through it. Not everyone has that core belief that they can do anything they put their minds to, and not everyone has a good support system to help them through the tough things. I want to start an after-school program for kids who don't have a good place to go. Show them that they can be strong and get through anything if they believe in themselves. That strength is already inside of all of us, and we just need someone to open the door."

Yep. Cam's answer had definitely been better, and Kailani wilted in her chair. The winner would be based off of more than just one interview question, but her gut was telling her

Cam had won, and rightly so. That was okay. She would be disappointed, but she and Cam were more than their gyms. Everything would work out exactly how it should.

"I don't know about you," Brad said to the audience, "but it definitely sounds like I picked the right people. What do you think?"

The audience clapped and cheered, though they may have been taking cues from a screen or big posters. The lights were too bright for her to see much beyond the stage.

"Let's see what other people had to say about our contenders," Brad continued.

Wait, what?

Suddenly Isla's face was on the screen, though she'd never mentioned anything about doing an interview. "When I lost my leg, I thought I would never walk again," she said, way too happy for someone talking about losing a limb. "But Kailani never gave up on me. She was so much tougher than my PT, but it was her push that got me on my feet again. Well, *foot*."

The audience laughed, but another face had already filled the screen. The trainer at Cam's gym that enjoyed glaring at Kailani. Cam leaned his elbows on his knees, his eyebrows pulling low as he watched. Kailani felt the same way. Where was this going?

"I've never met anyone like Martinez," the trainer said. "He has this way of pushing people past their mental blocks, not because he wants to see results but because he cares about them. He sees them so much better than they see themselves."

Kailani's trainer, Magda, was next. "You can just see the passion in her eyes, you know? Like she can see the end result and can't wait to get there with the person she's working with. But she's been so busy trying to keep the gym open, and you can tell she misses being on the floor with people."

A guy Kailani didn't recognize. "I never thought I would look in a mirror and like what I saw. Working with Cam, I started to forget to check my reflection because it was never about appearances for him. Now I'm healthier than ever, and I don't even think about sucking in my gut when a pretty girl walks past. Good thing I don't have one anymore, so I don't have to."

One of Kailani's clients. "She helped me find confidence. I've never had that before."

Kit. "Cam has always been able to see a person's potential, but he's never been good about seeing it in himself. He has spent his life for other people, and his gym is the first thing I've ever seen him want for himself. And even with this, it's all about how many people he can help. There is no one in the world more selfless than Cam Martinez, and he deserves so much more than what he allows himself."

Kailani's mom.

Kailani stiffened on instinct, immediately recognizing the front room of her family home. When had they filmed this? Mom hadn't known about the show until yesterday...

"My Lani has always been one to defy expectations," Mom said, eyes glimmering with tears as she spoke into the camera. "I remember the first time I held her in my arms. It was weeks after she was born because she was so tiny, and they didn't think she would even live. But I knew she would prove them wrong. And she did! She showed me that no matter how difficult life may seem, there's always a way to push through it and make the most of what you have. I am so proud of my little girl, and I don't tell her that enough. Lani, I love everything about you, and I know you'll do remarkable things."

Kailani didn't have time to react before the video switched to a fuzzy and distorted video of a man in fatigues with cinnamon eyes and Martinez stitched over the right breast. "Hey, *mijo*," the man said.

Cam's elbow slipped from his knee, his eyes going wide as the color rushed from his face.

"I only have a couple of minutes before we gotta head out, but I wanted to tell you how much I wish I could be there for your birthday. Rosa says you've grown a foot since I was home last, but I'm pretty sure she's exaggerating." He narrowed his eyes at the camera. "I hope she's exaggerating. Otherwise, you're gonna be way bigger than me. That's okay, though. You got that big heart of yours, so you have to make room for it somewhere. Anyway, I want to say I'm so proud of you, Cameron. I know it hasn't been easy, losing your mom, and me being over here, but you keep pushing through. You're so strong, and you can do anything. I knew that from the first day I held you. I knew you would be something special."

Some noise in the background made him turn, and he said something incoherent to someone off the screen. When he turned back, he looked sad. "Gotta go, *mijo*, but I'll be back home soon. Remember what I told you, okay? Even when I'm gone, I'm always right here." He patted his chest over his heart. "Doesn't matter how far away I am or how long it's been. I'll never leave you. I'll send this when we get back to base, okay? I love you, Cameron. Always."

The screen flickered to black, and the whole room was quiet.

Moving so slowly that it was almost imperceptible, Cam turned to Brad. Kailani couldn't see his face, but he was shaking. So was she, but she was recovering quickly. Yes, she was overwhelmed by the growing realization that she had *definitely* been wrong about her family, but Cam needed her right now.

He'd been there for her last night; now it was her turn. She could process later, as soon as she knew he was okay.

Brad had tears in his eyes. "We'll edit this part out if you don't want it shared," he said quietly. "But I thought you wouldn't watch that video if I just gave it to you, and I felt you needed to see it."

Wait, he'd never seen that video of his dad before?

"Where...?" Cam whispered.

Brad smiled. "I did some digging when all this started. Doing my research. The camera belonged to one of his fellow Marines who never thought to see what was on there after the platoon was attacked. I'd been hoping to get some quotes or insights about you from anyone who knew your dad, and he remembered your dad had borrowed the camera right before he died. It's a miracle the file was still good after all these years."

Kailani reached out and took hold of Cam's hand, hoping to offer some sort of comfort, and she breathed a sigh of relief when he lifted her fingers to his lips. Though he didn't look at her, the gesture meant he was going to be okay.

They both were.

"Thank you," Cam said, a little stronger now. "And you're right. I wouldn't have watched that if you hadn't... Thanks."

Brad shrugged as if he hadn't just given Cam something amazing. "Whenever you're ready, we'll announce the winner."

Kailani wasn't sure if she would ever be ready, and she couldn't imagine how Cam was feeling right now. With the way he'd been talking about breaking Oliver's nose earlier, she had a feeling he'd already been through some pretty high emotions today. Could he handle any more? Could *she*?

"Hey," he said, pulling her out of her thoughts. "As much as I like seeing you worried about me, as long as you're next to me, I can make it through anything. *We can do this*." He reached over and brushed his palm against her cheek. He seemed to be waiting for something, a question in his eyes as he studied her face.

She smiled. "I'm terrified right now," she whispered. "But whatever happens, you're what matters to me more than anything. We can get through this, right?"

He touched his forehead to hers and took a deep breath. "Pretty sure we can get through anything."

Stealing a quick kiss, Kailani steeled her nerves and turned back to Brad. "I think we're ready."

He grinned wide. "Are you sure?"

"Don't push it," Cam replied with a nervous chuckle.

Brad turned to the audience. "Are you ready to find out who will be running my fancy new gym?"

The cheer was almost deafening, and Kailani couldn't fathom why so many people cared this much. Though maybe they were all hardcore exercisers, she highly doubted the *entire* crowd would be signing up for memberships at any gyms, let alone the one Brad would be sponsoring. Did they not have their own lives to cheer for?

Laughing at the response, Brad turned his attention back to Cam and Kailani, who gripped each other's hands tightly as they waited. "The winner of my competition," he began as an intense music started up around them, "is…"

Kailani *hated* when they drew these moments out on TV shows, and she hated it even more when she was the one waiting.

Brad's grin widened. "You."

Kailani turned to Cam, who turned to her at the same time. In unison, they looked back at Brad. "Who?"

"You."

"Which you?"

"Both of you."

If Kailani still had a heart in her chest, she could no longer feel it. Her voice had disappeared as well, and she was pretty sure she'd forgotten how to breathe. She had been so sure that Cam would win, and technically she'd been right. But she'd also apparently been very wrong.

"Both of us," she whispered, somehow getting the words out despite having no air in her lungs.

Cam looked like he was about to burst into tears.

Scratch that—he was already crying. If nothing else, the big, burly weightlifter was proving to the world that it was okay for men to cry.

As if sensing how overwhelmed they both were, Brad approached slowly and knelt on the floor in front of them. "I know I like my games, but I want you to know that I always planned on giving you both this opportunity. Even before you each told me you wanted the other person to win."

Kailani met Cam's surprised eyes with her own. He'd told Brad that he wanted her to win? But when? It must have been after their last challenge, when Chase called her.

Brad beamed at them. "It was never about one beating the other."

Cam swallowed hard. "Then why—"

"I had to make sure the two of you could work together no matter the circumstances. That this relationship you're building would last. I couldn't very well invest in something that would fall apart at the first sign of trouble, now could I?"

"So…" Kailani was still trying to understand. "So you're going to invest in *both* of our gyms?"

But Brad shook his head, making the tiny sliver of hope she'd been harboring disappear. "This week has made it clear that the two of you are better together than apart. We're going to start a brand-new gym that combines both of your strengths. It will be a place that anyone can go, no matter their goals or their starting points."

"Together," Cam repeated, and he had finally found the strength to smile. "I like the sound of that."

"I hoped you would," Brad replied. "And you, Miss Adams?"

Kailani was still reeling, but when Cam gave her hand a squeeze, she nodded. That was about as much as she could handle. As Brad launched into his exit speech, talking both to the audience and to the camera about how there would be forthcoming information about the new gym, Kailani leaned into Cam as if he could share his strength.

He wrapped his arm around her and held her close.

"I'm dreaming right now, right?" she asked.

"Maybe. But if that's the case, I hope we never wake up."

The next several hours turned into negotiations and planning. Brad had already picked out a location that was so much better than anything either of them could have afforded on their own, and he wanted to hash out design ideas so he could get the ball rolling sooner than later. He had contracts ready to go and also provided unbiased lawyers to help Cam and Kailani feel comfortable with signing, but as far as she could tell, Breakout Brad was being more than generous in what he was offering them.

She would have been fine with him handing her a check for a thousand dollars and calling it good. He'd pretty much already done that with the month's overhead and the apartment. Instead, she was getting thirty percent of the shares of the new company and full control over her half of the training and the after-school program Brad was fully on board with.

"This is unreal," Cam said as he signed the first page of the contract. He'd listened to his lawyer for about ten minutes before deciding to agree to everything as it was. "I feel like I'm in a Nicholas Sparks movie. But, like, one of the happy ones."

Kailani stared at him.

"What? I have a heart. And you can't tell me this doesn't feel like it was manufactured by a happy ending factory. Our strange relationship, the mysterious benefactor loaded with cash, finding a long-lost message from my dead dad… Tell me that's not straight out of one of those movies."

He had a point, though Kailani was still hung up on the fact that he not only had seen a bunch of Nicholas Sparks movies but had apparently enjoyed them.

She signed her part of the contract, moving through the pages in a daze. "I'm still waiting for someone to say the magic word and I wake up realizing I've been hypnotized."

"Fun Cam fact: I can't be hypnotized. People have tried. Kit, on the other hand…" He paused, looking at the page she was on, and then he pointed to it. "What is that?"

Kailani glanced down. "My signature?"

"That's not a signature. There is nothing remotely close to your name in that scribble. It's the worst thing I've ever seen."

"Yeah, well, it's for security. No one can recreate it."

Cam flipped to an earlier page, pointing to the place where Kailani had signed her name. "Not even you can, apparently."

She had to admit, the two signature lines looked pretty different. She snorted, which turned into a full-blown laugh the more she thought about it, and soon she was falling into Cam's arms from laughing so hard.

"Not that I'm complaining, but…" Cam muttered, clearly concerned about her sanity.

She wasn't sure she could explain properly, but as soon as she could breathe again, she tried. "I've spent my whole life trying to be perfect so my parents would love me, and I can't even sign my own name."

Cam frowned. "I wasn't trying to make you feel bad. It's not a big deal."

"Exactly."

"You lost me."

Taking a breath that felt like the first full one she'd had in years, Kailani smiled. "I am never going to be perfect, and that's okay. I was never going to be enough kid for my parents, and *that's* okay. I may still have a hard time seeing it for a little while, but I know now they love me. So it's okay. I'm going to fail at a lot of things, big and small, and I'm never going to be able to make a proper pizza. And you know what?"

Cam grinned. "That's okay?"

"That's okay," she repeated.

For a moment, Cam looked thoughtful as he wrapped his arms around her waist and examined her face. Then he gave her a soft smile paired with a kiss to her forehead. "Can I ask you a question?"

Her heart leapt, jumping into double time. "Is this…"

But he shook his head. "Just a normal question."

"What?"

"Can I make you dinner tonight?" He kissed her temple. "And maybe tomorrow?" He kissed the tip of her nose. "What about the day after that?" The corner of her mouth.

Kailani threw her arms around his massive shoulders and grinned. "You can make me dinner any day you'd like, Nelli." And she pulled him in for a long, delicious kiss that made her forget she had ever had a life without Cam Martinez in it.

EPILOGUE

"CAN WE TAKE A SELFIE with you?"

Cam looked away from his client only long enough to get an idea of what he was dealing with. Four girls, likely in their early twenties, stood a few feet away, all of them clad in Isla-designed Spandex and tank tops with not a drop of sweat among them. Cam had seen them earlier, lightly bouncing around on the exercise balls on the second floor and more interested in watching viral videos than actually working out.

But, like everyone else inside the building, they paid the membership fee, so Cam couldn't be too annoyed. After all, one of the big draws of Horizon Tide was the variety. Anyone could get any level of fitness they wanted.

"Breathe through this last one," he told his client, hands hovering beneath the bench press bar as she heaved one final time. "Nice work, Becca! You got ten more reps than last time. Take a breather and acknowledge the way you feel right now. Do you feel strong?"

Becca grinned and nodded as she grabbed her water. She'd come a long way in the six weeks since she started, and her doctor had high hopes for her recovery after she'd checked into rehab a few months earlier.

Cam loved all of his clients, but he had a soft spot for the ones that came to him through the nonprofit that sent him the pro bono clients. The ones who truly needed someone to tell them they were strong enough to handle anything.

"Sorry about that, ladies," he said, turning back to the girls who hadn't budged.

"It's okay," one of them squeaked. "So, uh…?" She held up her phone.

Cam's online popularity had definitely died down a bit over the last couple of months, but he had a feeling that as long as he was on the floor at Horizon Tide, there would always be someone hoping to cash in on #hotbodycam.

Pictures were generally banned inside the gym for the privacy of the patrons, but there was one corner—courtesy of Brad—designed to be a photo backdrop for anyone wanting to document their progress. "Tell you what," he said, folding his arms as he stared them down. "You drop and give me twenty, and I'll let you take a selfie."

The girls blinked, one of them looking down at the wallet attached to the back of her phone.

Cam resisted the urge to laugh. "Push-ups," he clarified. "How about five each for a total of twenty?"

They still hesitated, likely because none of them had the muscle to do one push-up let alone five. Maybe a picture with him would motivate them to put in a little effort going forward.

He sighed. "I'll take my shirt off." Why was he even trying this hard?

Immediately the girls were on the floor, straining through the worst push-ups he'd ever seen. One girl had gotten smart and dropped to her knees, and her form wasn't half bad. The others… Well, maybe they would sign up for beginner training sessions if he nudged them in the right direction.

Without waiting for the girls to finish, Cam headed for the stairs to the second-floor balcony, where the picture wall waited. Thankfully, the nearby area was empty, though half the bottom floor would have a pretty decent view.

It was a good thing he'd gotten over being camera shy months ago. That was what happened when a famous fitness guru decided to document the entire process of building and branding a new gym and its co-owners.

The girls arrived just as he slipped his shirt over his head, and their squeals had him regretting the offer. Especially when they crowded in close and several ice-cold hands pressed against his skin. At least it made him tense up and flex so he would look better in the picture. One girl lifted her phone, they all made kissy faces—Cam stuck with a smile—and then the girls took several dozen pictures before they skittered off to the stairs.

"Make sure you talk to Henry at the front desk," Cam called after them. "You could work out with me every week if you sign up for training."

They all giggled and headed straight for the door. All but the one who'd had decent form. She paused at the desk, scanning the QR code that would take her to the sign up.

Cam called that a win.

Someone whistled behind him, and he pulled his shirt back on before things got out of hand.

"Oh, don't cover up on my account."

He was never going to get tired of that voice. Spinning around, Cam located Kailani sitting atop a tall stack of plyo boxes and headed right for her. The kids must have just left, leaving the area a mess that he tried to ignore before it drove him crazy. Tugging on Kailani's foot, he pulled her into his arms and nuzzled her nose with his.

"What idiot came up with the rule that we're not allowed to kiss inside our gym?" he growled.

Kailani laughed. "That would be you, Nelli. That was definitely your rule."

"I don't remember making..." He stopped, immediately putting Kailani on her feet as his stomach swayed angrily.

She rubbed his back. "I don't know why you even try," she said with a sigh.

"Yeah, me neither," he grunted. Though, it was probably a good thing his nausea had killed the mood. He couldn't very well break his own rules.

Sasha had already threatened to quit multiple times because of their "nauseating displays of affection."

"By the way, Kit called while you were training," Kailani said, picking up a couple of resistance bands that had been left on the floor and hanging them on the wall as she walked away. The staff would take care of the rest, but Cam was itching to put it all away.

The only reason he didn't was because Kailani was heading for the back office. They needed to leave soon if they wanted to make it to Madi's baby shower on time.

Besides, there was no rule about kissing in the office.

"What did he want?" Cam asked.

"He invited us over to dinner tomorrow."

"That's the third time this week." Cam frowned as he stepped into their shared office space. Kit wasn't usually this pushy about hangout time, knowing the Wonder Boys all stayed pretty busy. But lately, he'd been not-so-subtly pressuring Cam into spending time with him. School wasn't even out yet, so it wasn't like Kit had all that much free time on his end either.

Slipping her bag over her shoulder, Kailani patted Cam's chest and smiled when he grabbed hold of her hand and held it tight. "I was talking to Isla the other day."

Cam groaned. "I hate when you start a sentence like that." Isla was great—just like all of Kailani's siblings—but she seemed to think Cam was desperate for a makeover every time they were around each other. In addition to designing Horizon Tide apparel, she had also taken over their social media for them, which meant she was constantly hounding Cam for new content.

Isla didn't understand the concept of chill or relaxed, but at least she had been good for business.

"She thinks Kit is hiding something," Kailani said.

Tensing, Cam swallowed the queasiness that lately seemed to rise even before he told a lie. Somehow, he still hadn't said anything about Kit's failed engagement to anyone. Not even Kailani. But he wasn't sure he was going to be able to keep it in this time if Kailani asked a question.

But she laughed and leaned up to kiss his cheek. "You don't have to tell me anything," she assured him. "I just think Isla might be onto something."

"Isla and Kit drive each other crazy," Cam argued. "It's not like she knows him very well."

"Yeah, well, I love his best friend, and *I* don't know him well. The man's a mystery, Cam. It's like he's got this whole world inside him that no one knows about except him. Maybe he's just lonely."

Taking Kailani's hand, Cam led the way out to the parking lot as he considered that thought. While it was true that Kit didn't always share everything about himself, could there really be more than what even Cam had seen? His gut told him yes, which was a sobering thought. If Kit wasn't comfortable being himself around his friends, would he ever be comfortable with anyone else?

What if his failed relationship had made it impossible for him to trust anyone? He had gone out with Isla a few times—they definitely didn't work together, no matter how hard Isla tried—but he remained adamant that he preferred being alone and hadn't been on any other dates in years. It was going to take a special kind of person to break through that, and Cam wasn't sure that person existed. If Kit didn't show his true self to his friends, how would anyone be able to get to know him enough to love him?

"There's been a lot of change in his life over the last year," Cam admitted, hoping Kit's problem wasn't any deeper than that. "First Madi and Oliver getting married, then Ben falling for Allie and me for you." He said that last part with a kiss to her temple right as they reached his car. "Now that Madi's about to have her baby, he's probably in maximum panic mode."

Though he'd opened her door for her, he paused with his hand on the door and stood in the way. A thought had popped into his head, one that was probably a terrible idea but would keep him up at night unless he followed through. Being impulsive wasn't always the best option, but in this case… What if now was the perfect time, when everything was already in flux?

"Probably a good idea not to throw any more changes at him for a while," Kailani said after stowing her bag in the trunk. Then she frowned when she realized he hadn't moved. "What's wrong?"

"Will you marry me?"

Her eyes went wide. "What?"

The words were out, so he couldn't take them back, but the longer he thought about it, the less he wanted to take them back. "Marry me, Tease."

"Wait, you're serious?"

He held his arms out, showing her that his stomach was perfectly settled.

She took a step back, but he wasn't worried. She was stronger than anyone he knew, and she wouldn't run away from this even if she was scared. The worst she could do was say no, but he wouldn't have asked if he didn't think he already knew the answer.

He was hopeful, not delusional.

Rubbing her hands on her thighs, she studied him for a long minute. He probably could have picked a more romantic place than the open car door after a long day of work, but she would have caught on to the question before he ever had a chance to ask it if he'd tried planning something. She was too smart for him, and he definitely didn't deserve her, but he knew in his heart that he was going to spend the rest of his life with this woman.

He wanted to tell her as much, but the words stuck in his throat. Maybe he was more nervous than he'd realized.

"Cam," she said slowly, "this is quite the question you're asking me."

He swallowed. "I know. But it's an important question."

That was when it clicked. Her whole expression changed, shifting from wariness to a teary smile full of hope as she took a step closer. "*The* question," she said, this time in a whisper, and she seemed on the verge of laughing.

Cam nodded.

And the smile that lit up her face was one he would remember for the rest of his life.

"Don't leave me hanging, Tease," he begged, even if he wasn't all that scared. He still wanted to hear her say it.

Laughing, she jumped into his arms, knocking him into the door before he caught his balance. "You know the answer was always going to be yes, you dork," she said before claiming his mouth with hers in a wild kiss that had him melting. Not a great state to be in when he was holding her full weight and was the only thing keeping them from crashing to the pavement. But he didn't care, putting everything he had into that kiss because she agreed to marry him and be a part of the rest of his life. What could be better than that?

Nothing.

When his smartwatch buzzed the alarm that he'd set in case he got caught up in training—it happened more often than not—Cam groaned and reluctantly put Kailani back on her feet.

Kailani grinned as she splayed her hands against his heaving chest. She always managed to make him feel like he'd run a half-marathon when she kissed him like that. "You can breathe now."

"Fat chance of that," he replied, running a hand through his hair. He'd cut it a couple of months ago when Felipe nearly had a breakdown trying to get it to cooperate for Brad's continuing episodes about the gym, but it was already getting long again. "I don't know if I'm ever going to breathe again if you keep doing that."

She rolled her eyes as she tucked a piece of hair up away from his face. "I can stop kissing you if you—"

He cut her off with another kiss that lasted long enough for his backup alarm to go off.

Groaning again, he took a step back and stuffed his hands into his shorts pockets. "I can't tell you how happy I am that you said yes, but now I have to tell the Boys that we're engaged. That could get interesting."

She pursed her lips, clearly holding back more laughter. She'd spent enough time with the Wonder Boys to know that they wouldn't take this news calmly. Not when Cam—the commitment-phobe—had only been with Kailani for a few months. "They might be a little shocked, but they're going to be happy for you, like they always are."

Probably, but as Cam helped Kailani into her seat before sliding into his own, he couldn't get his fist to unclench. Oliver, Madi, Ben, and Allie would be thrilled, but he had no idea what this was going to do to Kit.

"Relax," Kailani said when he gripped the steering wheel tight. "Kit is stronger than you think. He'll be fine."

Cam hoped she was right, and as he drove across town with his fingers laced with hers, he relaxed more and more. Maybe Kit would have a hard time with another of his friends moving on without him, but at least the Wonder Boys would always be there for each other. No matter what happened, good or bad, they would get each other through.

"I love you," Cam said when they reached Oliver and Madi's house. "Have I told you that lately?"

Kailani laughed, leaning over and capturing his mouth in a kiss just as bone-melting as the last one. "You have, but that doesn't mean I will ever tire of hearing it." Then she squealed a little. "We're getting married!"

If Cam had anything to do with it, that was going to happen sooner than later.

The End

⫘—⫘

Special sneak peek of Book 4 in the Wonder Boy Series,

Love in Disguise

Excerpt from *Love in Disguise*

Something Kit never would have considered until he was stuck wearing the same two outfits several days in a row: it's not a great idea to push laundry day to the limit every single time, particularly on the last week of school when every day involves something especially messy.

You never know when a water main might burst and leave an entire townhouse complex without water.

The men working on it said they would hopefully have things fixed in three days. Three days without any kind of water.

When Kit stepped into Maravilla for his weekly burrito after failing to figure out the laundromat machines down the street from his house, the whole place felt off. Like everything had been shifted two inches to the left and the lightbulbs had been changed from warm to cool light. Not enough to look all that different but enough for Kit to get the itching sensation that always accompanied something new. He might have been able to ignore the feeling if things really had changed, but in reality, everything was exactly how it had been last week. And the week before. And the week before that.

Kit was pretty sure he hated burritos.

"Hey, Kit!" Gloria at the hostess desk waved at him, but instead of her usual million-dollar smile, she wore a deep frown. "Sorry, but your food's not ready yet. We had a huge family come in for a birthday party or something, and—" She paused when something shattered around the corner. "I'll go see how long it'll be, okay?"

Kit mumbled something unintelligible—he didn't even know what it was—and sank onto a vinyl waiting bench. Of course he couldn't even get a stupid meal this week. That would have been too convenient. Dropping his head against the wall, he closed his eyes and wished he could speed up time to the point where everything was back to how it should be.

As much as he hated the monotony, at least he knew what to do with it. After everything that had gone wrong last week… it was like junior high all over again, when he was suddenly surrounded by the unfamiliar and feeling like anything could happen.

The problem with that was the equal chance of the happenings being bad instead of good. Junior high? That had been bad. This chance to find something new? It was too soon to tell. For now, he just needed some time to process before anything else changed or knocked him even further off balance.

"Christopher?"

He jumped up so fast that he hit his head on a light fixture screwed into the wall. Cursing, he rubbed out the pain as he tried to figure out why he would respond to that name so quickly. Usually he had to think about it, like he often forgot his own name.

The twenty-something woman who had spoken cringed, her green eyes bouncing to the light fixture before returning to him. "Sorry," she said. "I didn't mean to scare you. But you're Christopher Morgan, right?"

Kit squinted. She looked moderately familiar, her skin pale and flawless beneath strawberry-blonde hair that hung in waves around her shoulders. Was she a parent of one of his students? He usually remembered them pretty well, and nothing was ringing a bell. Besides, they usually called him Mr. Morgan, which he hated. He was Kit to his students unless administration was around.

Whoever she was, she was painfully pretty. Kit wasn't even sure what *painfully pretty* meant, but looking at her was making his chest hurt.

"Yes," he said suddenly, his brain finally recognizing she had asked him a question. "Yeah, that's me."

She took a step closer.

Kit took a step back.

That made her lift an eyebrow, like she found all of this amusing. Then she started examining him, her eyes running from his hair to his shoes as if this was an entirely normal interaction.

He didn't know what to do. He wasn't usually this awkward, but he also didn't usually have to wait for his boring food after going through the week from hell. Was he supposed to just stand there and let her inspect him like a horse up for auction?

He cleared his throat.

Her eyes snapped up to meet his. "You look good," she said.

"I look awful," he replied. He was standing there in a rumpled shirt and tie, pizza sauce on his slacks and two days' worth of scruff making his face itch like crazy. He probably smelled, and his hair was a mess, and he was just now noticing a fingerprint smeared on his glasses that was probably part of the reason he had a massive headache right now because everything was just a little blurry in one eye.

For some reason, the woman smiled as she made her way up to the hostess desk just as Gloria returned. "I said what I said," she told Kit before turning to Gloria and announcing, "I have a reservation under Skyler Montague."

Kit's knees gave out, dropping him back onto the bench with a thump.

"Of course," Gloria said breathlessly. "Just so you know, it's probably an hour wait for food, so—"

"That's fine. I'm here for a business meeting anyway."

"Kit? Is an hour okay?"

Kit waved a hand without looking away from the worn carpet under his feet. Skyler Montague. Skyler Montague was in Maravilla. Now he was more convinced than ever that all of this was just some nightmare because there was no way *Skyler Montague* was in Diamond Springs and telling him he looked good.

Outside of a painful pinch to test if he was dreaming—he wasn't—he didn't move until Gloria had taken Skyler around to the main dining area, and then he got to his feet to start pacing—only to realize Gloria had taken Skyler to a booth right on the other side of the half wall that separated the waiting area from the dining. Kit dropped back down before either woman noticed him.

"This is perfect," he heard Skyler tell Gloria. "I have a few different people meeting me, but only one at a time. They should know to ask for my name."

The more she spoke, the more Kit wanted to hit himself for not recognizing her voice earlier. She had such a unique voice, so velvety that it made him shiver. It had gotten deeper over the years. Sexier.

This time Kit *did* hit himself, just in time for Gloria to come back around to her podium.

"Fly," he croaked when she gave him an odd look.

"Do you want a table or something? You can have some chips and salsa while you wait."

Kit might have agreed—despite the tension that filled him at the idea of doing something out of the norm—if a man who looked like The Rock hadn't come through the front door just then. Kit was used to strong people—Cam and his fiancée

Kailani both were made of pure muscle—but this guy was freakishly huge. He made Kit feel tiny as he passed, which didn't happen often. Kit was well over six feet, and he liked to think he packed a decent amount of muscle.

This guy made Kit feel like a preteen who spent all his days inside on the computer.

Gloria greeted him with wide eyes. "Welcome to Maravilla. How many in your party?"

He looked around the restaurant with narrowed eyes. "I'm meeting a Skyler Montague," he grunted.

Kit stiffened, meeting Gloria's gaze and sharing a worried look with the hostess. What kind of meeting had Skyler set up? Was she looking for a hitman? No, that would be ridiculous. But after the week Kit had had, ridiculous wasn't all that out of the question. Part of him was convinced he had been thrown into the Twilight Zone.

"Right this way," Gloria squeaked.

As soon as they were around the corner, Kit hopped over to the bench on the other side so his back was to the wall that separated him from Skyler's table.

"You must be Pete," Skyler said. "Have a seat."

The table creaked, probably Pete squishing himself beneath it. "Let's make this quick," Pete said.

"Of course. Here is all the information you need to know, as well as the amount you'll be paid if I decide you're the right candidate. Half up front, the other half when the job is done."

Kit's stomach twisted itself into knots. The hitman idea had been a joke! But maybe it was more accurate than he wanted. He hadn't seen Skyler in nearly two decades, so it wasn't like he knew anything about her. For all he knew, she was some government official here to call out a hit on someone who was causing problems.

Problems in Diamond Springs? Kit shook his head. Nothing happened in this city. Nothing but budget cuts and water main explosions.

Pete was quiet for a second except for some shuffling papers. Maybe he was looking at the target. "How many people?" he asked.

"As many as it takes."

As many as… Was Kit supposed to call 911 in this scenario? Was he about to become an unwitting accomplice to murder? It wasn't like he was helping a mass murderer, but he was aware of it. Not doing anything was technically doing something, wasn't it?

"I need to know your commitment to discretion," Skyler said. "There's a lot at stake here, and no one can suspect a thing."

"I've been doing this for years, lady. I'm a professional."

Where was Gloria? She hadn't come back yet. Had they dragged her into their scheme somehow? Holding her hostage under the table?

Kit shook his head again. He needed to get more sleep. The restaurant was full of people, and surely someone would have noticed a twenty-four-year-old being held against her will. Unless somehow the whole restaurant was filled with government agents, all of them here as backup for whatever Skyler was doing…

That was even more ridiculous. He needed more information.

"Your website has quite the list of names," Skyler said. "I haven't seen anyone with your level of variety before."

"I like to keep things interesting."

Did hitmen have websites now? Had Kit been living in the dark, so sheltered that he hadn't realized contract killing was a common business nowadays?

"Ever shot a gun before?"

"No, ma'am. Why would I need—"

"Ever dealt with kids before?"

"Hang on." Pete sounded nervous now. "No one said anything about kids."

Kit felt sick. Was Skyler planning on having some kids *shot*? He grabbed his phone, his hands shaking as he considered his best plan of action here. He would probably need proof of something shady for anyone to believe him. Could he sneak his phone over the wall and record the rest of the conversation without being noticed? Probably not.

Skyler let out a sigh. "I don't think this is going to work. The kid thing is non-negotiable. And here I thought I was dealing with a *professional*. Thanks for your time."

"Wait! I need this job!"

"And I need someone willing to do whatever it takes."

As something banged on the table—Pete's knees maybe— Kit jumped back to his original bench so it wouldn't look like he'd been eavesdropping. He meant to keep his eyes down, but when Pete came around the corner, Kit accidentally met his gaze.

And found the man crying. *What the...*

Wiping his nose, Pete hurried for the door and nearly slammed it into another man who was on his way in. "Sorry," he grunted before disappearing into the rain outside.

The newcomer frowned, glancing back at the door for a second before pausing when he saw Kit. This guy looked nothing like a hitman, so he probably wasn't there for Skyler, but Kit still didn't like the look of him. With a combover and pants hiked up high to cover a beer gut, he stood there with shifty eyes and fidgety hands.

"You here for the Montague chick too?" he asked.

Kit immediately went on high alert. "Yeah," he said, even if it was a lie.

The guy settled on the edge of the bench next to him. "It's crazy, right? What she's offering?"

Kit narrowed his eyes, gripping the vinyl on either side of his seat. Skyler had given a dollar amount to Pete at the meeting, but it seemed like this one knew that information already. "She hasn't told me," he said.

The guy chuckled. "Me neither. But the ad said it would be worth our while, right? I mean, how could it not? All I had to do was take one look at her and know she'd be a good time. Fine piece of a—"

Kit moved so quickly he surprised even himself, grabbing the guy by the collar and shoving him against the wall. "I'm going to give you five seconds to leave," he growled, making sure he was too quiet to be heard in the dining area.

Thank goodness the man didn't question his ability to follow through with his silent threat. He pulled himself free of Kit's grasp and stumbled back out into the rain without a backward glance.

"What have you gotten yourself into, Sky?" Kit muttered, grabbing his phone again as Gloria returned to her station without a clue of someone else having been in the lobby.

"Sorry about all this craziness," she said. "Did you want a table?"

Kit shook his head, typing Skyler's name into his phone to see if he could find this so-called ad. Whatever she was doing, it was going to get her into a lot of trouble. That much was clear.

* * *

Skyler had hoped more people would show up, but as her hour ticked down, her disappointment grew. Pete had been a bust the minute she saw him, but despite the fact that he was physically all wrong, she'd wanted to give him the benefit of the doubt. His resume had been the best out of everyone who contacted her, with a whole bunch of acting gigs over the years. But if just the mention of kids made him nervous, he would never last.

Sebastian wouldn't have been her first choice either, but he'd been the most eager of all of the applicants when he messaged her. The fact that he hadn't shown up had, quite honestly, been a relief. She didn't like to judge, but she really needed someone young and at least decently handsome. Sebastian was…not that. The combover in his profile picture had nearly made her laugh out loud.

At least Freddie showed up, but from the minute he'd sat down, he'd been so nervous. If he couldn't even pass an interview, he definitely couldn't make it with the real thing.

Two others had agreed to meet her tonight, but Skyler had been sitting at her table for twenty minutes now with nothing but chips and salsa to keep her company.

She should have known this tactic wouldn't work, but she had still let herself hope. Clearly she had been watching too much of the Hallmark Channel lately. She didn't even like Hallmark movies! They were too full of unbelievable romance, like a wealthy and successful woman falling for the down-on-his-luck guy she hired to be her fake boyfriend. *So ridiculous.* That would never happen in real life.

This was a waste of her time, but she couldn't bring herself to leave.

Nibbling on a chip, Skyler resisted the urge to poke her head over the wall and see if Christopher was still there. Despite him growing up—and growing up *well*—she'd known it was him the minute she saw him, but he definitely hadn't recognized her. That shouldn't have been a blow to her ego, but it was. She'd thought about the guy pretty frequently over the last seventeen years.

He had clearly forgotten about her.

Middle school in Diamond Springs had been all of four months of Skyler's life, but those four months had been some of her favorites.

"Miss Montague?"

Skyler turned to the man who had approached her table and nearly squeaked in surprise. She recognized Max from his photo, but he was a million times more handsome in person. "Yes! You must be Max. Please, have a seat."

He sat and flashed a bright white smile that knocked the wind out of her lungs. "Sorry I'm late. Traffic was crazy, and you didn't give me your phone number to let you know I was running behind."

Skyler grabbed a menu to fan herself. "No problem."

"Have you ordered yet? I'd love to buy you dinner to make up for it."

Almost bursting into laughter at the ridiculousness that was suddenly her situation, Skyler shook her head. "Not yet. Apparently there was a problem in the kitchens or something."

Seriously, Max looked like he had stepped out of a magazine photoshoot, touch-ups and all. He had the kind of smile that made women swoon and sparkled in the sunlight and probably sent old ladies to the hospital with heart attacks.

"Order whatever you want," he said. "I hear everything here is delicious."

Skyler couldn't remember the last time anyone had told her to order whatever she wanted; that was usually her line because she made a whole lot more money than any of the guys who agreed to go out with her. Or, she *had*. Before she moved back to Diamond Springs.

"So," she said after a waitress had taken their orders, "what made you respond to my ad? Most people have been in it for the money." And this guy didn't look like he needed a dime.

Max flashed another megawatt smile. "I'll admit, I was more intrigued than anything. You don't usually see stuff like this outside of movies and books."

"And you have some acting experience?" Though, at this point, Skyler wasn't sure that needed to be a requirement. All Max would have to do was smile, and he would win everyone over.

Taking a sip of water, Max nodded. "Not a lot, mind you. Just local theater things. I love working with the kids."

Skyler wished the waitress hadn't taken away her menu. She was ready to swoon. "That sounds perfect," she breathed as she slowly overheated from the inside out. But she should probably dig a little deeper before she hired the guy. "And you're free the first week of July?"

"I was supposed to be on a business trip, but it got canceled."

"How fortuitous."

Max laughed, and it was the most beautiful sound she'd ever heard. "Fortuitous. I like that word. Though, I thought this felt more like fate."

Though she tried to hold it back, Skyler let out a giggle followed closely by an unflattering snort. "Sorry."

"Don't be sorry for being adorable."

What in the world was happening? This couldn't be real. Skyler reached for her water glass to try to cool herself down, but she got caught up in Max's smile and, instead of grabbing her own glass, slammed her fingers into his and knocked it over right into his lap.

"Oh!"

Max jumped up in a flash, running right into a waiter with a tray full of food. Both of them went crashing to the ground in a sea of sizzling fajitas and way more beans than any one group of people should be allowed to eat.

Skyler clapped a hand to her mouth as she watched the scene descend into chaos. Though Max repeatedly told the terrified waiter he was fine while shaking beans from his sleeves, he still looked furious as he marched to the bathroom to clean himself up. That had definitely been Skyler's fault. But before she could drop down and help clean up the mess, someone slid into Max's abandoned seat.

"You're hiring a fake fiancé?"

Skyler blinked, too caught off guard by Christopher's sudden appearance to realize what he'd said at first. "Uh, yes?"

His thick eyebrows slid downward. "Are you completely crazy?"

Skyler rolled her eyes. "Hey Skyler, nice to see you again. I can't believe it's been seventeen years since I kissed you under the bleachers. You look great! How have you been?"

He had the decency to turn crimson as he continued to stare at her. "Hey Skyler," he growled out. "Nice to see you again."

She lifted her eyebrows when he didn't continue.

This time *he* rolled his eyes. "I can't believe it's been seventeen years."

"Since…"

He sighed, finally losing the scowl. "Since I kissed you under the bleachers." His scowl shifted into an almost-smile. "You look great. Really."

Though she'd told him the same in the lobby, that had been a lie. Christopher Morgan looked like he had had the worst week of his life. Even worse than Max getting showered by queso and sweet pork. He was a mess and looked like he hadn't slept in days.

That didn't make him any less attractive, though. Seriously, who would have thought Christopher Morgan could have such a glow up?

"How've you been?" she said.

He sighed again. "How have—"

"No, I'm asking you. How have you been, Christopher?"

"Kit."

"What?"

He shrugged as he slumped in the seat. "I go by Kit."

"Oh." That actually fit him better. When they met on the first day of sixth grade, Skyler had struggled to call him Christopher, but he had insisted on everyone using his full name. It wasn't like she'd known him for very long, but the nickname Kit felt more like him.

She wished she'd known that back when they were friends. *More* than friends.

He wasn't looking at her anymore, his focus currently on the empty chip bowl in front of him. But then he glanced down. "Is this seat wet?" Then he seemed to notice the absolute mess on the floor next to him, his eyes going wide.

Skyler snorted, which turned into a giggle, which turned into a full-on laugh complete with several more snorts as she finally processed the last five minutes. "Wanna get out of here?"

Kit's eyes went even wider as he glanced in the direction of the bathrooms. "But what about—"

"Oh, I highly doubt Max wants to come to my family re-union with me and pretend to be my fiancé. Not after that fiasco. I'd rather pretend I was never here and be just a strange dream for the rest of his life."

Kit grinned, looking more alive than he had a minute ago. He may have looked different, but that smile was exactly how she remembered it. And Skyler had to wonder if it was coincidence that had brought them together again after so long or if it was fate.

Also by Dana LeCheminant

The Wonder Boys
Love on Camera
Love in Writing
Love in Disguise

Simple Love Stories (Sweet Love Stories)
Simplicity
Growing Young
Bittersweet Brews
In Front of Me
As Long as You Love Me
Dear Dalia
Let Go

Terms of Inheritance (Sweet Romance)
Forever You and Me
Holding On to Everything
A World without You
Love, Strictly Speaking

Historical Romances
The Thief and the Noble
A Twist of Christmas (part of The Holly and the Ivy Christmas anthology)

About the Author

Dana LeCheminant has been telling stories since she was old enough to know what stories were. After spending most of her childhood reading everything she could get her hands on, she eventually realized she could write her own books too, and since then she always has plots brewing and characters clamoring to be next to have their stories told. A lover of all things outdoors, she finds inspiration while hiking the remote Utah backcountry and cruising down rivers. Until her endless imagination runs dry, she will always have another story to tell.